# Secret Lament

## Roz Southey

First published in 2009
by Crème de la Crime
P O Box 523, Chesterfield, S40 9AT
www.cremedelacrime.com

Copyright © 2009 Roz Southey

The moral right of Roz Southey to be identified as the author of this work has been asserted by her in accordance with the Copyright, Designs and Patents Act, 1988.

All rights reserved. No part of this publication may be reproduced or transmitted in any form by any means, electronic or mechanical, including photocopying, recording or any information storage and retrieval system, without prior permission in writing from the publisher nor be otherwise circulated in any form of binding or cover other than that in which it is published.

*All the characters in this book are fictitious and any resemblance to actual persons, living or dead, is purely coincidental.*

Typesetting by Yvette Warren
Cover design by Yvette Warren
Front cover image by Peter Roman

ISBN 978-0-9557078-6-5
A CIP catalogue reference for this book is available from the British Library

Printed and bound in Germany by Bercker.

**Praise for Roz Southey's inventive historical mysteries:**

*... points for originality... different, absorbing, and with an unhackneyed setting...*
– Alan Fisk, Historical Novels Review

*what really makes the novel come alive is its setting... she seamlessly incorporates the historical information into the novel... The dialogue, too, rings true: just ornamented enough to feel right for its time... A charming novel...*
– Booklist, USA

*A fascinating read, and certainly different.*
– Jean Currie, Round the Campfire

*... plot as intricate as a fugue... wickedly pointed characterizations and the convincing evocation of the sounds and stink of a preindustrial city. Southey deserves an encore...*
– Publishers Weekly, USA

*... a masterpiece of period fiction that delights while it provides an intriguing puzzle that keeps the reader riveted until the end.*
– Early Music America

*... it is good to see a publisher investing in fresh work that... falls four-square within the genre's traditions.*
– Martin Edwards, author of the highly acclaimed Harry Devlin Mysteries

*Creme de la Crime... so far have not put a foot wrong.*
– Reviewing the Evidence

**With thanks**

... to Lynne Patrick at Crème de la Crime for her unfailing support and belief, and to Lesley Horton for her clear-sighted assistance as editor. To Larisa Werstler for all her hard work in America. And to Jeff, for his entertaining company at various books signings, book fairs and conventions, including that fantastic trip to Philadelphia and Baltimore...

... to my sisters, Wendy and Jennifer, and to my brother-in-law John, for their generous help over the years, and to all the family (including Billy, who is much too young to know anything about the matter at all). Thanks too to Jackie, Laura and Anuradha for their continuing support.

... and especially to my husband, Chris, who as usual has obliged with endless cups of tea and a shoulder to cry on when things get rough. And thanks too for his enthusiastic organisation of trips all over England and even to America. I said there'd be a few good holidays...

Roz Southey is a musicologist and historian, and lives in the North East of England.
**www.rozsouthey.co.uk**

For Wendy, Jennifer and John

# 1

**Indeed, sir! There is nothing to be compared with the conviviality of a troupe of comedians!**
[*Reminiscences of a theatre manager*, Thomas Keregan (London: published for the Author, 1736)]

If ever a man was born to be murdered, it was John Mazzanti.

I was not in the mood to be tolerant. My head ached with the June sun beating in through the windows of the makeshift theatre, catching clouds of dust and sawdust in its rays. Outside, in the timber yard, sawyers could be heard shouting and clattering; inside, the resinous scents of the pine and cherry and rosewood that were normally kept here made me giddy. The store had been swept clean and the stage raised at one end for us to stand on, yet the scents still lingered.

But it was Mazzanti who tried me most. Here he came again, pounding up the wood floor of the warehouse, a tall thin man with a sour twist to his mouth. The very worst kind of theatrical director. He called imperiously, "Violino! Quiet! Damn it – can't you play more softly than that!"

Amongst the assembled company gathered on the stage, someone tittered. Mazzanti swung round on them. His gaze settled on Ned Reynolds, our leading man, playing the role of the dashing hero. "You laugh, sir!"

Ned stared at him, with an insolent little smile. Mazzanti reddened but snarled. "You have nothing to be proud of, sir! You began the song too slowly. And you!" He rounded on elderly Mrs Keregan, resting her bulk against a table on the stage. "Yes, *you*, madam! Do not breathe so loudly in your dialogue!"

"Want me to stop altogether, eh?" Mrs Keregan wheezed.

Her husband, the company manager – kind, gentle, inoffensive Mr Keregan – fluttered and stuttered unhappily.

The real problem – the reason we all disliked Mazzanti so much – was that he wasn't even Italian. All could have been forgiven if he had been – or at least swallowed with some resentment. Everyone knows that Italians are the crème de la crème as far as music and the musical theatre are concerned. Or at least it's fashionable to say so. But Mazzanti might have had an Italian name, and an Italian father, even a performance or two before the nobility of Europe, but he was as English as I am.

Besides, I had a personal grudge against him: he had been hired to lead the band for the concerts in Race Week and throughout the winter. That had been *my* job.

"Very well," Mazzanti snapped. "Let us start again – from the beginning of Julia's song."

Someone groaned. That damn girl. Julia, John Mazzanti's daughter, his pride and joy, his rising star of an actress and singer, even now hesitating with modest innocence at the front of the stage. Seventeen years old, golden-haired and blue-eyed, demurely dressed in white and pink. A limpid melting gaze. She turned to smile coyly at Ned Reynolds. He was playing her lover in this nonsensical little musical entertainment and did his best to look adoringly down at her, but I saw his jaw clench as he fixed his smile hard.

"No, no!" Mazzanti said. "Hold her hand, you fool."

A muscle worked in Ned's cheek; he took the girl's hand. Yes, surely someone must have planted a punch in Mazzanti's face before now, maybe several times. I was tempted myself.

We began again. The sun beat in and bathed us in sweat. The players in the company walking the stage around me were surrounded by a bright glare that made my head ache. I screwed up my face in a desperate attempt to play quietly enough so that Julia's song could be heard. She had the worst singing voice I have ever known, a breathy little girl's voice that you could hardly hear a foot away.

My sweaty fingers slipped on the violin neck; the squeak was loud enough to be heard over the shuffling of the actors.

"Damn it, violino!" Mazzanti roared. "Are you completely incompetent?"

"Play it fortissimo, Mr Patterson," advised a Scotch voice above me. Glancing up, I saw a huge cobweb – a single line drifting in the sunlight – and on the end of it a bright gleam. A spirit. Timber yards are dangerous places at the best of times and many a man has met his death here; three days later, his spirit disembodies and – as spirits cannot move from the place of the living man's death – joins the throng already here, happily spending their eighty or hundred years before final dissolution in the company of their friends and fellow workers.

I knew the spirit on the cobweb of old; the living man had been killed when a stack of oak fell on him and the spirit, once disembodied, insisted it was the best thing that had ever happened to him. To be confined to a snug warm wood-scented building was apparently his idea of heaven, particularly during the winter months and in June's Race Week when the building was cleared of all its wood and transformed into a theatre, and he was given plays and farces and pantomimes for free.

"As loud as you can, sir," the spirit whispered, swinging dangerously on the end of the cobweb. "Drown the girl out! She's not worth hearing."

Mrs Keregan took a hand, saying loudly, punctuated by heavy breaths: "Ignore His Foreign Highness, Charlie boy. I've been in this business fifty years and never yet cowtowed to no Italian." The Keregans' daughter, Athalia, spirited and red-haired, said: "You tell him, Mama." But then Athalia was jealous of Julia Mazzanti who, she insisted, had stolen the leading role from her.

Mazzanti flushed bright red, clearly remembered just in time that it was unwise to shout too often at the wife and daughter of the theatre manager, and took out his ire on the spirit instead. "Get those damn cobwebs out of the way! They're catching the light and blinding me!"

He stood immoveable until young Richard the errand boy brought a broom and swiped at the cobwebs. The spirit scuttled away to a corner beam, and Richard hurried after to apologise. Never offend a spirit if you can avoid it. Eighty or a hundred years is plenty of time for them to wreak revenge on someone they don't like.

Mazzanti banished me to the back of the stage where I could 'scratch away' without overwhelming the singers. On his way back to his place, he glowered at Ned Reynolds. "Take your hands off my daughter!"

I stifled a grin at the thought of Ned putting hands on any woman, then stared in astonishment as I saw him flash a smile at the girl. Anyone would have thought he genuinely admired her.

Of course Mazzanti paid the price for offending the spirit. No sooner had delicate, demure Julia started once more on her song, than the spirit struck up from a high beam with a Scotch song so bawdy it would have embarrassed a married man. The actresses in the company sniggered, Mrs Keregan looked grimly triumphant, and only young Richard, who is barely sixteen, blushed.

In the aftermath, while Mazzanti was shouting and Mr Keregan trying to calm him, and the spirit crooning happily in the rafters, the rest of us retired to the costume boxes and fanned ourselves against the overwhelming heat.

"Someone ought to see to that man, they should," Mrs Keregan said darkly. "Beer, Charlie boy?"

I took it eagerly.

"I hope the spirit isn't offended," young Richard said anxiously, staring at the cobwebs in the corner.

Athalia preened her red hair to an even greater pitch of curled perfection. "I'll sort him out," she said in warlike tones and pranced off across the stage.

The afternoon sun was slanting across me; I shifted the box backwards into the shade. Outside, in the bright yard, barechested workmen hauled huge timbers about and shouted instructions to the apprentices darting here and there. And one dark face appeared at the window, peering in with a leer. An unshaven face, scarred on one cheek and surrounded by dirty tousled hair.

He met my gaze. Instinctively, I pulled back. He grinned and was off.

He was following me, had been for nearly three months now, along with two or three other fellows. Back in March, I tangled with some ruffians in one of the chares down by the Keyside, and they had been after me ever since. They trailed me down the wide daylight streets, grinned at me if I thought of venturing into an alley, embarrassed me by coming up and addressing me by name when I was talking to respectable gentlemen and ladies. I had even seen them lounging outside my lodgings.

They were trying to frighten me, of course, revenging themselves for the defeat I had inflicted on them and their leader. They were succeeding. And I suspected that they would not stop at frightening but would sooner or later press on to give me a beating. I would have felt safer if my great friend Hugh Demsey had been in town to lend me a little practical help, but he was in Houghton-le-Spring, teaching the country ladies and gentlemen to dance, and I didn't expect him back for another week or two, until Race Week itself.

At the front of the stage, Athalia was cooing over John Mazzanti's shoulder.

"She's after him," her mother said with a sigh.

I was startled. "But he's married." Signora Mazzanti, who is also English, lingers in her lodgings, annoying the neighbours by practising her scales. She is a much better singer than her daughter – very good indeed, I'm told.

Mrs Keregan rolled her eyes. "Marriage? Why should Athalia want that? It's money she's after."

I kept quiet. I had one hundred guineas hidden beneath my mattress, the proceeds from selling a chamber organ which I had won in a raffle despite the fact that I had not bought a ticket; there were two people who might have bought me a ticket without telling me, and I didn't much like the idea of being beholden to either of them. Athalia would think one hundred guineas amply worth her attention, although, if the rumours were right, Mazzanti had a great deal more. He certainly dressed like a wealthy man.

He allowed himself to be cosseted out of his bad temper and called for us to begin again. I sent young Richard to whisper a polite request to the spirit not to annoy Mazzanti further; the boy looked dubious but went off willingly enough.

As I got up to play, I saw Julia Mazzanti turn. Her golden hair glittered in the bright sunlight, the twin yellow ribbons danced and gleamed. She gave me the sweetest of looks, winning and winsome.

I stared stonily back and glimpsed something else. A trace of anger? Or even desperation? Abruptly she looked very young, almost lost.

She turned her shoulder and began her song once more.

An hour or so later, as the company was rehearsing some dialogue and Mazzanti was busy offending everyone even further, a man slipped in beside me. I was dozing at the back of the stage and started in alarm, thinking the newcomer was one of the ruffians. But it was Matthew Proctor, the wandering psalm teacher, a slight, reserved man with a soft voice and a hesitant manner. In his mid-thirties, perhaps eight or so years older than myself. He slid down on to the wicker costume basket with a nervous nod of greeting, clutching his bassoon case to his chest.

"Proctor," I said in surprise. "I thought you were spending Race Week in Carlisle."

"Yes. No," he said. "Very well, thank you."

He was staring at Julia Mazzanti in patent adoration. Heaven help us, did she have all the men trailing in her wake? Even young Richard was offering shy homage, darting here and there to bring her lemonade, or her shawl, or a sweetmeat. They were much the same age of course, and I had seen them chattering together in odd moments – Julia artlessly innocent, Richard innocently adoring. He longed to act upon the stage himself and I had overheard Julia offering sage advice, which Richard would do well to ignore.

But it was Ned Reynolds's behaviour that startled me most. What the devil did he mean by solicitously handing Julia into her chair like that, or leaning over to murmur something that made her laugh? Proctor certainly didn't like it much. He leant close to me, without taking his reverential gaze from Julia.

"Who's that fellow?"

"Ned Reynolds. One of the company."

"He's too encroaching."

I could have told Proctor he didn't need to worry about Ned Reynolds as a competitor for Julia's affections. Whatever pose he might strike in public, Ned wouldn't even glance at the girl – any girl – in private. But such things are obviously never to be talked of, given the penalty the law demands.

Proctor's thoughts had already moved on. "She is going to London, you know."

"Julia? Is she?"

"To play Lucy Locket."

Yes, I thought, Julia would look very well as the virginal heroine of *The Beggar's Opera*. A pity she couldn't sing.

"I may go there myself," Proctor whispered. "To see her acclaimed at Covent Garden would be magnificent."

I said nothing. Proctor was clearly enamoured of the girl – he was unworldly enough to think of her as an angel come down to earth. That was no doubt a part she could play very well too. Providing she didn't have to sing. Or act.

She could not remember her words. She was rehearsing a love scene with Ned and stuttered over a commonplace: "Tonight, but – but – " I saw a flash of annoyance in Ned's eyes. That was much more like the man I knew. No one is more dedicated to his profession; it is a point of honour with him to do the best he is capable of. Which is considerable.

"The book!" young Richard said eagerly and snatched the playbook from Athalia Keregan's hands.

Before he could hurry to Julia's side, Proctor leapt up and seized the book from him, shyly presenting it to the lady himself. But Julia was already turning away, receiving the correct lines from her father. Proctor stood ignored at her side.

I have never seen a man so disconsolate. Proctor looked so woebegone that I leant forward to say something consoling. But the spirit leapt in first, sliding up the wicker work of the costume box and gleaming on a broken piece of cane. "She's not worth it," he said, in his broad accent. "There's not a woman in the world worth crying over."

Proctor gasped and leapt away.

I stared at him as he stood trembling on the edge of the stage. This was nervous behaviour even for the unworldly Proctor. Mr Keregan took his arm kindly. "Proctor, my dear fellow. Come and say good day to my wife – she'll be delighted to see you again."

He bore Proctor off and the spirit hung on the edge of the basket. "Not my day," it said, philosophically. "Anything wrong with me, Patterson, you reckon?"

"Not in the least. It's the heat, I daresay. Everyone gets tetchy when it's so hot." I glanced towards the window again. Yes, the fellow was still there, grinning in at me.

We should have given up then, before tempers frayed still further. But we played on, sweating and drinking ale by the tankard-full, getting hotter and more irritable by the minute. The sun slanted in through the windows, dazzlingly bright and fiendishly hot; even the spirit retreated to the coolest corner of the barn-like warehouse.

Mazzanti grew, if anything, more annoying, snapping at Ned for talking privately to Julia, complaining loudly when Proctor, clearly still upset, played a hatful of wrong notes. Young Richard grew very quiet, looking from Julia's face to Ned's with real unease; did he believe Ned was really attracted to the girl? Athalia muttered over the attention Julia was getting; her mother breathed yet more heavily. My violin was suffering so badly in the heat that I could hardly play a line in tune and Mazzanti made sure I knew it. I toyed with the idea of knocking him down with one well-aimed blow.

And the ruffian still grinned in through the window.

Mazzanti let us go at last, with a final contemptuous: "We will have to do better tomorrow. If you *could* all make sure you know your songs and your words…"

I pushed my violin into its case, slung it over my shoulder and strode off the stage. If I stayed a moment longer, I would say something unworthy of a respectable, god-fearing man. Or, worse, do something. The thought of punching that sour face grew ever more attractive.

I barely got as far as the door before the fellow strode up. "Where the devil are you going, violino?"

Yes, someone was going to do away with him soon and if he picked at me again, that someone was going to be me.

"If you want me to play for you," I snapped, "you could at least do me the courtesy of using my name!"

His lip curled. "Think a lot of yourself, I see."

"I could say the same thing."

I swung away, then stopped, heart racing. The dark-haired ruffian who had been staring through the window all afternoon – surely I had just seen him again. But there was too much of a crowd. We were jostled by workmen; a man with half a tree trunk across his shoulders blocked my view...

Mazzanti was snapping at me again. Something whined, hissed between us, thumped on the door jamb. We stood for the briefest of moments in startled immobility. Then Mazzanti ducked back inside the warehouse.

I ran the other way. After the man who had fired the shot.

# 2

**The political situation is at the present time very complex.**
[Letters from London, *Newcastle Courant*, 5 June 1736]

I glimpsed a figure behind one of the huge stacks of Baltic timber and dashed for it. The heat struck me as soon as I was out in the open, like the heat from a bread oven when the door is opened. What chance did I have of catching the ruffian in this heat? And with the violin bouncing against my back too?

I reached the stack, swung round it, found the open gate of the yard. A cart rumbled past in the street outside. I grabbed for the side of the wagon. "Did you see a fellow running?"

The carter grunted and jerked his whip. I tripped on the cobbles, staggered upright again and found a side street.

It was well-nigh deserted. No ruffian, no grinning filthy villain. Only a burly man halfway down it, wrapped in a heavy coat as if it was midwinter. He carried a bag over one shoulder and was staring back down the street.

I stumbled to a halt, out of breath, gasped out my query again. "Did you see – a fellow – running?"

The man turned to me; he had a good strong face, sallow skinned. "I saw him," he agreed with good-humour. He was a little out of breath himself. "I only wished he'd seen me. Sent me flying against the wall." He brushed dust from his coat. "You'll not catch him now. He's long gone."

I went after him anyway. I was damned if I'd let ruffians intimidate me. But the hot air clogged up my throat and sent the sweat running down my back in rivulets; by the end of the street, I knew I could go no further. In any case, as I looked right and left, I saw such a bustle and a hurry of people – women with chickens and children with hoops and men with heavy bags of tools – devil take it, I'd never find the fellow.

The man in the coat came up behind me, stood contemplating the crowds. "What's the villain done?"

"Shot at me," I said shortly.

"At you?"

I turned to eye him – I didn't like the incredulity in his voice, as if he didn't think me worth shooting at. He gave me a benign stare. He was a good-looking man, very dark in hair and eyes; the sallow skin branded him a foreigner although he had no accent and sounded entirely English. About a decade older than myself, thirty seven or so, I guessed and three or four inches taller than me, and I am not short.

"Well, well," he said. "Never believe a chaplain. I met one on the coach down from Edinburgh who said nothing ever happens here."

"Scotch, was he?"

"Well-nigh incomprehensible."

"Then how do you know what he said about this town?"

He grinned. "Touché! My dear sir, I invented the whole tale." The frankness with which he admitted lying took my breath away. "You ask why. Of course you do. The last two weeks of my life have been the dullest of my entire existence and here you have plunged me straight into excitement. I must thank you. Allow me to buy you wine – or would you prefer beer?"

I was so thirsty I could have drunk the Tyne dry. And sitting in a crowded tavern with my back to a wall was probably a lot safer than walking the streets.

The fellow professed to know nothing of the town, having arrived barely an hour before, so I took him down on to the Key, to one of the sailors' taverns, all rushes and wooden benches and the stink of sweat and coal. But it served a surprisingly good beer and we took it out into the cool shadows of the keels waiting at the wharfs.

I lowered myself on to a crate of candles waiting to be loaded on board one of the keels. My companion stretched and arched his neck, stripped off his coat and dumped it in a heap over his bag. Under the coat, he was dressed in drab brown, clearly with an eye more to practicality than fashion.

"I have not introduced myself," I said. "Charles Patterson, at your service."

"A violinist?" He gestured at the case on my back.

"I prefer the harpsichord. But I play whatever I must to earn a living." In truth, I preferred the organ, but my opportunities to play are limited to acting as deputy at All Hallows' Church.

He inclined his head. "Domenico Corelli, at your service."

I spluttered through my beer. "Domenico – "

"The great composer himself was my father."

I did not have the honour of being acquainted with the gentleman in question because he died when I was three years old. But I knew he had no son called Domenico.

"Illegitimate, of course," he murmured.

"I am a musician, sir," I said tartly. "You cannot pull the wool over my eyes!" I began to think him not as respectable as he looked and told him so.

He fanned away a little cloud of flies. A trickle of sweat ran down his cheek – he was not as impervious to the heat as he had pretended. "And you, sir?" he said lazily. "Are you respectable? What sort of respectable man has fellows shooting at him?"

"Ruffians," I said shortly. "They tried to rob me a couple of months back and I fought them off. They didn't like it and they have long memories."

He sipped at his beer as if it was an overlarge glass of wine. "And no one was hurt, I take it?"

"Hurt?"

"When they fired at you? I see you came away safe but were

there others around you?"

I swore. I had a momentary vision of John Mazzanti ducking back into the theatre. Or had he fallen? I tossed back the beer. "I had better go see."

He stood, lazily, a big man and, I realised with some surprise, intimidating. "Then if you'll direct me to a decent inn with comfortable rooms?"

I gave him instructions to get to Mrs Hill's in the Fleshmarket and turned back to Usher's timber yard.

My legs were aching by the time I had climbed the Side and reached the gates of the timber yard. I have never enjoyed weather as hot as this; it weakens me and leaves me disinclined to do anything. I wove my way across the yard towards the warehouse that served as our theatre, tired of darting looks left and right to be certain I was not being followed. The worst of it was that it was all my own fault; I had taunted the ruffians when we clashed – I should have had more sense.

All was chaos inside the theatre. Some of the timber yard apprentices had been attracted by the excitement and were laughing and shouting about the back of the theatre, miming firing a pistol and shrieking, "Bang, bang!" At the stage's edge, Julia was drooping in the arms of Ned Reynolds, who looked both embarrassed and annoyed; young Richard was hovering behind them unhappily. Proctor looked on from a corner – the psalm teacher clutched his bassoon case to his chest almost as if he thought it would protect him. Above, the spirit swung from cobweb to cobweb singing a rousing hunting song.

On the stage itself, Mrs Keregan sat in majestic isolation and indifference on one of the costume boxes, chewing her way through a large chunk of bread. Below her, the rest of the company were gathered in a huddle and I heard the mellow, soothing tones of Gale the barber surgeon.

Athalia saw me and came dancing across, her red curls

bobbing. "I don't suppose you caught the villain?"

I bridled at her mocking tone, said brusquely, "No, I didn't." I noticed with some satisfaction that her face was flushed with the heat and was almost redder than her hair. I pushed past her and marched up to the affecting little scene.

Mazzanti was sprawled in a chair, his eyes closed as if he was in a faint. One hand clutched affectingly at his chest; little moans escaped his lips. Gale had removed Mazzanti's coat, rolled up one shirt sleeve and was bleeding him to relieve the shock; Julia, who cannot have been able to see a thing for Ned's encircling arms, murmured distractedly, "The blood, the blood…"

"Was he hit?" I demanded.

Gale glanced up at me. "Mr Mazzanti has suffered a great shock." In other words, no.

"Most distressing," kind-hearted Mr Keregan murmured. "It must be most upsetting to be shot at – "

So it was to be Mazzanti who had been attacked, not me. Well, I was not tempted to claim the dubious honour. I had friends who would have been distressed to know I was in danger, and I had long since decided not to tell them.

Julia groaned and pushed herself from Ned's arms. He let her go without protest; I caught his eye. He was grim-faced; his mouth twisted in a cynical curl. What the devil was he doing?

Mazzanti moaned as his daughter caught hold of his trailing hand. I fancied she must have accidentally dug her sharp nails into his fingers for he started with pain. His eyes opened; he stared at her.

"Dear father," she said brokenly. "You are safe now. We are all here, we will look after you."

He feebly tried to wave her away; she brushed away a tear. "And I had thought there was no danger here…"

"Danger?" I said sharply.

She turned her lovely face up to me. Her hair glinted in the sunshine, bright ribbons gleamed amongst the curls. "This isn't the first time he's been shot at." She gripped his hand forcing another grunt of pain from him. "Twice before. Once in London and once more on our way north."

Mazzanti struggled to sit upright. "It is nothing. Nothing at all. Just some madman." He wiped a hand across his brow, leaving a faint trace of blood. "Nothing of any moment at all."

I stared down at him. I had told myself half a dozen times in the few days I had known him, that Mazzanti was the kind of man his acquaintances long to murder. Could it be that the shot I had thought meant for me, had really been aimed at him?

# 3

**We must strenuously condemn this modern tendency to lawless behaviour.**
[Letter from JUSTICIA to Mayor of Newcastle upon Tyne, printed in the *Newcastle Courant*, 15 May 1736.]

"Was he hurt?" Esther asked absently. She twitched a curtain back into place as we passed through the drawing room into the library of her house. The evening was cooler than the day but not by much.

I swung my violin off my shoulder and laid it carefully on the harpsichord stool. "He says so."

Mrs Esther Jerdoun (the title is purely honorary and the lady, I thank God, unmarried) comes from an impeccable family with aristocratic connections (albeit remote). She is my most constant pupil; I give her a lesson in harpsichord playing almost every day. But more than that, she is my delight. I met her more than half a year ago and fell under her spell at once. The strong sunlight is perhaps a little unkind to her, showing that she is a woman of mature age – thirteen years older than my twenty-six years – but she is still lovely in face and figure. I could have looked at her for ever, at the tiny strands of pale gold hair clustering at the back of her neck and gleaming in the sunlight, at her faint smiles and cool mischievous glances...

And, dear God, here I was again, longing for what was out of my reach, in all respects. Her age, her social position, her wealth all come between us. She was one of the two people whom I thought might have bought me that ticket for the organ; I avoided asking directly if she had – how could I take such a favour from a woman about whom I felt so strongly?

And there was of course the question of how she felt about me...

She stared out of the window into the garden at the back of the house. "Perhaps the ball ricocheted?"

"It did not," I said forcibly. "We dug the ball out of the door jamb."

She was still musing over the sunlit roses. I looked at her with some concern. She is the most practical of women, the most astute, the most down-to-earth. But here she was, staring absent-mindedly out of the window into the enclosed garden beyond, as if I was not even in the room.

"Does it matter?" she asked.

"Yes," I said sharply, then bit my lip and brought my attention back to the matter in hand. I had not told her about the ruffians and I did not intend to tell her; she would worry. So it was difficult to explain why I thought Mazzanti might be lying. "He said later that he had offended some rich aristocrat in London by dallying with the actress the lord had in keeping. His Lordship evidently sends his hirelings from time to time to remind Mazzanti to keep away from the lady."

I reconsidered Mazzanti's hurried man-of-the-world explanations, confided with a knowing air to the men in the company. They were just about unlikely enough to be true. Yet it struck me that there was something else, something he was hiding... That look in his eyes when Julia started telling me about the previous attempts on his life – I could have sworn he was genuinely afraid.

Esther glanced round at me, broke suddenly into a wry smile. "Oh, Charles, do forgive me! I am in the very worst of humours but I should not take it out on you."

I could forgive her anything when she used my name like that. We had fallen into this casual way of speaking, in private at least, some weeks ago; it was inappropriate and unwise but I could not regret it.

She took a little key from her pocket and unlocked the harpsichord; I helped her fold back the lid and prop it up, revealing a garland of dancing nymphs and shepherds. I pressed a few keys to see if it was in tune – hot weather plays havoc with such things – but I was distracted by the way Esther lingered beside me. Her perfume was bewitching; the pale green of her wide gown complimented her colouring perfectly. But there is more than that: an air of decision, of cool independence – these are the things that I –

No, the word is inadmissible. A foolish self-indulgence.

She traced the dancing nymphs with idle fingers as I adjusted the tuning. We were alone in the room; Esther's maid, Catherine (whom we told everyone chaperoned her mistress during the music lessons) had taken herself off to examine the linen cupboard as she usually did. This of course was disgraceful. A single man and a single woman – no matter how unequal their ages or status – are not to be trusted in a room together for fear they will be overwhelmed by the worst of human nature. Or for fear, rather, that everyone will assume they have been.

For that reason, when I first started teaching Mrs Jerdoun the harpsichord two months ago, we used the harpsichord at the Assembly Rooms, with Catherine sewing industriously in one corner and the gregarious Steward of the Rooms easing in and out from time to time to enquire hopefully if we had everything we needed. A perfectly innocuous situation – nothing secret about it at all. But not long since, we had, without discussing the matter, removed to Esther's house.

"The harpsichord is very much out of tune," she had said.

"Do you wish me to tune it for you?" I had said.

"Indeed – and you may give me my lesson at the same time."

At the time I had been wary. I did not like Esther's house in Caroline Square for it had once been the scene of the most extraordinary events which had left me unnerved and shaken. It was a gateway, in some mysterious inexplicable way, to a different world entirely, one that ran parallel to our own, almost identical but not quite. I had met my own self in that world, and had nearly come by my death.

But all this had happened last November, well before Christmas – seven months ago now. It had in some respects the quality of a dream; distance had blunted the edge of my fear. In many ways I would have been intrigued to experience something similar again. But I could not open and close the gateway at will but had merely to wait and see if it opened of its own accord. So far it had not.

"Esther." I cleared my throat; she started.

"What? Oh yes. Now where is my music?" She started to sort through the books that lay on top of the harpsichord. Her bare arm, and the fall of lace about her elbow, brushed my sleeve; I caught my breath.

"Tell me what is wrong," I said.

She stared at me then let out a sigh. "You are right of course. But it is only a small thing. There is no need to worry about it."

"I always worry when someone tells me not to."

She laughed ruefully. I loved that laugh, that smile. (But I would never press myself on her, and no woman, of course, would be so immodest as to proposition a gentleman. Dear God, why was I even thinking about this?)

"It *is* a little thing," Esther said. "But come and have a look."

I followed her out of the library into the rear quarters of the house, where the wooden floors gave way to cool flagstones, and servants clattered in the kitchens. The windows at the back of the house looked to the west, and the sun, slanting down the evening sky, cast a red glow through the glass on to the lime-washed walls. I heard a male servant laugh.

We passed open doors – I glimpsed a wine store and a pantry

before we came to the scullery, scattered with tubs and buckets and other mysterious machines. Here a door gave on to the garden. Esther took down a key that hung on a hook beside the door and pushed it into the lock. The key turned smoothly, well-oiled and well-kept.

When Esther pulled open the door into the sunlit garden, I was assailed by the scents of herbs, mint and sage, thyme and rosemary; a border of chives was in full purple bloom, lavender heads were forming on bushes beyond. I walked out on to a path that bordered cropped lawns. It was a rectangular garden, not large but well-tended and surrounded by a high wall that was almost obliterated by climbing roses; two apple trees stood in the far corner.

Esther brought my attention back to the house door. "Here. Look." She fingered the lock plate and I bent to examine it. The plate was shiny and polished, relatively new; the tiny scratches surrounding the lock were very visible.

I straightened. "Someone has been trying to get in."

She nodded. For a moment I saw weariness in her and was tempted to – I took a step back.

"The gardener will have it that Tom is being careless with the key but I cannot believe that."

Tom, if I remembered correctly, was the only male servant in the house; the gardener lived elsewhere with his family.

"When did this happen?"

"Last night, quite late. We had all gone to bed."

"The servants heard nothing?"

"Not a sound."

"And George?"

George, my former apprentice, is the only spirit in the house. He was, fortunately, a boy when he died, at that stage of being both fascinated by women, and frightened of them. He adores Esther but keeps his distance bashfully; we can guarantee therefore not to be interrupted by him.

"Did he not hear anything? Spirits, after all, do not sleep."

"George," Esther said with exasperation, "has discovered that if he opens the kitchen window on a windy night, the pots and pans all clatter together and wake the household. Charles, however did you put up with him as an apprentice?"

"Fortunately, he was only with me a few weeks before he died. What was he doing when your intruder attempted to get in?"

"Thinking, he says. He believes he heard a scratch or two but took no notice. He thought it was probably a stray cat."

I stepped back carefully, on to the lawn. The path was of gravel and held no mark. I retreated to the herb beds, scanning for footprints in the soft well-tended soil. There were none. I looked across the garden, squinting against the low sun.

"Is there a gate to the street?"

Esther pointed to a place where rose blossoms flourished.

I walked slowly down the path, scanning the flowerbeds on either side. Beyond the beds stood three damson trees, then the path turned sharply right along the wall; the roses trailed long thorny stems to snag at my coat. The gate was set back under a fall of heavy pink blossoms; I lifted the latch. It did not open.

"It's locked," Esther said behind me. Silently, she handed me another key. Her hand brushed mine; I shivered with its warmth.

This lock too opened smoothly; I pulled open the gate and saw outside a narrow cobbled lane, bordered on both sides by high garden walls. It was a dead end; Esther's gate stood at the blocked end.

I checked the lock on both sides. There were no scratches.

I walked down the alley. The garden walls were high and well-maintained; no crumbling mortar offered handholds that would have enabled someone to climb. A ladder might have been set up, I supposed, and would have left no marks on the cobbled alley but the thorned roses would have made it impossible to get down on the garden side.

The street at the end of the alley ran at right angles, passing the back walls of the houses in the square. As I stood looking along it, several people trudged past, casting me incurious glances. Late at night, drunks sauntered along here; the lower sort of thief would think Esther's house worth breaking into; even if all he got were a few silver spoons or lace cloths, it would repay the risk handsomely. But how could he have got into the garden?

I went back to Esther who was standing by the back door of the house, turning the house key in her hands.

"Perhaps the gardener was right and the scratches were caused by Tom," I said. "No one could have got into the garden."

She hesitated then shook her head. "There was someone. I saw him."

I stared at her in horror. "But you said – "

"That none of the servants heard anything. They did not. But I did."

She breathed deeply. In the strong light of the setting sun, I saw how tired she was, and how unnerved, and that worried me more than anything. Esther is not a weak woman to break down in fearful tears at the first hint of danger. I've seen her outface a whole gang of ruffians.

"Last night I had a headache when I went to bed," she said. "I was restless, could not sleep. I heard a noise, after midnight, I think. A kind of chink."

"Like keys?"

She considered. "Perhaps. The only thing I could think of was that perhaps a fox had got into the garden and knocked something over. So I got up to look."

"And you saw something – someone."

She was breathing more easily now, as she thought back to the events of the previous night, as if it was a relief to explain what had happened.

"It was very dark, unfortunately – the moon had not yet risen. But I saw a shadow moving away from the house, along the line where the path is. I distinctly saw him where the path turns, as if he was going down to the gate. Then I lost him." She gestured in annoyance.

I took the key from her, ushered her back into the house, locked the door firmly. "This is intolerable," I said. "We will report it to the constable."

She laughed, seeming to relax a little. "Charles! What good will that do? I can give no description of the man. And he took nothing because he did not get into the house."

"But if he comes back! You are alone here!"

I stopped, suddenly realising that she might misinterpret my words. How tempting it was to suggest that I should stay tonight, to make sure the fellow did not come back or, if he did, to make sure that she was protected. And if I stayed –

Esther said wryly, "Alone except for four or five servants!" She smiled and leant closer confidentially. Her skirts rustled, her hair drifted across my cheek. Dear God. "And a pair of duelling pistols," she murmured.

Esther is an accomplished user of pistols. And fearless, when she sees the need. But what if the would-be intruder was a large, well-built man? What if he disarmed her?

I looked back through the window at the gate hidden amongst the roses and the setting fire of the sun. There was of course one way he could have got into the garden. If he had a key for the gate. And if he had a key to the garden, who was to say he did not have a key to the house?

# 4

**This town, sir, is infested with ruffians.**
[Letter from Sir John Hubert to his brother-in-law
on visiting Newcastle, May 1732]

By tacit agreement we made light of the affair. Esther promised to inform the constable if there was another attempt to break in; she herself would double check that the servants had closed and secured all the windows and doors before retiring for the night.

By the time we had talked the matter through, the sun had fully set and it was late. We were both tired, so I shut up the harpsichord again and bid Esther goodnight; as I took my leave, she hesitated a moment as if she was about to say something more, but then evidently decided against it.

I had reached the hall before Tom, the young manservant who acted as footman, butler, and general factotum, appeared. His face was red as if he had been rushing; his coat sat askew on his shoulders. I told him I could see myself out and he disappeared back into the servants' quarters with a grateful smile of relief. I fancied I had caught him in the middle of his supper.

The hallway echoed as I walked across the shining black and white floor tiles. Behind me, an impressive staircase with a carved wooden banister rose towards an ornately plastered ceiling. Esther has only recently inherited the house and one of her first acts was to bring in a small army of painters, plasterers and glaziers to refurbish the rooms. Remembering its slightly shabby appearance of last year, I was inclined to admire.

A voice called: "Papa?"

A child's voice, a young girl, I thought. I turned on my heels, shivering. And as if a veil had been drawn across the hallway, the fine paint peeled, the windows cracked, the curtains frayed. The door to the drawing room stood slightly ajar but the view of the room I glimpsed showed not Esther's elegant new décor but a grimy expanse of wall. Looking out of the window by the front door, I saw not the elegance of Caroline Square but a narrow busy street. It was still day, overcast and drizzling with rain.

The gateway to that other world had opened, and to a slightly different time of day.

I stood for a moment, reorientating myself, wondering why this should happen now and not at another time. Could it be mere chance? A trace of my old fear lingered but I was intrigued too, no doubt of it. I went cautiously to the drawing room door, scratched on it. There was a moment's silence then the door was pulled open.

A girl confronted me with a wary, almost frightened look. She was maybe twelve years old, a wisp of a girl with thin brown hair neatly tied back with a ribbon and a clean but faded apron covering a shabby green dress. Her wary look faded; she curtsied politely. "I beg your pardon, Mr Patterson, I thought at first you were the landlord. Was it Papa you wanted to see?"

She talked as if she knew me. Resigned, I realised she must have mistaken me for my counterpart in this world – a man who bore my name, spoke like me, looked like me, but who was a great deal wealthier. Indeed, I saw she was frowning at my clothes as if wondering why I was wearing such poor things.

Who on earth was 'Papa'? "Er – yes," I said.

"He's not here, sir. But I expect him back at any time. Will you wait?" Her politeness was almost painful. She opened the door wider, to let me in.

The whole room had fallen on hard times. The ceiling, though cobwebbed, was in tolerable condition although a chunk of plaster had detached itself from one corner and showed the grimy laths beneath. The wallpaper, flaunting the bright colours of former days only in places, was torn and faded; the fireplace chipped and cracked. The grate was empty. A curtain cut off a corner of the room and I glimpsed a bed behind it. A chipped cup or two and a pewter plate stood on a large table together with a cloth covering what might have been a chunk of bread.

It was all scrupulously clean but unutterably dreary.

The girl had settled in a chair by a rickety table. A workbasket stood on the table; she plucked thread from it and started to thread a needle.

"I often wonder what this was like when the house was owned by the old family," she said, with the air of a hostess entertaining morning callers. "Of course we are very lucky to have so big a room between the two of us. The Forsters upstairs have a room only half the size for six people!"

So the house in this world had been sold and divided into tenements for the poor. The last time I had seen it had been eight months ago and it had been bright and smart then. Could time pass more quickly in this world? Surely the house could not have got in such a state in only a few months?

The girl was sewing ribbons, yellow strips of material on which she was setting tiny blue flowers each with a bright bead at the centre. She went on with the work as if it was automatic, something she did not have to think about, setting tiny fine stitches with quiet assurance. On the table beside her, was a neat pile of gauzy fabric, perhaps intended for a dress.

"I'm sure Papa was going down to the theatre," the girl said, picking up a bead to sew on to the ribbon. "Was he not there?"

"No."

"Then perhaps he has gone for a bowl of buttered barley. He's very fond of that."

While his daughter chewed on that chunk of dried bread under the cloth on the table, no doubt. "Yes. Of course."

"Did you want him for another concert?" she asked with sudden eagerness. "I'm sure he'll be available. He's often said how much he likes playing for your concerts." Her anxiety to obtain work for her papa was almost heartwrenching. "I'm sure he'll come home soon," she added wistfully. Her gaze wandered to the window. "He does usually tell me if he's going to be long."

She broke off, staring out into the street. "I'm so sorry." She hurriedly gathered herself up. "A customer – "

"Of course." I walked to the door with her.

"I hope you understand."

"Of course."

"I'm sure Papa will have gone down to the theatre."

"I'll go and look."

And I glanced out of the hall window into the street. Just as a chill took me, and the world began to blur, I saw a woman walking to the front door.

Julia Mazzanti.

I was standing on the steps of Esther's house looking out at the central gardens of Caroline Square. Stars were gleaming brightly, the full moon just sliding over the roofs of the surrounding houses. There had been another discrepancy in time; I had spent only a few minutes in that other world, yet an hour or two seemed to have passed here.

I shivered. The night was stifling warm but 'stepping through' to the other world was always accompanied by a cold that chilled me to my bones. I eased my violin on my shoulder and set off round the square. There is a drunken spirit in the gardens who enjoys a gossip too much and it is always less time consuming to take the long way round.

The streets were quiet; remembering what Esther had said about the moon rise the previous evening, I knew it must be the early hours of the morning. I heard St Nicholas's church clock strike but halfway through counting the chimes, I stopped.

Someone was following me.

Cursing, I strode out more quickly. My lodgings were across town from Caroline Square, on the far side of the Lort Burn. This stream cuts Newcastle in two from north to south; the only ways over it are by the Low and High Bridges. But to reach the bridges, I had to traverse some dark streets – the householders in this part of town are notoriously lax about putting out lanterns. In five or six streets, I saw only three lamps, all above houses of ill repute.

Not far from the High Bridge, I crossed from one side of the road to the other deliberately, so I could glance back at my pursuer. I was lucky, caught sight of him as he passed under a rare lantern. It was the man who had been staring in the theatre window at me. Had he been the one who fired too?

And – dear God! – could he have been the man trying to break into Esther's house? The ruffians had seen us together; it would not have been hard to discover who she was and where she lived. Were they trying to attack me through her?

If Esther was in danger, this had to be stopped. And now. But how? I was unarmed and any musician hesitates to get in a brawl for fear of an injury that will ruin his profession for life. I had my violin too which I didn't want to damage.

I walked on, glancing behind me, listening for a rush of footsteps. We were coming into the darker part of town now; half a dozen men might be hiding in the alleys for all I knew, to spring an ambush. I glanced down one of the alleys – and quickly stepped into it.

Someone had abandoned an old spade against a wall. The blade and the handle had parted company and the blade fell over with a clatter as I snatched up the handle. I pressed back into the shadows of the doorway, awkwardly trying to protect the violin on my back.

The footsteps were quickening, faster, faster, until they were almost running. I held my breath, gripped the spade handle.

Here he was, swinging into the alley in a panicking rush. I caught a glimpse of his face as I swung. Yes, it was the same man. Then he went down in a heap, hands clutching at his head where the handle had cracked against it.

I vaulted over his prone body and hurried on to the High Bridge. His groans followed me. I had not killed him then, which was a relief. But perhaps I had taught him I was not as defenceless as he had thought.

Perhaps.

My lodgings were eerily quiet when I walked in. Only a few months ago, there would have been the chatter of Mrs Foxton, my landlady (a spirit of many years standing) and the seamstress in the back room on the ground floor. But death, alas, paid a visit and the seamstress collapsed and died in Brewer's shop, amongst all the bales of cloth and silks and lace. An ideal place for a seamstress to die, you'd think, but I've heard that she plaintively sends messages backwards and forwards to my landlady until all the other spirits are sick of it. I've hardly had a word out of Mrs Foxton since, except when the rent's due.

My room is on the second floor; as I pushed the door open, something caught beneath it. A note, folded and sealed, with a great grimy fingerprint in one corner. I lit a candle, locked the door. Automatically, I lifted the mattress to check that the little bag of coins was still there. It was. I must make a decision soon about where to invest it – it was hardly in a safe place here.

The note was from my great friend, the dancing master, Hugh Demsey, and was dated two days previously. I have known Hugh since we were in petticoats, and over the past years he has been in many a scrape with me, though never more so than in the last year. Not long since, Hugh was shot while we were attempting to apprehend a murderer and he has only recently recovered his full health. He was still apparently in Houghton-le-Spring, which is tolerably near to Durham.

*Dear Charles* (he had written), *I trust that now you are wealthy you have not forgotten your friend languishing in this god-forsaken spot with only flat-footed yokels for company.*

Thank God the seal had been unbroken. I had told Hugh to keep my good fortune private. And if the ladies and gentlemen of Houghton-le-Spring knew their dancing master's opinion of them, they would look for a new teacher.

I scanned the rest of the letter briefly. Hugh was a wicked observer of weaknesses and told a good tale but I was in too much of a hurry at the moment to read his stories properly. One thing that did catch my attention was the last paragraph.

*Have our Italian Guests arrived yet? Is the Signora as fat as all operatic Sopranos? Is her husband as bad a Violinist as we were promised? And is the young Signorina delightfully virginal? I trust you have not forgot the phrases of Italian I taught you? I have been hearing Tales here that the Signor is not a man with many Friends – perhaps someone will take it into his Head to rid you of him and then you can take up your rightful Position as Musical Director again.*
*I am*
*Your Obt Servt Hugh Demsey*
*I am entrusting this to a Welch miner to deliver.*

That clearly explained the grimy fingerprint. I put Hugh's letter in a book for later detailed perusal, and blew out the candle. I was more than half inclined to go out again and patrol the back of Esther's house in case the intruder returned. But the household was on the alert now and if it had been an opportunist burglar he surely would have realised that the house was too stoutly defended.

The ruffians decided me. When I crawled across the bed, to draw the curtains aside and look out, I saw two men across the street, lounging against the wall. One was smoking a pipe. They were standing directly under a lantern and must have seen my curtain move for they looked straight up at me and grinned. I let the curtain drop. To go out again would simply get myself in trouble and not help Esther in the least.

Oddly, as I lay sleepless in bed, it was Hugh's letter that preoccupied me. Mazzanti was 'not a man with many Friends' he had said, implying that he was a man with a number of enemies. I still had quite not decided whether that shot had been intended for me or for Mazzanti. Was Mazzanti really in danger of his life? The previous shootings, in London, had suggested so, if Julia Mazzanti was telling the truth of course. I felt an obscure guilt; Mazzanti's death would make my life a great deal easier for I would be in possession of my old post and the money that went with it.

I turned over to make myself more comfortable. To acknowledge such self-interest was not to wish Mazzanti dead.

I wondered who did.

# 5

**I think there is no better place for company than this town; there are some very genteel people here.**
[Letter from Lady Hubert to her sister-in-law,
on visiting Newcastle upon Tyne, May 1732]

I slept surprisingly well although the June sun woke me earlier than I wished. I lay in bed staring at the dim ceiling and the line of bright sunshine that lay across the room, sliding in through the gap where the curtains did not quite meet. Sometime in the night I had thrown off my blanket, and it lay in a rumpled heap on the floor.

I dragged myself out of bed and splashed cold water from the bowl over my face. Was Esther all right? Had the burglar made another attempt to break in? I thought of sending a message by the spirits but that was out of the question; my interest in Esther would be all over the town in seconds; nothing moves faster than information amongst the spirits. I would have to make the enquiry in person.

Half an hour later, hastily dressed and unshaven, I was standing at Esther's door, learning from a yawning Tom that nothing untoward had happened. Mrs Jerdoun, he said, was breakfasting in her room. Did I want to go up?

I did. I said, "No," and made a hasty exit.

A flutter of white caught my eye as I turned, a flash of yellow. Like ribbons. I swung back.

Tom had already shut the door.

Perhaps I had caught a flash of sunlight reflected from the door as it closed. It had reminded me of the girl last night and the glimpse I had had of Julia Mazzanti in that other world.

And hadn't the Julia of my own world been wearing yellow ribbons too, yesterday at the rehearsal?

The sun was as yet very low but already very hot. As I walked down to the Sandhill, near the Keyside, I kept to the shady sides of the streets, cut through alleys where the sun never penetrated, dodged through back yards of houses and shops. Whatever Mazzanti said, *I* had been the one shot at yesterday; I was the one who had been followed last night. I wished I'd brought the spade handle out with me but it was tucked under my bed. Besides, in daylight it would excite comment. But I was sick of glancing into alleys and shop doorways in case a ruffian leapt out at me. Never mind that it was all my fault – how long were they going to bear a grudge?

I saw no one. Or at least no one who looked likely to attack me. It was probably still too early. The people who strode down the steep streets to the Keyside were the respectable folk with business to do; ruffians like the ones who threatened me had probably been up half the night, attacking unwary revellers, breaking into shops, or making off with the coal heaped on the Keyside for loading into the keels. And they would be gin-sodden too; they would still be wrapped up on the floors of their hovels, snoring in a drunken stupor or nursing headaches fit for the day of judgement.

The only person acting suspiciously was the unlikeliest. As I passed, I glanced up the street where the Mazzantis were lodging in Mrs Baker's house and saw Proctor the psalm teacher staring up at a window, longingly. Well, he was hardly a danger; he probably wouldn't kill a rabid dog, on the grounds that it was one of God's creatures.

And he wasn't going to win Julia Mazzanti's adoration either.

On my way down the Side, I called in at a tiny house just beside the breeches shop and chatted to a fellow there who lived on the floor below me until a month or two ago. He is a barber by trade, and had the good fortune recently to inherit his master's business. He was looking more prosperous than he had, and gave me a shave at his old rates 'for friendship's sake'. He does a good job and I felt a great deal better for it.

After a breakfast of bread pudding and a tankard of ale, I made my way along the Key for my only lesson of the day. June is a bad month for musicians; indeed the summer is a bad season. All the gentry and many of the richer tradesmen are at their country estates; if I could make a patron amongst them who would invite me out to a country party, I would be off myself, with alacrity. If it wasn't for that hundred guineas under my mattress, it would be a very hard time indeed.

Lizzie Saint, sixteen-year-old daughter of Thomas Saint the printer, had been offered a chance to venture out into the countryside with her friend, Miss Hawks of Gateshead, but chose not to take up the invitation. Instead, she stayed in town to practise her music and her feminine wiles. Lizzie has a gentleman in mind as a prospective husband and the gentleman is musical; Lizzie, who is pretty without being beautiful, knows that her harpsichord playing may be the factor that tips the scales in her favour in Mr Philip Ord's eyes. Ord is the nephew of an old friend of mine, but I don't like him. I suspect that Lizzie doesn't much like him either, but he has coal mines and mixes with the best people in society.

So Lizzie practises on all summer, providing a little income for me, and since she is a good student and a better harpsichord player than some professional players I know, I have no objection to her assiduity. I spent a pleasant morning with her in a cool room, and her widowed sister provided a little entertaining conversation and a dish of tea afterwards. I fancy they had not seen company for several days and were eager to talk to anyone available.

I lingered longer than I had intended and my plan of indulging in a little harpsichord practice on my own account was abandoned when I went out on to the Key and heard a clock strike eleven – I was due at the theatre just after noon. I decided to take refreshment at one of the coffee houses instead, and try and get this matter of Esther's burglar out of my mind. Houses were burgled all the time, I told myself; it was not necessarily connected with the ruffians who were after me. I trudged on along the crowded Key, the stifling sun nagging at me.

A man took hold of my arm.

I swung round, brought up my fist...

"Devil take it, man!" Philip Ord snapped. "What's the matter with you?"

A tradesman does not shout at a gentleman; I did not trust myself to be polite so I kept quiet. What in heaven's name did Ord think he was doing, leaping out of the crowds like that? He was a slim man of thirty or so, with a fashionably small wig sitting on top of a thin face and a distasteful expression; he let go of my arm and rubbed his hand against his coat skirts as if my sleeve had been dirty. It was not. Ord himself was dressed remarkably well, as if he was going courting. Given that he was heading in the right direction for Lizzie Saint's house, he probably was.

He was also sweating in the heat – more than I was, I saw with some satisfaction. A fine sheen of moisture coated his red face.

"What's this I hear about the Mazzanti girl?" he demanded.

I frowned. "She was well enough when I last saw her, yesterday." I was having difficulty remembering when I had last seen Julia – that experience in Esther's house last night had disorientated me. I had seen her when I left the theatre, that was it.

"The word's all about town she was shot!" Ord said impatiently. "They say you caught the fellow!"

Never believe gossip, I reflected. I explained what had happened – the shot, the chase, the fact that the fellow had got away. I was reluctant to add to Mazzanti's importance by supporting his lies but I did not wish to mention the ruffians who were after me; gentlemen look askance at such associations, even if they are unwanted or unlooked for. So I ended with "It was Signor Mazzanti who was shot at, not Julia."

He looked at me stonily, as if trying to judge whether I was telling the truth or not. "Her father?" he said at last. "Is that all?"

And he walked off without a word of farewell.

I plodded on along the Key, wending my way round heaps of stinking coal, round boxes of biscuits and candles and kegs of beer, dodging yellow-waistcoated keelmen, and black-coated preachers prophesying doom. I could not see any of the ruffians but Ord's sudden appearance had reminded me that I could not afford to lose concentration. But even as I scanned the shadowed corners of the Key and the entrances to the dark chares, and scrutinised the faces of the crowds through which I pushed, I could not help but reflect that Ord's concern for Julia did not sit well with his courtship of Lizzie Saint (which I had heard was all but settled). Was he not the man who had been sent down to London to negotiate terms with the Mazzantis? Back in March, I thought. He must have met Julia there.

I wondered how strongly he had expressed his admiration for her there, safely out of the gaze of friends and acquaintances. Of course a little harmless flirtation would not have been too offensive. All the same, whatever his own behaviour, Ord would be the first to condemn my interest in Esther as socially unacceptable.

The Guildhall, an impressive though extraordinarily ugly building, sits between the Keyside and the Sandhill, and is always festooned with notices for one thing and another: the theatre performances, the dancing assemblies in Race Week, the Races themselves. And – I stopped as I passed – a new notice dazzling white in the sunshine, offering a reward of one guinea for information on who had shot Mazzanti.

I read through it with some impatience. Mazzanti was making the most of his opportunity. Notices like this would keep the shooting alive in people's minds and, as far as Julia's appearances in the theatre and her mother's appearances in the concerts were concerned, that was all to the good. Advertisement of any kind attracts audiences. But the offer of a reward was foolish in the extreme; half the petty thieves in town would be besieging his door with false information.

The whole affair was irritating me. I stood in the hot shade, watching the carters battle along the Sandhill and two women arguing over a basket of eggs, and half the gentlemen of the town discussing the latest news from Georgia and Florida, and frowned over the matter. If I could have dismissed it as simply an attempt by Mazzanti to gain extra profitable notoriety, I would not have been concerned. But my experiences at Esther's house the previous night suggested that it was something altogether different.

I was not thinking of the burglary, which was clearly either a chance event or an attempt by the ruffians to punish me – I could deal with either of those possibilities. But what teased me was that I had again stepped through to that other world that ran alongside ours, so similar and yet so different. It was the third time such an experience had occurred, and on the two previous occasions there had proved to be an intimate connection with events in our own world, as if the shock and commotion caused by dramatic events in our world had prompted the gateway to open to similar events in the other world.

And in that other world, I had not seen the ruffians who threatened me. I had seen Julia Mazzanti. Were the Mazzantis at the heart of something strange? Were they what linked the two worlds at this time? And, if so, why?

I sighed and turned for Nellie's coffee house. John Mazzanti was the most obnoxious of men and if no one murdered him sooner or later, I would be extremely surprised. But it was none of my business; I would not be dragooned into the affair. I had enough to occupy me with the ruffians and Esther's burglar, and nothing, not even my growing fascination with the interlinked worlds, was significant enough to distract me from those matters, particularly where Esther's well being was concerned.

I had not calculated that the matter would not leave me alone.

# 6

**Travel is regarded as an everyday matter in this country. The gentlemen hop into their carriages and make off for the metropolis on the merest whim. Even the dreadful weather does not deter them.**
[Letter from Philippe de Breton to his sister in Paris,
1 March 1736]

Nellie's coffee-house was crowded and the snatches of conversation I overheard were all political. One elderly gentleman was insisting to a friend that Walpole was doing a fine job running the country; the friend said dismissively that Walpole was the worst thing that had ever happened to us. The first gentleman said Walpole was right to keep us out of European affairs; the other insisted that we risked losing a huge amount of influence by doing so. A military looking man in the corner gave his newspaper a sharp irritated snap and muttered something about the damage to trade in the American colonies.

I looked for a quiet corner. I have never taken an interest in politics – it seems irrelevant when you are preoccupied with the day to day business of earning a living. All I wanted was a bite to eat and something to drink, before I went back into that furnace of a theatre. But someone was signalling to me from a cluster of armchairs in a window embrasure: Claudius Heron. Heron is a gentleman of considerable wealth and astuteness who does me the honour of being my patron, and is the other person who might have bought me a ticket for that organ. He is widely read and well-educated, and can be a pleasant conversationalist – when his jaundiced view of human nature does not take possession of him.

He was with a small plump man, with an alarmingly red face and an irascible expression; a ludicrously tiny wig perched on top of a rotund head. Heron himself wears his own hair and, like many other fair-haired people, bears the heat badly. A trickle of sweat ran down his cheek as he waved me into an empty chair.

"Patterson, you know Wright, don't you?"

I could not say I knew him as we had never been introduced. But I recognised him by sight – William Wright of Dockwray Square in Shields was an eminent shipowner. I bowed and the gentleman harrumphed back; it was plain he had no idea why Heron should have sought my company.

"Wright was telling me about John Mazzanti," Heron said.

The girl came to serve me and I ordered ale and game pie.

"Fellow's a fraud," Wright said irritably.

"He can't play the violin certainly," I murmured. Heron gave me a sharp look; he was one of the gentlemen who decided that Mazzanti was good enough to take my place in the concerts – though, to do him justice, he had argued against it.

"Doesn't have a penny to his name!" Wright said stridently, attracting attention from men around us. He was wearing a thick coat more suitable for winter than summer, a rich shade of plum. No wonder he looked hot and irritable.

"But his wife sang for Handel last winter," I said. "She was rumoured to have earnt two hundred guineas."

"Then they've spent it," Wright snapped.

"The daughter," Heron murmured.

"Over-indulged," Wright said.

"And Signora Mazzanti is not beyond extravagance herself," Heron said, in a tone that suggested this was only to be expected of women. Though he would have used exactly the same tone for a spendthrift man. "She has an excellent voice, of course. Have you heard her sing, Patterson?"

Praise from Heron was praise indeed. I accepted my pie and

ale with a smile to the girl that brought it. "When I was in London, I went to the Haymarket Theatre to see her but she was ill."

"You will have a pleasant surprise at the Race Week concert then," he said. "There was a time she could silence the crowds with the first note."

In her youth, he meant; only the young nubile singers had powers like that. Once they are grown older and fatter, the crowds continue chattering even if the voice has matured and grown even more golden.

"I don't care how well they can caterwaul," Wright snapped. "The fellow's a damn leech. He fastened on me in London and he hasn't got his teeth out of me yet."

Did leeches have teeth? I wondered. But then Wright was notorious for loving the bagpipes. He didn't need my encouragement to tell his story – again, for he had plainly told it already to Heron.

"I was at Drury Lane, damn it, enjoying the company and getting an eyeful of the actresses." He leered at me. "You only get the sour-faced hussies up here, you know, the good-looking ones all stay in London. Stands to reason – that's where they make the money, on their feet and on their backs." Heron made a gesture of distaste; Wright ignored him and plunged on with his tale.

"And I'm hardly outside, climbing into my carriage at the kerb, when I hear this bang!"

I swallowed a mouthful of pie hastily. "A shot?"

"Women shrieking all over the place! Men shouting for the barber surgeon! And when I got there, the Mazzanti fellow is standing there with blood streaming down his face and his wife swooning in the arms of a gentleman. And d'you know all it was? A damn ricochet shot. Hit the wall, stone chipped, flew up in his face and cut him. Damn it, Heron, any more coffee?"

Heron signalled to the nearest girl.

"Should have walked away but he clutched at me, asked me to protect him!" He snorted. "Any Englishman could have protected himself. But there was that pretty little daughter of his pleading with me for help." He grinned. "Couldn't resist her. Took them back to their lodgings in my carriage. Next thing I know I'm agreeing to let them travel north with me."

He regaled us with tales of horror from the journey north – how Mazzanti had never had enough money to pay for his family and beds, how Signora Mazzanti had been finicky over her food, how Julia had made up to every ostler, stable lad and boot boy in every inn they stopped at. How they had wheedled him into letting them use his servants, for they had none.

"Taken ill," he said, contemptuously. "That's what they expected me to believe! I kept the bills, sir, all of 'em – presented the fellow with them when we got here. And what has he paid me?"

I was obviously expected to contribute to the conversation. I said: "Nothing?"

"Not a farthing! And I don't believe I'll ever see any of it!"

"I was told there was an attempt to shoot Mazzanti on the way north," I said respectfully. Another sharp look from Heron – he knew me too well.

"York. On a Sunday! Outside the Minster. You'd have thought they'd be Papists, wouldn't you, being foreigners, but they came to church, bowed and sat and stood in all the right places." He preened himself. "The little thing's not all bad – she was very respectful to me, chatted away inconsequentially like they all do. Very nice, very nice."

"And the shooting?"

"Damn near took the Precentor's hand off. William Mason, you know. Decent fellow. Very decent about the injury, though it bled like the devil. Missed Mazzanti by a hair's breadth." He collapsed into gloom. "I wish they'd got him."

"Then you would never have got your money back," Heron

pointed out.

Wright snorted. "Never will."

I could not resist an ignoble impulse. "Why do you not approach him in person, sir?"

"Don't know where to find the fellow."

"He will be at the theatre in Usher's timber yard," I said. Mazzanti had been devilishly rude to me yesterday; an unpleasant encounter with a creditor was only a small price to exact.

"Devil take it, is he?" Wright wrestled himself out of his chair. "Damn it, if I don't do it. Much obliged to you, sir, much obliged." And to my horror, he stopped as he passed me, fiddled in his waistcoat pocket and pushed a coin at me. "Much obliged."

The coin was a penny, about what I'd give a boy to take a message for me. I had a grim view of where Wright thought I was in the social scale. No wonder he had been horrified when Heron beckoned me over.

Heron's face was set hard in anger. He did not speak for a moment; the girl brought the extra coffee Wright had asked for but not stayed to drink. Heron leant forward and poured me a cup – a kind of apology, I thought.

"I hear Mazzanti was shot at yesterday," Heron said, sitting back with some effort. The heat outside was bad enough; in the coffee house, even with the windows open, it was stifling. He looked almost overwhelmed by it.

I won a little time by sipping coffee. I did not want to tell Heron about my encounters with the ruffians; not only would I have to admit to the scuffle that had earned me their enmity, which would not reflect well on my own behaviour, but I was certain Heron would insist on taking action against the fellows, calling out the constable, or putting out the hue and cry. And if that happened, sooner or later the entire business would come to Esther's ears and she would worry.

"Apparently," I said.

"And you gave chase."

"The fellow got away." I sighed. "It was much too hot to be running through the streets."

"Did you get a close look at him?"

I shook my head and frowned. "Do you have any particular interest in the matter, sir?" He had after all known, or thought, that I would be interested in Wright's stories on Mazzanti.

Heron hesitated. "I wondered," he said finally, "if the shot had been meant for you."

Damn it, he knew about the ruffians already!

"I'd advise you to take care, Patterson," he said. "Except that I've made the same plea in the past and you have never taken any notice of me."

I winced. "I beg your pardon, sir. Matters always seem to overtake me. But in this case, I'm inclined to think Mazzanti is the target of the assassin. The attacks in London and York would indicate that."

"It indicates the assassin is an abominable shot!" he retorted. "And to try and kill him under such circumstances! Ridiculous!"

"The crowds, you mean?" I had not thought of that; the London street would have been crowded with playgoers, in York the worshippers would have been taking their leave. Here in Newcastle the theatre company and the sawyers were moving about. "You're right," I said. "Why not merely trap him in some dark deserted alley?"

Heron swore. "Now I've encouraged your interest. Leave it, Patterson, for God's sake. Have you not learnt from your experiences last time?"

I grimaced. "I beg your pardon, sir, but I've never been able to let a puzzle go. And my interest was already piqued."

I told him about the glimpse I had had of Julia Mazzanti in that other world. Heron is the only man in this world who knows about that other world, for on one occasion he was even dragged into it with me. I felt some relief in telling someone what had happened and outlined my theory about dramatic events opening up the gateway. He listened to me with increasing grimness.

"I can honestly say that that was one of the worst experiences of my life," he said. "There was a time you shied away from it too."

I nodded. "Once. When I didn't know what was happening. Does it not intrigue you, sir? Do you not admit to even a trace of curiosity about that other world, about what it means?"

He shook his head wearily. "I know what it means. It means trouble. Disaster. Danger. I got you out of it last time, Patterson – I don't guarantee to do the same again."

# 7

**The most exhilarating time is at rehearsal, when the creations of the masters take shape, lovingly delineated by the best geniuses in the acting profession.**
[Reminiscences of a theatre manager by Thomas Keregan (London: published for the Author, 1736)]

We argued over the matter. Claudius Heron is the only gentleman I can argue with for he does it, as he does all things, in a civilised manner. He listens to views contrary to his own, admits if he is wrong, and gives way if he believes it the right thing to do. Unlike all the gentlemen around us, expounding their own political views to each other and dismissing any opposing view.

In the end, we agreed on one thing: that the shot had in all probability been intended for Mazzanti. It was too great a coincidence if he had been attacked several times already and then suffered from a shot meant for me; moreover, the ruffians were clearly out to frighten and torment me, not to kill. The opening of the gateway to the other world alarmed Heron; he agreed that it was probably caused by a coincidence of events in the two worlds and that, he said, meant that the danger was acute.

"But to Mazzanti," I said. "Not to myself. I am merely a bystander in this. It is merely that for some reason I can sense the other world where no one else can."

He nodded. "Then there is an easy solution – keep away from Mrs Jerdoun's house."

I kept silent. Quite apart from the fact that I could not tell him why this was impossible, I had once sensed the world opening up in a different place altogether.

Heron was musing on something else. "What is it about Mazzanti, I wonder, that makes him a target?"

"His obnoxious character," I said tartly. "The man is a self-important charlatan."

Heron permitted himself one of his rare smiles. "You are an impartial observer, of course."

I sighed. "No, but an accurate one nevertheless. The man is destined for a violent end."

"I must meet him. I trust he is not as bad as you paint. I have a great respect for his wife's abilities." He cocked his head as we heard the chimes of the Guildhall clock through the open window. Twelve o'clock. I started.

"I should be at the theatre." I quickly drank the remains of my coffee. "Forgive me, sir, I must hurry."

Heron nodded but detained me a moment longer. "Is it worth my while buying tickets for the theatre in Race Week?"

I had never known Heron patronise the theatre – much too trivial an occupation for him. He prefers the Italian opera of Signora Mazzanti to the English opera of her daughter. "Save your money for the concert the Signora is putting on," I said. "Unless you simply want to see your friends. The play won't hold your attention."

He laughed softly. "I'll take your advice."

It was not the sort of weather to rush but I rushed nevertheless, climbing the steep Side from the Sandhill to Mr Usher's timber yard at the top, not far from the Post Office. I did not neglect to keep my eyes open for the ruffians, but my talk with Heron had settled my mind somewhat. I had not been the target of the shot, therefore I was not to blame for the injury to Mazzanti, therefore I could concentrate on my own affairs, and Esther's.

Just inside the yard, I paused in the shadow of a huge pile of timber, getting my breath back from the steep climb. I was thirsty again, and the sweat was dripping from me. Two or three young apprentices were swearing over a large tree trunk.

"Complaining, complaining," said a spirit high above me. "Always complaining. You'd think they didn't know what sunshine was."

I started. That business back in March involved one or two very bad spirits and it had shaken me and taken me some time to regain a semblance of trust in them. I still disliked being startled by them. I squinted up at the timber yard gate. There was an old spirit there who had died run over by a cart. I sighed in relief; no harm in him at all.

"In my day," he said, "we really had hot summers."

The shade was beginning to feel surprisingly chill; I shivered. Then, as the voice of the spirit began to fade, I realised what was happening. There are no spirits in that other world – that is one of the chief differences between that world and ours. I was stepping through again. But why here? Why in the timber yard?

I put out a hand to steady myself against the pile of wood which seemed to exist in both worlds. But in this other world that ran alongside ours, it was already evening – the sun was sliding down behind the theatre, the last rays winking above the roof; the evening star was gleaming in the turquoise sky. And despite the warmth, a thin drizzle dampened the backs of my hands.

A woman strolled from behind the wood pile: Julia Mazzanti, looking demure and innocent. But there was something different about her. I couldn't quite fathom what it was. An extra edge of decisiveness perhaps? A sense of self-assurance unusual in one so young. She was wearing yellow ribbons in her hair – ribbons that had blue flowers scattered across them with a tiny bright sparkle in the centre of each flower. The young seamstress had finished her delicate task.

The contempt in Julia's amused eyes was new too.

"Too much to drink, Mr Patterson?" she said mockingly.

But before I could speak, the chill took me again. A momentary darkness, then I was in the hot shade, with the spirit droning above my head and a carter yelling at me to move.

I moved. Wondering what, if anything, the spirit and the carter had seen. Had they seen me disappear for a second or two? Or had they seen nothing at all? What had the Julia in that other world seen? I could wonder, but not do anything about it — I could hardly ask.

Inside the theatre, there was the usual chaos of people milling about before the beginning of the rehearsal. Mrs Keregan slumped in a chair, yawning hugely and calling for breakfast; young Richard was concentrating with bit lip on carrying a tray laden with tankards. Two or three lads were hammering at scenery on the stage.

And over by the prompter's desk a little knot of people fussed over John Mazzanti. His face was purpling with bruises; he exaggerated a limp as he hobbled to a chair. Athalia hovered over him like a red-haired angel, prettily making him comfortable. Mr Keregan said hopefully that he supposed Mazzanti could not go on.

At the back of the theatre, young Richard was offering a tankard to a scowling Ned Reynolds. Ned took the tankard but didn't even look at Richard; the boy scurried away, obviously distressed. Damn Ned, what was he playing at? I strolled across.

"Mazzanti's still making a fuss, I see." I contemplated the little knot of people; Mazzanti was saying in a long-suffering tone that he could not in any circumstances let the company down. Keregan looked disappointed. "Although how the devil a shot to the head can produce a limp, I can't imagine."

"You're behind the times," Ned said sourly. "That was yesterday's attack."

"There's been another?"

For a moment, I thought him disinclined to tell me. There

was a look of bitterness on his handsome face that took my breath away. Ned is a careless fellow, living from day to day with supreme indifference to such matters as money or rent – a devil-may-care approach that is both engaging and infuriating. But there was an ugliness in his expression that alarmed me.

"You see the hero of the hour," he said, sneering. "Some fellow tried to break into the Mazzantis' lodgings last night and damn near killed Julia. But Mazzanti dashed to the rescue and drove the fellow off."

I started. Another burglar? Or the same man who had tried to break into Esther's house?

"And here comes my darling colleague," Ned said dryly. I began to suspect that he was drunk. I glanced where he was pointing. Julia was pausing in the doorway, charmingly modest, with downcast eyes. Overdressed perhaps, with too many ribbons and too much lace, but properly white and pink. Except for – yes, those two yellow ribbons in her hair, exact copies of the ones her counterpart in the other world had been wearing. Though – I squinted for it was difficult to be sure at a distance – were the blue flowers a little paler?

She was hanging on the protective arm of Mr Philip Ord.

Ned Reynolds swore, softly, fluently. "Behold," he said. "My rival. What d'you reckon, Charlie? Do you think she'll prefer me to a fortune and high social position?"

"Prefer you?" I frowned. "Ned, what kind of a joke is this?" I glanced round and saw young Richard, watching us; he looked away quickly.

"Joke, Charlie?" Ned grinned wolfishly. "This is no joke. I intend to marry the lady."

And as I stared at him open-mouthed, he thrust his empty tankard into my hands and moved in on the little group.

Ned was courting Julia; Philip Ord was courting Julia. I didn't know which was more unlikely. Ord was hardly going to marry an actress, especially not with Lizzie Saint and her father's money in prospect. Yet he was looking at Julia with surprising devotion, and to allow himself to be seen in public with her, even if it was just in the presence of the theatre company, was surely significant. But as for Ned – the whole idea was preposterous.

Mrs Keregan cackled with laughter from her chair. "Enjoying the show, Charlie boy?"

"I don't believe it," I said forcibly.

"Oh, our Ned's serious all right." She rubbed her fingers together. "He's after the money. She's the worst singer and actress I ever saw, but she knows how to woo the gentlemen. She'll make a fortune for her husband – while her looks last at any rate."

"But Ned…" I trailed off. Some things are acknowledged but never spoken of.

Mrs Keregan was watching with some cynicism. "There's more than one gentleman with tastes of *that kind* who escapes the attention of the law by marrying." She cast a glance at Richard.

"It'll be a disaster."

"Oh certainly, but don't worry about it. Papa will never allow it."

I looked across to where Mazzanti was still playing the wounded hero. "I wouldn't have thought he'd approve of Ord, either."

She crowed. "He's after a duke, at least!"

That hadn't been what I meant. "I'm surprised he's contemplating marriage at all." The moment Julia married, her income would pass into her husband's hands, which meant that John Mazzanti and his wife would be dependent on the Signora's income. And the Signora was getting older and fatter, I was told.

Mazzanti looked round and saw his daughter, and Ord and Ned facing each other over her pretty little head. The change in him was remarkable. He leapt up, strode across and seized Julia by her arm. She was distributing her favours equally, it seemed, simpering at both Ord and Ned as Mazzanti raged about so-called gentlemen who took advantage while his back was turned. And – was it my imagination – or did he have just a touch of desperation about him too?

Mrs Keregan sighed. "That's no way to handle a girl of her age. It'll end in disaster, mark my words."

Mazzanti bore his daughter off, up the stifling theatre towards the stage, calling for the rehearsal to begin. The sunlight through the windows haloed the girl with gold. Mrs Keregan, a much more mundane figure, extricated herself from her armchair with difficulty, and went off fanning herself furiously with a piece of paper. Ned followed the Mazzantis, still with that predatory air about him; Ord, more inhibited, or more cautious, fumed impotently at the doorway.

Richard fussed around me, gathering up the empty tankards; his head was down, his shoulder turned. When I spoke, he muttered an incoherent reply. I started to talk to him then Ord interrupted, strolling across to me with as much insouciance as he could manage. Richard hurried off.

I slid my fiddle from its case, plucked the strings to check its tuning. Ord was gazing about with his usual insolence, but there was an edge of bravado to it. Well, if he was ashamed, so he should be. I could sympathise with Ned's plight even if I disliked his idea of using marriage as nothing more than a smokescreen and a source of money; Ord, however, I could only condemn. Not so much for the idea that he was thinking of taking a mistress – after all, so many men did – but to be courting an actress at the same time as negotiating his engagement was unfeeling.

Besides Lizzie Saint would get wind of it – someone would tell her. Someone always did.

"Miss Mazzanti is a fine performer," Ord said, as they began rehearsing some dialogue. I said nothing; there was nothing diplomatic I could say. "As a music-lover, I admire her greatly."

He was trying to pull the wool over my eyes. I was outraged that he should be so hypocritical and that he should think me gullible enough to believe him. "She is, of course," he added, "not a lady."

I could not contain myself. "Not like Miss Saint," I said.

Ord flushed. "Damn it, Patterson, it's not your place to bandy about the names of ladies!"

He stalked off.

I started to tune up; Mazzanti on the stage swung round angrily and demanded silence. I retreated to a hot little room off the theatre, which at other times Mr Usher used as a counting office. Richard was in there, cutting up chunks of bread and cheese; he glanced round, coloured, bent over his task. I plucked at the E string of the violin and it broke. Cursing, I loosened the peg to take off the broken ends.

"Do you think he will marry her?" Richard asked.

I hesitated. "Ord?"

He nodded. "He has lots of money," he said eagerly. "She's bound to like that." He offered a shy smile. "Julia likes money. Those ribbons she's wearing – the yellow ones? They have a diamond in the centre of each flower."

More like paste, I thought cynically, unwinding the last fragments of the broken string at last. "She might marry him, he'll not marry her."

"There was talk of it in London."

"You saw him there?"

He nodded. "He came to the theatre to see Julia."

"Did he show any partiality for her?"

Richard sniggered. "That's not what Ned called it."

"I can imagine," I said dryly. The new string was proving recalcitrant, refusing to wind round the peg properly. And it was my last spare too.

Richard said again, "Do you think he'll marry her?" He was plainly not referring to Ord any longer. From the theatre behind us, we heard the tones of Ned's voice; it was a love scene with Julia but something had annoyed Ned – the loving words were in distinctly unloving tones. And I couldn't hear a word from Julia – someone ought to tell her to speak up.

"She's so beautiful," Richard said wistfully, "And so kind. She's always happy to talk to me."

I didn't know what to say. Or what was the truth. "Don't concern yourself," I said. "He'll come to his senses."

"Yes," Richard said, sounding older than his years. "That's what I feared."

I watched him walk off into the theatre, feeling sombre. My own situation with Esther was difficult enough but nothing like the difficulties Ned and Richard faced, with the full force of the law and the revulsion of society against them. I myself found the whole affair rather odd, like a man who hates turnips stares at another who thinks them the best food in the world, but I couldn't for the life of me see what harm they were doing anyone.

Which was the point, I supposed. If Ned did succeed in marrying Julia, he risked doing a great deal of harm indeed – to Julia's happiness, to Richard's and to his own well-being. For I'd known Ned a long time, long enough to know that he found it dangerously easy to despise himself.

Through the open door into the theatre, I could see part of the stage. Julia was prettily shrinking away from the unlit candles along the stage edge and saying something inaudible. Mr Keregan was giving a fine performance totally against his own character, of the despotic father. Ned was simmering in fury even as he pronounced his undying love for the girl from whom he was about to be parted for ever (or at least until the last scene).

Dear God. The idea came to me with a start. Ned was set on marrying Julia, for her money and for the disguise she could give him. Mazzanti would never agree. Which meant that if Ned's plan was to succeed, Mazzanti needed to be removed from the scene.

Was Ned the one trying to kill Mazzanti?

# 8

**All the world meets in a town of this size.**
[Letter from Lady Hubert to her sister, 9 April 1732]

Halfway through the afternoon, Signora Mazzanti came into the theatre and sat at the back of the hall. She was accompanied by her landlady, Mrs Baker, who lets her house for lodgings and frequently accommodates members of the theatre company. Signora Mazzanti was not fat – certainly nothing like Mrs Keregan – but the plumpness was eating into what had plainly been a remarkable beauty. She sat well and smiled well, and moved well, and pretended that she didn't mind the company ignoring her very well indeed.

Mrs Baker, a comfortable homely woman of about fifty, gave me an expressive roll of her eyes. With one accord, we strolled towards the back of the theatre and met over the rickety old table that Richard had set up at the back of the theatre, with a dozen tankards and two or three glasses, a cask of beer and a bottle or two of poor wine. Bread and cheese were covered in cloths, reminding me of the chunk of bread I had seen in the other world, in the girl's room.

"Mrs Baker." I gave her an admiring look. "I wonder if you would introduce me to the Signora?"

Her look was flirtatious. "Would you not rather speak to me, Mr Patterson?"

"Much rather," I said, promptly. "But alas…"

She laughed but looked at me shrewdly. "You are getting quite a reputation, Mr Patterson, as the man to go to when trouble looms. And now you want to speak to Mrs Mazzanti. Is this anything to do with the attack on her husband? And the attempted burglary last night?"

It was and it was not. I had resolved to leave the matter alone, but that glimpse of Julia Mazzanti in the other world had undone my resolution. She had sneered and looked at me with contempt, but there had been something in her eyes that the Julia in this world did not have – spirit. I admired that, even while a little feeling of disloyalty to Esther prodded at me. Besides, there was the matter of the burglaries – one at Esther's house, one at the Mazzantis'. If they were connected, solving one puzzle might help me solve the other.

As Mrs Baker led me to the Signora, I saw Proctor the psalm teacher come into the theatre, sheened all over with a thin film of sweat, hugging his bassoon case to his chest. He looked lost. I smiled at the Signora, bowed over her hand. The skirts of her dress were so vast that I could hardly get near her. The fabric was embroidered with a thousand tiny flowers – silver thread on white material; I wondered how many seamstresses had lost their sight over it. Like Julia, she wore too much lace and too many ribbons, and much too much jewellery, though whether the latter was real or fake I could not tell. Her hair was improbably gold, her skin improbably white. She murmured pleasantries and I realised she was as English as her husband; she even had a grating London twang in her voice.

And only lastly, after taking in all this ornamentation, did I look at her face. She was not looking at me, but at the stage, even while she acknowledged my greeting. And there was such bleakness in her expression...

"I was distressed to hear, madam, that you were burgled last night."

"It's my fault," she said. On the stage her daughter was prettily wheedling her supposed father, Mr Keregan; as usual, Julia was inaudible at the back of the theatre.

"But surely..."

"Now, love," Mrs Baker said comfortably, coming round to pat the Signora's arm. "You know it's nothing of the sort."

"If only I got more engagements. They don't ask me like they used to." She probably had not even heard my reference to the burglary, I thought. "Julia should not have to bear such a responsibility," she said.

I frowned at Mrs Baker; she mouthed "Money" at me and gave me a knowing look.

It sounded more like envy to me; I said: "Your daughter still has a lot to learn."

For the first time she gave me her attention, in a slightly startled, almost shy way. I saw her daughter in her very clearly. "You think so?"

"Stagecraft and the art of singing and acting well only come with experience," I said, truthfully. "We should acknowledge maturity, not worship callow youth."

Mrs Baker gave me a look, as if to suggest I was a flatterer. The Signora was preening herself a little, in a charming way – she plainly did not realise she was doing it.

"Sometimes," she said, "I think one must simply have faith in God that all will come right in the end."

I nodded.

"Always bearing in mind that God needs a little push from time to time," Mrs Baker said with a wink. "He helps those that help themselves."

"Yes," the Signora said dubiously. She held out her hand gracefully. "My dear sir, do come to visit us when you have the chance. We are always glad to see friends."

And, immensely graceful, she gathered up her skirts, got up and swept out of the theatre.

"Don't come," Mrs Baker said out of the corner of her mouth as she prepared to follow. "You won't like it, Mr Patterson. The whole house stinks! Drink. Him, not her."

And shaking her head, she hurried after the Signora.

I didn't know what to make of this conversation; in a way I was embarrassed to find myself in the middle of what was plainly family jealousy. But I was tempted to take up the offer of a morning visit, to see if after all I would have a chance to quiz the Signora about the burglary. I was standing irresolute when Proctor came hurrying across. "Who's that fellow?" he said urgently. He gestured at the stage. "He's making up to her!"

"Ned? He's supposed to. He's the hero, she's the heroine."

Oh Lord, I thought, looking at the thin nerve-ridden face. Proctor, the unworldly, ineffectual soul, was in love with Julia. He is four or five years older than me – thirty or thirty-one – and I felt a decade older. Anyone less likely to appeal to Julia I could not imagine.

"Ned's like that with everyone," I said soothingly. Which was a lie, but if it soothed Proctor, it hardly mattered.

I was about to say something more but then I caught a flash of light in the corner of my eye. Proctor shrieked and flinched away. God, he was in a state! "It's only a spirit," I said. "Look."

But the spirit had taken offence and darted off to a high cobwebby corner. Proctor retreated to the door, his gaze never leaving the spirit's gleam.

It was a tedious afternoon. Mazzanti was intent upon rehearsing the love scenes, which he said were at the heart of the comedy. They weren't. The machinations of the villain, playing first upon the father with false promises of wealth, then upon the daughter with visions of fine dresses and jewels – those were at the heart of the play. Julia only had to look pretty and Ned handsome and dashing, which they could both do effortlessly.

But Mazzanti wanted Julia to shine. She had to be at the centre of the stage at every moment and Ned was always to be behind her, obscured by her if necessary. I saw Ned gritting his teeth in an effort to stay calm – he knew, I thought wryly, that any outburst would ruin his chances of getting Mazzanti to agree to a marriage with Julia.

Mazzanti was seconded in all things by Philip Ord who stayed an hour or two, calling advice from a chair placed in solitary splendour in front of the stage. Mazzanti ignored him almost totally, but Julia played to him, simpering and smiling coyly, and, at one point, bending down provocatively to consult him, showing off her immature breasts. Ord plainly enjoyed this and looked set to stay the afternoon, until a servant came in to remind him he had a business appointment.

Julia insisted on seeing him to the door, and they stood in private conversation for a good five minutes. She seemed to be impressing something on him, for she stood as close as she dared, and a good deal closer than was proper. Oddly, he looked less than happy – he looked round once or twice as if embarrassed. When he met my gaze, his chin lifted defiantly; he smiled with renewed vigour at Julia. He must have known I was thinking of poor Lizzie Saint.

Then I saw Julia's expression as she turned away from Ord to go back to the stage. For a moment, the demure smiling child was gone and in its place was an almost wretched young woman – heavens, did she want Ord that much?

I spent the afternoon with my violin in its case, fuming because Mazzanti didn't want me to play, yet refused to let me go. I consoled young Richard as best I could – at least the boy had the sense to pretend unconcern in public even if he could not stop talking about the matter to me. We were all bad-tempered. Mrs Keregan grumbled all afternoon, Mr Keregan fretted over box office receipts with so bad a performance. Proctor gazed adoringly at Julia and kept asking why Mazzanti didn't tell Ned to move further away from the girl. Athalia came off the stage in a rage because Mazzanti had told her not to 'flaunt herself' so much; we all knew that Athalia's red-headed vitality threw pale Julia completely into the shade.

"I'll strangle that girl myself," Athalia hissed. "Will someone tell her the whole point of singing is to be heard!"

I drank too much. And the heat ate at us all.

After two hours or so, not long after Ord had departed, I went outside for a piss and came back in to find my acquaintance from the street standing at the door staring calculatingly at the stage. I didn't for one moment believe his name was Domenico Corelli but I certainly believed he was Italian, or possibly of Italian ancestry; his sallow skin and black hair gave the game away even if he was tall enough and bulky enough for two men – all the previous Italians I'd met had been slight.

He gave me an amused look as I came up behind him. "I can't hear a word she's saying."

"No one can."

"The other fellow's good."

"Ned?"

"Should be in London."

"He plays there sometimes."

Silence. As if he knew I was wondering why he was there, Corelli said, "I came to see the father."

"Mazzanti? Do you have business with him?"

He shook his head. He was still dressed in his heavy coat, even in the stifling theatre, and still did not appear to be sweating. "I am intrigued. He was the fellow shot at, wasn't he? I was there when he was attacked in London."

"In Drury Lane? You didn't see the attacker?"

He laughed. "Half the world was there! The theatres had just turned out and the street was crowded. The villain lost himself in the crowds. And everyone was fussing over the victim, or running for cover."

I watched Mazzanti gesturing Ned and Mr Keregan further

back on the stage. "I can understand why someone might take offence at him."

"A man of no talent making a living from those that do," Corelli said. I thought I heard a trace of bitterness in his voice.

"Julia has no talent."

"Her mother does. She has a magnificent voice – do you think Handel would have accepted anything less?"

"I'm surprised she hasn't sung more for him."

Corelli laughed, showing white teeth. "Mazzanti got too greedy and the great man wouldn't take it. Handel's a great composer but a greater businessman – Mazzanti's demands would have bankrupted him!"

So Mazzanti had been the architect of his own downfall. That did not surprise me. "One of these attacks is going to be successful sooner or later."

Corelli shrugged his coat from his shoulders. "Never," he said confidently, then smiled at my surprise. "The worst of men always live charmed lives. I hear they were burgled last night."

He wanted to know all about it; he wanted to know very much, brushing off my casual dismissal and pressing me further. "It's no use asking," I said. "I don't know." I eyed him curiously. There was something that didn't quite smell right about him, even apart from his ludicrous name. He was good-humoured and pleasant enough but his interest was too great for it to be casual.

His gaze slipped from Mazzanti to Julia and back again. It was the father that interested him most, I thought, and wondered why. One possible explanation came to mind. Mazzanti would certainly have creditors who might be getting impatient for their money; it would not have surprised me if Corelli had been sent by one of them. He would naturally be interested if anyone was threatening Mazzanti and might kill him before his debts were paid.

For the first time, he wafted a hand across his face as if to cool himself. "You look like a busy man," he said.

I did not dignify that with a reply.

"I need advice," he said. "I'm thinking of setting myself up as a fencing master, and a teacher of French and Italian. Do you reckon there's a market for it in the town?"

I did not believe him for a minute. He was looking for an excuse to justify his lingering in Newcastle. "Fencing, yes," I agreed. "Foreign languages? I doubt it."

He grinned. "You surprise me. Allow me to treat you to a beer or two and pick your brains on the best people to apply to. Where should I set up my school? Who is likely to patronise me? The trades people or the gentry?"

It was clearly an attempt to get me on my own and pump me for information; I was ready to wager we would talk more about the Mazzantis than about fencing. But devil take it, I was merely kicking my heels here and acting as consoler for all the miseries of the company. And if Mazzanti was dunned by his creditors, it would be some small measure of revenge for the annoyances he had inflicted on me. In any case, a man ought to pay his debts.

"I have an engagement in an hour or so," I said. "A rehearsal of Signora Mazzanti's solos for the Race Week concerts."

"I'm happy to wait," he said.

# 9

**No one can ask for a straight path, sir. There are daily difficulties that call for our full attention.**
[*Instructions to a Son newly come of Age*, Revd. Peter Morgan (London: published for the Author, 1691)]

The rehearsal was in the Assembly Rooms on Westgate Road and I had expected it to be a quiet affair. The Signora was an experienced singer and would not need extended practice of her songs. A little effort to get the band to play in time and tune and an hour would be more than ample.

But I walked in to find a full complement of gentlemen, all the directors of the winter concerts presumably come to hear what they were paying so large a sum of money for. (One hundred guineas!) Mr Jenison, director in chief, greeted me at the door with some impatience. "Ah, Patterson. At last. We are all ready for you."

I glanced around. Three or four violinists stood at the end of the room, with the Rev. Mr Brown, who was tuning his cello. The harpsichord was positioned to one side. Signora Mazzanti was ensconsed in a comfortable armchair, picking at a bowl of sweetmeats. I began to understand what Jenison meant.

"You wish me to direct the band?"

He must have heard the frost in my voice. They had replaced me with John Mazzanti but still expected me to stand in for him when they demanded it.

"Signor Mazzanti is still engaged at the theatre, directing his daughter's performance," Jenison said. "Someone must deputise for him here."

Signora Mazzanti was near enough to hear what he said;

she reddened, I noticed. But she merely said, in a little girl's voice, "Mr Jenison…"

"Dear lady!" And he swooped on her, bore her up to the front of the room solicitously. And this from a man who openly regrets that the whole world is not English. But then Italian musicians have a certain glamour about them, a cachet which allows one to turn a blind eye to their unfortunate birth.

Signora Ciara Mazzanti also had a wonderful voice, and an innate, instinctive musicianship that was a joy to work with. She was not in the least disconcerted by the wrong notes in the band, or by having to repeat the opening of her first song three times so I could be sure all the band would start at the same time. More than all that, she had the ability to silence every one of the listening gentlemen and that is rare indeed.

Although, as I closed up my books at the end of the rehearsal, I did hear one gentleman say: "A pity she's so fat. Past her best."

Corelli and I spent the evening in the taverns, starting respectably at Mrs Hill's in the Fleshmarket and working our way down the social scale from there. At least that way we drank decent beer while we could still appreciate it. I left my violin with Mrs Hill for safekeeping which was as well because some time in the evening Corelli left his coat in a tavern and couldn't remember which.

He was good company, even if he did ask too many questions. I started by asking "why do you want to know?" to every question and ended by giving him practically an entire history of the town. He asked about me too – even in my hazy state at the end of the evening I had the feeling he already knew a great deal about me before he started asking. By then, it struck me as flattering rather than odd. I was a great personage – everyone in the town knew about me.

Corelli wanted to know about the Mazzantis too and I gave him a blow by blow account of the attack at the theatre. I even told him about the ruffians who were after me and he exclaimed in horror at their audacity; we talked at great length about the evils of society and agreed that the country was going to the dogs, Walpole or no. He told me about the low orders in Venice and Ferrara, all of which I promptly forgot. I told him about the last time Hugh Demsey was in Paris and was attacked by some knife-wielding thug; Hugh did a cotillion around him and got the fellow so confused he ran off in despair.

I wished Hugh was in town now, instead of in Houghton-le-Spring. He'd help run off the ruffians. And talking to him always clears my mind.

We were drunk well before eleven. We were not the only ones. I saw Philip Ord at one point, on his own, distinctly the worse for wear, going into Mrs Hill's just before midnight. Heaven help us, even Proctor the psalm teacher was wandering the streets forlornly. And in a tavern on the Keyside, I glimpsed Ned and Richard with a fellow I did not know; they were arguing violently and Ned stormed off on his own.

When I heard St Nicholas's church clock strike midnight, I decided to go home. I was not sure where I was but I was grubby and sticky with spilt beer and surprisingly hungry – I couldn't remember whether I had eaten or not. I remember saying goodnight to Corelli, who was lodging at Mrs Hill's, and I remember turning for home. But then I found myself staring up at St Nicholas's church spires and realised that I was going the wrong way.

I knew in some distant instinctive way that I needed to cross the High Bridge over the Lort Burn to get to the other side of town and my lodgings. I thought I knew where High Bridge was but St Nicholas's spires were falling over and I needed to hold them up so I was hampered somewhat. As I struggled with them, I called out for someone to give me a helping hand. A fellow came trotting up. Or possibly two. Or more. He was filthy but seemed remarkably helpful. He patted me on the back.

The next moment I was lying in the gutter, my head was exploding and my guts were on fire.

There were three or four of them. I smelt the bitter reek of gin as one leant over me, leering. He seemed to be in charge. I had fought a man who looked remarkably like him two months ago, I remembered, beaten him too. He didn't seem to be pleased.

I curled into a ball on the hard cobbles of the street, suddenly sober. A kick landed in my back and I screeched in pain. Then someone kicked me in the head and the world exploded in lights. Lightning streaked across my sight. I could hear someone screaming. It was me.

And then the sound of shouting and of running feet.

Silence.

Corelli propped me against the churchyard railings, forced me to drink spirits from a bottle he pulled from his pocket. I choked, spat and vomited up all the beer I had drunk into the gutter.

I lay back against the railings, exhausted, while Corelli squatted on his haunches in front of me. He looked none too healthy either but he grinned, despite his obvious weariness. "They didn't even resist – just ran away from me. Six of them!"

Perhaps they had been frightened at the bulk of him. More like, they preferred easy prey.

I staggered to my feet; Corelli grabbed me and pulled me upright. "I'm grateful you came by."

"Taking the air," he confessed, as if it was a mortal sin. "Trying to stop my head spinning."

I squinted at him. I was not so drunk now. Fresh air was not a convincing excuse; had he been following me? But why the devil should he?

I stumbled; he slipped my arm over his shoulder – I protested but only for form's sake.

"Where to?" he asked.

"The High Bridge."

"You'll have to show me where that is."

I nearly collapsed as we moved off; there was a stabbing pain in my back that wanted to double me up. As we limped along, I noticed that Corelli was keeping a sharp eye out for trouble. I ought to be doing that, if only I could think straight.

I couldn't remember if I had thanked him; I said, "I owe you…"

"Nothing," he said, firmly. "This is payment for all your free advice about my fencing school."

I couldn't remember talking about his fencing school. I couldn't remember anything we'd talked about. Everything was hazy. I limped on – and came to an abrupt halt as Corelli stood stock still.

He was looking down Amen Corner, the street that runs round the back of St Nicholas. In the middle of the cobbles, just before the street turns a corner to the right, was a white heap.

We looked at it for a long moment.

"A sack," I said, finally. "Or abandoned copies of the *Courant*."

We both knew it was not. Corelli left me clinging to the railings and went quickly down the street. I hobbled after him. My head throbbed, my back ached and it didn't matter. All that mattered was that pale heap abandoned on the cobbles.

It was a white bundle of muslin and lace and ribbons. As I reached the place, Corelli was lifting a layer of cloth and revealing what lay beneath. A pale face, frozen in death.

I had been wrong. No one had murdered John Mazzanti. They had taken his daughter instead.

# 10

**We must not close our eyes to the dangers of life.**
[*Instructions to a Son newly come of Age*, Revd. Peter Morgan
(London: published for the Author, 1691)]

Aches and pains forgotten, I bent to tweak away a further inch or two of fabric. The light was poor – the nearest of two or three lanterns that burned in Amen Corner was twenty yards away – but the bruises on the girl's neck were very visible. The dark marks of fingers.

"Strangled," Corelli said. I glanced at him. One of the lights was behind him; he was a dark shape squatting down beside me, his face hidden by the shadows. But I heard his fury in his voice.

Julia Mazzanti lay face down on the hard cobbles, her left cheek pressed into the ground, her once pretty features distorted. Blood was matted in her hair at the left temple and stained the length of looped ribbon that tied up the long blonde strands. Some of the hair trailed free, stiff with blood. Her hands were by her neck as if they had been raised to prise away her murderer's hands; scratches from her nails marked the fair skin by the bruises.

I drew back to take in the full slight length of her – and saw blood on the white muslin. I was beginning to feel a fury as great as that which obviously possessed Corelli.

"I'd lay odds she's been raped."

I was scanning the surrounding area of cobbles to see whether the attacker had left some clue as to his identity – a button, a scrap of torn cloth, even a dropped piece of paper – when I heard Corelli's shocked whisper. He had drawn back slightly and the light fell across his horrified face. Dear God, he had the air of a man of the world; he must know the injuries men are capable of doing each other. But he stared numbly at the girl's body as if this was the last thing he had imagined might happen.

"Corelli!" I raised my voice and spoke loudly. There is no point in being sympathetic on occasions like this – only brisk efficiency stops people falling apart. "We must alert the constable, Bedwalters. You must go for him – I'd take half the night to get across town with this sore back."

He pulled back so quickly that he almost overbalanced. He put a hand on the cobbles to steady himself. "No."

"It's not far," I said, talking as calmly as I could. "Bedwalters is a writing master – he lives at his school on Westgate."

He scrambled to his feet. His face was shadowed and unreadable. "I don't want to get involved in this."

"Damn it –"

"I'm not going."

"You can't walk out on a murdered girl!"

He snarled at me. "You go if you're so concerned!"

My back was aching with bending over the girl; I stood to face him. "Bedwalters lives next to the Assembly Rooms," I said evenly. "You can't miss the house."

"Go yourself!" he roared. And walked off.

I could not believe the callousness that would leave a young girl dead and uncared for on the cold cobbles of a public street. I drew the thin muslin over Julia Mazzanti's head and called for a spirit. After a moment, I heard the thin wail of a child, two or three years old, crying for her mummy. Damn it, there must be more spirits than that in the street! But I had to walk out of Amen Corner and down the street into one of the poor alleys around the Castle Gate before any replied to me. Half of them must be feigning deafness; that feeling of distrust returned in full force now. Not that living men were much better – how could Corelli walk away?

The spirit who finally answered had been a middle-aged woman in life by the sound of her, who clucked and tutted and promised to send a message for Bedwalters straight away. I walked back to Amen Corner. There was a pain in my back and a stitch in my side and I found it difficult to catch my breath. I had to stop once or twice, leaning against a wall to ease the pain. At last I turned back into Amen Corner –

There was a man bending over the body.

I thought at first it must be Bedwalters. Perhaps he had been close by and received the message almost at once – spirits can send a message across town in the time it takes a living man to draw a breath. But the figure was too slender and slight a figure to be Bedwalters. Uneasily, I called out. The man's head jerked up. Damn the poor light. He took a step or two backwards. Did I see a flash of light on metal? A knife? I bellowed in rage. The man jerked back.

Then he started to run, and I started to run, and he was gone down a side street in a flash, and I was left staring at empty air and cursing.

And after that, there was nothing to do but sit on the stone base of the churchyard railings and wait for Bedwalters. And pray that the ruffians did not come back.

# 11

**Died: Suddenly, Miss Julia Mazzanti, in the 17th year of her age. By her death, the theatre has been robbed of a promising ornament.**
[*Newcastle Courant* 19 June 1736]

I sat in the drawing room of Mrs Baker's lodging house listening to the sounds of grief. The door was ajar to the hallway; it was a small house and sounds carried. Upstairs, John Mazzanti was shouting with rage – I heard Bedwalters the constable raising his voice unwontedly in an effort to calm him. Across the hall, Ciara Mazzanti was sobbing, melodramatic hysterical wails; Mrs Baker's soft consoling murmurs were hardly audible.

And there was Philip Ord too, raising his voice to snap at Bedwalters. Ord was closer, halfway up or down the stairs.

The ornate clock on the mantelpiece ticked; a fox barked outside in the street. I could not stop thinking about the events of the night, as if reliving them might somehow change them.

Bedwalters had taken twenty minutes to reach Amen Corner; he must have been in bed and needed to dress. He looked worn, as he increasingly did these days. He stared down at me as I hunched against the stone base on which the churchyard railings stood, then at the bundle of white fabric. He bent to examine the body.

I was disorientated, still half-drunk and aching, still stunned by Julia's death. I could not get out of my mind that vision of Julia in the other world, that exact copy in looks yet subtly different in demeanour. In my stupefied state, I kept thinking that it was she who had died. But I gathered my wits sufficiently to give Bedwalters an account of the night. I explained away my dishevelled state by telling him Corelli and I had tangled with robbers, not wanting to have to admit to my argument with the ruffians. I could see Bedwalters thinking we must have been easy prey; drunken men always are. Bedwalters does not drink or at least nothing more than the communion wine. I told him everything else truthfully, about the shot at the theatre, the attacks on Mazzanti in London and York, about the attempted burglary at the lodging house. And at the end of the recital I was no wiser for all the words I'd expended and doubted that Bedwalters was either.

"Why Julia?" I said stupidly. My head was thick with drink. "If it had been her father, that would have made sense."

He stared at me for a moment, then said, "She was abused, Mr Patterson, grossly abused. Perhaps there is nothing more to it than that."

"A passer by who took advantage of the fact she was on her own? Her father is attacked three or four times but she is the one who dies? I don't believe it. Too much of a coincidence."

"Stranger things have happened," he said.

"And what was she doing out of doors at this time of night!?"

Bedwalters sent for two labourers and they bore the girl back to Mrs Baker's lodging house, five or six streets away. Bedwalters went ahead like the chief mourner; I stumbled behind like the drunken village idiot. And somewhere in the dark streets, Philip Ord came running up to us and let out a great gasp of horror that turned into impotent rage. In heaven's name, had he really felt that strongly about the girl?

At last we reached the door of Mrs Baker's lodging house; Bedwalters hesitated then rapped the knocker twice, sharply, almost wincing at the loudness of the noise. It did seem disrespectful. Mazzanti himself opened the door, reeking of drink and looking befuddled; Bedwalters was forced to repeat his dreadful news three times. When the message finally sank home, Mazzanti stared down at Julia's limp body with something akin to desperation. Quite apart from the natural love a father must bear his daughter, the girl had been his sole secure source of income; he was looking at the certainty of poverty.

Finally, he said, "He took her instead of me."

Bedwalters was confused. "Who would that be, sir?"

Mazzanti gestured helplessly. "There was a woman," he said, "In London. And some noble lord. I didn't know…" He put a hand to his face, hiding his eyes. "Patterson will tell you."

Hurriedly, I outlined the story of the courtesan Mazzanti had laid siege to and the anonymous aristocrat who had taken offence. Bedwalters's face grew longer with disapproval and set hard. I could not blame him; if it was true, it was hardly a story that rebounded to Mazzanti's credit. When I had finished, he turned his calm gaze on Mazzanti; in a voice that oozed incredulity, he said, "And you think this lord has killed your daughter in order to warn you off trifling with his mistress?"

Mazzanti burst into tears.

We all stood around, looking at the door, the walls, the ground, in helpless embarrassment.

The clock chiming brought me back to the present, to Mrs Baker's comfortable drawing room. I heard footsteps on the stairs and glanced out of the half-open door. Philip Ord was hesitating on the bottom step of the stairs, as if he didn't know whether to leave the house or not. He was wearing drab clothes, fashionable but dull; at some point in the evening he must have lost his wig, and his scalp, freshly shaved that day, gleamed in the fitful light of candles on a small table in the hall. He half-turned, turned back, turned again. With a sudden burst of energy, he took the stairs in bounds of two and three. They creaked loudly. From across the hall came a fresh burst of wailing.

I got up from the too comfortable chair and walked about in front of the empty fireplace. My back still ached, but the first sharpness of the pain had gone. All this noise – Mazzanti's shouts, his wife's wailing, Ord's rants: it was as if I was still at the theatre, listening to the comedians strut their parts. When my own mother died, I was twelve years old; I did not speak to a soul for a week. That was uncomprehending grief – not this weeping and wailing fit to wake the whole street.

A knock at the street door. In the flurry of disbelief, no one had thought to take the knocker off the door or to mute it. A scurry of footsteps in the hall, a murmur of conversation. Then Mrs Baker's little maid, no more than fourteen years old, appeared in the doorway with a scared little bob.

"Mr Heron, sir."

She fled. Claudius Heron shut the door and came across to the fireplace where I stood. He knew what had happened, that was certain, for he was dressed in respectful dark colours.

"Mrs Baker sent for me," he said without preamble. "Signora Mazzanti is apparently uncontrollable with grief; Mrs Baker thought I might have enough influence to calm her."

We listened to the wailing, still loud even through a closed door. "Foreigners," Heron said, without heat, "tend to indulge their emotions."

The mantelpiece clock chimed two in the morning as I explained to Heron what had happened. He was not as credulous as Bedwalters or perhaps knew me better, for he had the true story of the ruffians out of me, with a few deft questions.

As we talked, we heard the sound of John Mazzanti and Philip Ord, shouting at each other upstairs.

"Is the girl's body up there?" Heron asked.

I nodded. "Gale the barber surgeon has been sent for to examine it but the merest onlooker could see what was done to her. Raped and strangled."

"And they are arguing over whose fault it was, no doubt."

The door of the drawing room opened and Bedwalters came

in, looking wearier than ever. The shouting from upstairs did not cease. He was plainly disconcerted to see Heron.

"This idea of Mazzanti's," I said, "that some lord in London must have had Julia killed as punishment for her father flirting with his mistress – it's preposterous."

"Indeed," Bedwalters said.

"But the shootings are real enough. I was there when the last shot was fired and Mr Heron knows someone who saw the incident in York."

Heron nodded.

"He's justifying his neglect of her," I said. "If he hadn't been drunk, if he'd kept a better watch on her, she wouldn't have got out of the house." I remembered how the stairs creaked; had Mazzanti been too drunk to hear that?

Bedwalters lowered himself wearily into a chair. "This fellow you saw bending over the body, Mr Patterson. Did you recognise him?"

I shook my head. "Much too dark."

"Could it have been the Italian fellow?"

"Corelli?" I said, startled. "No, not in the least – he is a much bigger man."

"The attacks on Mazzanti himself, the burglary, and the death of the girl would suggest a feud against the family," Heron pointed out. "And who more likely to be the perpetrator than another Italian?"

"Corelli could not have killed the girl," I said. "He was with me all evening." But then I stopped because there had been a little while between our parting at Mrs Hill's and Corelli's rescuing me. But surely that had been not long enough for Corelli to rape and murder Julia? And how could he possibly have known the girl would be out of doors and an easy target?

"I automatically suspect someone with so obviously an invented name," Heron said.

Bedwalters shook his head, eased his shoulders against the back of the chair. "It is an invented name, certainly, but for a reason."

"You know him?" Heron asked sharply.

"He came to me yesterday," Bedwalters said. "He is a government agent. Looking for spies."

I stared at him incredulously. But why not? Newcastle is a port, regiments are stationed at Tynemouth and the political situation in the Indies is perilous –

"But why invent an Italian name?" I demanded. "The fellow could pass for English – he speaks without an accent, perfectly fluently. If he had an English name no one would notice him. But to draw attention to himself with a foreign name!"

"He thinks Mazzanti is a spy," Bedwalters said.

To me this was perfectly ridiculous. To Heron and Bedwalters, apparently, it was at least possible. They discussed political implications at length. I listened and posed questions that were never answered. Bedwalters had evidently seen Corelli's papers and had no doubt as to their authenticity. I wanted to know why, in that case, Corelli had so obviously wanted to get away and refused to fetch Bedwalters. Heron speculated that a musician of some international stature (or married to one) was ideally placed to travel and examine sensitive areas without rousing suspicion. I asked why, if Mazzanti was a spy, his daughter was the victim. And why had Corelli been open about his real purpose with Bedwalters, who was after all a mere constable? How could that have benefited him? But I didn't voice that last question – it was hardly complimentary to Bedwalters.

I let the two talk, rearranging the ornaments on the mantelshelf. There was, of course, the usual way in which deaths were resolved. In three days' time, or thereabouts, Julia Mazzanti's spirit would disembody and could be questioned about the circumstances of her death. But the victims of violent deaths are often traumatised and confused by the experience and their testimonies are not always reliable; besides, we had found her face down, with a wound to her temple. Had she fallen, been dazed, perhaps knocked unconscious? Had her attacker raped and strangled her while she was unconscious? Julia might have seen or known nothing.

Perhaps her testimony would clear up the mystery but it was unwise to count on it. And any help she could give us was three days away, at least, and meanwhile the murderer could still make another attempt on Mazzanti's life. Did I care? I wasn't sure I did. But I cared about Julia – or rather, I cared about the woman I'd seen in the other world. She had had an edge of something extra about her that drew my sympathy. But she had not died; her counterpart – an altogether more unsympathetic person – had.

Damn it, why didn't I just leave it to Bedwalters?

He was looking at me intently. "I understand," he said, "that you left Signor Corelli at Mrs Hill's?"

"Yes – "

"And the attack did not occur until some time later."

The sentence hung in the air. I stared at him; he looked back wearily. It was a moment or two before I took in his meaning. I had been wondering all this time if Corelli had had time between our parting and his rescue of me to attack Julia; Bedwalters had turned the matter around and was wondering if between our parting and Corelli's rescue of me, I had had time to attack the girl.

My God, he suspected me.

# 12

**We shield our daughters from the perils of this life
and this is only proper; it is the duty of a good father.**
[*Instructions to a Son newly come of Age*, Revd. Peter Morgan
(London: published for the Author, 1691)]

I was abruptly aware how tired I was, how far from sober. I took a deep breath. Bedwalters was obliged to ask questions about the girl's death – it was natural that he should want to know what I had been doing. But before I could speak, Heron snapped, "Are you accusing Patterson of this foul crime?"

Bedwalters was plainly as weary as I. "I am investigating whether – "

"It is patently obvious," Heron said, with a voice like steel, "that it is the work of some ruffian who came across the girl by chance."

"Like the ruffians chasing Mr Patterson for instance?" Bedwalters suggested. "Do you wish Mr Gale to examine you, sir?"

Lord, now he was suggesting I might be faking my injuries.

I began to think Heron was just making matters worse but he wasn't finished yet. He was obviously making a great effort to control his temper. "Patterson is hardly likely to have called for your assistance if he had perpetrated the crime!"

"He might have, if he thought the girl's spirit might accuse him." Bedwalters might be weary but he was proud of his office and he would not compromise it. And he would not be less than civil, whereas Heron, usually so cool and collected, was showing signs of being heated.

I hurried to defuse the situation. "It's my opinion Julia will accuse no one," I said and outlined my theory. "And I think it looks like the villain took the precaution of attacking her from behind in which case she will have known nothing. Why was she out so late? Do you know?"

Bedwalters hesitated; Heron turned away, poured himself wine and downed the glassful in one gulp. "She was eloping," Bedwalters said.

We stared at him.

"With whom?" Heron demanded.

Bedwalters shook his head. "We do not know." He reached into a pocket and unfolded a note, looked at it for a moment then held it out to me. I took the note to the single branch of candles on the sideboard; Heron looked over my shoulder.

*Dearest father* [the note read] *Love cannot be denied. I am flying to my love despite your refusal to entertain his proposals. Your ever loving daughter, Julia.*

Heron snorted in derision. "Dramatic twaddle."

"It is somewhat melodramatic," Bedwalters agreed. "It is not a quote from a play, Mr Patterson?"

"Not that I know of. But Keregan would be a better man to ask." The wording of the note made me uneasy. *Dearest* father? And *your ever loving daughter*. What odd phrases to use in such a note – I would have expected something a little more defiant. And was the word *proposals* significant? Did she mean a formal request for her hand in marriage?

"You think the writer of this note might have killed her?" Heron asked.

"He would have had no need to do anything of the sort," I said. "She was 'flying' to him – he could have borne her off and taken advantage of her somewhere warm and comfortable."

"Unless she changed her mind," Bedwalters pointed out. "He might have tried to force her to go with him."

"But to rape her in the street? What kind of man tries that?"

"A fool," Heron said. "I presume there is a chance some spirit overheard the whole?"

"Alas, no," Bedwalters said. "There is a chambermaid in this house who died in the attics; I asked her spirit to enquire for me. No spirit apparently heard or saw anything. He may have forced her into an unspirited alley."

I turned the note over. The paper was worn and dog-eared; the folds had dirt in them and had plainly been made some time before. On the reverse side, the word Papa had been written with a great flourish; below, something had been crossed out vigorously. I angled the note to better catch the light. It was a date. After a struggle, I made it out: 26 March 1736.

I stared in disbelief. "It is an old note." I showed Bedwalters the date.

"She had tried the trick before," Heron said contemptuously.

Bedwalters looked tried almost beyond endurance. "If she had," he said, "the note would have been in the hands of her father."

"Maybe it was," Heron said dryly.

"You're suggesting Mazzanti left it out?" I said, incredulously. "To persuade us that Julia was eloping? But why?"

Heron laughed shortly. "Perhaps he killed her himself."

Bedwalters and I exchanged glances. This was just Heron's innate cynicism talking, but nevertheless it was undoubtedly true that the note was puzzling.

"Perhaps she intended to elope in London but was prevented," I suggested. I recalled that Ord had been in London in March. "She kept the note and used it here for the first time."

"Intending to elope with the same man both times?" Heron asked sceptically.

"It's too much to believe surely that she had plans to elope with two different men?"

Bedwalters nodded. "If it's the case that her inamorato

murdered her, then at least we have narrowed down the possibilities. The man must have been in London in March and here now."

This of course eliminated me, I thought with some relief, but I could not avoid saying again, with some reluctance, that it was unlikely her lover would have needed to attack her in the street. Heron said nothing; Bedwalters merely stood silent for a moment then turned back to the door. "I believe I need to talk further to Mr Mazzanti."

We followed, of course.

The house was small; upstairs were only three rooms and the stairs to the attic. Philip Ord and John Mazzanti were trading insults at the foot of the attic stairs; on either side the doors to the rooms were firmly shut. Ord was accusing Mazzanti of exploiting Julia without regard for her welfare, Mazzanti was accusing Ord of trying to seduce his daughter. I thought both accusations were probably true.

Bedwalters said, in a quiet voice, "Gentlemen."

Both men looked round; Ord glowered at me, sneered at Bedwalters, then flushed when he saw Heron's cool gaze.

"I believe you have no more business here, Mr Ord," Bedwalters said implacably. "Mr Heron will let you out of the house – he is going down to comfort Mrs Mazzanti."

It was a masterly stroke, getting rid of both gentlemen at once. For a moment, I thought neither would co-operate; Ord was red with fury, Heron tight-jawed. But the laws of civilised behaviour, inculcated in us all, and in particular the gentry, since birth, won; Heron drew back to usher Ord ahead of him, which was strictly impolite, as Heron was the older, wealthier and better-connected, but it established at once who was the master. Ord clattered off in a great rush and could be heard furiously tugging at the bolts of the door.

Bedwalters apparently had no intention of requiring me to go, which I took as a compliment, and as a tacit admission that his question to me earlier had been a matter of form. He regarded Mazzanti steadfastly, the note in his hand. "Where did you find this?"

Mazzanti looked half-drunk, half-dazed. "On her bed," he said thickly. "I told you."

"When?" I said.

"When we laid her body there." He might be half-dazed but he was still capable of guile. "The labourers were there," he said. "They saw it."

"When did you put it there?" I asked.

He swung a fist at me. I was half-expecting it and ducked, but stumbled against the wall. The muscles in my back groaned in pain.

Bedwalters took hold of Mazzanti's flailing arm. "If you would leave this to me, Mr Patterson. You have seen the note before, I believe, Mr Mazzanti."

Now Mazzanti looked more confused than ever. "Before?"

Bedwalters showed him the crossed-out date. "She eloped once before in March – in London, I presume."

"No." Mazzanti put a hand to his head. "No." He swayed. "Never. She was a dutiful daughter." He drew himself upright with some difficulty. "She would never run away. I was going to make her the best actress in London. The richest."

He started to weep, a thin keening sound; he stood at the foot of the stairs, his face contorted, a thin mewling sound drifting from his half-open mouth. A single tear trickled down his cheek. Bedwalters reddened with embarrassment; I hovered, without the slightest idea of what to do.

"Come downstairs, sir," Bedwalters said at last, and, hand on Mazzanti's arm, helped him down the stairs to the hall. I limped behind, stumbling on one of the stairs, which creaked alarmingly. Mazzanti was still weeping. Our descent was noisy and brought Heron out of the drawing-room. Through the half-open door behind him, I could hear the women conversing, Mrs Baker in soothing murmurs, Signora Mazzanti in broken, helpless phrases. I had a brief glimpse of the Signora, holding a crumpled handkerchief; she seemed no longer to be sobbing. Heron's presence had apparently had a calming effect.

Mazzanti shook off Bedwalters's grip and, only a little unsteadily, made his way past Heron, into the drawing room. "Do not fear, my dear," we heard him say. "We will not be penniless. I will find someone else to take Julia's place."

He closed the door, very pointedly.

Heron broke the silence. "She is not a woman of business," he said. "I have recommended lawyer Armstrong to her if she and her husband require assistance."

I have become accustomed to hearing what Heron did not say; the Signora, he implied, was one of those women who sink thankfully into the metaphorical arms of a capable man; I suspected she had hinted that Heron might like to fill the part and he had recommended another. Thank God Esther was not of that kind.

"There is little more I can do here, I fancy," Bedwalters said. "It looks very much as if the girl was eloping and was attacked by a chance passer by. She had a little money and jewellery on her person and that was untouched, so robbery could not have been the motive. Whoever attacked was a villain of the worst kind. I will put the hue and cry in Thomas Saint's paper on Saturday and I will attempt to find the man with whom she intended to elope."

He cast a glance at me. "Could it have been one of the theatre company, do you think, Mr Patterson?"

Dear God. Ned.

## 13

**Never be surprised at the unexpected vagaries of
your acquaintances; it is not polite.**
[*Instructions to a Son newly come of Age*, Revd. Peter Morgan
(London: published for the Author, 1691)]

Nobody is more suspicious than a man hovering on a doorstep at three in the morning, shivering in the unexpected chill of a cloudless June night. Behind me, I could hear the murmur of Mazzanti's voice in the drawing room and Mrs Baker's sharp protests. Bedwalters had just gone, striding off towards his house on Westgate Road; Heron's carriage had been waiting for him, the coachman walking the horses up and down the street. He had driven off without a word to either of us.

My own lodgings were not far away but I still lingered, going over in my mind the route Julia would have had to take to get from this house to Amen Corner. Not an easy one and she was a near stranger to the town too, with only two weeks' acquaintance with it. And I warrant she would not have walked very far during her stay. Why had she gone to Amen Corner? Had she been attacked there or elsewhere? If elsewhere, why should her body have been taken to Amen Corner? And Amen Corner, as it turned out, had very few spirits in it; a three-year-old girl is no danger as a witness.

Bright stars flickered over my head, the Great Bear swung slowly round the pole star, the full moon rode high down the street, making it almost light as day but washed of all its colour.

Had Ned killed Julia? I did not doubt that he was capable of it – I had seen him in huge tight-lipped rages. But he had apparently wanted to marry the girl – why should he kill her?

Had she spurned him?

A lazy voice spoke above my head. Mrs Baker had relit the extinguished lantern on our arrival to light the way for the barber surgeon, and a spirit lodged on the hook from which the lantern hung.

"Busy tonight," the spirit said. A young man in life by the sound of him, and, I'd warrant, dissolute.

"I didn't know Mrs Baker's house had a spirit," I said.

"Chambermaid," he said. "Keeps herself in the attics. I'm next door." I looked closely and saw the hook was indeed hammered into the neighbouring house's masonry.

"Pity," he added. "She was just the kind of girl I like."

"The chambermaid?"

"Nah," he said. "The other one. Yellow curls, yellow ribbons. Kept her head down but gave you a sly glance out of the corner of her eye."

Those ribbons again. And something started to nag at me; I had seen something without properly noticing it...

"You saw her come out of the house last night?"

"Midnight," he agreed, sliding down the lantern hook to hang on its lowest curlicue. Moonlight gives the gleam of spirits an odd greenish tinge. "The bewitching hour. She was certainly one to bewitch a man."

I did not disagree. "How did she leave the house?"

Now he was surprised. "By the door, sir. How else?"

Perhaps I had been infected by the melodrama we acted out at the theatre. I'd been imagining she'd climbed down a ladder into the arms of her lover – wasn't that the traditional method for elopements?

"She was alone?"

The spirit chuckled. "Except for my good self."

"Did you talk to her?"

"A word or two, sir. She was not in a good mood but I restored her humour with a compliment or two. She was – ahem – waiting for someone."

"Her lover?"

"So she said."

"But he didn't arrive?"

"Never a sign of anyone," he said. "She sighed, and she walked about, and she sighed some more, then she muttered, then she cursed. The entire history of a love affair in ten minutes, sir. Then she stalked off to the corner and was gone. Never saw her again till you brought her back dead."

"Did you see which way she turned at the corner?"

"Right. Certainly right, my dear fellow."

*Right?* But to get to Amen Corner she would have had to turn left.

"Are you going, sir?" the spirit asked with sudden querulousness. "I have told you everything and you have not reciprocated. I am annoyed, sir, annoyed."

Never offend a spirit; they can do you too much harm. I turned back to him. "If you like a good tale – "

"I do. I do."

"Then I promise to come back and tell you one – when I know it myself. In the meantime, I would be much obliged if you could ask your fellow spirits if they can trace the lady's movements last night."

"Umm…" Heavens, but he was lazy; he sounded as if pondering if he had energy enough to stir from the lamp hook. Then: "It's a deal, sir. Anything to beguile an hour or two. God, but it's dull being dead!"

The streets at night are unnervingly quiet and the sounds of carousal that come from every tavern on every corner only make the silence in the streets more complete. Lights are few and far between, even in those streets where householders are conscientious and put out their lanterns; in any case, in the early hours of the morning, many are guttering and dying. As I turned from street into street, the sense of being watched, of having a gaze steady upon my back, was almost tangible. I told myself that the ruffians would be out housebreaking or lying dead drunk in some house but could not quite convince myself.

There was something I had to do before going home, something that made me brave the streets longer than I had to. I was going after Corelli. The hard-hearted villain who would leave a young girl lying dead in the street rather than get involved, who sought out the constable in the afternoon with some wild story of spies, but who ran off rather than face him in the evening. I knew what that meant. Corelli was a trickster with some sort of knavery in hand, involving money, no doubt; my only surprise was that Bedwalters had been taken in by his tricks.

And the knavery must involve Mazzanti; two Italians in town at the same time was too much of a coincidence. The Mazzantis flaunted themselves as if they had plenty of money and that was what villains like Corelli wanted. Was he simply planning to rob Mazzanti? Or was he involved with the shootings? Suppose Corelli threatened to kill Mazzanti unless he was given money and the shootings were warnings that he meant business? Or was there something more complicated going on? Could there be an accomplice involved?

I warmed to this latter idea. The unknown accomplice was part of a plot to kidnap Julia and hold her to ransom. A wild idea perhaps but I'd heard of that sort of thing happening in London. The accomplice had enticed Julia out of the house, perhaps by courting her, but something had happened; she had resisted perhaps, and he had accidentally killed her. That would account for Corelli's horror on seeing the body – he had anticipated she would be safe and sound in some hideaway; after all, a dead body is difficult to bargain with.

No, no, none of this would work. Strangling was not an

accidental way of killing. And the accomplice, if there was one, had not kept his appointment – Julia had had to go in search of him. Had her death been the result of a chance encounter after all?

One thing was for certain, Corelli's behaviour was suspicious and I wanted to talk to him. Even more importantly, he was the only person who could confirm that what I said about discovering Julia's body was true.

Mrs Hill's in the Fleshmarket was still open – only in the middle of the morning would it be quiet. I ducked in through the low door and found a cluster of butchers, still in bloodstained aprons, shouting drunkenly over a game of nine men's morris. A youth of no more than twelve years old was drooling over a beer, and one of the serving girls looked inclined to encourage him. Mrs Hill herself, as fresh as morning dew, was chuckling over a conversation with a friendly spirit; I knew that spirit – never short of a good joke.

The lady turned a smile on me. "Out late, Mr Patterson?" Mrs Hill was fifty at least but she wore well, one of those women whom maturity only improves. "Your usual beer?"

Landladies, as well as spirits, should never be offended. Tiredness was beginning to make me feel heavy and weary but I made an effort to stifle my yawns. "Looking for one of your lodgers, Mrs Hill. The Italian gentleman."

She raised a knowing eyebrow at me. "Now there's one who'll never have trouble with the ladies. But he's gone, Mr Patterson, paid up and left."

Damn, I should have guessed it.

"When?"

"An hour or two back. Said he was off to Shields for a boat. Had to catch the tide. He left you a note though. Mary!" She raised her voice. "Where's the note for Mr Patterson?"

The serving girl tore herself away from the leering youth with a scowl, and hunted through the rags and dirty tankards that surrounded her. Eventually, the note was found, stained with circles of beer and stinking of ale. A single sheet of paper of the cheapest kind, folded and sealed with a blob of red wax. Corelli had evidently been in a hurry and had inadvertently used too much wax so that little blobs clung to the paper all over. The ring, or whatever Corelli used as a seal, was engraved with a large ostentatious musical note – a quaver with a flying tail.

I broke open the seal. Inside were scrawled six hurried words in a watery ink that was already fading.

*Don't trust him*, Corelli had scrawled. *He's a devil.*

Him? Damn it – who!?

# 14

**Friday we went to the theatre and had moderate entertainment. One actress was tolerable-looking; the others were nothing.**
[Letter from Sir John Hubert to his brother-in-law on visiting Newcastle, May 1732]

A bright light was slanting across the bedclothes – the June sun shining in through a gap in the curtains. The room was as stifling as it had been when I stumbled in at around four o'clock this morning. Downstairs, I could hear the tramp of miners leaving for work and my spirit landlady's querulous complaints about dirt. I lay staring at the ceiling in blank incomprehension. It was early morning, I had slept very little and I had a huge hangover. And…

And Julia Mazzanti was dead.

I dragged myself upright. The movement set my stomach roiling. Julia Mazzanti had been raped and strangled and I had found the body. No, Corelli and I had found the body, and now he had left the town. That made him chief suspect in my eyes.

There was no point in lingering in bed; I knew I would not sleep again. I threw back the blankets and waited for the room to settle. A white rectangle lay on the floor; I bent to pick it up and the room reeled around me. Damn all hangovers. Why had I drunk so much?

The note was the one I had found at Mrs Hill's; I must have dropped it as I crawled into bed. *He's a devil.* Did *he* mean the murderer? I remembered the look of shock on Corelli's face when we found Julia. It had been a surprise certainly. Surprise that she was dead? Or just that the body was not where he had expected it to be? And – a worse idea occurred to me – could it all have been part of a plot by Corelli? Had he arranged for me to be there when he found the body? Had I been as credulous as Bedwalters?

The voice must have spoken two or three times before I registered it. My landlady, Mrs Foxton was outside the door, asking if she could enter. I grabbed for a blanket, for I had stripped before going to bed to try and cool myself.

When I called entrance, the spirit came creeping in, hanging on one of the door hinges. There was a dullness about Mrs Foxton's spirit these days, a lack of sharpness, a certain lack of caring; in the old days before the seamstress's death, for instance, she would never have allowed miners to lodge in her house. Now she grumbled and argued but took them in nevertheless. "Money's money," she'd said to me not so long ago in a dull sort of way.

So I was pleased to detect a note of disapproval in her voice, which reminded me of her old self. I had a clear conscience; I had paid the next quarter's rent before times, thanks to the money beneath the mattress, and did not fear her annoyance.

"You have a message, Mr Patterson." One that had been passed from spirit to spirit across the town, clearly. "From a young person. By name of Catherine." Mrs Foxton pronounced the name with disdain.

I sat up, grabbed the blanket as it threatened to slip. We had agreed that if Esther needed to send me a message she could use her maid Catherine as courier to avoid speculation. There must be something wrong.

"She would like you to call, urgently," Mrs Foxton said coldly. "And if you don't mind, Mr Patterson, I would request that in future you avoid implicating me in your affairs."

She probably thought Catherine was pregnant. I suspected something much worse than that. Had the burglar tried to gain entry again?

I pacified Mrs Foxton and she slid out of the room again. I threw on some clothes, splashed my face with cold water and grabbed some music books to suggest a reason for my visit. A church clock was striking six when I tumbled out into the street; the air was already thick with heat and clamped itself around my aching head.

Six o'clock. No one had a music lesson so early – I would have to hope that no one saw me arrive. But of course all the servants in Caroline Square were up and about, and half of them were on the doorstep shaking out cloths or looking for someone to gossip to; six or seven pairs of eyes followed my progress across to Esther's door. There was nothing for it but to walk straight up the steps to the door and to tell Tom as loudly as I could that I had come to give Mrs Jerdoun her music lesson. I raised my hand to the knocker –

The door swung open.

Alarmed, I walked in – and was assailed by the sharp stink of mildew. A strong aroma of beer too. The sweeping stairs in front of me were chipped and cracked, the varnish on the curving banister scratched. Plaster had fallen from the ceiling and been casually kicked aside into corners; the old elegant wallpaper was curling from the wall, showing black mould underneath.

I had stepped through into that other world.

Cursing, I stood still to listen. I could hear voices distantly, and the barking of a dog. God knows, I was fascinated by this intersection of worlds; it was a puzzle and I have always been partial to puzzles. But for this to happen at this moment, when I was worried about what might have happened to Esther!

The voices were sharp and angry. Two women. A high childish voice – that one I knew belonged to the young seamstress, and was subdued and humble. Then a lower voice, almost contemptuously amused. A grown woman who enjoyed impressing on her social inferiors how low they really were. A woman who was demanding information — I could hear the words 'want to know' and 'tell me' but beyond that nothing much more. I recognised the voice, however.

Julia Mazzanti.

A dead woman talking. The thought sent shivers through me in this cold house. I had to remind myself that I was not in my own world any longer; there, Julia Mazzanti lay dead. Here...

Here, a door opened, and Julia paused in the open gap, caught by surprise when she saw me. In her hands was a folded package wrapped in tissue; behind her, the young girl was curtseying with pathetic gratitude.

"Mr Patterson," Julia said, coyly. She waved a hand to dismiss the girl and the child obediently shut the door behind her. Julia strolled forward. "Have you come to see Flora too?"

I reddened. There was no mistaking what she meant by that. Her gaze was fixed steadily, mockingly, on my face. The Julia in my world had been demure, all cast-down eyes and coy, darting glances; this Julia was taunting and direct, her mocking gaze meeting mine as equals. It was that kind of directness of gaze that attracted me to Esther. But there was something else there too, a kind of contempt.

"Or her father?" Now there was something else; I saw a tension in her, a watchfulness.

"Flora's father." Dear God, yes, yes, Flora had said he was a musician. "Yes, indeed. Have you seen him?"

Her gaze flickered over the music books I held, which I suppose gave credence to my story.

"Not for several days," she said. Her manner was strained; I frowned and she smiled sweetly on me. "I believe he has gone out of town. But I do not keep watch over every poor musician in Newcastle." She reached out a daring hand and drew a caressing finger across my shoulder. "Only the rich ones..."

One of the less welcome aspects of this world is the knowledge that my counterpart is a wealthy man, far more successful than I. I reflected wryly that this Julia at least was plainly not an inexperienced girl; no innocent could have infused her voice with just that perfect edge of invitation – sufficient to make her meaning clear, yet not sufficient to make a withdrawal, if spurned, embarrassing for either party.

"Why do you wear such shabby clothes?" she murmured and lifted a contemplative gaze from my coat. The sharp intelligence in her eyes was alarming. "It's almost as if – "

"Yes?"

Now she was frowning in puzzlement. "Sometimes, Mr Patterson, I think you are quite a different man altogether."

"I – I can't imagine – "

"I like this version better," she said meditatively. "The other you is all politeness and genteel manners and 'don't you worry your head, my dear'. As if I was still a child. Do you think I am a child, Mr Patterson?"

She was talking as if I was quite a different person from my counterpart. Surely she could not suspect the truth?

"Not in the least," I said, my mouth dry.

"Then why do you sometimes treat me as if I am?"

I foundered. "Nothing but the good manners a gentleman is taught to show to a lady."

She laughed softly. "A lady, Mr Patterson? Not in the least. I am nothing but a singer and an actress, and you know what society thinks of such creatures."

It thinks that they are prostitutes; all too often young women who wish to pursue a singing career can only get apprenticeships by being 'friendly' to their teachers. First society offers only one course of action, then it condemns.

"But we are flesh and blood," she said. I almost imagined I saw tears sparkling in her eyes. "We hurt when we are insulted.

We fear when we are forced against our will." She must have caught my frown. "Oh yes, Mr Patterson," she said with a nod. "Yes, that is what I mean. And the most unexpected of men too. Can you blame me for having a low opinion of your sex?"

I could not stand for that. In that mildewed, sour-smelling hall, I went as far as I could and said, "We are not all cut of the same cloth."

She stood, head on one side, contemplating me. "Indeed."

"I am a musician myself. A mere tradesman. I have suffered some small indignities." But how, I thought, reddening, could those compare with what she had suffered?

The door opened behind her. The young girl, Flora, came out of the room, with her basket over her arm and a shawl thrown about her shoulders. Julia Mazzanti cast a quick look back at her, then leant towards me. Her whole body, her smile, her knowing look suggested flirtation. What she said, however, was a desperately urgent: "I must talk with you. *Please*. Tonight, midnight, outside Mrs Baker's house."

"But…" I saw the girl looking at us. Was that contempt in her expression? I said lightly, "People will think we're eloping!"

Now she raised her voice so the girl could hear. "Elope? Me? Now, Mr Patterson, you know I am a respectable young woman."

And she swept past the girl with head held high and a smile of wicked mischief.

The girl stared after her with a private little smile of contempt. Even the poorest members of society can find reasons to despise their social superiors; all too often, I reflected wryly, they are given just cause. "Do you want to see Papa again, sir? He is not back yet."

I had no wish to see her papa, whoever he was, but I did not wish to rouse too much suspicion so I entered into the conversation dutifully. "Do you know when he will be back?"

"No," she said bluntly. This time I was certain I saw tears; she bit her lip. A child in distress, plainly, not knowing what to do – could it be that the father had abandoned her? I started towards her but she gasped and fled into the street.

I stood irresolute in the hall, at the foot of the battered stairs. In truth, I did not know what to do. On previous occasions, the chill and the darkness had briefly taken hold of me and transported me back to my own world. But on this occasion, they did not. I merely stood, waiting for something to happen.

It did not.

I walked about a few steps, wondering if there was a spot I must stand on for the stepping through to take place, as if there was an invisible door in the air which I must find. Then I stood still and closed my eyes and tried to conjure up the cold and the darkness. No, that did not work, either.

Was I to be stuck here for ever?

In growing desperation, I tried again, several more times. I walked to the door, opened it, stared out into the drizzle-dampened street that in my own world was replaced by Caroline Square. It obdurately remained a street. I closed the door, went to the door of the girl's room, came back to the foot of the stairs. I willed something to happen.

It did not.

Cursing, I threw open the street door again and went down the steps to the cobbles. And shivered and foundered in darkness, and found myself staring out into Caroline Square, bathed in early morning light, and hearing Tom saying urgently behind me.

"Mr Patterson – thank God you've come!"

# 15

**Sir, only a few days since, an innocent young girl was sadly killed in the street by ruffians of the lowest kind. It is time to clear the streets of all such dangers...**
[Letter from AB to *Newcastle Courant* 15 June 1736]

I knew the worst the moment I turned to face him. A huge purple bruise disfigured Tom's temple on the left side, the eye was swollen and almost closed. He was so agitated that he had come to the door in shirt sleeves and breeches, a breach of correctness which would normally have horrified him. In the house I could hear the clatter of pans, the calling of women. And Esther's voice, unusually sharp.

I pushed past Tom into the house.

"He came back!" he said, following me breathlessly. His voice had more than a trace of glee. "But we saw him off!"

Catherine was just leaving the drawing room, ushering a flustered chambermaid before her. She looked relieved to see me, but said warningly, "She won't be cosseted."

"She was magnificent!" Tom said.

I flung open the door of the drawing room. The curtains were still half drawn and for a moment I had difficulty in seeing Esther. She was sitting on one of the delicate fashionable chairs, a glass of wine between her fingers although she was not drinking. She had set her head back against the chair and had closed her eyes.

She must have thought me one of the servants back again for she said without moving, "I told you to let me be!"

"What the devil is going on!?"

Her eyes snapped open. She started up and was in my embrace

before I was halfway across the room.

Behind me, I heard the door click closed and Catherine's voice in the hall, ushering the servants away. The drawing room was perfectly quiet except for the sounds of our breathing – Esther's slow and steady, mine coming far too unevenly for decorum. She was warm and fragrant against me; her pale hair drifted against my cheek, her head was heavy against my shoulder. And she sighed with deep contentment.

Dear God, what folly was this? I eased her away from me and lifted her face. A bruise lined her jaw on the right, an ugly line of purple. It looked like the result of a punch.

"I wasn't quick enough on my feet," she said ruefully. "My night robe tangled around my legs and I half-tripped. He lashed out wildly and caught me on the chin. I wished I'd thought to put on my breeches – much more convenient in such a rough and tumble."

I made her sit down and sip her wine, resisting as well as I could the temptation to hold her hand. "Tell me from the beginning."

"The spirit woke me," Esther said, with a weary sigh. "George. He had heard someone in the garden. So I told Catherine to wake Tom, and I came down myself to see what was going on. I had my duelling pistols," she added ruefully, "but such things are to no purpose if you are not prepared to use them. And I'm afraid I baulked at shooting him, Charles."

"*I* would have shot him," I said, tartly.

She smiled. "In the dark? Knowing that at least two servants are up and about? In any case, I never got the chance of a clear shot. By the time I got down to the scullery he was outside the back door trying to pick the lock. Tom hopped out of the kitchen window, I flung open the back door and we both grabbed for him." She sipped the wine. "It was so dark neither of us could see a thing! The fellow was swinging his arms wildly. I tangled myself in my night robe and one of his fists hit me on the chin.

Poor Tom took a couple of blows too."

"I've seen him."

Esther was clearly beginning to see the amusing side of the affair. "I cried out, Tom screamed for the watch, Catherine shouted to Cook to go for the surgeon and Cook fainted! In the meantime, of course, the burglar got away! Really, Charles, you would have enjoyed the scene enormously. Better than any ballad opera. I was tempted to burst out singing!"

I breathed a hidden sigh of relief. In truth, I had known her injuries to be slight, and Esther was more than capable of looking after herself, but my instinct was still to worry. If the burglar had been armed, he might not have been so reluctant to fire, and I could have arrived to find Esther dead or dying.

The horror of the idea made me shake. I gathered my wits, said, "What time was this?"

She considered. "Gone one this morning, I think. Charles – " She was as expert in reading my expressions as I was in reading hers. "What is the matter? Something else has happened."

"The Mazzanti girl," I said. "She has been raped and murdered."

I told her what had happened as best I knew it, omitting only to tell her the full extent of my drinking with Corelli. Esther was silent, out of a kind of respect, I think. The morning sun crept into the room through the half-drawn curtains and touched the back of Esther's chair, as I relived that half-hour spent in Amen Corner in the near-darkness, with only the girl's silent huddled body for company.

At the end of my tale, Esther asked for more wine; I refilled her glass and poured a glass for myself. I pulled back the curtains to let the light flood in, as if that could dispel the horror of the night.

"What was Julia like?" she asked, curiously. "I never met her, you know, although I encountered her parents at one of Jenison's dinners a week or so ago."

"What did you think of them?"

She considered. "*He* was all bombast and self-importance. *She* was more intelligent, or at least she could converse intelligently on musical matters. But she was –" She thought carefully. "I think the Signora is afraid of her husband. He was very disparaging about her, and to her face too. Saying things like *you always talk nonsense, dear* and *really, Ciara, why must you be so stupid?* I heard that he was very dogmatic on political matters over wine after dinner." She gave me a wry look. "But we ladies were of course discussing fashion over the teacups at the time."

I sympathised though I felt the gentlemen had probably got off lightly. Esther can be very decisive in political discussion too, and makes me greatly ashamed of my ignorance.

"And their daughter?" she asked.

"A mere girl. Pretty, demure, respectful."

Esther waited.

I added, "Sly, manipulative and vain."

"And as a musician?"

"She didn't know the meaning of the word."

Esther contemplated her wine. She was more at ease now; seemingly distracted from her aches and pains by the tragedy of Julia Mazzanti. "Philip Ord was at the dinner too. He eulogised the girl. *A great find*, he called her. *An enchanting performer.*"

"Philip Ord's musical tastes are not sophisticated."

"Indeed," Esther agreed mischievously. "He admires Vivaldi." (She knows Vivaldi is a pet hate of mine.)

"And I think," I added unrelentingly, "that a man engaged to be married – or as good as – should not be thinking about actresses!"

"He is promised to Elizabeth Saint, is he not? The printer's daughter?"

"She's barely sixteen and head over heels in love with him."

"And he is a man of near thirty," she mused. "Fourteen years between them."

A little silence fell, for that was only a year or two more than the difference in age between Esther and myself. Only she was the elder, and that made a great deal of difference.

"So who killed the girl?" Esther said finally.

"There are two possibilities," I said, pondering on my wine which glowed ruby in a stray ray of sunshine. "Either it was a random attack – she was unlucky enough to be caught by a passing villain – or the fellow Corelli was the culprit. Although I can't quite see that he would have had sufficient time. He would have had to seize her in the time it took me to get from Mrs Hill's to St Nicholas…"

I stopped. No, it was not possible; there was simply not sufficient time. And it was not possible that Corelli had killed her earlier in the evening – the spirit had seen her leave her lodgings around midnight. (Though of course a spirit cannot give evidence in a court of law.) No, Corelli must be innocent; he had fled for some reason of his own, because he was a trickster and was afraid of being found out.

So who did that leave? Only Ned.

"Charles," Esther put a hand on my arm, and I started. "I asked who Julia was eloping with."

"God knows!"

Esther reached out and tugged the bell for the servants. Her weariness seemed to have completely dissolved; she looked lively and determined. "Let us be systematic. Who would benefit from Julia Mazzanti's death? Ah, Catherine, pray bring some tea and something to eat for Mr Patterson. A piece of pie or some cold meats. Whatever there is in the kitchen. And some hot chocolate for myself. And make sure Tom takes care of that eye."

Catherine went off, grinning.

"If it was a random attack," I pointed out, "no one would benefit from Julia's death – not in the sense you mean."

"I don't believe in chance," Esther said firmly. "Now, what

about the father?"

"He wouldn't kill her!" I protested. "She was his only sure source of income."

"Her mother killed her from a motive of jealousy?"

"Julia was raped," I pointed out.

"Philip Ord?"

"Ord! He wanted to bed her – "

"She *was* raped," Esther pointed out. "Perhaps Ord encountered her in the street eloping with another man, lost his temper and attacked her."

"While the other fellow stood by and watched?"

She considered. "The would-be lover ran off in fear."

"A poor fellow to abandon the woman he loved!"

"Such men do exist," she said, with unwonted cynicism. "Someone from the theatre then?"

So we came back to Ned.

The maid brought the food and drink and we ate and drank in pleasurable near-silence. I thought that I was becoming dangerously at home in Esther's house, and that I was coming dangerously close to not caring. It occurred to me that if I had succumbed to temptation the previous night, and stayed, as Esther had hinted I should, she might not have been injured.

"There must be something in this house he wants," I said aloud.

Esther apparently had no difficulty in following my train of thought. "The burglar? I should imagine the spoons would be attraction enough to a poor man. But I am not the only householder with silver spoons – why does he so persistently want mine?"

"He might try again tonight."

Esther sipped at her chocolate. "I should imagine so." She did not look at me.

I speared a piece of beef on to a chunk of bread. "Particularly if he has realised there is only one man in the household."

"I don't want Tom hurt again," Esther said severely. "I have ordered him to keep to his bed. And after so disturbed a night, he will of course be very tired."

"Perhaps you need someone else to help. A friend… "

Dear God, what was I doing?

It was too late to back out now; I agreed to return in the late evening and left the house in a hurry before I could commit more folly. I did not like the amused look Esther gave me just before I left.

On the doorstep, I paused. To begin a secret liaison with Esther – could I do that? Could I pretend indifference in public? Could I keep the secret without fear of inadvertently letting it slip? Could I deny my feelings for her and hide them as if I was ashamed of them, or her? But what else was I doing now?

I fanned myself with my hand. The sun was already warming the day to the limit of what was comfortable, and it would certainly become hotter in the middle of the day. The theatre would be unbearably stuffy.

The theatre. The company. There was still a production to be put on; Keregan could not afford to cancel Race Week performances – they would finance the company for the next three months. He would have to replace his leading lady of course; Athalia would have to play the part.

The servants were still the only people around; the ladies and gentlemen in these genteel squares would not be up and about till nearly lunchtime. Once I was out on Westgate Road, however, I saw more of the tradespeople and working sort about. A chapman tried to get me to buy ribbons – cheap dull things compared with Julia's gaudy embroidered possessions. How odd the differences between the two worlds, I thought; both Julias had the same ribbons. The ribbons were identical but the Julias were not. And there was something else too – for a moment I was haunted by that sense of something missed, or overlooked. No, I could not think of it. Perhaps I would remember later.

I trudged through the stifling streets towards the theatre, reviewing the possible culprits. Athalia benefited from Julia's death but of course could not have raped the girl. To think of gentle Mr Keregan – courteous, contented, happily-married Mr Keregan – as a rapist and killer was preposterous. Richard? No, he had adored the girl in a platonic kind of way; he was starstruck – he would never have considered her carnally. Matthew Proctor? He had been as admiring as Richard but was the least violent man I knew; I didn't think he could have brought himself to hurt the girl he loved. Philip Ord? Now that was the most ridiculous idea yet! Ord would consider himself perfectly capable of seducing the girl without having to have recourse to violence. And Julia would probably have been willing enough, considering his wealth.

There were various other men in the company too of course, the scene shifters, prompter and so on. But I'd never seen one of them show any interest in the girl.

Except Ned.

It was time I talked to him.

# 16

**Only disaster can result when men of the lowest sort
get ideas above their station.**
[Letter from AB to *Newcastle Courant* 15 June 1736]

My mind was full of Esther's burglar as I started down to the theatre. He could not be a petty opportunist thief if he had come back. Did this have anything to do with the attempted burglary at the Mazzanti's lodgings?

I was wishing that Hugh was back in town, and wondering whether to send him a letter asking him back again, when a man stepped out of an alley in front of me. I was on the lower reaches of Westgate, by St John's church, and the only grace in the situation was that there were plenty of people about.

We stood stock still, staring at each other. He was not one of the ruffians but a poor labourer, with third or fourth-hand clothes on his back and a shirt that was more holes than material. He was perhaps twenty years old and too tall for his age, so he hesitated, bent over as if about to beg some favour of me.

"Mr Patterson." His voice was a whisper. If this was a plot to persuade me close to him I was not falling for it; I strained to hear him from where I was. "I've a message for you."

The lower sort like this man would not have been able to write so I did not ask for a note. "Say it then."

The lad looked as if he was nervous enough to forget the message, certainly anxious that he would do so. "He says that if you want the girl's killer, he can give you him."

"He?"

"But he wants you in return."

"To the devil with that," I said shortly.

"But if the villain should kill again?" the lad said slyly. "How would you feel then?"

"I've got my wits about me," I said. "I can find the murderer without help."

Well, that sounded fine enough.

"You don't understand," the lad said laboriously. "If you don't come to him, he'll come to you. In force, with all his men. If you go to him, it'll just be him and you."

Did I believe that? "I'll think about it," I said shortly and strode off towards the Side. Damn the ruffians. When I had bested their leader back in March, I had not thought he would be so persistent in his search for revenge. But I would not dance to his tune. And I wasn't going to believe any of his promises.

I thought I might be too early for the theatre company but many of them were already gathered in the stiflingly hot theatre. Mrs Keregan had thrown on an old dress in her hurry and had food stains on the voluminous shawl that covered it. Athalia was beautifully dressed but looked like a woman who had not slept well; her red hair was loose and tumbling about her shoulders. She came racing across the open theatre and seized hold of my arm.

"Is it true? The spirits have been going on and on, and not telling a sensible story..."

"I resent that," said the convivial spirit, swinging low on a cobweb – apparently his favoured lodging place.

"Oh, go away!" Athalia said in a frenzy. "Charlie boy, is it true? The girl's dead?"

"It's true."

Mrs Keregan said, "Heavens!" faintly, and leant back against her husband's arm.

"Raped and murdered," I said. There is never any need to be delicate and roundabout in such matters with theatre women.

"Who was the malefactor?" Keregan asked, with real tears in

his eyes. "That poor, poor girl."

"He did the world a service," Athalia retorted. "Where is he? I want to thank him."

This was bravado; I could see the fear in her eyes. Perhaps she was thinking that she might have been the victim. "Alas, no one knows his identity."

They made me sit down and tell them what had happened. In the middle of my recital, young Richard came stumbling into the theatre, still struggling to put on his coat; by the time I had finished, almost all the company had gathered. But none of my surreptitious glances spotted Ned.

There was silence when I had finished; I wanted to ask after Ned but under the circumstances I thought the request might be interpreted in the wrong way – or indeed, the right way. Richard, I noticed, was looking unhappy and would not meet my eye. Was that just natural distress at the death of someone he had admired? But he must have feared Julia too, because she had seemed to be the object of Ned's affections. Had he taken action to remove her?

Richard a murderer? Never. And I'd lay odds he'd never so much as touched a woman, let alone lain with one.

But hadn't I seen him around during that drunken indulgence with Corelli? Richard and Ned and some other man in a tavern on the Keyside? Or was it on Silver Street? I'd seen someone else too but I couldn't quite remember who...

"Well," Athalia said, at last. "I'd better go and con the lines, hadn't I?"

Mrs Keregan sat bolt upright. "The play! Dear God, we'll have to recast the play!"

Keregan stared at her. "Quite right, my dear. Where's my book? Athalia will have to take Julia's part of course. Now, what other changes will have to be made?" Kind-hearted or not, he was all business-like theatre manager at heart.

As the group broke up, I managed to accost Richard; he would not look me in the eyes but glanced round and mumbled something about being needed to fetch breakfast. Sweat was running down the line of his jaw.

"Where's Ned?" I demanded.

"Somewhere – in the back, I think."

"No, he's not."

He cast a quick half-glance at me. "Yes, yes, I forgot. He went out."

"Where?"

"To – to see a friend."

"Richard – " I started warningly. But I was not quick enough; he darted round me and out into the sunny yard. Well, I could hardly have asked outright if he and Ned had been together all night; he would certainly have said no.

Dust motes danced in the sunshine flooding through the door, the shouts of the workmen outside filtered in, muffled and indistinguishable. The spirit swayed lazily on the cobweb above me and murmured appreciatively. "This is the life, eh?"

"The death, certainly," I agreed.

"Uh-ho," he said. "Here's that preachy fellow again." He chortled. "I had fun yesterday, I can tell you. Frightened the life out of him four or five times – easy prey. Reckon he'd be frightened of his own shadow."

Turning, I saw Proctor the psalm teacher halfway across the theatre towards me. Red-eyed, dishevelled, distraught. Then his gaze lifted over my head and he stopped dead. The spirit said regretfully, "Too easy, ain't it? I'll have pity on the fellow and let him be." And the spirit slid up the cobweb on to a roof beam and away.

Proctor was in a dreadful state, dark circles round his eyes emphasised by the pallor of his face. He had certainly been crying and looked as if he had never been to bed; he was dressed in the same clothes as the previous day, though that was hardly surprising – I fancied he was not well off.

"It's true?" he said bleakly. "She's – she's – "

He couldn't bring himself to say the word. I quashed the feeling of irritation that I felt – how could he be so feeble? "Yes," I said. "Julia's dead."

He stared at me a moment longer. Then he seemed to crumble. "I killed her," he said.

I took him by the arm, turned him about and led him out into the open air. There was a tiny breeze which relieved the worst of the heat. I found a shady corner and sat Proctor down with his back to a stack of newly sawn timbers. I eased myself down beside him; the beaten earth beneath me was hard and dusty but at least we were out of the way here and no one was likely to overhear us.

"I loved her," Proctor said, tears coursing down his cheeks. "From the moment I saw her." He was lost in the world of the past; trying to rush him by asking questions would do him no good at all. I kept silent.

"I was in the Golden Fleece, bespeaking stabling for my horse when they arrived in town. I saw the servant hand his mistress down from the coach."

The Mazzantis had brought no servants with them, according to William Wright; no doubt Proctor meant one of the Fleece's servants. I did not bother to correct him.

"But I'd already seen her, leaning out of the coach window as they drove into the courtyard. Such golden hair, such delicate skin. Almost angelic and yet – " He paused for a moment, lost in reverie. "So human. No one could be more beautiful. And when I told her so, so gracious."

Proctor had evidently gone straight up to Julia, almost before her foot touched the cobbles of the yard, and murmured his adoring compliments. Julia had, he said, gazed on him with kindness and gratitude. Papa had hustled her away.

"I didn't expect anything else," Proctor said simply. "I am a poor psalm teacher – she deserves the highest in the land, a duke or prince at least. I could not have imagined she would be so kind as to notice me."

His voice trailed off again. I left him a moment or two, then felt it necessary to prompt him. "Did you see her again? Outside the theatre?"

"I kept watch over her," he said. "Night after night, hoping for a glimpse of her, not grieving if I didn't. It was enough to be outside the house, knowing she was safe."

It was Proctor I had seen, I realised, sometime last night. In my drunken stupor, I had registered his existence, though I could not recall where. I'd seen Ned too and Richard, and yes, it came back to me, albeit hazily – Ord as well.

"What time was this?" I asked.

He seemed to come back from a distance. "About nine – yes, nine o'clock. But he saw me."

"John Mazzanti? Her father?"

He nodded. "He threatened me. Told me he'd call the watch if I didn't move off. He accused me of wanting to harm her." A low bitter laugh. "As if I could have injured such an angel."

Alarm bells started to ring in my mind. What an odd thing to say when he had admitted not five minutes ago that he had killed the girl. I rubbed sweat from my cheeks. "You did hurt her," I pointed out.

He was slow to react. He turned his head against the pile of wood, frowned, looked at me as if I had just said something extraordinarily stupid. "Yes," he said, nodding. "I did hurt her, as much as if I had twisted the knife myself. I did as her father told me and went home."

He stared off into the distance again. "If I had stayed," he said.

"If I had kept watch. I could have prevented this. I would have seen him – the murderer – and prevented him."

I set my head back against the timber and could not help but feel a pang of bitter disappointment. The hope that this matter was almost over before it had begun disappeared. Proctor was racked by guilt, not at what he had done, but at what he had not done. He had not kept his love safe; he had betrayed her by leaving his watch. And if I needed anything more to convince me he was telling the truth, it was his apparent belief that Julia had been stabbed.

"I was afraid," Proctor said. "Afraid of the consequences to myself, so I ran away. Scared. And left her to die."

I could not think what to say and the silence lengthened in the hot yard. A sawyer stretched his aching back as he passed and gave us a curious look; a cart rumbled in through the gates. Someone called loudly for small beer.

"When did you talk with Mazzanti?" I asked as gently as I could.

Proctor seemed to come back from a great distance. "About – about ten o'clock. He saw me from the window and came out to me."

"Did you see Julia herself?"

He stared at me blankly.

"Was she with her father?"

"No. She was in her room. I did see her," he said reverentially. "When she heard me outside, she came to the window and looked out."

"But you did not talk?"

"Her father came out," he repeated.

"And you went off as he told you to."

He nodded numbly.

"You did not see anyone else hanging around?"

No, of course, he had not. He had probably walked away

backwards, straining for a last look at his love.

A silence fell between us. I wiped sweat from my temple. "There's nothing else you've not told me?"

He hesitated, rubbed his fingers together, whispered, "No."

"Nothing else you saw or heard?"

"No."

"You don't know who might have wanted to hurt her?"

He hesitated again. "No," he said wretchedly. "If only I'd stayed." Something like a sob escaped him. "If only I could have made her listen to me."

I sighed. "How did you hear what had happened?"

I had to repeat the questions. He had heard in a tavern. He could not remember which tavern. I could guess how he had spent his night. Drinking, sleeping fitfully on a tavern bench, drinking some more.

"Go back to your lodgings," I said gently. "Get some sleep."

"Lodgings," he muttered. "Yes, my lodgings."

"Get some sleep," I repeated. "And some food. You'll feel better for it."

I had to help him to his feet and he stumbled away as if drunk, shying away from the friendly spirit at the timber yard gate and almost staggering under the wheels of another cart. I watched him go with wry irritation. So much for an easy solution to the matter.

I was back where I had started. With Ned.

# 17

**We hear that an engagement will soon be announced between Mr P—O and a delightful young lady of this town, known for her sweetness of character and her admirable musical abilities.**
[*Newcastle Courant* 17 April 1736]

*Dear Hugh* (I scribbled) *For God's sake, I hope you are enjoying Houghton-le-Spring for I am not in the least enjoying this town. The Italian girl has been murdered and no one has the least idea who has done it*

Bedwalters said: "May I have a word, Mr Patterson."

I started and blotted the ink on the paper. Hastily, I turned. Bedwalters was looking at me with calm impassivity, although his face was red with the heat. I had stripped off my coat and had sat down in shirtsleeves to scribble my note. Around me, the members of the theatre company scurried; Athalia was prowling backwards and forwards with a book in her hand, muttering lines.

"A word?" I brought my attention back to Bedwalters. He looked uncomfortable and I fancied it was not entirely owing to the heat.

"I am looking for the Italian gentleman."

"Mazzanti?"

"No, the gentleman who was with you last night."

"Corelli?" Hell and damnation. "He was staying at Mrs Hill's, I believe."

"She says he paid his bill and went off to Shields for a ship."

"Indeed?"

"As I believe she told you when you sought him out."

Bedwalters's tone was respectful but his eyes were sharp and watchful.

"Yes, she did," I said. "I had forgotten."

He waited but I knew better than to elaborate. The longer the explanation the more likely you are to dig a hole for yourself.

"You did not know him before he came to this town?"

"No, I met him the afternoon after Mazzanti was shot."

"But you went drinking together like old friends."

Yes, that was odd. Why had I done that? It was all lost in an alcoholic daze.

"I face a difficulty, sir," Bedwalters started.

I finished for him. "If you can't talk to Corelli, you can't be certain my story was – " I was going to say 'truthful' but did not want to put ideas in his head. "Accurate."

"Indeed," he said. "Was there anyone else who saw you?"

"Mrs Hill."

"In the later part of the evening."

Ned, Richard: I could not draw them into the matter – not at least unless I found there was evidence against them. I didn't know the man who'd been with them. And as for mentioning Ord!

"I can't remember," I confessed.

To my surprise, Bedwalters seemed to believe me. He nodded. "If you do recall anything later, sir – "

"Of course."

"It could be important."

"Of course."

"To yourself, particularly."

And on that ominous note, he walked away, passing through the dazzling slanting sunlight out into the timber yard. I looked after him, very uneasy indeed.

Across the theatre, Keregan clapped his hands. "We must begin. Quickly, quickly. Mr Patterson, we will rehearse only the dialogue and movement today with the new players. Do not allow me to keep you. If you could return tomorrow?"

I seized my coat, crumpled my half-written note to Hugh into a pocket and made my exit. Behind me, I heard Keregan saying, "Now where is Ned?"

There were half a dozen things I wanted to do: find Ned, question Mazzanti, talk to Philip Ord, talk some sense into Bedwalters. I was too exhausted for all of it, and the overindulgence in ale the previous night was making my head ache. Besides, I needed to be rested if I was going to sit up watching for Esther's intruder in the coming night. (And I *was* going to sit up, decorously, in the kitchen or the scullery, as far from Esther's bedchamber as I could manage.) So I abandoned everything, went home, drew the curtains and, lulled by the raucous shouts of carters outside, went straight off into a deep undreaming sleep.

When I woke, the sunlight slanting in through the gaps in the curtains was low and reddening and the racket in the street was that of children. I washed, dressed and visited my friend on the Side for a shave. As the sun sank down below the roofs and spires of the churches, I walked down to the Cale Cross at the foot of Butcher's Bank and bought myself a bowl of buttered barley. It was a foolhardy place to be, perhaps, as the day lengthened, for I was not far here from the filthy chares where the ruffians lived. But there were still plenty of people about and I felt safe enough.

I was wondering whether to make a direct approach to Bedwalters when I heard a voice accost me. Philip Ord swung down from his horse and led it towards me. The horse was sweating, as if it had been ridden too hard.

"Patterson. I've a job of work for you."

That disconcerted me. Not so long ago, I had been thinking of questioning him about his relations with Julia; now he was his old commanding self, making me feel acutely aware of our respective social positions. I was conscious of the bowl and spoon in my hands, and the drab clothes on my back. And what kind of work could he want me to do?

"I know your reputation," he said curtly, squinting against the low sun. His face was red, his wig askew; his manner might be cool but I was very sure he was in the grip of strong emotions. "You can fathom these sorts of mysteries. Find out who killed Ju – Miss Mazzanti."

After Bedwalters's hints, I'd probably do far better to keep out of it. Not that I intended to let the matter drop, not while there was a chance it was connected with Esther's burglar. But I disliked Ord, I objected to his behaviour towards Lizzie Saint and I wasn't averse to punishing him a little.

"Why?" I demanded.

He stared at me. "Damn it, the girl was an innocent. Find me the devil who murdered her."

"And raped her," I said, watching him closely.

His jaw clenched with fury. "Find him!"

I could have sworn his emotion was genuine. Had he really cared for her that much?

"You want payment, is that it?" he demanded. He sneered. "Very well. If you find the villain, I'll make sure my wife continues to take lessons from you after her marriage."

The horse shifted restlessly, dragging him a step or two backwards. I was ready to hit him – at the insult to me, in thinking he could get me to leap into action simply for the sake of money, and at the insult to Lizzie Saint.

"You'll pay me to give lessons to your wife, in return for finding the murderer of your mistress!"

He was fiery red and snarling. "How dare you insult her memory!"

"Oh come," I said, with dripping sarcasm. "A singer, an actress

– what else was she good for?" Then the obvious occurred to me. "Damn it, you were the one she was going to elope with!"

"No!" He glanced about, seemed to realise for the first time that there were passers by glancing curiously at us. He visibly curbed his anger, yanking on the horse's reins and causing it to jerk its head in pain. He lowered his voice, said very deliberately: "I was not going to elope with Julia Mazzanti."

His gaze dropped away from mine; he seemed to chew on resentment. I knew he must be lying. He glanced about again, waited until the chaplain from All Hallows had walked past, bowing acknowledgement to us. Ord tried to meet my gaze, looked away again. In the soft evening sunlight, I saw his mouth work.

"I met her in London," he said abruptly. "When I went down there to negotiate with her father on behalf of the concert directors. She was – " He hesitated. "She was an innocent child, Patterson! With an angelic face and a sweet nature. Is it wrong to have admired her?"

I thought of Richard who had succumbed to Julia's attractions in much the same way. But Richard was a naïve boy and had nothing but admiration on his mind. A man like Ord is not looking for pleasant conversation and a song or two when he encounters an actress, however young and innocent. And I did not believe Julia had been innocent.

He swallowed hard. "I – I may have been precipitous."

He had made promises. I sighed inwardly. What was it about Julia that made sensible men lose their wits?

"You made promises."

"No, no, I did not. I – I may have led her to believe, purely accidentally, without intending to – that my admiration was – rather deeper than it actually was."

"You told her you loved her."

"Not directly."

The lowering sun was now shining in my eyes; I shifted to get a better look at Ord. He was gritting his teeth. I felt a reluctant admiration; confessing such stupidity, and to someone his social inferior, cannot have been easy. But he must have been in desperate straits even to contemplate it. I had an inkling I knew what that meant.

"You wrote her letters," I guessed.

He nodded, jerked on the reins as the horse fidgeted. "Damn it, Patterson, I have to have them back! If I don't get them, my chances of marrying Miss Saint are finished. You know what a puritan her father is!"

Thomas Saint is a decent man with admirable morals, and very well named.

"Where do you think they are?"

"In her room, damn it! Tied up with ribbon and placed with a pressed rose amongst her handkerchiefs. Damn it, where do young women usually keep such things!"

"How many letters?"

It cost him a struggle to tell me. "Eight or nine."

He had been in London only three weeks as I recalled; he must have written one every other day.

"So," I said, "how much will you pay me?"

That made him straighten. He was sneering again, plainly feeling he was back on familiar ground.

"I've told you – "

"Not enough." I said ruthlessly. Lizzie's trusting gaze was in my mind's age; she was a serious girl but of excellent character, and I objected – I objected very strongly – to what was going on behind her back. And to what would no doubt go on behind her back after marriage. The least I could do was to exact payment from her prospective spouse.

"You want money." Ord smiled unpleasantly. "I should have known."

"I want the directorship of the winter concerts."

He stared at me. Real fear showed in his eyes. "I can't. Mazzanti – "

I shrugged and pretended to move off. He snatched at my arm.

"Damn it, I can't! How could I persuade the other directors?"

"You've seen Mazzanti trying to direct the play. You've seen how incompetent he is. He'll ruin the concerts within a month. Persuade the other gentlemen of that fact."

He drew back. I knew he had wit enough to see I was right. He looked sour but he said harshly: "I'll try."

"Not enough."

"Very well," he said sharply and bit his lip as a passing merchant raised eyebrows at him. "Very well. I'll do it. Somehow. I'll do it."

He swung away suddenly, as if he could stay still no longer, swung himself up on to his horse.

"Damn it, Patterson." He looked down with defiant contempt. You'd better succeed in this. If you don't – " He hauled on the reins. "If you don't, I'll break you. I promise you that – fail me and that'll be the end of you."

# 18

**Tickets for the Concert may be obtained at the coffee-houses, at the Golden Fleece, of the Printer of this Paper, and at Mr Mazzanti's lodgings in Piper Row.**
[*Newcastle Courant* 5 June 1736]

That last look of Ord's stayed with me as I turned towards Mrs Baker's lodging house; I would have sworn he had been genuinely in love with Julia. What an odd pair they must have made. The strait-laced disapproving man of thirty and the actress who had not, I swear, been as innocent as she looked. Would he have married her? I fancied he had been tempted.

But surely he would not have been so blind to the social consequences of such an act? She would never have been received in company and he would have been ostracised by all respectable matrons; they would have rallied to Lizzie Saint's support without hesitation. The gentlemen would have continued to deal with him, of course, and some would have envied him in some respects. But they would all have felt it cast doubt on his judgement.

Letters indeed! For a sensible man, Ord had been remarkably silly. Esther and I had never exchanged more than a receipt for her payment of my bills.

Where to start in the business? I was wandering around in the dark, suspecting first Corelli, then Ned, then anyone else who came to hand. I needed some good solid facts. And I knew someone who would provide me with reliable information.

The street in which Mrs Baker's lodgings stood was narrow, but respectable, the haunt of lesser tradesman – Mrs Baker herself was the widow of a cheesemonger. Few people were about; a gentleman idled at the far end of the street ogling a saucy young fisher girl, a Quaker in black paused to contemplate a notice on a wall. Mrs Baker's door stood open slightly.

The house seemed silent. I wondered whether to call out. It seemed disrespectful when the girl's body was lying upstairs. The hall seemed to be in Stygian gloom, shutters and curtains drawn, a single candle burning on a small table.

Mrs Baker came up behind me in the street, making me start. She was dressed in dark purple, as a gesture towards mourning, and carried a jug of ale.

"You've timed it right, Mr Patterson," she said with a satisfied grin. "Come and have a bite with me."

She thrust the jug into my arms, shut the door, snatched up the candle, and led me into the back of the house. As she opened the door to the kitchen, sunlight leapt out, blinding me. The shutters were not drawn here, and the heat was immense.

Mrs Baker fussed about as I stood for a moment to let my eyes adjust. In only a second or two, she had bread on the table, and cold beef and half a cooked pheasant which smelt very high indeed. She winked. "One of the butchers is a particular friend of mine, Mr Patterson. Sit yourself down – you look like a man who needs food."

The effect of the buttered barley had not lasted long, I found. I dragged a stool up to the table, while Mrs Baker reached down another plate from the dresser and a knife from a drawer. She was a remarkably good-looking woman, full of life.

"You're not looking for his highness, are you? Mr Mazzanti?"

"No."

"Or herself?"

"His wife? No."

"Then you wanted me." She plumped herself into a chair, set her elbows on the table and grinned at me. Her pose gave me a fine view of her neat breasts. "Want the whole story do you?" Another wink at my sigh. "You're becoming well-known,

Mr Patterson. They say your talents extend to more than music."

There had been a time I had wanted nothing more than to be left alone to play and compose. Now I could not remember the last time I had set pen to paper to plan a concerto. And I did not miss it. To tell the truth, solving a mystery or two had been far more profitable.

"Well," she said, "what do you want to know?"

I took a grip on my wits. "I want to know what happened last night. Why was the girl out of the house?"

"Eloping, so they say."

"And no one heard her leave?"

"Apparently not. I didn't. But then I sleep sound."

The sign of a clear conscience, I'm told. But there was that butcher – I knew what Mrs Baker meant by particular friend. And she was so open about it!

"They all dined here last night?"

She shook her head and slid a piece of meat on to my plate. "The ladies did. He had an engagement with a friend." She snorted. "A tavern, more like. He was as drunk as a lord when he came home. Had an altercation with Mr Proctor on the doorstep. Accused him of harassing his daughter." She chuckled. "Mr Proctor! Doesn't even use his whip on his horse for fear of hurting it."

There was a mixture of amusement and contempt in her voice. Proctor can engender that feeling all too easily.

"What time was that?"

"About nine."

"Not very late."

"He said the friend had been called away and demanded I serve him dinner. Well, there was nothing left! Mrs M eats for six and there was none of the missish attitude about the young lady. Not that that surprised me. Any rate, I brought in some bread and meats, much like you're having now." She poured ale for me. "And he turned his nose up at them." She gave me a slice of pheasant. "Likes his fancy sauces, he does. Come of being a foreigner, I daresay."

"Complained, did he?"

"To the air," she retorted, breaking off a chunk of bread and chewing on it. "I left him to it."

"Then what happened?"

She gave the matter some thought. "Oh, yes, I remember. I took tea into the ladies, and the young missy said she was going to bed. Feeling unwell, she said." Mrs Baker gave me a significant look, which was entirely lost on me. "Her mother fussed over her a bit but let her go. Then his highness came into the drawing room with the brandy in his hand." She chuckled. "Most of it was already inside him! Mrs M took one look at him and said she thought she'd go to bed early too."

I picked at the meat, played with the bread. "And what did Signor Mazzanti do?"

She shrugged. "I tidied up the dishes, locked the doors and went to bed myself. If he did what he usually does, he stayed up all night, drinking himself into a stupor."

"He does that every night?"

"Every night he's been in this house."

"Then conjugal relations – "

"Non-existent," she said with glee.

I tried to work out what Julia must have done. She had gone upstairs, waited until the house seemed quiet, gone down, left by the front door and waited in the street. But the house was narrow-fronted and Julia must surely have been visible from the windows on to the street.

"Did Mazzanti usually stay in the drawing room all night?"

She nodded. "Sleeps in a chair. And he's there every morning till noon at least. I have to turn any visitors away at the door, or show them into the dining room." She gulped at ale. "And he stinks. The room stinks. He gets so he doesn't know what he's doing and the stuff goes all over the chairs. Over the curtains too once – tell me how he managed that!"

When Bedwalters and I had brought Julia's body back, Mazzanti had opened the door himself. He had been dazed, like a man that has just woken from a deep sleep. And yes, he had smelt of brandy, a little. Perhaps he had not had time to drink as much as usual.

"You definitely locked the front door before you retired?"

She gave me a reproachful look as if I had just insulted her.

"Mrs Baker," I said tactfully. "The door was ajar just now when I arrived, and your neighbours are after all trustworthy people. It would hardly have been surprising if you had left the door unlocked."

"Not after that burglary on Monday night," she retorted.

I had not forgotten about that. "Tell me about it."

She was only too glad to oblige and I devoted myself to her meats which were excellent; I knew the butcher Mrs Baker was *friendly* with – one of the more respectable ones. Mrs Baker wiped sweat from her brow, fanned herself against the hot sun flooding in through the kitchen window, and told me all between gulps of beer and mouthfuls of bread.

The evening before the burglary had apparently passed much as usual: Mrs Baker in the kitchen, the ladies in the drawing room, Mazzanti lingering too long over his wine after dinner. At some point, he had gone into the drawing room and disturbed the ladies with talk of money troubles.

"Had his wife in tears, he did," Mrs Baker said. "When I went in to clear the tea things, he was berating her for getting old – losing her looks, he said, not attracting the gentlemen any more. The young lady was smirking at that." Mrs Baker stared contemplatively into her ale for a moment. "None of them liked each other, you know. Well, I can understand trouble between husband and wife – it happens all the time. My own case… " She stopped and gave me a rueful look. "Married, Mr Patterson?"

"Not yet." I caught myself up, cursed. Why the devil had I not just said no? What if Mrs Baker had heard rumours…

Apparently she had not. "That's well," she said approvingly. "Take your time over it. That's what caused half the trouble in this case. The young lady wanting to rush into marriage. Anyhow she went off to bed early."

"She seems to have made a habit of it."

Mrs Baker chuckled. "With her parents quarrelling all the time? Wouldn't you?"

My father had been one of those quarrelsome men but as a son I had seen little of it – my mother had taken the brunt of it. I said nothing.

"So she went up to bed," Mrs Baker said. "And her mother followed her and I went off too and left the Signor to get drunk. Much the same as every other night."

"And the house was all locked up?"

She winced. "I may have left the back door unlocked."

"The butcher?" I suggested.

She set her head on one side. "Now, Mr Patterson," she said, "a gentleman should know better than to ask a question like that."

Which was an answer in itself, I reflected. "And then?"

"Nothing, sir, till the middle of the night, when I heard a tremendous noise on the stair and went out to see what had happened. I thought – " she looked coyly at me.

"The butcher?" I prompted.

"He will insist on coming up without a candle in case someone sees it and he's as blind as a bat! So I went out to pick him up again. And there was Julia lying on the stair, clutching on to the banister to stop herself tumbling down. She'd hit her head and was dazed. I went to her to ask her if she was all right.

And then I heard the sound of someone running, down in the hall."

"What did you do?"

"What any sensible woman would have done," she said. "I picked up the poker I keep under my bed in case of such emergencies and I went down after him. To tell the truth, I still thought it was my butcher friend, thrown into a fright by the young lady appearing. But it wasn't – my friend told me next day he'd not left his wife all night. So who it was in my house the Lord alone knows."

"You didn't see him?"

"Not a hair of him. Only his highness."

"Mazzanti?"

"He'd heard the fellow too, and came out to catch him." She sniffed. "Drunk as he was! No use at all. He was blundering around in the hall and walking into doors and crying out that the villain had hit him, and bleeding all over my furniture and meanwhile the fellow was getting away!" She poured more ale for both of us. "Foreigners," she said, placidly. "Useless."

"Did Mazzanti see the intruder? Could he describe him?"

"Not he!"

"Was anything stolen?"

"Not a penny." She contemplated a slice of the pheasant, speared it with the point of her knife. "There was one odd thing though. Miss claimed the fellow had tried to throw her downstairs." She nodded at my surprise. "Aye, I thought she was imagining it too. But after what happened last night… "

I finished off the meats in silence. If the burglary had been an unsuccessful attempt to kill Julia, how did that relate to the attempted burglaries at Esther's house? From what she'd told me, she'd been injured as a result of her own courage in tackling the intruder. But what if that had been his purpose in trying to get into the house?

Nothing made sense. What connection did Esther have with Julia? She'd told me they'd never met. And, if there was a connection, it would surely rule out the idea that a passer by had taken advantage of finding Julia in the street. And who could it be?

Philip Ord was known to both ladies, I thought, and he had a motive. What if Julia had threatened to use those letters against him? Had the burglary been an attempt to find the letters and remove them from Julia's possession?

Philip Ord – a murderer?

I'd seen him on the night of the murder, hadn't I? At Mrs Hill's, I thought.

Ord?

Mrs Baker got up to clear away the meat and bread, and to set down a huge bread pudding. I brought my attention back to the present. I was after information and I would not get it if I daydreamed. "Where are Signor and Signora Mazzanti now?"

"*He's* out organising the funeral. Chaplain of All Hallows was first on the list to be honoured with a visit, then the organist and the undertaker." Mrs Baker cut up the pudding. "Oh, and the tailor – he doesn't have mourning, he says. *She's* being looked after by Mrs Jenison and Mr Heron. You know, sir, I never met a lady who so expected to be looked after. I daresay the quality are like that, but the rest of us know it's hard work that brings home the meat."

I nodded absently. If Mazzanti was looking for the organist of All Hallows, he would be out of luck; the organist was in London introducing his mother to the youngest of his six children. I was his deputy and Mazzanti would no doubt be seeking me out before long. I had better practise the funeral psalms. Not that I was likely to be paid, if William Wright's assessment of the Mazzantis' financial dealing was correct. Still it meant that Mazzanti and I would have to have a conversation; I'd have plenty of questions for him.

Mrs Baker tucked into her pudding. "Mrs M seems to think that now his highness will dedicate himself to her again. They'll console each other, weep on each other's shoulders and devote the rest of their lives to her singing." She snorted. "Any fool can see her days are over."

"She has a wonderful singing voice."

"She's almost as old as I am," Mrs Baker said tartly.

"That proves my point," I said. "I never met anyone whose days are so clearly *not* over."

She told me to get away with me, but her smile of pleasure at the flattery lingered. "I stick to what I say," she added. "It doesn't matter how you look when you're letting out lodgings. When you get up on a stage, though, that's different. You've got to attract the gentlemen. And it's a rare gentleman that likes a mature woman." She preened herself a little. "His highness will find another young lady," she said. "Mark my words."

I thought of Athalia.

"Not that Mrs M'll see that," Mrs Baker said, waving her tankard at me. "She's the sort of lady who doesn't see what she doesn't like. The day after the burglary she never gave it a second thought but went straight out visiting the next morning as if it hadn't happened. And Miss – she sent a note off."

I considered for a moment. "Fixing up the elopement?"

Mrs Baker nodded approvingly.

"Are you sure? How do you know?"

"Saw her. She gave the paper to a boy in the street."

"Did you hear where she told the boy to take it?"

She shook her head. "Too far off." She paused for a moment, looked at me shrewdly. "Want to see her, do you? The body, I mean."

I did not. I had seen quite enough in Amen Corner. "No, but I'd like to look at her room."

"Well, so you shall. They've laid Miss out in the spare room, her own room being a trifle *disordered*."

She finished off her bread pudding, stacked the dishes and wiped down the table. Then, in the airy kitchen bright with the last sunshine of the day, she took up a candle and lit it. We went out into the shuttered gloomy hall; as we went up the dark stairs, our shadows danced and flickered, the banisters cast grotesque shadows.

At the top of the stairs we saw the three doors, all closed and the tiny narrow stair to the attics. Up here the heat was heavier than ever. "The maid lives out with her mother in the tavern," Mrs Baker said. "I have the top floor to myself. Keeps the place private for my lodgers."

We paused outside one of the doors. Mrs Baker was in contemplative mood. "She's a nice girl," she said. "The maid, I mean. Not bright but plenty of commonsense. Though I daresay she'll have her head turned by some good-looking young man one day, just like young Miss M." She sighed. "What makes young girls so foolish?"

"Youth, I suppose," I said lightly. I felt hypocritical; older men do foolish things too. Look at Ord. Look at myself. "Young people fall in love so easily."

"Falling in love is easy and harmless enough," Mrs Baker retorted. "It's the falling into bed that's foolish."

I stopped with my hand on the door, turned to stare at her. Dear God, why had I not thought of that before?

"Julia was pregnant," I said.

# 19

## THE LADY'S MISCELLANY
## Available at Willliam Charnley's on the High Bridge.
[*Newcastle Courant* 24 April 1736]

Julia was pregnant. Somewhere there was a man who had bedded her and fathered her child. Someone who didn't want to acknowledge the child. Someone who was married or as good as. Someone who wanted to get rid of her. Ord? The pair had met in late March; it was now mid-June – he could have been the father.

"Are you sure?" I asked Mrs Baker.

"I'm the mother of five children myself," she said comfortably. "I'm sure."

"Did her mother know?"

Mrs Baker laughed. "Not her! I told you, she doesn't see anything she doesn't like. And his highness certainly didn't know. Can you imagine how he would have reacted if he did?"

She threw open the door. I hesitated, feeling a little daunted, then went in.

The room in which Julia had lodged was small, with one window that gave an unattractive view of the next house across a narrow alley. I went straight across to the window; starlings cocked their heads at me from the sill and flew off in a flurry of annoyance as I threw up the sash.

The alley outside was one of those dank places where the sun never penetrates even in weather as hot as this; a cat was slinking along and paused, one foot raised, to stare up at me. The alley was scarce wide enough for two persons to pass, and to put up a ladder to the window would have been well-nigh impossible.

The faint lingering possibility that Julia's elopement was traditionally romantic died. Julia must indeed have gone out of the front door – which confirmed the spirit's evidence.

I turned to glance over the room. Mrs Baker was still at the door, looking both interested and expectant. A narrow bed with a great wooden headboard and foot, and a heap of neatly made bedclothes, was topped with a beautiful pastel-shaded patchwork quilt. A small table to one side of the bed held a candlestick with a half-burnt candle; a set of drawers stood on the other side of the room, an old-fashioned bowl on top full of dried flowers. A travelling trunk rested by the window, covered by a shawl; a stool had been pushed against the wall beside it.

And the clutter! Mrs Baker had been understating the case when she referred to disorder. Every available surface was covered with knickknacks and ornaments. A scatter everywhere of scent bottles, all half-used, combs, brushes, a cheap trinket or two, hair ribbons of every hue. A book on top of the trunk had a ribbon in it as a bookmark – surprisingly, it was a book of sermons. I flicked through it. It had been for show; half the pages were uncut.

A paper or two: the *Lady's Miscellany*, a copy of the latest *Newcastle Courant*. The latter was folded with the inner pages displayed and I saw a paragraph ringed. I bent to read it.

*We hear that Miss Mazzanti has lately made a great impression with her depiction of the Portuguese Princess and is shortly to appear as Lucy Locket in London. It is a great triumph for Mr Keregan to have obtained her services and we hear that she will sing in the Race Week concert.*

Julia was to sing in the concert? It was the first I had heard of it. And not a mention of her mother. I wondered what Claudius Heron had thought when he read that paragraph. Or the Signora for that matter. Perhaps that had been another of the things she thought it politic to ignore.

Mrs Baker coughed gently. "If you don't mind, sir, I have one or two things to do in the kitchen... "

I was startled. "Oh. Yes. Of course."

She smiled and gave me another of her significant looks. Her gaze rested for a moment on the travelling trunk.

I waited until I had heard her steps recede down the stairs. I was already feeling guilty. It was one thing to have a look at the room – I was probably not the only person Mrs Baker had shown the room and most of the others would have had only the most prurient interest. But it was quite another thing to go rooting amongst the dead girl's private possessions.

The worst of it was that Mrs Baker plainly trusted me not to take anything, but if I saw Ord's letters I would certainly abstract them. Not only had I agreed to return them to him – I needed to know how far the affair had progressed. I wanted to know if Ord indeed could be the father of Julia's child. That fact would have ruined his chances with Thomas Saint and his daughter and been ample reason to want to be rid of Julia. Of course I could only know such things by reading the letters and that was hardly civilised behaviour, but Ord's behaviour to me was not very civilised either. And neither was murder.

I dragged the shawl off the travelling trunk and dumped it with the books and papers on the patchwork quilt. The trunk had a key in the lock but was unlocked; I threw back the lid.

A miasma of scent rocked me back on my heels; I waved my hand in the air to be rid of it. Another shawl lay across the top of the trunk, as if it had been laid there to protect what was underneath. I lifted it off – and saw, lying on a froth of white material, a yellow ribbon embroidered with blue flowers, each with a spark of brightness at the heart.

I ran the ribbon through my fingers. At one end it was stiff with a spot or two of blood. I saw in my mind's eye that still body on the ground, gauzy fabric rucked about her, one thin layer drifting over her head. I had drawn back the layers of muslin and seen Julia's dishevelled hair...

Yes, there had been one of the yellow ribbons in her hair. In one side of her hair. On the other side, the hair had hung limply.

Julia must have had two ribbons in her hair. The murderer had taken one as a souvenir.

I bit back the nausea in my throat and laid the ribbon carefully aside. If Julia's attacker had been after monetary gain he would have taken both ribbons; to a poor man they would have represented riches. Could the man I had seen bending over the body later have taken it – an opportunist thief who had not had enough time to take both ribbons? No, I remembered distinctly that there had only been one ribbon when Corelli and I first found her.

I must hurry before Mrs Baker returned. I lifted out the delicate dresses made of yards of fabric, expensive embroidery, spotted with pearls or edged with lace. Each would have kept me for several months. Undergarments, stockings, more ribbons. Under a chemise, I felt something hard.

I dragged out a wooden box, long and thin with charming if awkward carvings on the top. Just the sort of place a young girl might keep personal treasures. I eased back the lid.

The box was full of newspaper cuttings. *We hear Miss Mazzanti is to honour us with her presence... The latest sensation is a certain Miss M ---- whose virginal beauty and charming innocence...* Half the regional papers of the country were there – from Bath, Oxford, Exeter, Leeds...

At the bottom of the box, beneath all the cuttings, were the love letters, in a little bundle wrapped with pink ribbon. Nine letters, the folds pressed flat. I hesitated to pull the bundle apart to check that they were indeed from Ord but luckily a few words were visible; I read – *your ever loving....* . and recognised Ord's hand.

I slipped the bundle into my pocket.

Mrs Baker was humming over a bowl of dough; flour dusted her arms and the apron she had donned over her purple dress. She smiled knowingly at me as I came back into her hot kitchen. I had put back Julia's dresses as tidily as I could, and left everything there except the letters, but the consciousness of their presence in my pocket was making my face burn.

"Funny, isn't it?" Mrs Baker said. "How one little girl can fascinate so many. I even had the psalm teacher in here earlier on."

"Proctor?"

"Wanted to see the girl's body. Well, I thought he'd say a prayer over her, or sing a psalm, but no, he bursts into tears and weeps and wails till I thought the whole street would hear." She turned the dough out on to the floured table; the sunshine laid long fingers across the wood. "I had to ask him to go."

Poor Proctor, still feeling guilty at leaving Julia to her fate. I slipped Mrs Baker a coin or two in thanks; she beamed at me and I saw myself out.

The sun was behind the houses as I left Mrs Baker's and the street was already in twilight. I was wondering what to do next. It was too early to go to Esther. I would creep in the back way when it was fully dark; to arrive early would run the risk that she had visitors or was perhaps entertaining friends to dinner. Finding somewhere to read Ord's love letters would be best; I would look for a tavern and read them over a beer.

But oh dear God – what a furore there would be if Ord turned out to be the murderer! Would Bedwalters dare to do anything? But wait – how did the attacks on Mazzanti fit in with all this? Surely Ord could not have carried them out – he was certainly in Newcastle at the time of the attacks in London and York.

I turned to go down the Side to the Keyside, to one of the sailors' taverns. The streets were full of people, both purposeful and idle, walking home with baskets, or gathering idly to chat.

A merchant climbed down from his horse to lead it up the hill. Someone grabbed at me.

## 20

**The idea that comedians are men and women of loose morals is not at all correct; they are god-fearing decent people.**
[*Reminiscences of a theatre manager*, Thomas Keregan
(London: published for the Author, 1736)]

I swung my fist – a couple of women close by scattered in alarm. "For God's sake!" I drew back.

Ned Reynolds was breathing heavily. "Charlie! For God's sake, don't desert me too!"

I stared at him. He was dishevelled, in crumpled and stained clothes, smelling of drink, yet plainly stone cold sober. Behind him, an alley led to a flight of steps climbing the Castle mound, house doors on either side. On the bottom step was a jug of ale and a tankard.

I shuffled Ned back into the alley, sat him down on one of the steps. "I've been looking for you all day. Where the devil have you been?"

"Hiding," he said with bitter self-contempt. "Trying to pretend nothing's happened. Trying to get drunk. I've heard about the way you solve mysteries, Charlie. Well, this one's no mystery. Anyone can see what an idiot I am!"

"It's a mystery to me," I said firmly. I had never seen Ned like this before, confident, brash, ruthless Ned reduced to a self-pitying heap. "Why the devil were you courting Julia? And don't tell me for her money, because I've never known you care about that. Nor for respectability – when did you last meet a respectable actor?"

He laughed shakily, then his face crumpled. "Richard," he said thickly, burying his head in his hands. "To protect Richard."

I sat down beside him, pitched my voice low so that casual

passers by climbing the hill could not hear.

"Julia found out about you?"

He snorted in derision. "She didn't need to dig too far. Devil take it, Charlie, does everyone know? Have we been that careless?"

"No one in the company would give you away."

"One did," he said dryly. "Guess who, Charlie."

I sighed. "Richard himself."

He nodded, rested his elbows on his knees and stared at the cobbles. "She befriended him, chatted away to him, told him all about her triumphs. He adored her, Charlie – he was starstruck, told me all her *bon mots* as if they were pearls. And of course, since she told him all her secrets, he told her his – or hinted at them at any rate."

"And then she tried to blackmail you."

He nodded. "Not overtly, of course. She started to hint that she was interested in me. At first I thought she was just trying to annoy her father – whenever she was with a man, he'd rush into a fury and try and run the fellow off."

I poured myself beer, into Ned's tankard. "She was his sole source of income."

"The Signora's too old, I take it."

"Not in voice, but in looks, yes."

He nodded. "Well, after a while I realised she was serious. She said she wanted me to marry her. That's how she put it. Not that she wanted to marry me but she wanted *me* to marry *her*. When I laughed at her, she turned nasty. She said that if I did as she told me, she would keep quiet about Richard. She even said that once we were married, we could do as we liked and she'd pretend she didn't notice, that she'd turn a blind eye to what was *going on*." He laughed bitterly. "Do you know how much contempt you can get into just a couple of words, Charlie?"

"She was pregnant," I said.

He straightened sharply, stared at me as I drank the dregs of his beer. "Devil take it, the little... " He laughed again, unwillingly. "And she called *me* immoral. I don't fall into bed with anyone who asks, Charlie. It's Richard or no one. And that girl wanted to foist a bastard on me! Who's the father?"

Ord's letters hung heavy in my pocket. "I have a good idea but I don't want to say before I'm sure."

A woman with a toddler on her hip climbed wearily past the entrance to the alley, wiping her sweating face; a boy of thirteen or so came running down the steps and leapt past us. We let them get out of earshot.

"So," I said, "to cut a long story short: Mazzanti forbade the marriage, Julia insisted, you had no choice and you arranged to elope."

"Elope?" Ned echoed blankly. "No."

"You didn't arrange to meet her outside the lodging house at midnight?"

"Devil take it, no!"

I'd swear he was telling me the truth. It must have been Ord after all, for all his denials. What in heaven's name had Julia been playing at? Engaging herself to one man then promising to elope with another?

"When did you last see her?"

"At the theatre in the afternoon."

"Was she as insistent on the wedding as ever?"

He thought for a moment, staring out at the Side where the shadows lengthened, and the last sun touched the upper windows of the houses. "As far as I can tell," he said finally.

"You were her last resort," I said. "She had someone else in mind, someone, I'm afraid to say, rather richer than yourself, and probably the father of her child. But if he didn't come up to scratch, you were there to fall back on."

He swore, took the tankard from my hands and drained it.

"Where were you last night?" I asked. "I have a vague memory of seeing you in Mrs Hill's."

"I probably was," he agreed. "And a dozen other places. We drank the night away. My way of pretending everything's all right, Charlie."

"You're not the only one who does that," I said. "Were you alone – just the two of you?"

He shook his head. "We met an old friend of mine, a fellow from London in service somewhere. And no, I won't name him, Charlie. How the hell do you think I originally met him? We have certain *tastes* in common."

I nodded. "And you don't remember much of the night?" I knew that feeling myself.

Ned grimaced. "Almost nothing. I was in a rage, I remember that. Wanting Richard and knowing I was the reason he was in this mess…"

"If you're going to be self-pitying," I said, "I'll leave you to sort it out yourself!"

He laughed shakily. "I *could* have done it, Charlie. Killed her, I mean. I don't remember. Not after leaving the Golden Fleece and God knows what time that was!"

"But Richard would remember, and this friend of yours. Either they would have been with you and seen you do it, or they would know you'd gone off on your own and could have done it. And neither of them has said anything?"

He stared at me. "Richard would never be party to anything like that! And he couldn't keep it a secret either. And this morning, he said we were together the whole time. He said they had practically to drag me home."

"Then you're worrying about nothing," I said.

I was far from certain this was the case. Not that there was any point in talking to Richard; true or not, he would insist Ned couldn't have done it. In any case, there was no way anything he said could be used as evidence in Ned's favour. Nor the other fellow for that matter. Their inclinations would immediately make them unreliable witnesses in the eyes of any court. Still, I believed him, which meant that I could continue looking in other directions without worrying about Ned.

His mouth twisted into a bitter smile. "Not out of the woods yet, Charlie. Not yet."

A cold dread took hold of me. "What do you mean?"

"The constable, Bedwalters. Came round to our lodgings this morning and was asking for me. That's why I slipped out. He'd got wind of the fact Julia and I wanted to marry – her father told him evidently. Bedwalters wanted to know if Julia and I had an argument. That's a roundabout way of saying he thought I'd killed her in a temper, I suppose. But I didn't talk to him. One of the other fellows saw him and sent him off in the wrong direction. Luckily, Richard wasn't there – he'd already gone to the theatre. But now he's saying that if I get arrested, he'll go off to the constable and tell him we were together. All night."

"In heaven's name!"

"Might as well be hanged for a true crime, than a false one, eh, Charlie?"

"Keep Richard's mouth shut," I said forcibly. "Tell him I know who the murderer is and he's only got to have patience and I'll prove it."

Ned frowned. "Is that true?"

"Not yet but it will be." I pushed myself to my feet, looked down at him. "Ned," I said. "Go home, keep your eye on Richard and don't let him do anything stupid. If Bedwalters comes to see you, tell him you were simply after Julia's money – that means you wanted her alive not dead. You are broke, aren't you?"

"Always." He pulled out his pockets and showed me his wayward, charming, feckless smile. "Charlie, you can make this all right, can't you? All of it?"

"That might be too much to ask," I said dryly. "But for you and Richard, yes, probably. Just don't do anything rash!"

# 21

**Modern fashions are extraordinary; women seem to trick themselves out in the most ridiculous of finery. But there is no arguing with them.**
[Letter of Sir John Hubert to his brother-in-law, May 1732]

In the darkness of Esther's kitchen, I sat and restlessly smoothed my fingers along the edge of the table. That wild promise to Ned weighed heavily on me. Make everything all right for him? I could only do that if I found the real murderer and just at the moment, I realised, I had no idea who it might be. Ord was my only suspect now and I couldn't convince myself of his guilt.

The cook had put out a tankard of beer for me and a plate of cold pie which I hadn't touched after my meal with Mrs Baker. I drank the beer, though, cautiously; drinking in the dark is surprisingly difficult.

Esther had been all business-like when I arrived. I had crept up the back alley and into the garden as if I was the intruder; Esther had met me at the gate, her perfume drifting over me like honeysuckle, and had brushed past me as she bent to latch and lock the gate behind me. She was wearing breeches and a loose shirt over which a waistcoat hung unfastened: "I'm not getting caught out again, Charles. No more tripping over skirts!" I knew from her mischievous gaze that she knew exactly what effect her appearance was having on me.

She led the way through the garden to the house, the light from the open back door of the house showing us the path. Esther's long pale hair had been loosely twisted back and pinned up to keep it out of her way; wisps danced in the lantern light.

Inside the house, a pair of duelling pistols lay on a small

table by the door. They were loaded, Esther told me, and extra ammunition and powder lay beside them. I didn't want to touch them; I am incompetent with guns – I never had the opportunity or desire to become proficient. But Esther took one up and offered it to me. "Tom will take the other. I have another pair of pistols upstairs."

I took it with distaste. It was heavy and warm in my hands.

Esther had locked up the house in my presence and taken her maid Catherine upstairs; the window in Esther's bedchamber looked down upon the garden and would give advance warning of someone entering that way. I had detailed the spirit of my former apprentice, George, to watch the front of the house, looking out on to the square, more to keep him out of the way than because I thought the intruder would come that way; George still had the ebullience and bad judgement of youth and would do something rash if not watched carefully.

In the butler's pantry, Tom was snoring. He was allegedly keeping watch from his window for movement in the garden; the view from the kitchen window was obscured by lavender and rosemary bushes. Restlessly, I got up, felt my way around the table, looked out into the garden. Nothing more than a gleam of moonlight; otherwise the darkness was impenetrable.

My mind wandered inevitably back to Julia Mazzanti's death. Ord's letters were still heavy in my pocket. If he was guilty, would he have asked a third party to recover the letters? Would I dare to accuse him if I did find evidence against him? There would be plenty of people who would point out that Ord was a man with hundreds of acres of land and several coal mines and shares and many families relying on him for a living, and Julia was only an actress, a young woman who was immodest enough to perform in public and therefore had invited undesirable behaviour.

Poor Julia. I had disliked her greatly – most people had, it seemed. Did it all turn on her character? She had conformed to the general expectation of actresses, and fallen into bed with some casual suitor and then found herself in predictable difficulties. Or had I done her an injustice? Had she been forced to give her favours? I wondered what that other Julia would have done – the Julia in the other world.

And, as if I had conjured her up, in she walked, with a candlestick in one hand, and her gaze fixed carefully on the obscured flags of the kitchen floor. I must have moved for she started and looked up quickly. For a moment, I thought she might flee but then she clearly decided to brazen the situation out. She set the candle on the kitchen table and I saw there were now two glasses on the table, set beside a bottle of wine, as if waiting for guests.

Julia was shivering. She was dressed in the flimsiest of gowns with a cobweb-thin shawl thrown over it. Jewels glittered at her throat, in her ears, in her hair. Was she about to go out? Or had she just come back from a party? It had not occurred to me that she might be lodging in this house – surely she could not, it was much too shabby. So was she visiting someone here?

She gave me a flirtatious smile. She was remarkably like her counterpart in my world; her face was a little broader, perhaps, her hair a little darker and straighter. But she had the same wild, self-centred look as the murdered girl – and an added hardness, an added determination. "What are you doing here, Mr Patterson?"

I was still unsettled by having stepped though into the other world so easily, without any of the forewarnings I had previously received. As if I had willed it myself. But I rallied. "I could ask the same of you."

Even in the flickering candlelight, I saw her flush. She leant across the table to pour wine into one of the glasses, looked at me provocatively across the top of the glass. "Forgive me for not inviting you to share, Mr Patterson, but I am waiting for… someone…"

There was no mistaking her meaning. The boldness of it took

me aback. I thought that there was a trace of bitterness in her voice; was she deliberately inviting me to judge her by common prejudices?

"And you," she said. "Are you visiting someone? One of the *ladies* upstairs, perhaps?"

The house must be the haunt of prostitutes. That's what she meant. I surprised myself by saying: "I would not condemn you for doing something I myself would do." Oh Lord, that sounded as if I meant I *was* visiting the women upstairs. "I mean," I corrected myself, "there is a great deal of hypocrisy in the world which I deplore. Men may apparently do as they please but women must do as they are told."

Her head lifted slightly. "I had not thought you so advanced in your thinking, Mr Patterson. Of course it is easy to talk."

I found myself disturbingly anxious to appear in a good light to her. "I am not visiting prostitutes," I said. "In truth, I hardly know why I am here."

"You should take greater care." She pulled the shawl more tightly about her, still shivering. "You are so well known in this town, Mr Patterson, that your movements cannot go unnoticed."

"Nor yours, I think."

She laughed softly. "Mr Patterson, I have ceased to care." She regarded the wine in the candlelight; she had not drunk any, I noted, but merely held the glass in her hands as if for want of something to do. "I have appeared on the public stage since I was six, and I have heard every proposition and proposal men can make. And yes, I have agreed to some of them." Her mouth twisted bitterly. "You are right, Mr Patterson, a woman never has any choice about what she will do. Except in the choice of jewels." She fingered her necklace. "And ribbons."

I began to wonder how she was so sane and sensible. Had her counterpart in my world led the same kind of life?

"And then I did something really foolish," she said. "I fell in love."

She laughed again, more loudly. "Your face, Mr Patterson, tells everything. You never can disguise your feelings. You don't believe me? Very well, an infatuation only, of course."

"I've fallen in love a good few times myself," I said lightly, more distressed by her confidences than I had expected to be. "Particularly as a youth. And with the most unsuitable of women."

"Actresses?"

I reddened. "Servants – " But that was just as bad.

"Oh, chambermaids," she said. "Or the milkmaid? The fishmonger's daughter?"

"And I fell out of love again very quickly," I said steadily. "It seems to be the common lot."

"So all I must do is wait a little and all will be well?"

"Possibly."

She drained the glass. "But I am the spawn of Satan, Mr Patterson. I have it on excellent authority – the best. Creatures like me are set on earth to tempt good men into sinfulness."

"Ord?" I suggested.

She frowned. "Philip Ord? What is he to the purpose?"

I was in danger of treating this world as if it was a mere reflection of my own, I realised, as if I could solve the mystery of Julia Mazzanti's death in my own world by understanding the life of her counterpart in this world. I had had ample evidence in the past that, similar as the two worlds were, they were not identical. The woman standing before me was proof of that. She lived while her counterpart lay abused and murdered in my own world. And a little part of my mind was disturbingly pleased that it was the Julia in my world that had died, not this woman before me.

Julia was still musing on her own difficulties. "Don't you see, sir, that my reputation is already gone, simply because of my profession. So why should I not simply go my own way and do as I please? The world cannot think worse of me than it already does."

And yet, I thought, this second world seemed only to open up when there was a crisis in my own world, and it opened up to the same moment, the same situation. Surely that could not be coincidence? Surely there was something to be learnt here?

"But don't fret yourself, Mr Patterson," Julia said with a knowing smile. "I am not one to give the world up for love. Marriage without money is not to my taste." She fingered the jewels in one ear. "Your face, Mr Patterson, your face! Such contempt."

"No," I protested, but she swept on, setting the empty glass neatly down on the table.

"Well, I must get back to my wicked ways. You have not seen him, have you, Mr Patterson?"

"Him? Who?"

Her lip curled in contempt. "You are like the rest of them, sir. He's beneath your notice, is that it? Because he's poor and living in a place like this? Well, don't condemn my morals, Mr Patterson, until your own are beyond reproach, or until you have learnt some Christian charity."

I was stung. I had only the greatest admiration and sympathy for her and she insulted me. "I do not think we need to prolong this conversation," I said.

And I was alone in the darkness of the kitchen again, hearing Tom's rattling snores.

A whisper in the darkness. I was still recovering from shock at the realisation that I could govern my entrance to and exit from the other world, and stood dazed until a hand touched my arm. Then I knew Esther by her faint perfume. She leant close and I saw her face as a pale blur, her hand on my arm as a faint leavening of the darkness.

"The spirit heard someone at the garden gate," she breathed

in my ear. "We must wake Tom."

"I'll do it." I thought about telling her to go back to her room, and leave Tom and me to deal with it. It's what I would have said to any other woman. I did not say it to Esther. We felt our way to the butler's pantry, and Esther waited outside while I went in to wake Tom. He had one candle burning and I blew it out before putting a hand on his shoulder. He came awake at once, said eagerly: "Is he here?"

I heard the scratch of metal against wood as he picked something up. "I have the pistol," he whispered excitedly. I pushed it aside with some trepidation.

Esther was waiting for us impatiently, a slim shadow in the darkness. "Tom," she whispered. "Get to the kitchen and keep watch there. We'll stand by the door."

He looked disappointed but went without argument.

Esther and I took up our station on either side of the door to the garden. I stood where I could be seen when the door opened; Esther hid behind the door where she had a good chance of taking the intruder by surprise if need be. All I could hear in the darkness was my own breathing. And all I could see in my mind's eye was Julia Mazzanti – the woman from the other world, bejewelled, wrapped in her thin shawl, with an insolent tilt of her head and amused contempt in her eyes. She was a woman, that was the difference between the two Julias. She was a woman who had taken life into her own hands, and the Julia who had died had been a mere girl.

Esther breathed: "Here he is."

I heard a faint crunch of footsteps, a pause, then a scratching on the other side of the door. The intruder was trying to pick the lock. No, it sounded as if he was trying to push a key into it, like a man who hasn't yet realised it doesn't fit. Surely after three attempts to get in, he must know he had the wrong key!

An angry mutter. Not loud enough for me to be sure of more

than that it was a man. Or did I recognise the voice…?

The handle on the door twitched; the door shifted fractionally as if someone was pressing harder against it. Then a rattle as the intruder grew more frustrated.

Esther's pale face was just visible in the darkness. Her breathing was very steady. The oddest of burglars, I thought. Surely no thief of any experience would make a noise if he could avoid it. It was more like a man who unexpectedly found that he could not get into his own house.

The jerking of the latch stopped. Silence. I strained to hear something more. I felt Esther shifting, pressing her ear to the door. "Footsteps?" she mouthed. Yes, I could just catch the faint thud of footsteps on the path. Was he going away? What the devil to do now? Go after him? He'd run for the gate and be out of it before I had the door unlocked.

The sound of breaking glass.

"The kitchen!" Esther cried. I ran off in that direction, knocking over half a dozen things as I went. Pans clattered and rolled on the floor with a huge din. I blundered into something sharp that stabbed my thigh.

Behind me, a candle flared, casting my shadow dancing on the walls. By its light, I found the kitchen door. Tom was roaring in fury. A boy's voice called: "Help! Murder!" The spirit of my apprentice, George, was here, gleaming on a saucepan hung from a rack.

Shadows at the window. One man was perched on the windowsill itself, clinging on to the frame. Tom was reaching up for him, tugging at the intruder's clothes and trying to bring him down. The man kicked out at him. The light from the candle touched them both briefly, then a draught from the broken window caught the flame and snuffed it out, plunging us into darkness. Esther swore.

I levelled my pistol. I had only ever fired a pistol once before and was not confident of my ability to hit the intruder rather than Tom. I yelled: "Hold still or I fire."

The shadows at the window froze. And at that moment, the gleam of George's spirit slid swiftly along the wall and on to the window frame. "Got him!" George shouted gleefully. "Got him!"

He startled both Tom and the intruder. Tom yelped and let go. The intruder pulled free.

He fell backwards. I fired. Tom ducked and the ball hit the window frame square on the sash – I heard the wood crack and split. I threw down the pistol, grabbed Tom's arm.

"Hoist me up!"

He cupped his hands and I put my foot into them; he heaved me up on to the windowsill. The broken glass nipped my fingers as I tried to use the window frame to balance. Then I was jumping down the other side.

I crashed through bushes, landed on my hands and knees in soft earth. The scents of crushed mint and rosemary rose around me. I picked myself up, stumbled along the path towards the gate. Trailing rose stems caught at my clothes. In the darkness, I drifted into the shrubs bordering the path. I already knew I was not going to catch him. The gate into the alley was open. I could hear footsteps clattering on cobbles. He was well away.

Annoyed, breathing heavily, I went back. The back door of the house had been flung open wide and light flooded into the garden. I squinted against the brightness. Esther was holding a lantern high above her head; I glimpsed her slim figure in breeches and waistcoat, her pale hair loose about her shoulders.

"I suppose he's gone?" she said coolly.

I nodded, resigned. "He knew the path better than I. But at the very least we have given him a fright, and deterred him from returning."

She frowned. "I rather think he is too persistent for that. Come back in. I've sent Tom for brandy."

She turned back into the house. As she moved, the lantern light caught on something pale tangled in the bushes beneath the kitchen window. I stooped quickly to catch up the gleam. The bushes held it tight a moment, then it came free.

It was long and shiny, scented with rosemary. A yellow ribbon spotted with embroidered blue flowers.

## 22

**Do not ever consider abandoning your friends, if only because they may then abandon you in your hour of need.**
[*Instructions to a Son newly come of Age*, Revd. Peter Morgan (London: published for the Author, 1691)]

I did not tell Esther. She was already in the house, dealing with domestic matters. The noise – of the breaking window, I supposed – had woken the women servants. Cook had come down with a wicked-looking cleaver; the chambermaid had snatched up a poker. Both were threatening war on the intruder. The young kitchenmaid was cosseting Tom, much to his pleasure. I thrust the ribbon into my pocket, took the key to the garden gate from its hook and the lantern from Esther, and went back out outside.

What kind of a burglar had a key to the garden gate but not to the house? Of course, I thought, as I held the lantern high to see my way along the path, the intruder probably believed he did have the house key – that was the meaning of the scratching noises, he had been trying to fit the wrong key in the lock.

But why did he keep trying? Why had he not learnt the first time that the key did not fit? And, when he had given up on the key, why had he thought he could smash the window so noisily without rousing the occupants?

I checked the garden gate for marks, found none, shut and locked it. A closer examination would have to wait for daylight, but I hardly thought it worthwhile. I went back to the house.

Esther was alone in the kitchen, cleaning out the pistol I had fired. She had poured two glasses of brandy and had plainly been sipping at one of them. In the silence, I could hear the kitchenmaid giggling in the butler's pantry.

"It's very late," Esther said. "Or indeed, very early."

I was desperate for the brandy and drank it down. Esther's would-be intruder was Julia Mazzanti's murderer; I had proof now. He had taken a ribbon from Julia's body and he had dropped it here. But why was he after Esther too? And he must be desperate – to try to murder someone in a houseful of servants was preposterous. But this threw another light on that attempted burglary at the Mazzantis'. Had Julia been right and this was an early attempt to kill her? Again in a house full of people? It made no sense at all. The whole thing was impenetrable.

"You should not go out," I said brusquely.

Esther looked up at me in astonishment. "Why in heaven's name not?"

"This could be a personal attack." I threw back more brandy to gain time, to think how much I wanted to say. I did not want to alarm her by telling her about the ribbon but neither could I leave her to believe this was a mere burglar.

"There was an attempted burglary at the Mazzantis' lodgings the day before Julia was killed," I pointed out.

Esther set the cleaned pistol down, carefully, on the table. "She was murdered in the street."

"That's why I want you to stay in."

She laughed. "I cannot confine myself to the house, Charles! I have business to do, urgent matters connected with those wretched estates I inherited."

"Ask the lawyers to come here."

She picked up her glass and sipped thoughtfully at the brandy. "Well," she said at last, "it is undeniably true that the streets can be dangerous."

"Exactly."

"Particularly in the small hours of the night." Her hair had come loose and hung about her shoulders; I forced myself to look away. "Particularly," she persisted, "when a man has ruffians after him."

Too late, I recognised the trap into which I had fallen. I said, wearily: "I had hoped you did not know about that."

"Really, Charles," she said in exasperation. "You cannot stop spirits talking. And that former apprentice of yours talks all the time." She added, under her breath, "Most annoying," then lifted her head in challenge. "Well, there is one solution, is there not?"

I said nothing.

She put down her brandy glass with a little click of annoyance. "Very well, if I must be more direct, I shall be. There is one solution to the danger you say exists, Charles. Stay here. Stay with me tonight."

I panicked. I had just faced down a murderer but I could not deal with my own desires. I wanted to say yes, but the consequences of doing so were too far-reaching. To marry a woman of Esther's standing was out of the question; the disparity in age, station and wealth was too great. But to conduct an affair with her was the greatest insult I could imagine offering.

But I did not want to say no.

"The neighbours," I said, helplessly, searching for excuses. "Or rather their servants – suppose they saw me leave in the morning?"

"They would merely suppose you had been giving me a music lesson."

I felt a moment of hysterical amusement; that was certainly not the first idea that would occur to servants.

"Your reputation," I said, with some desperation. No, it was plainly out of the question. I did not trust myself where she was concerned. To spend an entire night in the same house would be a temptation too far. I took a deep breath, said more decisively, "No, I cannot. I will not."

She looked down at her breeches, absent-mindedly removed

a trace of dust. "This is not the end of the matter, Charles."

She must see how impossible it was. I had just drawn breath to say so when Tom came into the kitchen, followed by the kitchen-maid holding a branch of candles. Tom had arms full of wooden planks, a hammer under his arm. "Sorry, madam, but I need to make the window safe."

Esther gave me a long look, so long that Tom started to look puzzled. "Very well, Tom," she said. "Do what is necessary. Mr Patterson, I must thank you for your assistance this night."

That was a dismissal. I was both relieved and dissatisfied. But what was the point of discussing it further? I had made my decision, the only honourable decision I could have made. I nodded, uttered pious wishes for her health and a good night's sleep, and let Tom escort me to the garden gate so he could lock it after me.

He stopped me as I stepped out into the alley. "Is he going to come back again, do you think, sir?"

"Not tonight."

"But tomorrow? Only – " He hesitated. "The women are very game, sir and you've seen how up to it the mistress is. But they are only women after all and I'm not sure I can hold the house on my own." His voice wavered a little and I realised how very young he was, not even twenty perhaps. "Is he likely to bring others with him?"

"No," I said firmly. "I'm sure he's acting on his own. Don't worry, Tom, we'll deal with it."

"If you could come back again tomorrow, sir," he said, unsteadily. "I mean, tonight. If you were there, I'd do better."

"You do very well as it is," I said. How the devil could I come back again? I was dog tired as it was, and needed to spend the day looking for the murderer. Yes, that was the essential point – if I could find the murderer, I could remove Esther from danger without the need for heroics in the middle of the night.

"If it's necessary, yes, I will come back," I said. And walked away hoping it would *not* be necessary.

The church clocks were striking three when I walked out on to Westgate Road. I had decided to go back home by the main streets, hoping that some at least of the lanterns put up by public-minded householders were still burning. Many of the alleys never saw a lantern from one year's end to the next. But it was dangerous, nevertheless; Esther had been right about that. This *was* folly – half a dozen ruffians could be hanging about and I'd never see them. This was their territory, their time, and I should have left them to it, slept in Esther's library or in the butler's pantry. I should have been stronger-minded.

But no, I knew my own limits.

Westgate lay ahead of me, a long road gently tending downhill, full of looming houses and windows. Two or three lanterns did indeed burn, but at wide intervals, pools of brightness in a sea of darkness. Not a soul about. Silence as the echoes of the clock bell died away.

A shadow moved. My heart leapt – but it was only a cat lightly running across the road. A white cat lurid in the darkness. Silence again.

I started walking. It was still uncomfortably warm. I should have borrowed one of Esther's pistols. Or at least found myself a stout walking stick. Or a kitchen knife? I should at least have picked up a knife.

My footsteps echoed in the empty street. I tried to tiptoe. I could hear my breathing. I nearly broke into a run. The quicker I got out of these streets the better. But that would be admitting to panic –

I quickened my pace. A spirit murmured out of the darkness high above me. "Dark nights. I always hated dark nights." Heart racing, I broke into a run, tried to fall back into a walk, could not. I jogged on past the vicarage gardens. The sound of drunken singing, very distantly. A spirit? Or living men?

God help me, it was a living man. Reeling out of the shadows shrouding the garden and peering at me in a drunken stupor. He still held a bottle.

I recognised him at once. One of the ruffians. He peered at me, pointed waveringly. "You're – you're – Hey!" I heard more footsteps. Damn it, he was not alone.

There was no point in delaying. I put my head down and went for him. He staggered aside at the last moment and only my shoulder caught him, spinning him backwards. I clenched my fist and swung at him.

He stumbled. I connected only with air.

There were two others, staring blearily at me from an alley. God, but they were drunk. I barged into one of them, then pulled away. Discretion is always the better part of valour and discretion was telling me to run.

Something caught my ankle.

I went down, hit the cobbles with a thump that jarred the breath out of me.

The fellow had a fist around my leg. He tried to lever himself to his feet. Somehow his bottle had been broken; he had it by the neck and was waving the jagged ends at me. Beer dripped on to my face. He was weaving and staggering and his aim was not going to be good, but at this distance he could not miss.

And I could not move. I gasped for air, willed my legs to kick out. There was a roaring in my ears. The men were laughing, jeering –

The clatter of horse's hooves.

The men yelled, veered away. I heard their footsteps as they ran off. Still gasping for breath, I looked up into the face of a man sitting on a chestnut horse. He was smirking.

"Well, Charles," he said. "It's nice to be able to rescue you for

a change."
　　My good friend, the dancing master, Hugh Demsey.

# 23

**Late nights never profit a man.**
[*Instructions to a Son newly come of Age*, Revd. Peter Morgan (London: published for the Author, 1691)]

It took us an hour to wake the owner of a tavern at the top of Westgate where Hugh usually stabled his horse, and to rub the animal down and feed it. In the stable that smelt of hay and horse shit, and warmth, Hugh was as cheerful as a man in drink. I suspected that he *was* in drink.

"Nonsense," he said, struggling under the weight of his saddle as he slid it from the horse's back. "I only had three or four beers while I was waiting."

"Waiting for what?"

"For the farrier to shoe the horse."

He had set off from Houghton-le-Spring in late afternoon, it transpired, confident that with the long days he could still get home in the light. But the horse had cast a shoe and Hugh had had to go miles out of his way to find a blacksmith. Then the fellow had had to stoke up his fire again, and send for his apprentice who had gone off courting, and the blacksmith's wife had been very hospitable, and all in all it had been almost dark when Hugh set off again.

"And coming across Gateshead Fell in the dark wasn't fun, I can tell you," Hugh said, rubbing the horse down. "I still haven't forgotten the fellows who left the post boy for dead and stole his letters."

"They were hanged the other week at York," I said dismissively. "Why didn't you just stay overnight with the blacksmith? It sounds as if his wife had taken a fancy to you."

"That's precisely why I didn't stay!" Hugh forked hay for the horse, patted its flanks and reached for his bags. "And what an ungrateful thing to say when I've just saved your skin. Come to my rooms and tell me everything."

We walked down the street towards Hugh's lodgings. I could not help but glance about in trepidation in case the ruffians still lingered, but we reached the building in safety and climbed the narrow stairs past the clockmakers on the ground floor, Hugh's dancing school on the first floor, the widow and her children on the second, up to Hugh's attic room. Hugh owns the entire building, having inherited it from his late master; he does not look it and he certainly does not flaunt it (except in his clothes) but he is a wealthy man.

The attic was stiflingly hot, having been shut up for several weeks; it was difficult to draw breath. Hugh flung open the window, wafted a few papers around futilely and dropped on to his bed with a relieved sigh.

"It's been a long day. I was teaching all morning and afternoon."

I perched on the only chair in the room, an uncertain old dining chair that had seen much better days. Hugh had not bothered to light a candle and we sat in a darkness relieved only by the faint light of a lantern that still burned in the street outside.

"I'm grateful to you for coming back so quickly."

"Eh?"

"After getting my note."

"What note?"

"The one I sent you asking you to come back."

"Never got it."

Then I remembered I had never sent it. I fished in my pockets and found it, crumpled and bedraggled where I had thrust it after Bedwalters interrupted me.

"Come on, Charles," Hugh said with relish. "Tell me all about it.

What mess have you got yourself into this time?"

I told him in detail, from the beginning, lingering lovingly over Mazzanti's comments on my violin playing, his exaltation of Julia's very few merits, the attempts on his life. Hugh whistled when he heard of Ned's courtship of Julia and muttered something to the effect that Ned was the most foolish idiot he had ever met. I told him about Ord's infatuation and he obliged me by getting indignant on Lizzie Saint's behalf – she was one of Hugh's pupils too. I told him about discovering Julia's body, and about Corelli.

Hugh was silent for a moment at that. "As a matter of fact – "

"Yes?"

"It's owing to Corelli I'm here. I met the fellow."

"What!"

"In Houghton-le-Spring. In a tavern last night when I was having a nice quiet chop. Said he was a friend of yours."

I snorted.

"Then he said – Wait!" Hugh rose up off the bed and crawled to shut the window again – in case someone passing in the street overheard us, I presumed. In the darkness, he was an outline against the faint lantern light outside. "He said he was a government agent, looking for spies. Is that true, Charles?"

"The devil it is," I retorted. Then honesty reared its head. "He says Mazzanti is a spy. God knows he might be – the situation in Europe's complicated enough. And in America. And if Mazzanti is a spy, it might explain why someone is trying to kill him."

"He has stolen secrets that must never be allowed to get into the wrong hands!" Hugh said melodramatically, then came back down to earth. "Corelli's no government agent, Charles. I've met one or two of those in Paris and they're a different sort of men altogether. If you ask me, Corelli's a thief, trying to gull honest men out of their guineas."

I nodded. "I'd come to that conclusion myself. Did he try

anything of the sort on you?"

"No." Hugh shifted uneasily. "He came straight up to me, said I'd been pointed out to him and that he knew you. He said he was worried about you."

"Worried?" I said, startled. "Why?"

"Said you'd tangled with some ruffians and they were after you. Well, I know what *that* is all about – don't forget I was there during that business in March when you offended them, Charles. Though you didn't say they were still after you. I'd wager he was genuinely concerned, you know."

"I can't imagine why. I still haven't completely ruled him out as Julia's murderer. Or the accomplice of someone else who was."

"Never said a word to me about the Mazzanti girl." Hugh was silent for a moment, the only sound in the dark room our quiet breathing. "He wasn't a happy man, Charles. Kept a sharp lookout for strangers, insisted on sitting with his back to the wall, wouldn't stay longer than he had to. And I fancy..." he hesitated. "I fancy he was in a rage, Charles. He was having to bite his lip all the time, stop himself bursting out in a fury."

"At what?"

I dimly saw Hugh shrug.

We mused over Corelli's behaviour a while longer. He had told Hugh he intended to catch a ship at Sunderland, so either he had changed his mind or his intimation to Mrs Hill that he intended to go to Shields had been a deliberate misdirection. But at the back of my mind all the time we talked was the question of how honest I could be with Hugh. I had Ord's letters on me, and the ribbon I had found in the herb bushes outside Esther's kitchen window; I would happily sacrifice Ord's infatuation but Esther's reputation was a different matter.

I told him about Ord. Hugh condemned me for taking the letters but not for any reason of morality; he thought I should have left them for Bedwalters to find and let Ord take the consequences.

"He's the most supercilious, patronising fellow I know. Have you read them yet?"

"They're private correspondence, Hugh!"

"And he could be a murderer."

I shuffled a little uneasily. "That's what I was going home to do as a matter of fact."

I saw his teeth gleam as he grinned.

"And the other matter, Charles? What else are you not telling me?"

I sighed and told him about Esther's intruder. It was a relief to talk about it, to express my concern. Hugh listened without comment. He probably would have guessed that Esther and I were comfortable enough with each other for her to turn to me for help, for we had all taken a part in that fracas in March that led to my disagreement with the ruffians; he had seen us together then and had cautiously uttered one or two warnings a day or two afterwards. Which, of course, I had ignored, even while I realised I was foolish to do so.

When I had finished, Hugh was silent for a moment. Finally he said, "You're taking a devilish risk, Charles. The town is full of people who think they know exactly how society should be, and they have the power to get what they want. And to ostracise people who won't do as they say. And then she'll have no reputation, and you'll have no living."

"I'm interested in a murderer," I said, obstinately. "That's the issue in hand."

"Meaning that you're not going to listen to me. Again."

"You don't – you *can't* – understand fully."

"I do," he retorted. "I understand that when people start saying, *You can't understand how I feel* or some such thing, they're just about to do something really stupid and don't want to be talked out of it."

"The ribbon," I said, between gritted teeth.

He sighed. "Very well. Just don't say I didn't warn you. You think Mrs Jerdoun's would-be intruder is Julia Mazzanti's murderer."

"In all probability, yes. The ribbon proves that."

"So he's trying to murder Mrs Jerdoun too?"

I winced. "It's a possibility. But I can't imagine why. I'm not sure that the two women ever met."

"They must have something in common."

I gestured helplessly. "Nothing."

Hugh swung his legs over the edge of the bed. "I'm exhausted, Charles." He stripped off his coat. "I'm going to sleep. And if you've any sense you'll bed down here until it's light. Wandering the street at night is never a good idea, let alone when you've offended half the scum of the town. And give up all this traipsing about town in search of murderers. Leave it to Bedwalters."

"I can't," I said. "I can't tell him about the ribbon. He'd ask where I found it and I'll have to tell him about Esther."

"Bedwalters will keep his mouth shut."

I shook my head. "I can't be certain of that."

"Then get Mrs Jerdoun to give him the ribbon."

"That wouldn't work either! She'd have to tell him why she knows it's significant, which would mean admitting to her – her – "

"Intimacy?" Hugh suggested.

I ground my teeth. "Her friendship with me. Anyway, I haven't told Esther about the ribbon."

Hugh collapsed back on to the bed with a groan. "Charles, Charles! How do you get yourself into such messes?"

I took a deep breath. I'd never told Hugh about the world that ran alongside our own or my ability to step through into it. Only Claudius Heron knows about that. Should I tell Hugh? Or would he think me mad?

He rolled over to the far side of the bed and curled into a ball. "Go to sleep, Charles."

I tugged off my coat and hung it neatly over the back of his chair, sat on the edge of the bed to tug off my shoes.

"Corelli did say one odd thing," Hugh said out of the darkness.

"What?"

"He said it was all his fault. That if he'd had any sense, none of this would ever have happened. Do you think he was complicit in Julia Mazzanti's death?"

I lay down and stared into the darkness. Corelli had been horrified to see Julia's body. I was certain he had not had time to kill her himself but was her death a consequence of something he had done, a consequence that he had never intended? And if so, what?

# 24

**The love between a woman and her daughters
is one of the greatest blessings life has to offer.**
[Letter of Lady Hubert to her eldest daughter
on the birth of the latter's daughter, September 1731]

Hugh was his usual sleepy self in the morning; he had once told me he never felt awake until midday. I found this almost more annoying about him than anything else; everything had to be said three times before he finally repeated it correctly. We established, eventually, that he intended going down to the printing office to put a notice in this week's *Courant*, announcing he was returned to town early and was available for lessons.

I went down to Mrs Baker's lodging house. It was time I spoke to Julia's parents. I could not credit that they had no idea who had engaged their daughter's interest, so much so that she had contemplated eloping. And Mazzanti had not yet properly explained those attacks on him. This preposterous tale of spies!

I heard raised voices inside the house before I got to the door and had to knock several times before Mrs Baker herself answered it. She ushered me inside hurriedly. The hallway was stiflingly hot, the drawn curtains and shutters on the lower floor keeping in the heat of the previous day. Mrs Baker shut the door behind me and raised her eyebrows to heaven.

"Dear God, Mr Patterson, but we could do with some sanity in the house!"

Mazzanti's voice drifted down from upstairs, quibbling over the cost of mourners and horses and black draped hearses.

"Wants only the best," Mrs Baker said, "but wants to pay nothing for it."

I listened a moment longer. Mazzanti was clearly planning an extravagantly demonstrative funeral – a procession through the streets with half a dozen mourners, kettle drums and muffled trumpets. Where in heaven's name did he think he'd get kettle drums in Newcastle!? And trumpets? He'd have to call in the band of one of the regiments at Tynemouth and they charged the earth.

"Wants to make sure everyone sees how fond he was of the girl," Mrs Baker said.

"Was he?"

"Never a bit. Just wanted to make money out of her."

There was a little silence upstairs, marred only by the calm sorrowful murmurs of the undertaker.

"And Signora Mazzanti?"

Another sigh. "I can't do anything with her. And the maid won't go near her. Or him. Or the body."

"You need a rest," I said, eying her weary face.

"It'll all be over in a day or two," she said, philosophically. "And at least I'll have no spirits in the house. Thank God the girl got killed out in the street; I'd not want to put up with her whining the rest of my life." She looked at me. "That sounds hard, doesn't it? Uncharitable."

"Yes," I admitted.

"Well, I feel uncharitable," she said. "They're the hardest work I ever had. Comes of being foreigners, I daresay. She's in the drawing room, Mr Patterson. Go on in." She smiled mischievously. "Don't worry, she prefers the gentlemen. That's why you can't hear her crying now. Mr Heron's with her."

I went into the drawing room. In the plain room with its comfortable chairs and scatter of cushions and knickknacks, a vase of overblown white lilies struck an incongruous note. As did Signora Mazzanti, huddled in a chair in a froth of black satin, black plumes in her hair, black jewellery dripping over her bosom and wrists. She was sobbing quietly into a handkerchief as white as the lilies.

Across the room, Claudius Heron turned and met my gaze. He had been straightening books on an occasional table, as if in need of something ordered to do. I fancied I saw a trace of relief in his eyes. They were the only people present; there was no maid, no chaperone; perhaps Mrs Baker had been sitting with them. If so, she did not come back in.

"Signora." I hesitated, then eased myself into the chair opposite her, so that I could look her in the eyes – if I could persuade her to look up. "Signora, forgive me, but I want to ask you some questions."

She raised limpid blue eyes, swimming with tears. Heavens, but she must have been beautiful twenty years ago.

"About Julia," I said.

She gasped and buried her face in her damp handkerchief. Heron strode across to us. "Signora, you must answer. I assume you want to find the man who killed your daughter?"

His tone was brutal in its matter-of-factness. I winced, but to my surprise, Signora Mazzanti straightened, murmured, whispered, finally said, just audibly, "Yes, yes, of course."

She turned those pleading eyes on me again. "Do you know who – who *hurt* her, sir?"

"Not yet," I said gently. "That's why I need your help."

"I'm sure I don't know anything," she said with just a trace of – what? petulance? She glanced at Heron as if for approval.

He said curtly, "Go on."

"I was asleep," she protested.

"Yes, yes, of course." I did not like Heron's manner but it was clear that Signora Mazzanti responded better to it than to my cautious sympathy, so I tried to cultivate a little directness myself. "Do you know who she was eloping with?"

"No!" she said convulsively, then gathered her composure and spoke more firmly. "No, I'm sure you're wrong. She wouldn't do anything like that."

I fancied I heard Claudius Heron give the tiniest of exasperated sighs.

"Julia would do nothing to give us pain," Signora Mazzanti said. She dabbed at her moist eyes, stared fixedly at a point on the carpet. "You think me very foolish, no doubt, sir. But I know my daughter. She was a good girl. She knew – " She faltered.

"Yes?" I probed. The Signora glanced quickly up at Heron.

"She knew we depended on her."

"Financially?"

Her head jerked up; she sat a little straighter. "Yes, sir, financially," she said bitterly. "The world seems to prefer vapid prettiness to true worth!"

Vapid prettiness – was that how she had regarded her daughter? The vision of a contented, happy family that she had been trying to present was rapidly vanishing.

"She was aware of her attractions, I think," I said with a careful edge of contempt.

"Oh, yes," Signora Mazzanti said scornfully. "She knew she could attract the men and that they'd pay."

Was she suggesting that Julia had sold her body for money? Given Julia's pregnancy, that was clearly not impossible.

"But you don't know of one particular man?"

"One?" she snapped. Then she seemed to recollect herself, cast a fleeting look at Heron. In that look, I saw how similar mother and daughter had been – that was not a look pleading for help and support, but a quick assessment of the effect she was having on her audience.

"Who?"

She flushed. Yes, I thought, she certainly knew something.

"That player. The one who performed the young hero."

"Reynolds?" Heron asked.

"Anyone else?"

"Half a dozen gentlemen," she said contemptuously.

It was no good; she knew very little in reality, I surmised, and was intent upon making a great deal of it.

"She wouldn't be told," the Signora said. "She'd do anything to give me pain. None of it was accidental, you can be sure of that."

"What in particular?"

"Always taking her father's side. Always telling me how old I looked." The Signora's voice dripped scorn. "Telling me she'd teach me how to sing *English* opera instead of Italian. *She* – teach *me*!"

"And her father did not reprimand her?"

"Oh, yes," Signora Mazzanti said. "He reprimanded her all right."

The bitterness of this remark bewildered me and I saw that it puzzled Heron too. Why should she be annoyed that her husband had disciplined the girl who had been so rude to her? Or did she mean it sarcastically?

She was sitting bolt upright, an imperious figure, but then seemed to recollect herself. She looked up at Heron with watery eyes. "Please – I think – a little tea – would you be so good – " And she was drooping again, wielding that damp handkerchief.

Heron was still for a moment, then nodded. "I will go and find Mrs Baker."

He strode for the door, and I made my excuses and followed him; it would not do to be alone with the Signora, and in any case I fancied Heron wanted to talk. Why else should he go to the trouble of leaving the room when he could simply have rung the bell for the maid?

I had hardly shut the drawing room door behind me when he rounded on me. He kept his voice low and quiet but the venom in it took me aback.

"God damn it, Patterson, what fiends women are!"

I blinked at his fury, stuttered something incoherent.

"She plays the loving mother when she hated the girl!"

"Mazzanti was the same," I pointed out. "It's a household of enemies."

"And she sings so wonderfully." There was a bitter twist to Heron's mouth. "Tales of love and heroic sacrifice, of maternal selflessness and dutiful obedience. Oh, yes, Patterson, she knows how to act all the correct sentiments."

"Far from it," I said, in that level calm tone I knew he appreciated. "You wouldn't be raging at her now if she had not given herself away."

He was breathing deeply. The angry flush began to die out of his lean cheeks. I went on, to give him a little extra time to recover.

"She cannot be the murderer," I pointed out. "We know we are looking for a man – Julia was raped."

"If she had been a true mother, she would have known exactly who her daughter was seeing and would have prevented the elopement!"

"The Signora sees only what concerns herself."

In the silence that followed, we could hear Mazzanti, upstairs, still laying down the law to the undertaker. Heron grimaced.

"Hear that, Patterson? How much do you think a funeral like that will cost?"

"More than the Mazzantis have, no doubt."

"There are plans on foot to hold a benefit for the family. A concert or a theatre performance perhaps – anything to raise money for them. And the concert directors are talking of increasing the amount to be paid to Signora Mazzanti for singing in the concerts this winter."

"They'll bankrupt the series," I said in horror. "We can hardly afford what they are paying now!"

Heron sneered. "Don't worry – nothing will come of that idea! When did you ever know the directors to give away money? You'll no doubt find yourself playing in a benefit concert, however."

I nodded. All the musicians in town would be there, giving their services free of charge. Few would know the Mazzantis well, others would dislike them. But you never turned down an appeal to help raise money for an indigent colleague; next year you might be the one in need of help.

"And who knows," Heron said dryly, his calm quite recovered. "Maybe the whole affair will give the Mazzantis such a dislike for the town that they head straight back to London. And then you may lead the concerts as musical director after all."

He swung on his heels and strode off towards the back of the house. His parting shot was thrown back at me over his shoulder. "At least *something* good may come of this affair."

# 25

**But I go along with whatever Lady Hubert says;
marital peace is worth a little sacrifice.**
[Letter of Sir John Hubert to his brother-in-law, October 1731]

I was not sure I wanted to profit in such a way. To know that your good fortune may be the cause of someone else's destitution is not a palatable thought, even if John Mazzanti was so objectionable.

I had thought him destined for a violent death. I had never imagined it might be his daughter that died.

I was about to climb the stairs to see Mazzanti when I heard footsteps upstairs. Mazzanti and the undertaker must be coming down. Well, it saved me the effort of going up to him. And if he'd had his way in the matter of the funeral, he might be in a good mood to answer questions.

But to my astonishment, as the figures appeared at the top of the stair, I saw not the undertaker but Athalia Keregan, hanging on Mazzanti's arm. He was looking benignly paternal, patting her hand and murmuring consoling noises as she dabbed her eyes with a scrap of lace.

They did not immediately notice me. Not until they were almost at the foot of the stair did Athalia glance around and see me in the middle of the hallway. She looked startled, then gave me a wink from behind the handkerchief before turning her watery adoring gaze on Mazzanti again. She really was a remarkably fine actress.

Mazzanti murmured his farewells and Athalia lingered as long as she dared before rushing past me with a convulsive sob. She managed to give me an admonitory kick on the ankle as she passed.

Mazzanti was glowering at me. "I suppose you've come to gawp at my daughter's remains, Patterson?" His breath was stale with beer.

Athalia, no doubt, I thought, had come to 'pay her respects'.

"I want to ask you some questions," I said, borrowing Heron's curtness.

"Questions? What right have you to question me?"

Heron came from the direction of the kitchens, striding up behind Mazzanti. "Don't stand on your dignity, man! If anyone can find the murderer of your daughter, Patterson can. He has an expertise in these matters."

"An expertise in prying?" Mazzanti lifted a supercilious eyebrow. "How creditable. Out of my way, if you please, Heron. I must see my wife."

He walked towards the drawing room, with only a little unsteadiness. I wondered which had come first – the beer or the despair. For he was a man lost, confused, and bewildered; I had seen it in his expression when we had brought Julia's body home.

Heron went after him at once, his face set in disapproval. Mazzanti's casual use of his surname, without the politeness owing from a social inferior, was bad enough but the tone was beyond acceptance. I expected a reprimand; when I followed them into the room, however, I found Heron standing by the cold fireplace, contemplating Mazzanti in silence as the man poured himself a glassful of brandy.

The maid came in with a tray of tea; Signora Mazzanti looked helplessly at the dishes and spoons and all the other paraphernalia before her. I took pity on her, sat down and poured the tea. It was women's work but if I was to get any sense out of Mazzanti I needed to gain credit with him somehow and perhaps helping his wife would please him.

He showed every sign of ignoring her, however. He came round to the chair opposite me and sat down, crossing his legs nonchalantly, as if he was alone in the room. Heron and I exchanged glances.

"It cannot please you, surely," Heron said irritably, "that the man who raped and killed your daughter is still free. Patterson can help you find him."

Mazzanti took a dish of tea from me. "Julia was not raped."

"No, no," Signora Mazzanti protested. "I'm sure she wasn't."

"She has been examined," I said, "by Gale the barber surgeon, at the request of the constable, Bedwalters."

Mazzanti made a dismissive gesture. "What do fellows like that know? She was not abused, sir, not in the least."

Perhaps the natural partiality of a parent could not abide the thought; nothing would move him on the matter. Signora Mazzanti started fussing over the blend of tea; the shop had sent the wrong one, she had asked specifically for the one she usually had in London. I interrupted. "If she was not abused, why do you suppose she was killed?"

Mazzanti sipped his tea with cold indifference. "I deny your authority to ask me these questions, sir."

"And I suspect your refusal to answer me," I retorted, stung. "Sir!"

He sat up, slopping the tea on to the knee of his breeches. "How dare you! Do you have the nerve to accuse me of – of – "

"Of course not," Heron said smoothly, annoying me. I had worked hard to get a genuine reaction out of Mazzanti; an angry man would say more than he otherwise might. But Heron went on, obviously intending to calm him, although his own fingers were tapping irritably on the mantelshelf. "Patterson merely wants to establish what happened and to bring the culprit to justice – surely an outcome we would all desire?"

"Yes, yes," Signora Mazzanti said, the tea dish trembling in her hand, darting a little frightened glance at her husband. "We all want that."

I contemplated the odd emphasis she gave to that sentence. Mazzanti sat back, crossing his legs again and sipping genteelly at the tea. His hand, I noticed, was trembling.

"I repeat, Heron, I have yet to hear a good reason why Mr Patterson is interfering in this matter."

He turned his cold gaze on me, lifted his head and gave me a condescending sneer. The tea slopped from side to side in the dish. "He was after all the one who found Julia and he has no convincing explanation of what he was doing there."

Heron lost his fragile hold on his temper. "Damn it, are you suggesting Patterson killed the girl!"

Signora Mazzanti started to sob. I seized her tea dish as it threatened to spill.

Mazzanti remained unperturbed. "He made advances to Julia."

"The devil I did!"

"She told us all."

"I did not!"

"Didn't she, Ciara?"

Signora Mazzanti wept.

"The idea is preposterous!" Heron snapped.

"I hardly knew her," I said. How the devil had Mazzanti done this? He had turned the conversation against me. It was all self-defence, clearly. What more could I do but protest my innocence – aware that the more I protested, the less convincing I sounded? "Is this a distraction, sir? To hide the fact that you neglected your daughter?"

"How dare you!"

"If you had taken better care of her, she would not have been able to slip out of the house unseen."

"To meet you!" Mazzanti retaliated.

"Devil take it – " Heron began. I had motioned him to silence before I realised what I was doing; he turned away in annoyance, turned away, gripping the edge of the mantel.

"She didn't have to be killed," Signora Mazzanti said with a wavering sob.

"I suppose," Mazzanti said, "that you were annoyed by her rebuff and forced her." He was gripping his tea dish so tightly, I was surprised it did not crack.

"I thought you said she was not raped," I pointed out.

"It didn't have to come to this," Signora Mazzanti said, behind her fragment of lace handkerchief. "We were all so happy."

"Were you trying to persuade her to elope with you, Patterson? Did she change her mind?"

"What are we going to do?" Ciara Mazanti moaned. "We've no money, no engagements. How are we going to live?"

"So sordid, Mr Patterson," Mazzanti said scornfully. "To be running after young girls not old enough to know their own minds. Was it her money? Her future career? Or was it just lust?"

Heron snarled. "Damn it, I won't listen to this!"

Mazzanti leapt up, the tea spilling everywhere. Heron crowded in on him, all traces of the gentleman disappearing. Mazzanti shouted; Heron yelled back. Mazzanti grabbed a handful of Heron's coat; Heron cocked a fist and struck out. He caught Mazzanti on the chin and the Italian staggered back into the chair, stumbled, went down taking the chair with him in a great crash.

Ciara Mazzanti wailed in panic. I was trying to clamber over the teatable to separate the two men but only Heron was close enough to grab and I had already insulted him enough. But there was nothing for it. He was reaching down to seize hold of Mazzanti and was likely to do him real damage. Heron was the younger by a good fifteen years, and he wasn't half-drunk.

I was reaching across the table when Ciara Mazzanti caught hold of the skirts of my coat. "Don't! Don't!" she pleaded. Don't rescue her husband? Don't hurt him? The woman was mad.

I pulled free. Mazzanti was tangled in the chair, swearing in English and Italian – the first Italian I had ever heard him use. Heron had one hand entangled in Mazzanti's coat.

I seized Heron's arm. Beneath the brocaded coat, he was icy cold.

"Sir!"

Heron took no notice. "Get up, damn it."

"He'll send for the constable," I hissed in his ear.

Mazzanti was trying to crawl backwards across the floor. The door flew open. Mrs Baker burst in, brandishing a saucepan. I pushed past Heron, managing to pull him away from Mazzanti as I did so.

"Just an accident," I said brightly to Mrs Baker. "Signor Mazzanti tripped over the footstool."

She looked round at the scene: Signora Mazzanti weeping in abandon, Heron standing with his coat disordered and his fists clenched, his lean cheeks red with fury. And Mazzanti squirming across the floor, swearing as blasphemously as the ruffians who had attacked me.

Heron strode to the door, managing the sketchiest of polite bows to Mrs Baker.

Mazzanti rolled over on to hands and knees, crawled across the floor. I reached for his arm to help him up. He shook me off. Ciara wept on. Mazzanti used the overturned chair to pull himself upright. He looked at me, tried to draw himself up haughtily, and stumbled across the room in search of brandy.

I took Mrs Baker's arm and led her from the room. We shut the door on Ciara Mazzanti's weeping and her husband's sharp complaints.

"However do folks come to that?" Mrs Baker said, as we stood in the hall; she cradled the saucepan in her arms as if for consolation. "They were children once, hopeful and pretty and promising. However did they come to this?"

# 26

**What are a few secrets to a woman? Meat and drink.**
[Letter of Sir John Hubert to his brother-in-law, October 1731]

I escaped, feeling fraught and harassed. I have never known how to deal with weeping women. What had I learnt? That they were both turning a blind eye to the truth. Julia had not been raped, she had not intended to elope, she was a good girl. All this might have been the reaction of grieving parents, who cannot bear to think about what happened to their darling. But neither of them cared a jot except for their own well-being. *How are we going to live?* Signora Mazzanti had wailed. True, the removal of the one secure wage earner in the house made their situation unenviable, but I would have liked to have seen a little genuine grief.

I was in sore need of someone to pour balm on my soul – or at least someone I could complain to. I accosted the spirit that clung to the house next door to Mrs Baker's and asked it if it could find Hugh Demsey. There was a moment's silence, presumably while the spirit passed the message on.

"Such a coming and going," it said happily. "Though I could do with a little less of that psalm fellow."

"Proctor?"

"Stands outside here singing all the day. Last night, for instance. In a right state, he was. Told him to go home but he said he was keeping vigil."

The day was bidding to become as hot as any before it; I retreated to the thin strip of shade at the edge of the street.

"All night," the spirit said in amazement. "At least when I was living, I only had to go to church on Sundays. And that other fellow too."

"Which one?"

"Don't know his name. Never seen him before. Tall, dark, looks like he's not slept much."

Not much of a description to go on; at a pinch, it could have fitted both Philip Ord and Ned Reynolds, who were very different men in looks.

"What did he do?"

"Stare. Just stare. Stare, stare, stare." The spirit slid down the water pipe to confide in me; he was a bright excited gleam. "Like a man possessed. Eyes popping out of his head."

"Did he say anything?"

"Never a word."

"Did you see him here before the girl died?"

The spirit considered. "No, no, I can't say I did."

A sightseer then? Or –

"Not Bedwalters the constable?" I suggested.

The spirit sniggered. "I know him. He's plump – eats too much."

I couldn't remember seeing Bedwalters eat at all. "Have you found Hugh Demsey yet?"

"Oh Lord, yes, sir. Ages ago. He's looking for you as a matter of fact. Wants a chat. He's gone to the theatre in Mr Usher's timber yard."

"Thank you," I said. "And if you ever find out who the unknown man was – "

"I'll send a message to you straight away," the spirit agreed, and I knew by his excited tone that he indeed would.

I walked up the Side towards the timber yard at the top. If anything, the spirit's sketchy description sounded most like Corelli, though he would probably be at sea by now. But I wondered again why he had fled at all; any untoward activity could surely have been covered by the story he had given Bedwalters about spies. What had he really been doing?

The timber yard gates stood open and a heavily laden cart was manoeuvring through the gap. I stood back to let the men work, fanning my hand across my face to create a cool breeze. I could hear the regular scrape scrape of saws, and the thud of hammering. Men called encouragement to the cart driver; two very young boys sat on top of the tree trunks on the cart, squealing with glee.

The cart got through at last and I squeezed past, and walked across the busy yard towards the theatre. The double doors to the theatre were closed. Or rather one stood just ajar – a bad sign, for if a rehearsal was going on, surely the doors would have been wide open to let in the air. There was no sign of Hugh.

I was looking about me as I approached the doors, remembering the time in this yard when I had almost fallen at the feet of Julia Mazzanti – the other Julia, in the world that ran alongside our own. Then the sun went in and I felt rain on the back of my hand. Darkness gathered with extraordinary rapidity. I glanced up. Lowering clouds scudded across the sky; wind caught at my coat tails and tore the clouds apart to reveal the moon, a thin unhelpful sliver of light.

The day flickered out of existence and it was full night. I had stepped through again to that other world.

I must have brought this on myself by thinking of that other, still living, Julia. I stood, disconcerted, alarmed that a stray thought could have such an effect. Stars speckled the night sky above me, were covered by the fast-moving clouds; a flurry of rain splattered against my face, driven by the wind. Well, I was here now; I must be careful and learn as much as I could.

One thing was obvious. The worlds were not moving at the same speed. I had stepped from mid-morning to full night and from a hot heavy June to a chill wet – well, the temperature suggested perhaps October.

The rain splashed on my shoulders and dampened my hair. I ran to the shelter of the theatre, jerked open the door and hurried in.

And saw in the darkened, unlit theatre, two figures embracing.

They were twenty or thirty feet away, mere shadows in the darkness, and all I could tell from the outline of their clothes was that they were man and woman. The woman was resisting the embrace, pushing at the man, turning her head to avoid his kiss, trying to wriggle out of his hold.

I coughed, loudly.

They broke apart. The woman swung away from the man and came towards me, head held proudly high. From that stance alone, I recognised Julia Mazzanti. The man turned abruptly away. I stared hard as he stalked off into the darkness but in seconds he was a mere hint of movement. I had not the slightest idea who he was.

Julia Mazzanti came to a halt in front of me. Her face was just touched by the light of a guttering lantern burning somewhere behind me, outside the theatre. Her hair, slightly disordered, gleamed, as did the yellow ribbons wound through it. Her expression was defiant. I realised with a shock just how much sympathy I felt for her; she was a woman besieged but fighting back, and I admired that greatly.

Her gaze flickered over my clothes in distinct amusement again but she spoke cordially. "Good evening, Mr Patterson. Were you looking for me?"

"I'm looking for the truth," I said, then regretted my honesty. How could I explain what I sought without telling her that in my world her counterpart lay dead?

"Impossible," she said, with a gleam of bitterness. "Truth is always buried very deeply, Mr Patterson. She paused, then said with some determination, "I wonder, have you seen Mr Proctor, sir?"

"The psalm teacher? No." I wondered if in this world Proctor was as meek and uncertain as he was in mine. "Did you want him for any particular reason?"

"Tuition," she said, quickly. "He is giving me some advice on my singing."

Proctor is an excellent singing teacher. What would the Proctor of my world not have given to have Julia as a pupil? I reminded myself again that this was a different world from my own, and a different Proctor – he would bear a substantial resemblance to the man I knew, but there might well be pertinent differences. Perhaps here he was more decisive, less meek, less – I hesitated, but I could not deny it – Proctor was a frightened man; he feared the world, and his religion, real though it was, was a defence against that world.

Ciara Mazzanti turned away from what she feared, Ned ran away from it, Proctor took refuge in God. I thought of Esther and what she was asking of me. Was that not what I was doing too? Running away? Pretending that if I ignored the situation it would go away? Was I as timid and fearful as the others whom I despised for their timidity?

"You look shocked, Mr Patterson." Julia leant a little closer, spoke more softly. "You saw a certain affecting little scene when you arrived no doubt."

I brought my thoughts back to the present. "It was very dark."

"Come sir," she mocked. "Let's have honesty."

Was her mind running on the same lines as mine? "Is that buried as deep as truth?" I countered.

She laughed. "Oh *much* deeper, sir." She eyed me consideringly; there was no denying she was a daring woman, to broach such a topic openly, rather than merely to pretend it had not happened. "Well, do not judge me harshly, sir. You know how little power we women have, sir – at least allow us at least our power to attract."

"And to manipulate?" I murmured.

"But of course," she said, wide-eyed in innocence. "We see a man whom we think will help us in whatever we desire, then attract him, then use him." Her voice hardened and I remembered that she had been struggling to put off the embrace with the unknown man. She was not as honest as she appeared; she was acting out her defiance to deflect my disapproval. "What else is there to do, Mr Patterson? If I could act directly, I would, but society thinks me too weak and silly."

I thought fleetingly of Esther. She had the advantage over Julia of being of age and a wealthy woman, but even so, I could not imagine her stooping to manipulation – it was in itself a form of dishonesty. Yet who was I to judge Julia? Or any woman?

"I do not think you silly," I said. "In truth, I admire you for your frankness."

"Then perhaps," she said impishly, "I should marry you?"

I recognised this for the tease it was. "God forbid!" I said, equally lightly, "I would make a very bad husband."

She laughed with more genuine amusement. "And I would be a termagant wife, sir!" She sobered, hesitated, then lifted her head proudly. The lantern light from outside sparkled on her earrings and on the necklace at her throat. "I will have control of my own life, Mr Patterson. I will earn my own money, spend what I like, marry whom I like or not marry at all. And – "

She broke off as a voice sounded behind her. Lights sprang up at the back of the theatre, outlining the scenery and casting huge shadows on the theatre walls. I heard someone call for beer. Then a man came walking down the length of the theatre towards us with a lantern held high. Mazzanti. In the distorting flickering light, he looked harassed; a thin sheen of sweat gleamed on his forehead. He was thinner than in my own world.

"Mr Patterson, have you come to watch the rehearsal?"

"At this time of night?" I said blankly.

"We are behindhand because of dear Julia's illness." He gave her a fond, caressing look; she glanced off in another direction. "Are you sure you are quite recovered, my dear? This is not another false dawn?" He smiled at me. "She was ill yesterday too and we thought she had recovered but – alas – no."

The unctuous false concern in his voice grated. Julia said, without looking at me, "I am a great deal better, yes. I will go and change into my costume."

She walked off quietly, with no backward glance. But I had not missed the point of the conversation; it looked as if this Julia, like her counterpart in my own world, was with child. More importantly, in this world, her father knew.

"She is a sweet child," Mazzanti said, startling me by the syrup smoothness of his voice. "Do come and watch a while, Mr Patterson. We do not play the music tonight of course but I think you will still find it interesting. Julia is so graceful, do you not think, so beautiful?"

He cocked his head and smiled at me, like a merchant watching for a reaction to his wares. He was trying to sell her to me! He knew about her pregnancy and was looking for a marriage to save her reputation. And a wealthy husband too, one who could be guaranteed to be generous to his wife's family, particularly if he had taken from them their one wage-earner.

Mazzanti hovered, easing me into a chair and extolling Julia's virtues still further. She was an excellent manager, knew how to run a household, was frugal and could make a joint of meat go further than any woman he knew. She was quiet and respectful and of course deferred to the judgement of her betters. In short, although he did not directly say so, she would be an ideal wife.

I hurried to deflect him into another subject. "You are going to London soon, I hear."

"Indeed. Julia is to make her first appearance in the capital.

She will of course be a great success."

A *large* one, no doubt, if she was pregnant.

"Many gentlemen will admire her," he said, waving to another member of the company to hurry with their task. He treated me to tales of Julia's triumphs here, there and everywhere. A viscount had admired her in Exeter, a rich knight in Bristol. In Manchester, two merchants had almost fought over her. All of which might, possibly, be true, but I doubted any would have made a respectable offer for her – a disreputable one, possibly.

"She is of an ideal age to be thinking of marriage," Mazzanti said, abandoning roundaboutation. "Although, alas, the idea of her leaving me is torture. A daughter is always dear to her father's heart."

"No doubt." I wanted to ask if the father of Julia's child was so very unsuitable as a husband but courage failed me. Even if he told me, the same might not be true of my own world. Here for instance, John Mazzanti was clearly more inclined than his counterpart to find respectability for his daughter. Moreover, I was not the Charles Patterson who rightfully belonged to this world and I had no right to say or do anything that might make life difficult for him. I should not encourage Mazzanti but remain polite and non-committal. But his brazen canvassing made that difficult.

Just then Julia came back on to the stage. One of the company was at the edge of the stage, bending to light the candles that outlined it. Julia, in the demure virginal white of a heroine, stood talking to a middle-aged man of dissolute mien.

Mazzanti cursed. "She will marry to spite me," he said sharply. "I know she will!"

He leapt up on to the stage, took hold of the man's arm and led him away. Julia stood a little irresolutely in the middle of the stage, but she was, I noticed, smiling wryly.

I got up. The rest of the company were hurrying into the

theatre; some of the faces were familiar, though others were strangers. Not everyone in one world had their counterparts in the other. And there was a difference in their demeanour towards me; even those who knew me gave me a distant respectful nod as if I was a little above their station. In this world, I was rich, well-known, almost a gentleman, or as much of a gentleman as a musician could ever hope to be. If nothing else, the incident reminded me of the dangers of drawing conclusions from one world and applying them to the other.

But if I could learn no lessons from this world about events in my own, why was I here at all? Why did I have this ability to step between worlds and why did the ability only seem to manifest itself at times of crisis when events in the two worlds echoed each other?

Was it merely chance, of no significance whatsoever? Or was there something here that could help me find the man who had killed Julia in my world?

I looked at the woman standing on the stage, accepting a shawl from a young girl with an armful of clothes. This Julia Mazzanti was a strong-willed woman; I was sure she was not the kind of woman to put her child out to a wet nurse or a baby farmer and never see it again. She would unhesitatingly take on what she regarded as her duty. Married or no, she would accept the child as her responsibility.

That would hardly please her father, but there was one man who might have more at stake than Mazzanti in making sure the child was never born. The child's father. Had he killed the Julia in my world?

And might he think the same in this world? Was I here to prevent Julia dying here too?

# 27

**FOR SALE At Usher's Deal Yard, Timber of all Kinds, suitable for Housebuilding, Furniture making, &c. Orders promptly fulfilled.**
[*Newcastle Courant* 13 March 1736]

I suddenly panicked that my counterpart would also arrive and that I would find myself face to face with him. I retreated to the door of the theatre and looked out on to the dark night. The rain had stopped and the clouds were scudding away; stars glittered in a translucent sky.

It was time to go home, back to my own world. I took a step or two out into the darkness, expecting it to shift to bright June sunshine.

Nothing happened.

I stood in the warm darkness lit only by the moon, cursing. What the devil did I have to do to control this ability?

Then, simultaneously, I noted three things. Firstly, the moon was full. Secondly, it was stiflingly warm. Thirdly, the theatre behind me was silent and empty.

I had stepped back. I had stepped into my own world without noticing it, gone from a chill autumn night to a stuffy June night at the full of the moon. When I had left it, my own world had been in the middle of a day; now it was so late that the timber yard was shut up and locked against the world, and there was not a light in the place. I had been right; time did indeed move at a different pace in that other world. What had taken half an hour at most had allowed hours to pass in my own world.

I hoped it *was* only hours, not days.

The timber yard gate was locked and barred from the outside;

I rattled it to no effect. There was a smaller gate at the back of the yard somewhere but that would no doubt be locked too. Perhaps I could spend the night in the theatre – there would probably be sufficient costumes to make a comfortable bed, maybe even a little food. Not that I was hungry or tired – it still felt mid-morning to me. Still…

I heard a dog bark.

I stood very still. The dog sounded close.

It bounded from the shelter of a pile of timber.

A huge black shape raced towards me silently into the full glare of the moonlight. It might be a guard dog or a rabid wild dog – either way it was dangerous. I stepped back, took a deep breath then ran for the wall. At the last moment I leapt, grabbed for the top of the wall, hung for a moment by one arm before I could get a purchase with the other. Then I scrambled up to the top and sat astride, looking down at the snarling dog. A big ugly brute with a wide collar. Clearly Usher's guard dog.

I wriggled round until I could let myself down the other side of the wall, dropped to the cobbles. Behind me, the dog barked then subsided to yelps and frustrated whines.

I turned to go.

Then I saw the three ruffians waiting for me.

# 28

**No Godfearing man or woman dare walk the streets at night. Something must be done, sir!**
[Letter from JUSTICIA to Mayor of Newcastle upon Tyne, printed in the *Newcastle Courant*, 15 May 1736.]

I had one advantage over the ruffians: they were drunk and I was not; they had apparently been drinking for hours and could hardly stagger along. I wished fervently I'd thought to borrow a stick of wood from Usher's yard but even so I had the upper hand almost from the start. They got in a blow or two, connecting more by luck than by judgement, and one blow to my cheek half dazed me. But they were falling over each other and their own feet, and were kept awake only by their own fury. I snatched a cudgel from one of them and laid him out with it, skipped away from another.

There was only one nasty moment when I misjudged my position and got myself boxed in by them; at the same time, I saw two or three more men stagger out of the shadows. One man and a cudgel was no match for four or five others, and I couldn't run because I was surrounded. So I slipped the bar on the timber yard gate and it wasn't locked after all, as I had hoped, and the dog came raging out.

We scattered.

I raced off down the Side – totally the wrong direction if I wanted to get back to my lodgings but any way was good, as long as it was away from those ruffians. I heard a shriek as the dog found a victim. Then I was on the moonlit Sandhill, and running across to Butcher Bank and the climb to Silver Street. By the time I stopped outside All Hallows' Church, winded and desperate for breath, I was alone and safe.

I was tempted to go to Esther's house to see if the intruder had returned; I had intended to go back, I had told her I would be there. But I had no idea of the time and the church clocks refused to oblige me by striking. It might be three or four o'clock in the morning; I could not wake everyone up in the small hours. Clearly the best thing to do was to go home. I kept to the sides of the streets where the moonlight did not reach, started at every cat that crossed my path and made it to my lodgings without any further incident.

I could hardly expect to escape the spirit of my landlady, demanding to know why I was out so late, though I silently eased open the outer door of the house in faint hope that I might. But she was on me at once, her bright gleam whipping the door out of my hand and clicking it shut with a snap.

"Upstairs, Mr Patterson, quickly!"

The stairs were pitch black and I stumbled half a dozen times as I climbed. The drawing room clock chimed once and fell silent. Not as late as I had feared; why then was Mrs Foxton in such a flap? The miners in the house came home much later than this.

The door to my room flew open, letting out a flood of moonlight from the uncurtained window. Hugh Demsey grabbed my arm, pulled me inside. The gleam of Mrs Foxton's spirit, following us, whisked the door closed.

"Where the devil have you been?" Hugh demanded.

How was I to explain? I ummed and aahed.

"Charles, for God's sake!" His voice changed. "What the – did you know you're bleeding?"

One of the candles lit itself, courtesy of Mrs Foxton. Hugh snatched it up, pushed me in front of my fragment of mirror. In the flickering candlelight, I saw blood running down my cheek from a cut under my hairline at the right. I hadn't noticed

– I'd thought I was sweating with running.

"The ruffians caught me," I said, wiping away the blood with my handkerchief. "Why the flap, Hugh?"

"Bedwalters," Mrs Foxton said grimly.

"He's after you."

"What!?"

"I went down to the Printing Office this morning," Hugh said, "I overheard Bedwalters and Mazzanti talking. Mazzanti said you'd been making advances to Julia; he told Bedwalters that Julia was frightened of you."

I swore. I remembered that Mazzanti had accused me of something of the sort in his own drawing room but we had both known the accusations weren't true – he had been defending himself by attacking someone else. But to go as far as to take the tale to Bedwalters!

"And," Hugh pressed, "Ord's told him he saw you talking to Julia – *intimately*."

"Ord!" I said in outrage. That devil! To accuse me when he'd asked a favour of me! And such a favour too! He must be desperate to divert suspicion from himself but why in heaven's name did he not see the consequences for himself? What was to prevent me telling Bedwalters about the letters?

There was a hammering at the door.

"Oh God," Hugh said. Mrs Foxton's spirit disappeared.

"Bedwalters is talking of arresting you!" Hugh said frantically. "This is all your own fault!"

"*My* fault?"

"He only wanted to *talk* to you until he realised you'd left town."

"I did not leave town!"

"Of all the times to disappear!" Hugh said in despair. "Couldn't you see how suspicious it would look?"

"It wasn't my fault!"

Mrs Foxton's spirit came back, sliding between the door and

the frame.

"Quick, Mr Patterson, out of the back and over the wall. Mr Demsey, help him. I'll delay the constable."

And she disappeared again.

"This is preposterous," I said, trying to dig the letters out of my coat pocket. "Look, I'll talk to Bedwalters. I've got evidence." I waved the letters.

"Not now!"

"But they'll give the lie to Ord's story."

"Do you *want* to end up in gaol?!" Hugh demanded, bundling me towards the door.

"No, no!" I dug my heels in. "If I must go, there's something I must take." I pushed Hugh on to the landing. "Check that the way is clear."

Hugh was right; I had to go. But I had one crucially incriminating piece of evidence in my possession: Julia Mazzanti's ribbon. If Bedwalters searched the room and found it, I'd be in trouble for sure. I snatched up the mattress, retrieved the ribbon and stuffed it into a pocket. I also slid two guineas out of my store from the sale of the organ.

By the time I was finished, Hugh was in the room again, snatching at my sleeve. We ran for the servants' stairs, were only just on them when we heard footsteps pounding up the front stairs. Bedwalters must have brought helpers – he himself was not capable of such speed.

At the foot of the servants' stair, Hugh threw his weight against the door to the yard and it flew open. Across the moonlit yard, the back gate was bolted and locked. Hugh made a cradle of his hands, I stepped in them and scrambled over the wall, then reached down to help Hugh up. There were sounds of banging from the house, and shouting.

We dropped down into the cobbled street. I seized Hugh's arm.

"Go home."

"No."

"I don't want you to get in trouble. If you help me, Bedwalters will be after you too."

"I won't go."

More shouting. Someone appeared at the far end of the street.

Hugh shoved me in the opposite direction. "Run!" We ran, stumbling on cobbles, to the end of the street. Hugh gasped for breath. "Go right. I'll decoy them."

"Hugh – "

"Go!" he yelled.

I went right, dived into an alley and ran like the devil. Behind me, I could hear the shouts of the men dying away. They must be following Hugh. I prayed they did not catch him.

At the junction with the next street, I stopped and bent over, trying to recover my breath. I needed help. It was easy enough to outrun a couple of Bedwalters's men but I could not hide from the constable forever. I needed to be able to move around and find the murderer, and I couldn't do that if Bedwalters clapped me in prison to await the next Assizes. And all this because of this wretched ability to step through to another world. It was a skill that was like to get me hanged.

There was only one person who could help me. I couldn't get Esther involved in this mess and any attempt to explain what had really happened would met with derision. Except from one person.

Claudius Heron.

# 29

**The houses on Northumberland Street are those of the gentry and are fine monuments to history and good taste.**
[*Visit to the town of Newcastle upon Tine* by Harriet Brown (Edinburgh: published for the Author, 1703)]

Beyond the town wall, Northumberland Street is a great straight stretch of road that dawdles eventually into the country around Barras Bridge. Houses here are large and sit back from the street in extensive gardens; they always make me nervous – they look aloof and intimidating, reminding me that I am, after all, only a tradesman.

Claudius Heron's house is larger than most and older, a splendid ancient house with generations of Herons at the back of it. Hordes of Herons have died here; there is one room so full of spirits that it is shut up and left unused – no one could possibly get a wink of sleep in the old bed in which so many Herons have died.

I hauled myself up over the garden wall and dropped down the other side on to the soft earth of a flowerbed. My footprints were no doubt emblazoned there for all to see, so when I stepped out on to grass, I scuffed a toe across the place where I had landed.

The house was in darkness but the high-riding full moon cast an unearthly glow across it, glinting off glass. The windows have eyebrows in the old-fashioned style – stone decorations that make the windows look permanently astonished. A couple of weathered statues on the roof represent some indistinguishable deities.

My heart began to sink. The place was plainly entirely shut up for the night. No chance of a wayward servant rolling home late and half-drunk; any such servant would be dismissed within days of entering Heron's employment – or never get into his employment in the first place.

I went softly across the grass towards the square bulk of the house. As I neared, the shape resolved itself into a multi-gabled façade hinting at the many rooms behind. I knew Heron had in effect divided up the house into two parts – one where his own rooms were situated, a second where his young son's retinue lodged. I even thought I knew which part was which but precisely which window gave on to Heron's private rooms, I didn't have the least idea.

As I hovered indecisively on the dark path that ran round the house, a spirit said: "Can I help you, sir?" The spirit had been a pert young woman by the sound of it, deferential but with just a hint of sauciness.

I tried for a confident tone. "I have an important message for Mr Heron."

"If you'll just wait here, sir," she said, as polite as if she was answering the door. "I'll see if he's in. Who shall I say is calling?"

Nervously, I gave her my name.

I stood on the dark path for what seemed to be an age. Spirits are usually so swift in passing messages. Then, on an upper floor, I saw the flicker of candlelight. Another long wait. Candlelight in a second room. What the devil was going on? Then the spirit said close by my ear: "He'll see you sir. Go round to the door by the kitchen."

I felt my way to the back of the house. The moonlight was deceiving, casting impenetrable pools of shadow just where I wanted to step. An archway in a wall led to a stable yard; I heard horses snuffling, hoofs clattering against stone. I nearly fell over a mounting block, eased my way round a pump with a full trough below it. Candlelight flickered behind windows in one corner of the yard. I found a door and waited until I heard bolts shifting. The door was pulled open. I saw in the candlelight a shadowy figure; a voice said deferentially, "If you would enter, sir."

I ducked through the low door into a room with a deep chill in it. A sink in one corner, a washing tub in another. A night light stood on an old scarred table in the middle of the room.

The servant was bolting and locking the door; he came across to pick up the light. One of the reasons for the delay was that he had taken the trouble to dress – in shirt and breeches at least; he hadn't bothered to put on his wig and his scalp was covered by a dark stubble. He was tall, his face a trifle harsh though perfectly neutral in expression; he was in his mid-thirties, perhaps – Ned Reynolds's age. He gave every sign of being a personal manservant, although I had always imagined Heron's valet would be an elderly man, meek and silent.

"This way, sir." He was a Londoner by his accent. He led the way through the kitchens, past the butler's pantry, through the servants' door and out into the main part of the house. Dark rooms flickered around me in the candlelight; ghostly painted faces winked and leered. Then a staircase. I had seen the main stairs of the house and this was nothing like as large but it was far from being a servants' stair.

In the shifting candlelight we negotiated two flights of stairs without mishap. At a closed door, we stopped and the servant scraped his fingernail on the wood. Heron's voice called, "Enter!"

The opening door showed me an opulent room lit by a single branch of candles. Even in the flickering light, I could see the rich colours of the curtains around the disordered bed, the deep comfortable chairs by the unlit fire, a small Roman statue on an occasional table. Heron himself was dressed in a brocade gown hastily flung over a nightrobe; he had tied his fair hair back out of his eyes. He was clearly one of those men who can snap back into alertness whenever he chooses; it was the small hours of the morning but he looked as if he had had an undisturbed night's sleep. Beside him, in this elegant expensive room, I felt shabby, grubby and disreputable.

"I'm sorry to disturb you so late," I murmured awkwardly. Heron was looking at me with an enigmatic expression that I took a moment or two to decipher. Surely he was not amused? What in heaven's name was there to be amused about? I suddenly perceived the enormity of what I was about to ask. I wanted Heron to shelter me against the law, to lie, if necessary, and to run the risk of whatever penalties the law chose to impose should it find out his complicity.

I shook my head. "No, no. I should not have come. I will go."

He did not stir, merely pointed a finger at one of the chairs. "You will not." He dismissed the servant. "Sit down and tell me what has happened."

It is impossible to argue with Heron when he uses that tone of voice. I sat down. He strolled to a table in a corner and poured brandy into two large glasses, held one out to me.

I gathered my wits and told him what had happened. It was a long tale for I could only explain properly by detailing my visits to the other world. Heron was the only man I could confide in, for half a year ago he and I found ourselves stranded in that world with a murderer intent on killing us. He lit another branch of candles to improve the light, sat down opposite me and listened in silence. I hesitated to speak ill of Philip Ord for gentlemen tend to stick together clannishly against outside attacks but since he had spoken against me to Bedwalters, I felt I had no choice.

Heron did not defend Ord; his lip merely curled contemptuously.

Mazzanti was a different matter; when I told Heron that Mazzanti had regaled Bedwalters with the imagined tale of my advances to Julia, he said some very sharp things about fools and foreigners. When I told him about Bedwalters's visit to my lodgings, his anger boiled over.

"What the devil does the man think he's doing?"

I have a great esteem for Bedwalters. Even in these circumstances I felt obliged to defend him. "He is duty bound to investigate any information that comes to his attention."

"Nonsense," Heron snapped. "Why should he suspect you any more than this Corelli fellow? You discovered the body together, and he is an unknown quantity where you are not!"

"Corelli is probably at sea by now." I told him of Hugh's encounter with Corelli at Houghton-le-Spring.

"He wanted to warn you?" Heron demanded, going straight for the most interesting part of the puzzle. "Why should he care what happens to you?"

"I don't have the least idea. I think he may be back in town too." I told him of the spirit's testimony, how it had seen a man keeping watch outside Mrs Baker's house.

Heron pushed himself to his feet, the draught setting the candles flaring; he reached for the bell to summon the servant back. "Then Bedwalters has a far better suspect close at hand. And why the devil has he discounted the idea that the girl was attacked by a passer by? Fowler!"

The servant had appeared in the doorway so swiftly that I suspected he had been outside the door, indulging in the usual pastime of servants – eavesdropping. "Fetch my clothes," Heron said brusquely. "And wake one of the footmen. The tallest. I want him to accompany me through the town. Tell him to bring a cudgel."

"You're going to rouse Bedwalters?" I asked, incredulously as the servant looked out Heron's clothes.

"If you can rouse me, I can rouse him," he said tartly. "Have you told me everything, Patterson?"

I had not, of course. I had not mentioned Esther and her intruder. Nor the ribbon I had found in the bushes. "Everything I can think of that is useful," I said.

He looked at me for a moment, clearly suspicious. But he said nothing, merely nodding when the servant held up a coat for his approval. "There are rumours," he said, "that the murderer has killed before."

"There are always such rumours." But I mused over the possibility as the servant helped Heron dress. I could still not fathom how the attacks on Mazzanti fitted in with Julia's death or indeed if they had any relevance at all. And all this talk of spies – I saw the servant, Fowler, grin when I outlined this theory.

Heron pursed his lips as he leant close to a mirror to arrange his cravat. "Do you think that all this might simply be a smokescreen to cover up some other crime? Did Julia perhaps have something the murderer wanted?" He frowned as Fowler brushed down his coat. "Or perhaps Mazzanti possesses something. The girl was wooed and the villain persuaded her to bring this something with her, then killed her so she could not talk."

I thought of Ord's letters and could see that Heron was thinking of them too. They sat in my pocket still, as did the ribbon.

"But that would not work," I said. "Once the girl's spirit disembodies, she will tell all she knows. She will certainly reveal if someone has been trying to persuade her to some such plan."

I tried to work out days and dates. Spirits usually disembody three or four days after death, although it has been known to take longer. My trips between the worlds and the lapse in time caused by them confused me, but Julia's spirit must surely disembody soon.

"Bedwalters thinks that she may not have been killed in Amen Corner," Heron said. "He has found some more spirits there and they know nothing of it."

"Damn," I said. The spirit clings to the place of death, not to the body; were we to be reduced to wandering the local streets looking for the girl's spirit? It would not be the first time I had done something of the sort. I wondered what these spirits in Amen Corner had been doing when I was searching for help after finding Julia's body. Minding their own business, no doubt.

"Then the body was moved deliberately to confuse us."

"Indeed."

"But a man carrying a dead body is hardly inconspicuous! What if he was seen?"

"He was not," Heron pointed out.

He turned on his heels so Fowler could help him into his coat. "Bedwalters also told me that the murderer took a souvenir – one of the girl's ribbons. As a kind of memento of the occasion, I suppose. Logically, if we can find the murderer, he will have the ribbon in his possession, so we may be sure of his identity."

The ribbon was almost burning a hole in my pocket. "It could have been taken by a passer by," I pointed out. "The man I surprised bending over the body, for instance."

The servant smoothed the coat on Heron's shoulders. Heron stared into the air. "Possibly. But I don't like coincidences."

Nor did I.

And neither would Bedwalters.

# 30

**The law must be respected!**
[Letter from JUSTICIA to Mayor of Newcastle upon Tyne, printed in the *Newcastle Courant*, 15 May 1736.]

Only an hour earlier I had come alone through the night, with my heart in my mouth every time I saw a shadow move. Now I walked back with Heron and a footman tall enough to bang his head against every door in town. The footman carried a cudgel in one beefy hand; Heron himself, slight and lean, walked with his hand on his sword.

Across town we went. The night had become unexpectedly chill – not a cloud in the sky and the stars sparking like diamonds. We didn't see a single person though laughter echoed from behind tavern windows. An owl swooped along Pilgrim Street, a silent white shadow in the darkness.

In Westgate Road there was no lantern left burning. The hulk of the West Gate itself blocked out the end of the road as we crossed to the tall row of narrow-faced houses just below it. Bedwalters's writing school was shut up and in darkness. Heron thumped on the door. When there was no reply, he signalled to the footman, who used his fist. After a moment, a light flickered in an upstairs room. A window was pushed up. A woman's voice, shrewish and sharp, snapped indistinguishable words; a man's head ducked under the window sash.

I had never seen Bedwalters without his wig before; I stared at the bald head for a moment without recognising him. Then his gaze rested on me; he said, "I will be down," and ducked back inside. In the moment before the sash was pulled down, I heard him say, "Official business, dear."

When he pulled the door open for us, he was in nightgown and robe, but he had stopped to put on his wig and looked reassuringly more familiar. Heron pushed in without a word, cut me off when I started to explain our visit and said brusquely: "I am told you have been seeking to apprehend Mr Patterson in connection with the murder of Julia Mazzanti."

"Indeed," Bedwalters said with composure. He shut the door, picked up a candle from a small table, and led the way into the schoolroom. We stood in the middle of low tables and chairs, the feeble light of the candle glinting on pictures and bookshelves. Bedwalters cast me a measuring glance. I felt horribly self-conscious. What must this look like to him? He must think I had brought Heron and the dominating footman to intimidate him.

"Do you intend to charge Mr Patterson with this crime?" Heron demanded.

Bedwalters blinked at the repetition of Mr. It was a warning and both of us knew it. It meant Heron was treating me as his equal in this, that he chose to take me under his protection. Bedwalters took his time to respond. "Mr Mazzanti has informed me of certain matters – "

"Such as?"

"I understand that Mr Patterson had – if I may put it discreetly – "

"Come to the point, man!"

"That he had formed a liking for Miss Mazzanti," Bedwalters finished calmly.

I started to protest but Heron silenced me with a brusque gesture.

"And that she did not return his regard."

"Good God, man. Are you suggesting Patterson killed the girl because his pride was offended!"

"Mr Mazzanti says – "

"The man's a fool."

Bedwalters tried again. "He says his daughter had expressed concern."

"She had more after her than Patterson," Heron snapped. "Half the company wanted her."

I cursed silently. I did not want to point Bedwalters in Ned Reynolds's direction.

"And if she was concerned, she shouldn't have led them on!"

"I understand that Miss – "

"Devil take it, are you going to believe a silly girl above a man you've known for years?"

And so it went on. Bedwalters began his sentences patiently; Heron snapped back with all the brusqueness and hauteur of a duke. Bedwalters's suggestions were dismissed, Mazzanti's information condemned, and Julia Mazzanti's fears ridiculed. Everything Bedwalters tried to argue was quashed with a ruthlessness that made me feel sick. In the end, the bullying had its desired effect; Bedwalters ground to a halt, staring at Heron with flushed cheeks and a dull look in his eyes. I have never been so sorry to be involved with a matter.

"There is no evidence against Mr Patterson," Heron said.

"No sir," Bedwalters said dully.

"And this Italian fellow, Corelli, is a far more likely suspect."

"Yes," Bedwalters said.

"Moreover, it is likely that the girl merely got caught up with whoever is mounting these attacks against her father. That it is all one matter."

Bedwalters hesitated. "Possibly."

"Well?" Heron demanded.

"Yes," Bedwalters said.

"Very well," Heron said. "Then we may all go our beds. Good night."

Bedwalters's fists were clenched at his side. The candlelight flickered on his haggard face. "There is one matter left to clear up, sir."

Heron was halfway to the door; he swung back. "Which is?"

"Mr Mazzanti reports that one of his daughter's possessions has been stolen."

"Stolen? What?"

"A ribbon, sir."

I felt abruptly hot. A ribbon. Which I had pushed into my pocket at the last moment for fear Bedwalters would search my rooms. Damn, damn, damn.

"It was taken from Miss Mazzanti's hair by the murderer, sir. If Mr Patterson would not object – "

"You want to search me," I said.

"Damn it," Heron said furiously. "I thought we had dealt with this! But you are still accusing Patterson – "

"On the contrary," Bedwalters said. "I am attempting to exonerate him."

A moment's silence. I found I was holding my breath and let it out gradually. If Bedwalters searched me, he would find the ribbon. Five minutes earlier, I had been willing Heron to silence, now I wanted him to demolish Bedwalters again with that bullying, imperious manner.

"Oh, very well," Heron said irritably. "Let's be done with it!"

# 31

**New ideas should always be regarded with suspicion
until they are proven beyond doubt.**
[*Instructions to a Son newly come of Age*, Revd. Peter Morgan
(London: published for the Author, 1691)]

Apologetically, Bedwalters asked for my coat and waistcoat. I stripped them off and handed them to him one by one.

He went through each pocket in turn pulling out my meagre possessions and placing them in little piles on one of the low tables. The candlelight flickered over my grubby and bloodstained handkerchief, on three guinea coins and a handful of pennies and farthings, on my resin box which I had stuffed into my pocket the other day at the theatre and forgotten about. There was a loose button whose provenance I could not recall, and a scrap of note, which Bedwalters looked at closely. Fortunately it was the notepaper on which I had scribbled figures for Thomas Saint's bill before writing the account out neatly.

My heart stammered when he pulled out the thin bundle of letters from Philip Ord to Julia Mazzanti. The thin pink ribbon around them and the tiny silk rose tucked beneath the ribbon made it painfully obvious what they were.

"Damn it, Patterson," Heron said, without missing a beat. "Why the devil did you not tell me you had retrieved the letters?"

I had told him, so I kept quiet. Heron held out his hand imperiously. "Those are mine, Bedwalters. If you please."

Bedwalters looked from one to the other of us. It must surely have been in the back of his mind that love letters were not in

Heron's style. I said nothing. I was half-inclined to tell Bedwalters the truth; it would be awkward explaining to Ord but if he had been planning to elope with Julia, it would not hurt him to have to face the consequences. But to tell Bedwalters the truth would have been to brand Heron a liar which was plainly impossible.

"Patterson was retrieving them for me," Heron said. "From the lady in question. You understand – once an affair is over, it is only proper that letters and such like should be returned. Patterson was acting as my intermediary."

I prayed that Bedwalters would not ask the identity of the lady. An affair! Was there a spirit in Bedwalters's house? If so, the story would be halfway round town by dawn and half a dozen ladies would have their reputations in shreds.

"The lady's name… "

"I cannot divulge it," Heron said inexorably.

Bedwalters looked at me a moment longer.

"You're looking for the ribbon, man!" Heron snapped.

"Do you give me your word, sir," Bedwalters said to me, "that you did not write these letters to Miss Mazzanti?"

"Neither to her nor to any woman," I said, relieved to be able to tell the truth. "You know my hand, Bedwalters – look at the superscription."

He turned the bundle over and looked at which could be seen there, shifting the pink ribbon slightly. I had glanced at the topmost letter and knew that Ord had merely scrawled *Darling* in a dashing script as the direction.

Bedwalters looked a moment longer then silently handed the bundle to Heron. He was staring at me as he did so, in a manner that plainly said he knew something untoward was going on. Damn Heron for this; damn myself for bringing him into the matter. And yet – Heron was displaying a great deal of trust in me despite what might be considered to be incriminating evidence.

Heron slipped the letters into his coat pocket and proceeded to rub in his triumph. "I rely on your discretion, Bedwalters."

"Of course."

"If the story gets about, the lady might suffer."

I intervened. Bedwalters had suffered too, more than enough. And it was time to bring this farce to an end.

"There is another pocket you have missed in the coat," I said, and pointed it out. It was the pocket into which I had stuffed the ribbon. All I could do was to let Bedwalters find it, tell him the whole story of Esther's burglar and hope he believed me.

The ribbon was not there.

Hugh leapt out of the darkness of my room and practically bowled me over. "What happened!? Why are you back? Mrs Foxton says she's been told you've seen Bedwalters."

I hoped Mrs Foxton was keeping herself to herself and not eavesdropping. She usually respects her lodgers' privacy. Except for the miners.

I disentangled myself and locked the bedroom door. Sufficient moonlight came in through the window for me to see the room clearly, albeit drained of colour. I slumped on the bed.

"He didn't find it."

"Find what?"

"The ribbon."

"What ribbon? The one taken from the girl's body?" Hugh crawled on to the bed and sat with his back to the wall. "The one you found in Mrs Jerdoun's garden?"

I longed for some more of Heron's brandy. The non-appearance of the ribbon had been a shock and I was still worried about what had happened to it. Most likely it had dropped out of my pocket as I clambered over one of the half dozen walls I had scaled that night. Which meant that it probably lay in the back alley behind Mrs Foxton's house, or – heaven forbid – in Heron's garden. But all

I could do was bid Bedwalters a civilised farewell and walk off across town with Heron again. Heron had handed me back the letters without comment and had insisted on seeing me to my door with his footman before returning to his own house. And now here I was, telling Hugh as much as I could remember of the night's events.

And worrying about Esther. While I had been distracted by all this, was the murderer trying to gain access to her house again?

I heard the church clock strike four.

"You're swimming in dangerous waters, Charles," Hugh said at last with distinct amusement. "With Mrs Jerdoun particularly."

"I am not," I said sharply. "I am carefully avoiding doing anything of the sort."

He chortled.

"Damn it, if that's all you can contribute to the situation, go home! I need some sleep."

In truth, the whole affair was catching up on me, even though I had somehow missed half the day. I eased myself out and felt drowsiness creeping over me.

Hugh stuck out a foot and prodded me in the leg. "Hey, wake up! You don't get away so easily. I want to know where you were all day. It wasn't anything to do with the Julia Mazzanti thing, was it?"

Reluctantly, I dragged myself back into a sitting position. Outside, an owl hooted; otherwise the town was silent.

After a moment, I said, "You'll not believe me."

"Not with Mrs Jerdoun!"

"No!" I said irritably.

There was nothing for it. I told him about the other world, about how I had originally found it (or rather, how it had found me), how I could step through to it. How it bore so many resemblances to our world, yet was in some ways so different. How I existed there too, but spirits did not. How Julia Mazzanti existed there, still alive, so like her counterpart and so different. How I could only seem to visit that world in times of crisis, how I had at first feared it but now began to be fascinated by it. How I was coming to believe that what I learnt there might help me solve the mystery of Julia's death in this world.

He did not believe me.

# 32

**And I order especially that my son take good care of all his sisters, and ensure that no fortune hunter comes near them.**
[Will of Frederick Carlisle, 25 December 1712]

Hugh and I argued about the matter at great length. He had a huge store of reasons why I was wrong, why I was mistaken, why I was just plain confused and imagining things.

"I am not imagining it," I said irritably. "Ask Heron."

That was at about six in the morning and it silenced Hugh at last.

"Heron was there?"

I explained.

"Damn it, Heron's a sensible man."

"Hugh!" I said, outraged. "We've known each other since childhood and you'd rather believe Heron than me!"

"Yes," he said unequivocally. "For one very good reason. The fellow doesn't have an ounce of imagination in him. He couldn't possibly make up a story like that."

Heron hadn't lacked imagination in his story about the letters, I reflected wryly.

"Damn it," I said. "I need sleep." And I turned over and ignored his mutterings.

I dozed restlessly until around seven then got up and splashed water on my face. I could contain my anxiety about Esther no longer. Hugh was still sleeping; I left him to snore and went off to Caroline Square.

Once, not so long ago, I would have approached Esther's house in Caroline Square with trepidation; for some time it had been the only place where I could step through to the other world, and I had had no control over the act. But now I knew that I could to some extent choose whether I came or went, so I marched up to Esther's front door with no fears at all, and rapped at the knocker.

The servant, Tom, came almost immediately, impeccably dressed in his livery and beaming at me. He was plainly a man who had had a good night's sleep.

"We did it, sir!" he said enthusiastically, as he let me in. "Run him off, we did. Not a sign of him last night."

Esther's maid Catherine came running down the stairs as cheerful and bright as Tom. "Come on up, Mr Patterson. Mrs Jerdoun said I was to show you in as soon as you came."

So I went up the stairs after her and before I knew it I was walking through a door into what was plainly a private dressing room, and looking at Esther lounging in a chair with a dish of hot chocolate in her hands. She was still in her night robe with a gown drawn over the top of it; her feet were bare and her fair hair was loose over her shoulders and down her back. I stopped dead, my heart leaping into my mouth; she looked beautiful beyond expression.

And she looked up at me with an amused, sly look that told me this encounter was not accidental. She had intended me to find her this way.

I kept my back to the door, trying to control my breathing. I cleared my throat.

"Tom says your intruder has abandoned you."

"Alas, yes," Esther said with mock distress. "He took pity on us and let us sleep undisturbed." Her amused look lingered a moment longer, then she frowned and put down the dish with a snap on the table by her side. "You're hurt," she said.

She got up. I couldn't move quickly enough to stop her taking hold of my arm, and reaching up to where I had been bleeding earlier. She pushed back the hair at my temple. Her fingers were warm and smelt faintly of roses; her hair drifted across my cheek. I drew back.

There was a calculated look in her eye as if she could divine exactly what I was thinking and feeling. A smile drifted across her face; she remained where she was, close enough for me to embrace her. When I did not, she sighed, said coolly, "Very well, tell me what happened."

She settled herself back in her chair and indicated the chair opposite her.

I should have refused. I did not. I was in no danger of forgetting the difference between Esther's position and mine, in age, wealth and social standing, but I was weak enough to indulge myself a little. To use Hugh's metaphor, I knew the difference between shallow water and deep dangerous currents. I eased myself down, started talking to distract myself from her closeness. But hardly had I started than Catherine came in with a dish of chocolate for me.

"Cook says would you like some breakfast?"

Esther nodded. "And bring something for Mr Patterson."

Long before the breakfast arrived, Esther had flown into a temper. It straightened her spine, stilled her fingers and hardened her jaw. She stared directly at me with cold rage.

"You went to Heron for help?"

"I couldn't think of anyone – "

"It did not occur to you that I could have helped?"

"It occurred to me, yes – "

"Then why did you not come?!"

"It would have ruined your reputation," I said.

Esther put down her dish, pushed herself from her chair, prowled about the small room, straightened the curtains which were still drawn, pinched out a guttering candle. "This is abominable. Not to be endured!"

I wasn't entirely sure to what she referred. "I didn't want to – "

"Something must be done." She gripped the back of her chair, gave me a long hard look. "This wretched situation cannot go on."

Now I did know what she was thinking of. I didn't want to discuss the matter. I found myself suddenly in sympathy with Ned, and with Ciara Mazzanti; some things are better ignored.

"It is abominable that two grown people cannot do what they wish without society prying and complaining. We are not children!"

"Rules are there for a good reason," I said, as levelly as I could.

"To facilitate the working of society, not to hamper it!"

"If Julia Mazzanti had not defied her father," I said, "she might be alive now. Instead, she tried to elope, and that exposed her to fatal danger."

"Julia was a foolish child," Esther said. She took a deep breath to calm herself, leant on the back of her chair. "I am thirty-nine years old, Charles, and I have lived on my own good sense since my father died when I was twenty-three. I think that by now I know the ways of the world!"

"That does not prevent the dangers," I pointed out.

"But it does mean I know how to deal with them," she retorted. "Oh, really, Charles, how could anyone who knew us both think you a fortune hunter and me a fool who would fall for a villain's blandishments?!"

"Ord, Jenison, half the ladies in town," I murmured. "No, all of them."

She resisted for a moment then laughed shakily. "Charles, Charles!" She looked at me a moment longer. "I cannot persuade you to thumb your nose at society?"

I thought her right, in all respects. Why should society condemn us for not fitting into its conventional categories? It is hardly fair, yet it is not possible to ignore the fact that it does. So we are forced into a situation where we do as society requires, or accept the consequences if we do not. No wonder there are so many secrets in the world.

"No," I said. "Your reputation depends on society's good will."

She came round the chair to sit down again. "And your living too. I must not forget it. Charles…" She hesitated, then went on, with some determination. "I have a confession to make. I was the one who bought you the ticket for the organ – the ticket that won you the prize."

I breathed deeply. This had been another matter I had been avoiding assiduously. I had always known that it must be Esther or Heron who had bought the ticket; if it had been Heron that would have been at least tolerable, if oddly secretive and round-about for so direct a man, but for it to come from Esther! What would society at large say if it was known? It would inevitably think the worst.

She was looking uneasy at my silence. "I thought that if you had a little more money, it might make your feel a little more my equal."

I laughed, bitterly. "A hundred guineas makes me feel a great deal better, but it hardly compares with your thousands."

"No," she agreed, and added impishly, "but at least you would not come penniless to a marriage."

At that moment, Catherine scratched on the door.

♦

By the time the table and chairs had been rearranged, the curtains drawn back to let in the sunshine, the candles pinched out, and a breakfast of breathtaking variety set out, the moment to respond to Esther had gone. I was reprieved for the moment, but I knew it was only a temporary respite. Esther would raise the topic again. Marriage! How could I drag her into the furore that would cause?

I was ravenously hungry, could not remember the last time I had eaten. As I worked my way through eggs, ham, devilled kidneys, meat pie and local black-skinned cheeses, I finished the tale of my encounter with Bedwalters. Esther, I noted, was not one of those women who pick listlessly at food; she ate steadily, and with every sign of enjoyment.

At the end of my recital, she sipped at the remains of her chocolate contemplatively, stared at the sunshine striping the wall, then said, "What else aren't you telling me?"

I had contrived to omit the ribbon from the tale but as the need to do so had only occurred to me at the last moment, I supposed she had divined that the tale did not quite hang together.

She continued to muse. "The only reason you might leave out something," she pursued, "is that the matter concerns me." She set her head on one side, gave me a reproachful glance. "Charles, if you think anything would frighten me, I despair of ever teaching you my character!"

I gave in. It was a relief to do so. I dislike having secrets from my friends and in truth I am a bad liar. I told her about the ribbon and where I had found it. Esther raised an eyebrow.

"My intruder is the murderer?"

"I have come to that conclusion," I said reluctantly.

"But it doesn't make sense!" She frowned. "You think he has some grudge against me personally? But I have nothing at all in common with Julia Mazzanti."

"He must think you have."

She shook her head. "Preposterous. There is nothing, can be nothing. I never spoke to the girl or her parents. I have had nothing to do with them – in fact I cannot even recall talking about them except to you. I was not even at the rehearsal for the Signora's concert."

She sat up straight suddenly.

"Charles," she said in an odd voice. "I am wrong. We do have one thing in common, Julia and I." Her mouth twisted wryly. "You."

# 33

**Nothing ever reforms a thief, sir. There is nothing to do but step down hard on them and keep them underfoot. That is what transportation is for!**
[Letter from JUSTICIA to Mayor of Newcastle upon Tyne, printed in the *Newcastle Courant*, 15 May 1736.]

I stared at her in horror. Did the murderer know about my relationship with Esther? Had he believed me to be courting Julia? If Mazzanti had told Bedwalters that story, he might have told others too. No, no, if all that was true, it would be a reason to attack *me*, not Julia or Esther. Then why was the murderer trying to get into this house?

"The house," I said, weak with relief. "It's the house. He's not after you – he simply wants to get into this house!"

Dear God, was the murderer someone else who could step through?

"Charles!" Esther reached across the table and shook my arm. Her warm fingers sent a tingle down my spine. "How is the house significant?"

I had to tell her about the linked worlds. Unlike Hugh, she did not keep interrupting me with expressions of incredulity nor she did she snort or make deriding noises. But at the end of the tale, I saw her take a deep breath as if steeling herself to do something unpleasant.

"Charles – I – "

"I know, I know. It sounds preposterous. But Claudius Heron will corroborate everything I say."

I noted wryly that Esther, like Hugh, was more influenced by that than by everything I had said before. She frowned. "You swear this is the truth?"

"I swear."

"You do not think you could be mistaken?"

"No."

"Dear God," she said. "It is bad enough knowing that every day you walk out of my life, and I only know if you are well or ill, alive or dead, by the gossip or chance remarks of other people, or when you visit under cover of some acceptable excuse. But to know that when I don't see you, you might be in some other world, entirely, completely out of *everyone's* reach! Charles." She leant across the table and seized my arm again. "You must promise me you will never go into this other place again."

I drew back, startled. "That's not possible – "

"Then at least not alone."

"I can't do that either," I protested. "I can never predict when the world will open up. Oh, I am beginning to be able to say whether I go or stay, but – " I searched for words. "It's like a door. If the door is unlocked, I can choose whether I go through or not, but if it is locked, I cannot do anything. And sometimes it opens unexpectedly and I have no choice whether to go or stay."

She thrust back her chair and started walking about the room. I pushed my empty plate away and watched her. She seemed to be debating something within herself; once or twice she seemed about to say something then changed her mind.

At last she turned. "Charles," she said. "It is no good. I cannot live with this anxiety as well. If there is to be any to-ing and fro-ing between this world and the other, then it must be at least in some part under my control. I will not go through my days in fear at what might be happening to you. I want you here, Charles. I know daily business will take us in separate directions, but nonetheless I will be able to keep a closer watch on you for at least some of the time."

We stared at each other. I did not know what to say. For a woman to proposition a man – and with no word of love, or romantic flights of language, or the suggestion of undying devotion –

There was a little kernel of scandalised outrage in my heart. Not because of Esther's outrageous proposal. Because of my own temptation –

I got up, hurriedly. "I can't – I mean – I must think – "

A gleam of amusement showed in her eyes. "I won't give you long, Charles."

"Or what?" I retorted. "You will withdraw the offer?"

She strolled across to me, lifted a hand to touch the graze under my hairline. "No," she whispered. "Never that. I might just – "

I could hardly breathe. "Yes?"

"I might just take matters into my own hands," she whispered and leant closer.

Catherine scratched on the door.

In Caroline Square the heat was already burning off the houses, pressing close around me. As I crossed towards Westgate Road, the drunken spirit in the central gardens of the square called out to me; I pretended not to hear him and walked out on to Westgate Road, stood for the moment, calming myself.

Dangerous waters, Hugh had said. He'd been right. All too right. The currents were dragging me under and the devil of it was that I wanted them to. I knew I should keep clear of Esther, and I knew I couldn't do it. Moreover, she was a determined woman and would certainly take matters into her own hands if I did not fall in with her wishes. What in heaven's name was I to do?

I turned down Westgate towards St John's Church. I knew exactly what I was going to do. I was going to tell myself that it was silly to agonise over the matter at the moment, that I had far more important things to deal with. That I should concentrate on finding Julia Mazzanti's murderer and Esther's burglar, and then think about other matters, when I had time to do them justice.

If that is not cowardice, I don't know what is. But it was the only decision I was capable of taking at that moment.

I was looking for a tavern, a reasonably respectable one where I was not well known and where gentlemen did not generally go, so I could sit down and read Ord's letters without being disturbed. The idea of reading another man's love letters was distasteful – no man can ever appear sensible in love letters – but it had to be done. I was no nearer deciding who had killed Julia but I was certain that Ord knew more than he was saying. And he could fit the description of the man the spirit had seen watching Mrs Baker's house; he might at a pinch, too, fit the man I had chased from Esther's garden.

There was a tavern in a back street just this side of the West Gate itself; I crossed the road towards it and almost walked into Bedwalters who came quietly out of his house to stand directly in front of me.

"If I may have a word, Mr Patterson?"

I took a deep breath. "About last night? I owe you an apology – "

"I am grateful," he said with a flush in his cheek, "but I believe that matter is closed. I wished to inform you that you will have no more problems with the ruffians who have been following you."

I stared at him blankly. "No more trouble?"

"I have spoken with Jem Harris and represented to him that it was most unwise for him to pursue the matter."

I wished, not for the first time, that Bedwalters would speak plainly.

"Jem – ?"

"Their leader now recognises that sometimes it is wiser to let matters drop."

His steadfast gaze met mine. I saw how it must be. Bedwalters must know something to this Harris's discredit, something that might land him in jail waiting for the Assizes, for transportation or possibly even the hangman's noose. And he had chosen to remind Harris of it, to protect me. More than ever, I regretted that scene in the small hours. It had been my fault that Bedwalters had suffered that humiliation and yet he had gone out, perhaps straightaway, and taken it upon himself to help me.

"I am very grateful," I said humbly. The words seemed hugely inadequate. I was overwhelmed by his generosity. I added, "I did not kill Julia Mazzanti."

"I never imagined you did," he said and turned back into the house.

I found a tavern in a side street, took a pint of beer and wearily sat down in a corner to read Ord's letters. The matter of Bedwalters weighed heavily on me; half-distracted, I pulled the bundle from my pocket, slipped off the ribbon. It was expensive stuff; I pushed it into my pocket out of the way. The tavern was not busy; a carter was enjoying a joke with a couple of spirits across the room and two women at the door were quietly discussing the price of meat.

I took a deep draught of beer. It had been as I told Heron – Bedwalters was a conscientious man, who felt duty bound to follow up every piece of information he was given. And my absence from the town had been unquestionably suspicious. John Mazzanti's lies that I was pursuing Julia had to be investigated too, though why he should want to involve me, I could not fathom. And at the possible cost of letting the real murderer get away with it too!

A man pushed his way into the tavern, glanced about then came straight for me. It took me a moment to recognise him; tall, thin, harsh of face, a little out of breath, neatly dressed. Fowler, Heron's manservant.

He pulled out a stool opposite me and sat astride it without asking permission. "I saw you talking to the writing master but couldn't catch you up before now. I thought for a moment I'd lost you."

Out of Heron's hearing, he had lost the deferential manner and was a trifle over-familiar – nothing objectionable, just a little encroaching. He glanced round.

"I thought you'd want this."

He dug his hand in his pocket, pulled something out and pushed it under. Glancing down, I saw something bright crushed in his fist – and an end of yellow ribbon.

# 34

**Always have a good tale in mind to entertain the company
— but make sure it is a respectable story.
Nothing disgraces a man more than an indecent tale.**
[*Instructions to a Son newly come of Age*, Revd. Peter Morgan
(London: published for the Author, 1691)]

"Picked your pocket," Fowler said. "As you left Mr Heron's rooms." He grinned. "Used to do it for a living. Go on, take it."

I took it, slid it into my pocket. Fowler straightened, called for beer, and sat, smiling maliciously, until the girl had poured it. He drank deeply.

"Damn this weather. I can't take it. Heron was all for Italy last year but decided against it, thank God. I'd have been fit for nothing." He looked at me. "I'll not leave him," he said, as if I'd questioned his loyalty. "It's thanks to him I'm not six feet under. If he says Italy, Italy it is. But I don't have to like it."

"What happened?" I asked. He began to intrigue me.

He gave me a quick look and drank his beer. "That's between him and me. But I'll tell you this. I wasn't living a good life." He nodded at the ribbon, presumably implying he had been a thief. "Another man might just have left me to it. He didn't."

"In London?"

He grinned. "You can tell by my voice, I warrant!" He drank more. "You should be more careful, Mr Patterson. Left a good inch of that ribbon hanging out of your pocket."

"I was in a rush," I said ruefully. "How did you know what it was?"

"That missing ribbon's the talk of the town," he said. "And I saw it in the girl's hair myself."

"Then why didn't you report me as the murderer?"

He shook his head. "I've heard of you, Mr Patterson. You sorted out that matter of William Bairstowe's a couple of months ago and there was more funny business before Christmas too, wasn't there? Heron came home from that pretty shaken – I've never seen him that overset by anything before or since." He glanced around but the women had gone and the serving girl had joined the carter and the boisterous spirits; all the same, he spoke more quietly. "And I'm a friend of Ned Reynolds, if you take my meaning."

His gaze met mine and I saw in his expression a wealth of experience I could only guess at. I wondered again how he had met Heron and what had made Heron think he was worth saving.

"You've known Ned long?"

"London," he said. "When the company was playing in the Haymarket theatre. Before Richard came on the scene." He snorted. "Ned's a fool over that boy."

I sighed, checked that the ribbon was well-hidden in my pocket. "Ned's a fool, pure and simple," I said.

Fowler nodded. "But the best meaning of fellows. Always has excellent good intentions, heart good and sound – and no judgement at all."

"When did you see the girl wearing the ribbons?" I asked.

He drained his beer and called for more. "That night."

"The night she died?"

He nodded. "We were drinking. Me, Ned and the boy. Leastways, Ned was drinking." The girl refilled his tankard and he dropped coins into her palm; she went back to the carter. "The boy doesn't care for beer much and I know better than to overindulge – that's how I got myself into the trouble Heron rescued me from. Well, Ned got more and more drunk. And more and more angry."

"With Julia?"

Another quick glance around. "She knew."

"So he told me."

"She said that if he married her, she'd keep quiet about it. Well, what could he do? She even said he could keep seeing Richard. Wouldn't you have agreed?"

"What choice would I have had?" I contemplated sly demure little Julia. Or was it desperate, frightened little Julia? Desperate to find a husband so she could have her baby respectably. So desperate that she had courted two possible husbands at once – Ned and Ord. But was one of them the father of the baby? Not Ned certainly, but Ord? And if it was not Ord, why had she not turned to the real father? Because he was already married? "I would not have trusted her though," I added. "What was to stop her giving the secret away at a later date, if she wanted to be rid of Ned? What did you say to him?"

He laughed. "Told 'em to run off to the Colonies. Change their names, call themselves brothers and no one would be the wiser!"

"France would be better," I said. "I'm told they are much more relaxed about these things on the continent. Ned didn't think much of the idea?"

The tavern was hot and stuffy, the straw on the floor stinking in the heat. Fowler drank deeply, almost recklessly. I began to wonder if he generally drank little because once started he found it difficult to stop.

"He hates deception," Fowler said. "Me – it's a way of life."

"Keeping it secret from Heron?"

He smiled, said nothing, drank. "Ned wanted to – to *get rid* of the girl."

I sat up. "Kill her, you mean?"

Another glance round. The spirits were still recounting a long and hilarious tale; reassured, Fowler said, "It was all wild talk!

Richard and I kept trying to calm him down but he just got more and more foolish with the drink. In the end, he wanted to go to her lodgings, do away with her there and then. So off we staggered along the street, Ned swearing vengeance and Richard and me hanging on to his coat tails, and trying to bring him to reason."

"How far did you get?"

"The street where she lodged. And there she was walking up and down in her best. Including those ribbons." He picked up the tankard to drink again, looked twice and pushed it away. "Yellow ribbons with yellow hair. No taste at all. Her dress was all lace and flounces and bows too."

"No one with her?"

He shook his head. "She was all impatient. Waiting for someone, I reckon."

"What time was this?"

"About midnight."

"Did you see anyone else?"

His lip curled. "Philip Ord." He lifted the tankard in an ironic toast. "Want to know what Heron thinks of him?"

"I can guess," I said dryly. "Anyone else?"

"That psalm teacher fellow. All meek and mild and frightened. Jumping every time the spirit talked to him."

"He was keeping vigil. To make sure she was safe."

Fowler burst out laughing, making the serving girl glance round. "Didn't do it very well then, did he? And we saw her father too."

"You saw Mazzanti?" I said, startled.

"Staring out of the window."

"But he didn't come out?"

"Not that I saw."

"And was there a confrontation between Ned and Julia?"

"Never a bit." Fowler grinned. "I sorted him out."

With a sense of foreboding, I said, "What did you do?"

"Hit him over the head! Richard and I had a devil of a struggle getting him back to his lodgings, I can tell you, but no one thought it odd. Just thought he'd passed out. And in the morning, he didn't remember a damn thing!"

I thought of how scared Ned had been at that. How he had been frightened that he had killed Julia in a drunken stupor. "You could at least have reassured him."

"Nothing I could do. I had to get back and I was late as it was – I'm supposed to be back by midnight. I only get one evening off a week. Heron's generous with his servants but I won't take advantage of him. I told Richard to straighten him out. I suppose Ned ran off before the boy could tell him."

"And Julia?" I asked.

"Still there when we carried Ned off. Walking up and down, up and down. Waiting for some fellow who didn't turn up." He frowned. "But he did, didn't he? He turned up eventually and he murderered her."

"Yes."

"Do you know who it was?"

"No."

He laughed. "You will – if half of what Heron says about you is true."

I winced. "He talks about me?" I nearly added, *to the servants*, but thought better of it.

Fowler chuckled. "I told you. Ned's the one who likes everything out in the open, not me." He pushed the tankard out of his way, leant across the table. "Mr Patterson, I'm not a fellow who cares much about his fellow man. I don't see why I should bother. I don't care who killed the girl – he probably had good reason. But Ned I do care about." His mouth twisted wryly. "You have to look after your own, don't you?"

I said nothing.

"That's what I'm doing," he said. "Looking after them that aren't capable of looking after themselves. Very Christian of me, eh? I want that murderer. I want him out in the open and I want it clear that Ned wasn't the one who killed the girl. I want him free of suspicion so that no one looks closely at what he does and says. Get my meaning?"

"Perfectly."

"And you're the one to do it, so Heron says. That's why I pinched that ribbon from your pocket when I knew you were going off to the constable. Not just to keep you out of trouble, Mr Patterson." His face twisted with grim amusement. "I wanted to gain a little credit with you." He leant closer. "I want some thanks for helping you out, Mr Patterson."

I looked into his harsh face, the face of a man with few scruples and too much ill experience.

"I'll prove Ned didn't kill Julia Mazzanti," I said, evenly. "And I'll find the real killer. That's been my intention all along. You don't have to coerce me into it."

Fowler hesitated then sat back. "I'm not used to men of honour, Mr Patterson. Except Heron." Another wry grimace. He levered himself up. "I'll be off. I'm supposed to be running errands. Collecting some books. You needn't let me know when you've done the job. I'll know."

"You could do me one favour," I said as he turned to go. He glanced back. "Keep Ned from doing anything foolish."

He laughed. "I'll tell him to trust you to come up with the goods."

I only wished I shared his belief.

# 35

> **Never marry out of your station, sir.**
> **Only trouble will come of it.**
> [*Instructions to a Son newly come of Age*, Revd. Peter Morgan
> (London: published for the Author, 1691)]

I read Ord's letters. The serving girl and the carter flirted in the far corner while I worked my way through page after page of Ord's flowingly expressed devotion. He had been taught to write well but under the pressure of his passion, the copperplate handwriting deteriorated until at the end of some letters it was wellnigh indecipherable. If he had ever written Julia chaste little notes of admiration, or polite requests for meetings, she had not kept them. These were the outpourings of a man who believed himself in violent love, full of praise for Julia's beauty, for her innocence and her sweetness. He had deceived himself about her abilities as an actress and a singer, and effusively praised every song she had sung, every line she had spoken. He had not held back. This was silliness of the highest order and the oddest thing of all was that I believed it all sincere. I thought back to that time Ord had accosted me in a panic because he thought Julia had been shot. He was genuinely in love with her.

And here was the silliest of all.

*Darling girl, I cannot tell you how happy you made me last night with your sweet modesty. A thousand times I wished your mother out of the room so I could hear you own dear lips sealing my fate. But alas, she lingered and I must wait long tedious hours before I know your answer. I beg you to slip away at the theatre tonight and make me the happiest of men.*

And lest any casual reader should imagine he was merely urging her to a night of debauchery, he added,

*If your answer is yes, I can have the licence within hours and you may bear my name within a day.*

Why the devil could he not just have said *we can be married at once?*

Ord had offered Julia marriage. Had she refused or merely held him at arm's length, promising to give him an answer later? She had plainly not destroyed all his hopes or else he would not have been solicitously escorting her to the theatre the day after the attempted burglary. But of course she had not been pregnant when she dangled Ord on her apron-strings in London, or if she had been, she had almost certainly not yet known it. She had been indecisive; perhaps she had been looking for someone richer. But as soon as she did know she was with child, Ord became immensely valuable to her. He was already in her pocket.

I unfolded the last letter and drank the dregs of my beer. The serving girl was attending to two sailors who had just come in; one of the spirits had embarked on a rambling story too obscene for female ears.

There was a gap of two months between the letters I had just read – written in London – and the last letter written in Newcastle the day after the Mazzantis arrived in the town. It was shorter than the rest but still as ardent. *Nothing has changed my mind and heart. Darling Julia, do not hesitate any longer. Give yourself to me.* And it urged her to name the day and time she would fly with him.

Now I could see why Julia had clung to Ned Reynolds so fervently, to the extent of blackmailing him. In this letter, Ord made no mention of marriage; perhaps that was what he still intended but he did not say so. Perhaps returning home to his friends and neighbours, and the thought of the dowry Lizzie

Saint would bring him, had brought him to his senses, in practical matters at least. Julia must have known Ned was not a good match but he would be better than nothing. And again I wondered about the child's real father. Was Ord the culprit?

I folded up the letters and slipped the ribbon back round them. The spirit was whispering the end of his tale. It came to me that Heron's manservant, Fowler, had said something I should have taken more notice of. Some casual comment that had more significance than he knew. And Julia Mazzanti too, the one who still lived – there was something from my encounters with her that still nagged at me.

No, I could not recall anything of significance. Except that Fowler had said Mazzanti had been looking from the window of his lodgings. Surely he must have seen Julia? Why then had he not gone out to fetch her back in?

I tossed down payment for my beer and left the tavern. Well, that was one thing I could easily check. And perhaps on the way I would remember Fowler's more significant comment.

I turned into the street where Mrs Baker's house stood and saw Matthew Proctor standing in the full glare of the sun, staring up at the shuttered windows. He did not look at me as I walked up to him.

"The funeral is tomorrow," he said. "At All Saints."

No doubt, I thought, there would be a note waiting for me at home requesting my presence as organist. The spirit across the way, on the house next to Mrs Baker's, called a cheery greeting. Proctor flinched at the loud noise.

"Why are you here?" I asked.

"Keeping vigil over her body," he said fervently.

I felt a twinge of impatience, reminded myself of the virtues of Christian tolerance. But why such a sly unformed girl should inspire such devotion in two men was beyond me!

"Her father won't let me in the house," Proctor said. "He is so close about her all the time."

"He feels guilty, no doubt," I said dryly. "It is hardly useful to protect her now she is dead. He should have taken better care of her before." Too late I recalled that my criticism applied equally to Proctor, and I feared that I had prompted another bout of self-blame. But he turned a bleak face to me and said, "She was afraid of him."

"Of her father? Why?"

"He took advantage of her every day of her life," he said melodramatically. "He shouted at her, shook her, threatened to hit her." He was hot in rage now. "He used her so he could have an easy life of his own. He exploited her talents when he had none of his own!"

I could well believe that last part. I could also imagine that Julia had been at times infuriating to deal with; Proctor had seen only the outward face, the best of her. Now if it had been the other Julia, in the other world – I could imagine a man getting indignant at bad treatment of her.

"Go home," I said, fanning myself against the heat.

"I can't."

"Rubbish!" the spirit said with good humour. "You mean you won't."

Proctor cried out, clutched at my arm.

"Many a time I'd give a fortune to be able to lie on a soft bed again," the spirit said. "Not that I have a fortune. Or anything now, for that matter."

"Nothing is going to bring Julia back to life," I said. "We have to go on."

Proctor was trembling, staring at the place where the spirit gleamed on a stone above a window. I said slyly, "We must go on. It's what Julia would have wanted."

Proctor stared at me, screwing up his eyes against the sun. I wanted to shake him, tried to curb my irritation and put myself in his position. How would I feel if Esther died?

"Yes, yes, of course," he said.

I gave him a gentle push. "Go back to your lodgings."

"I haven't – I don't – Yes." He stared up at the window. "Go back. If only I could."

"You must try," I said, firmly. "It's what Julia would have wanted."

"Makes you wonder, doesn't it?" the spirit said as we watched Proctor walk slowly off at last. "Sometimes I don't know how some folks get by in the world. Silly as a baby."

"He's shaken by the girl's death," I said, trying to be charitable. "He's not normally as bad as this." I wiped sweat from my temple and wished I had put on a thinner coat. I moved over to the small stripe of shade along one side of the street. Proctor must have been truly in love with the girl, I thought ruefully. Meek and unworldly he had always been, but not so foolish. Last I heard he had intended to be in Carlisle for the Race Week there but Julia must have drawn him back to Newcastle.

"Once the funeral is over, he'll be better," I said, more in hope than in expectation, and gave myself over to squinting at the windows of Mrs Baker's house. The downstairs window on the left, I decided, was the drawing room window and the other, on the right, was the dining room. At midnight, Mazzanti must surely have been in the drawing room, preparing to drink the night away.

"Where was the girl waiting?" I asked.

"Right in front of the door," the spirit said.

Mazzanti must have seen her, I thought, even if he had to squint a little. Then the obvious question occurred to me. "Which door?"

"This one." The spirit slid down to hover on the lintel above the door of its own house. The door was particularly deep set,

235

with two steps leading up to it.

I sighed and contemplated the sight. If Julia had slipped inside that doorway, or walked up and down before it, then perhaps Mazzanti might not have seen her. He had been looking out, certainly, but perhaps Ned, Fowler and Richard themselves had attracted his attention. If Ned had been drunk, he might well have been shouting, or at the very least talking loudly. Mazzanti, half-drunk himself, might have misinterpreted everything he heard: if he had heard Julia unfasten the front door, he might have thought it a noise in the street; if he had heard her footsteps, he might have thought it the drunks outside. If he had heard voices –

"Damn," I said.

Nothing led anywhere.

I went off to find Ord.

Ord's house was new. Everything about it was new, up-to-date, in fashion, of the latest design, the latest manufacture. Its plaster ceiling, its gilded mirrors, its chairs, its pictures – all new. The echoing rooms even smelt new. As I waited in the library, I looked on rows of untouched books, obviously bought by the yard, identical spines, identical covers, all smelling of fresh leather. And a brand-new harpsichord in one corner, open to display the gorgeous new paintings of nymphs and shepherds inside. Waiting for the nimble fingers of Lizzie Saint, no doubt.

The instrument was horribly out of tune.

I turned on my heels. The house must have cost a fortune. The Ords were a wealthy family, but building on this scale must surely have been beyond Philip Ord's means. Coal mines he had in plenty, particularly since his father died a couple of years back – but coal owners were all hard put to for ready cash. No wonder he needed Lizzie's money.

I was staring out at the sundrenched gardens, the only part of the place to be less than perfect, for no money will persuade new plants to grow faster, when Ord came in briskly. He had only kept me waiting half an hour or so, enough to put me in my place but not enough to seriously annoy me. Looking at his agitated manner, which he was attempting to hide, I was surprised that he had managed to contain himself so long.

"The letters," he said without preamble. "Where are they?"

"I have them."

He held out a hand. I did not move. I was waiting for a 'if you please'. But it is usually useless to wait for politeness from the gentry.

His lip curled. "I see you want money, in addition to everything else I promised."

I was about to tell him no but he went straight on without giving me time to speak. "You are standing on very insecure ground, sir. I have heard the rumours that you killed Julia."

"Then you will also have heard that I did not do so," I said. "I will give you the letters – "

He held out his hand again.

" – when you tell me what you were doing in the street outside her lodgings the night she died."

"What are you talking about? I wasn't anywhere near the place."

"You were seen."

"By liars and thieves eager for some reward, no doubt."

"*I* saw you," I said levelly. "Drinking in Mrs Hill's less than an hour before Julia died." I saw him flinch – yes, there had been real feeling for Julia there. Enough to make him throw caution and Thomas Saint's money to the winds, and contemplate marriage to a penniless actress? "Other reliable witnesses saw you barely a street from Julia's lodgings while she waited outside for her lover to bear her off to a Scottish anvil. And – " I waved the letters. "In the last of these, written less than a week ago, after her arrival in Newcastle, you begged her to name the date she would marry you."

I had to bear a rant of five minutes or so berating me for every sin in the Bible, and every crime on the statute book. I had violated his privacy, the confidences of an innocent girl, the sacred feelings of love and admiration. I was a villain of the worst kind, a debaucher of maidens, the sort of fellow who undermines all the most sacred tenets of religion and society.

"You knew I was looking for Julia's murderer," I said. "Did you seriously imagine I would not read the letters?" He reddened, opened his mouth for another outburst. "Was she waiting for you that night?"

He came to a halt in the middle of his expensive, new, unused house that sparkled in the radiant sunlight. Red-faced and almost gasping for breath, he stared at me, then closed his eyes. I waited. When he opened his eyes again, he was calmer, but his hands could not stop fidgeting, twisting round themselves, fingering the buttons on his coat, dipping in and out of pockets.

"I didn't know what to do," he said.

"What happened?" I spoke as calmly and flatly as I could, to keep him calm.

"She wanted to elope," he said helplessly. "To Scotland, to marry."

"And you agreed?"

The hands went into pockets, came out again. "Yes," he said, almost inaudibly. "I – I thought I loved her."

Those words almost made me despise him more than everything else. He was already beginning to deny to himself that he had truly loved her, was already resigning the episode in his mind to that of a foolish infatuation.

"I knew from the moment I first saw her in London that I wanted her," he admitted. "She was as a girl should be, modest, retiring, obedient to her parents. Not like an actress at all.

And her parents – damn it, Patterson, they're not commoners. Mazzanti has aristocratic connections – he's some relation to the Count of Ferrara."

I didn't even know if there was a Count in Ferrara and neither, I suspected, did Ord, but even if there was, I doubted that Mazzanti would be related to him. Ord was just trying to make his actions sound more reasoned than they had been.

"And when she showed such quiet interest in me, when she so delicately indicated that she might not be averse to my approaches – "

"You sent her letters," I finished. "Did you also meet?"

"Only in public. Never anything else, Patterson! The most innocent of meetings. I wanted to marry her, for God's sake!"

"Did you approach Mazzanti to ask for Julia's hand?"

"He turned me away," Ord said, bitterly. He was plainly not accustomed to rejection. "The day I left London he took me aside and said that he had other plans for his daughter." His voice hardened. "He said they didn't include a member of the provincial minor gentry!"

That jibe had probably hurt more than anything else.

"I thought I had no chance left. I came home. Got on with my life."

Wooed Lizzie Saint, I added mentally.

Ord was getting into his stride now, literally, walking backwards and forwards across the sunshine that striped the floorboards, as if all his pent-up energy was too much to bear.

"You had no further contact with her?"

He looked at the walls, the floor, the pictures – anywhere but at me. "She wrote me a letter at the end of last month."

"From London?"

"Telling me when they would arrive and asking to see me."

"Where is this letter?"

"I burnt it," he said bleakly.

"After Julia died?"

"It was an innocent letter, Patterson," he said angrily. "A sweet letter, like any young girl might write."

Young girls know better than to make assignations, I thought. I did not say so – he would probably refuse to talk to me any more.

"So you saw her."

"Only in public."

"But you managed to make an assignation with her," I pointed out. "For midnight on the night she died. You agreed to elope with her and get married."

"I could not deny her! She put her reputation and her precious self in my care!"

I'd had enough; I said brutally, "She was with child."

He stared at me with stricken face. He had not known.

"Were you the father?"

He shook his head numbly. "No, no, I could not have been. We never – I did not – " He turned away so I could not see his face, rubbed his hand across his temple. "She wanted to marry me for respectability's sake," he said heavily. "She wanted a father for her child. That's all, isn't it? There was no feeling, no love – "

I said nothing.

"I suppose the father is married," he said after a moment.

"No doubt."

Another silence.

"She was desperate to get out of that house," he said, his mouth twisting. "She hated her father and despised her mother."

Such an odd word to choose for a mother, I thought. "*Despised* Signora Mazzanti? Why?"

He shrugged.

"I want to get back to the point," I said as patiently as I could. "I need to know what happened the night Julia died. You had arranged to meet her so you could elope but you had to spend all evening in various taverns, drinking, to try and summon up your courage to go ahead with the affair. How near to her did you get?"

Ord swung round on me. He had recovered himself. His expression was sneering; his demeanour confident and swaggering.

"Two streets away. Then I met that damn singing fellow."

"Proctor? He was keeping a vigil, to protect her."

Ord snorted in derision.

"And then you decided not to meet Julia?"

"I came to my senses, thank God!"

"So you didn't see her?"

"No."

"Was anyone else around?"

"Two or three drunks in the street."

Something was nagging at me. "What time was this?"

"Midnight."

"Are you sure?"

"I heard St Nicholas's church clock chime."

Midnight. That was significant in some way. But why?

"So you went back to the nearest tavern and drank some more."

"I went home," he said.

"No, you did not."

His head shot up at that. I was, after all, accusing him of lying. "You saw us carrying Julia's body home, remember. You came with us to the lodging house. But you already knew she was dead." I thought I could guess what had happened. "After your first attempt to meet her, you went back to a tavern to drink, but you still couldn't make up your mind whether to go or stay. Eventually, you decided you would elope with her and started back. But on the way, you saw her body in Amen Corner."

He turned away from me, pushed his hands into his pockets

and stared out of the window at his new, bare gardens.

"You bent over her, then when you heard me shouting, you took fright and ran off. And that's why you were so distraught at the Mazzantis' lodgings that night. Not only was the girl you loved and coveted dead, but you were afraid you'd been recognised in Amen Corner. You were afraid I'd seen you. That's why you told Bedwalters you'd seen me wooing Julia – if I then accused you of being the man bending over the body, it would look like a lie to try and discredit you."

Without turning, he held out his hand. "The letters, Mr Patterson."

I hesitated but there was plainly nothing more to be got out of him. His silence told me I was right. I took the letters from my pocket and held them out. His fingers snapped closed on them.

"They are all here?" he demanded. "You have not abstracted one?"

"There were nine letters," I said. "And there still are nine letters."

And then I knew exactly what was teasing me. Nine, damn it, nine letters!

Ord stared at me. "What the devil's the matter?"

"Nine letters," I said and started laughing. "Nothing. Nothing the matter at all!"

I knew who the murderer was.

# 36

**Mr Walpole is convinced we should stay out of this war in Europe; he says it will only swallow up men and money, and bring us no profit. Mr Walpole is an excellent man; but he is wrong.**
[Whit Sunday Sermon preached by Revd Edwin Plumb, afternoon lecturer at St Nicholas's Church, Newcastle, 13 June 1736]

Tiredness was beginning to catch up with me at last; I was yawning as I called in at Charnley's bookshop for a parcel of books I had ordered from London. There was irony in picking up a book of Corelli's concertos, but I had also sent for a copy of the songs from *Camilla*. An old opera, but with some singable tunes in it; when I had sent for it, I had thought I would have the direction of the winter concerts and the songs would come in useful then.

Well, they came in useful anyway. I told Charnley not to wrap up the books and strode up to Esther's door in Caroline Square with the music boldly displayed: Mr Patterson, the music teacher, come to give Mrs Jerdoun her lesson, sadly neglected recently.

Tom showed me into what he grandly called the estates room. It was a small room at the back of the house, with space for little more than a table and chair, and an array of bookshelves filled with heavy tomes dating back twenty years. Leases, title deeds, correspondence – all the paraphernalia of Esther's wealth, which the purchase of that ticket for the organ only served to emphasise.

Esther was sat at the table, figuring some accounts; she threw down her pen as soon as I was shown in.

"I have been cursing you all day," she said. "I cannot concentrate on these accounts for worrying about you." Then she saw my expression. "You know who the murderer is!"

I tossed down the music books down on the table. "I do. And I know how we can catch him."

"A trap?" Esther said with a gleam in her eye.

"Tonight. If you care to help?"

"More than willingly," she said, "What do you want me to do?"

I left the music with Esther despite her protestations that she loathed *Camilla*. "Such a silly plot!"

"All opera is silly," I pointed out. "The characters always burst into song at the least provocation and at the worst moments. And in the Italian opera, they sing about opening doors and buying oranges and all the rest of it." I was adamant about leaving the books however. "It will lend credence to my visit."

In truth, I did not want to have to carry the books in the disreputable part of town into which I was about to venture. I wanted to go home to sleep before springing the trap for the murderer this evening but I had two things left to do. One was easily dealt with; I scribbled a note for Hugh, went back into Charnley's and gave his boy a penny to deliver it. He is a reliable lad and eager for money to support his eight siblings. He went off with a will, and I turned towards the Keyside.

I was looking for the sailors' tavern where Corelli and I had ended our entertainment on the night of Julia's death, just before we parted and I reeled off to encounter the ruffians and find Julia's body. How long ago that seemed now! The tavern was spit and sawdust, not very respectable, and I recalled that Corelli had rather liked it. The place was crowded and stuffy, and I had to hunt through the sailors before I saw him, easing himself into a chair in a corner. He looked much the same as before but more sombre, more subdued. Two tankards of beer stood on the table in front of him.

"I saw you coming," he said, looking wearily up at me. "I reckoned you'd figured it out at last."

He indicated the beer and the stool opposite him; I sat down, pulling the stool aside to accommodate a cluster of raucous sailors. I didn't much like the 'at last' but I let it go.

"Thank you for speaking to Hugh," I said.

He shrugged. "Those ruffians would have got the best of you sooner or later."

"They've been called off. By a better friend than I deserve."

He nodded, not much interested. "And I wanted to make sure you didn't tackle Julia's death on your own. There's more to it than you know."

"You didn't think to enlighten me?" I asked tartly.

He gave a wry smile, glanced up as a serving girl called across our heads. "I know I had to get out while I still could. My original idea was to catch a boat from Sunderland and take in your dancing master on the way. But when I got to Sunderland, there were no ships sailing for three days." He shifted the tankards on the damp table. "Ample time for a great deal of thinking."

I reached for the beer. "Did you manage to pass the information on?"

His gaze jerked to my face; he began to speak, fell silent.

"I mean," I said to clarify my point, "the information you had on you when we discovered Julia's body. The reason you had to make a speedy retreat – just in case Bedwalters took it into his head to search us." I smiled on his obvious annoyance. "You told Bedwalters you were a government agent keeping an eye on Mazzanti because he was suspected of being a spy." I shook my head, sipped the beer. "You're the spy. And somewhere during that drunken spree of ours, someone slipped you some information, a paper of some sort. I didn't see it, I admit, but then I was a great deal more drunk than you were. What was the information about?"

He looked at me a moment longer, then grimaced, made a careless gesture. The noise in the tavern was briefly overwhelming; two or three men scattered as one Scotchman took a wild swing at another. No one was paying the least attention to us. "Details of the regiments at Tynemouth, their officers, their strength, their armaments. And yes, I passed it on."

"Who are you working for?" I said.

He laughed bitterly. "Whoever will pay me. At the moment, the Austrians."

Hardly surprising, I thought, since half of Italy is ruled by the Hapsburgs. But I had thought they were supposed to be our allies.

He gave me a considering gaze. "Are you going to turn me in?"

I let him stew on that. "Why did you come back?"

He sighed. A horde of keelmen suddenly pushed through the doors, bright in their yellow waistcoats, and sauntered across to tables on the far side of the tavern. "I'm the one who shot at Mazzanti," he said.

"Good God," I said, not expecting this in the least.

He leant forward, resting his weight heavily on his arms laid on the table; his tired face was sallow. "They say you should always start at the heart of the matter, don't they?" He sneered. "Only, there is no heart in the man at all, Patterson." He smiled at me, and I saw all the bitterness of years in that smile.

"He is my father."

# 37

**My dear sir, if you want history, go to Italy and see the Monuments – do not bother me with it!**
[Lord Eaglescliffe, in a coffee-house on the Strand, quoted in the *Daily Courant*, 8 March 1735]

He told the story quietly, as if it had all happened to someone else, in another age, long ago. John Mazzanti's father had been Pietro Mazzanti, a Venetian violinist of great ability who had had the misfortune to injure an arm in a carriage accident. With stoicism and great practicality, he had turned to trade instead and set up a music publishing firm with branches in Ferrara and in London; on a visit to his associates in London, he met and married the daughter of a clergyman by whom he had four children, all sons, all given good sensible English names. John was the youngest.

Time passed. The clergyman's daughter died of consumption, and, heartbroken, Pietro took his children back to Italy. Relations seem to have welcomed the children into their bosom, and all followed in their father's footsteps covering Europe with the publications of the family firm and spreading the music of Italy far and wide.

All but John, who could not settle. The heat didn't agree with him, the food didn't agree with him, the elderly relatives didn't agree with him. He pined for the attractions of London, the theatres where he had played in the rank and file as a precocious youngster; at the age of seventeen, he felt he had been cast out from all that made the world worthwhile. Except of course for the attractions of the servant girls. The inevitable happened; one of them fell pregnant and appealed to John to make her respectable and marry her.

John fled.

"Of course," Corelli said. "My grandfather Pietro would never have countenanced a marriage, not to the fourteen-year-old daughter of a peasant. But family is family and you don't ever disgrace it, or abandon your kin. He gave my mother a pension and a nice little cottage, sent her presents of food and drink on saints' days, and made sure that I was healthy and well-cared for, and that the priest taught me to read and write and to figure. Once a year, on my birthday, I was paraded in the family drawing room, and given presents." He flushed. "They made sure I knew my place, of course, but for all that they took good care of my mother and me."

He spread his large hands on the table, ignoring his tankard. The keelmen were deep in a discussion of politics, the sailors in debate about the serving girls. "I inherited not a jot of the family talent for music, so when it came to taking an alias, I amused myself by adopting the names of the great composers. My real name – "

"I don't want to know," I said. "At least I will be able to protest my ignorance with a clear conscience."

He laughed. "But fencing – that's a different matter. That's where my talents lie. And in a keen eye for a good opportunity to make money. Now, that is a family trait." He flung himself back in his chair. "Damn it, Patterson, you don't want to know my entire life history! I was apprenticed to a sword master and have earnt my living that way for years until I took it into my head to see how my father was doing in London. He seemed to be making a great deal of money and I felt I deserved a share of it, even if it was only a bequest in his will."

"You wanted acknowledgement," I said.

He nodded. "But my father's wealthy days were long over by the time I found him. Ciara is a great singer but she is getting older and fatter and no one cares any longer whether the voice is as good as it was. And as for Julia!" He made a gesture of disgust.

"So your father refused you money and you tried to frighten him by shooting at him."

"Devil a bit of it!" He leant across the table. "He hired me to shoot at him!"

"To kill him?" I said, bewildered.

"No – to shoot and miss."

I was no wiser. "In heaven's name, why?"

Corelli grinned wolfishly. "The publicity, of course! He was scared out of his wits at the way things were going. Ciara is losing popularity with every sweetmeat she eats, Julia is – was – nothing yet – just a pretty little girl playing in provincial theatres."

I thought back to those press cuttings I had found – all from provincial theatres, none from London. I should have realised the significance of that. "She'd never have been anything else," I said. "What about the engagement to play Lucy in *The Beggar's Opera*?"

"Oh, she had that," he said sarcastically, "but not in London. In a small company touring the Kentish towns."

I laughed wryly. "I thought Mazzanti was fooling himself over Julia's prospects, but he wasn't – he was trying to fool everyone else."

"Exactly." Corelli sat back, toyed with the splintered edge of the table. "He thought that if there were very public attempts on his life – and remember Ciara and Julia were both there at the time – the newspapers would pick it up and speculate, and the fashionable audiences would be intrigued enough to buy tickets, if only to see if someone would shoot him dead in the middle of a Handel aria."

"Did it work?"

The heat in the crowded tavern was beginning to be unbearable;

I drained the beer. Corelli must be the devil of a shot, I thought, if he could fire in the middle of a theatre crowd confidently expecting not only to miss Mazzanti but everyone else as well.

"Of course. The papers gave it some very good speculation – written by our correspondent at the theatre on the night."

"Mazzanti wrote it himself?"

Corelli pointed to his own chest. "Trouble is, novelty wears off very quickly. A week later someone else is eloping with a footman, or arguing over a tricorne, or some similar trifle. And the audiences get bored, because, of course, no one does shoot Mazzanti dead in the middle of his wife's aria."

"So he told you to make a second attempt."

Corelli nodded. "He got me to try the same trick in York to attract people to a private performance they gave there at the house of the mayor's wife. But the Newcastle papers didn't pick it up."

He laughed shortly. "I wish you could have seen the scene. In a grimy tavern like this one, outside Micklegate Bar. Father had the latest edition of the *Newcastle Courant* and was in a rage that the attack hadn't been mentioned. And what had the printer preferred?"

"Accounts of the debates in Parliament?" I suggested, remembering Thomas Saint's recent editions. "What else could he expect? The possibility of war is of the greatest moment to merchants and tradesmen whose livelihood depends on the safe movement of shipping and goods."

"He expected at least a paragraph or two," Corelli said. "Well, I sent it in – what more could I do?"

"Try again," I said. "In Newcastle."

He grinned sardonically. "You were never in any danger, you know. I was never going to hit you."

I was not going to let that pass. Good shot or not, he wouldn't allow for the unexpected. "Unless I'd moved, of course," I pointed out. "So that poster Mazzanti put up offering a reward for information – that was a further attempt to publicise the event? Did it have much effect?"

"Just what you'd expect – half a dozen rogues with some made-up stories. One or two ladies sympathised with Ciara and bought tickets for her concert. But they were probably going to do that anyway."

"So," I said, "when we found Julia dead, you worried about whether anyone knew you were the one who had shot at Mazzanti. If someone did know, they might think you had killed Julia to revenge yourself on your father. That and the document in your pocket gave you plenty of reasons to run."

Corelli glanced about the tavern. The sailors were now attacking what looked to be half a haunch of beef; the more respectable keelmen were paying their bills and drifting out in twos and threes.

"There's more," Corelli said.

"What?"

"Julia."

"Your half-sister."

He nodded. "I hated those birthdays, the patronising little jokes, the plain little presents when they could have afforded better, the severe exhortations to obey God, the priest and my mother. But, believe me, Patterson, I have never allowed my injured pride to make me forget that if it wasn't for those rich, condescending, pompous idiots, I would have died in the gutter and so would my mother. One thing is more important than anything else, Patterson, and that's family. You do not desert your family. Julia was a little fool but she was my sister and I'll kill the man who killed her."

A moment's silence while I wondered if I could prevent that. Or if I wanted to.

"I need your help tonight," I said.

# 38

**The law, sir, must be strengthened against these outrages.**
[Letter from JUSTICIA to Mayor of Newcastle upon Tyne,
printed in the *Newcastle Courant*, 15 May 1736.]

I stifled a yawn as I let Corelli into Esther's garden. I had managed a few hours sleep in the afternoon but it had not been enough and the onset of darkness had made me feel tired again. I knew it would pass. High above, the full moon rode in the sky, slipping behind a bank of cloud, silvering it from behind. That cloud was new – maybe we were in for storms and an end to this hot weather. It had to happen soon, surely?

Tom must have been watching out for us for he opened the back door before I could knock. Voices were raised in the kitchen. I gave Tom back the key to the garden gate. "I've locked it behind us."

He nodded. "They're all in the kitchen, sir," he said unnecessarily. I noticed his admiring gaze settle on Corelli's bulk.

Ned Reynolds's voice was audible as we negotiated the machinery in the scullery. "I'll say this for her, Athalia's a damn good actress. A few tears and a two or three flattering remarks about how no one could imagine him old enough to have a daughter Julia's age, and he's hers."

"He's taking her to London?" Esther asked.

"To play Lucy in *The Beggar's Opera*. Athalia as Lucy!" Ned laughed scornfully. "It's been a long time since she knew what it was to be a virgin."

"Ned," murmured a warning voice. Fowler – whose service had taught him what was and was not suitable to mention in the presence of ladies. I understood why Ned had forgotten his manners, however; as I pushed the kitchen door open, I saw Esther was dressed in her breeches again.

They stood in a little group about the kitchen table: Esther, turning to me with a smile, Hugh, casting an exasperated gaze to heaven, Fowler, looking uncomfortable, and Ned, not entirely sober. Catherine, Esther's maid, was pouring beer and apparently flirting with Hugh.

"Everyone's here, as you see," Esther said.

"I got your note," Hugh said, "and found everyone you wanted."

"Except Richard," Ned said, slurring his words slightly. "I'll not let him get mixed up in this."

Esther gave me a warning look. I was beginning to think that the biggest danger to Richard was Ned himself; Ned ought not to be talking of him in any company he didn't know and trust completely. He might know me and Fowler, but his acquaintance with Hugh was slight, and with the women and Corelli non-existent.

"And George?" I asked Esther, explaining to the others that George was the only spirit in the house.

"I've told him to stay upstairs," Esther said. "And to watch from the roofline. He's to let us know if the intruder tries to scale a ladder to get in."

I sighed; only the spirit of a child could have swallowed such a tale. But we needed George, and his exuberant rashness, well out of the way.

"So," Hugh said. "We're here to set a trap, right? For the murderer."

"How do you know he'll try to get in again tonight?" Esther asked. She had swept her fair hair up into a simple knot and her demeanour had altered subtly with the clothes she had put on; she was brisk and businesslike for which I was glad. That matter of the organ ticket weighed on me; it had altered something in our relationship – or perhaps merely brought it to my attention more acutely. "After we ran him off last time, I should imagine he'd not want to come near the place."

"I asked him to come," I said. "Though I did not realise it at the time."

There was uproar. Fowler said dubiously, "That's dangerous – the women – " Hugh laughed and said, "Devil take it, Charles, no wonder you're always in trouble." Corelli said, "Five on one, that's fair odds." "Seven on one," Esther said sharply.

"Devil take it," Ned said. "Leave the fellow alone. I want to shake his hand – he got rid of the bitch, I want to thank him."

Fowler took the tankard from his hand and shoved him down on to a stool. "Shut it," he said sharply, his accent coarser than before. "Shut it or I'll shut you. If you can't talk sense, I'll knock some into you. And stop drinking!"

Hugh gave me a weary look. "He's been drinking all day apparently, and talking to whoever wants to listen."

"Ned," I said, copying Heron for brutality. "Do you want to hang? Do you want Richard to hang?"

He blinked at me then started to tremble; he buried his head in his hands. Catherine pushed past Fowler.

"Leave him to me. You go on."

Ned was clearly a problem for later; I nodded and turned to explain to the others what I wanted to do. The household was apparently to retire as usual and to go through their normal routine so that if our murderer was watching he would not be suspicious. The house was to be locked up, with the exception of the back door. We knew that the murderer had the key to the garden gate but that his key did not fit the back door.

"He must get into the house," I stressed. "And I don't want any chance of him running back out again. Tom, you stay just inside the back door. Once he's well in, lock the door and pocket the key, then keep watch over it."

"He might not try the door," Esther pointed out, "knowing he couldn't get in that way before. What if he tries the kitchen window again?"

Catherine grinned. "Then he'll have half the saucepans wrapped round his ears! We'll take care of it." And she nodded meaningfully at Ned who still sat with his face buried in his hands.

"No," I said firmly. "You must let him pass. Just be ready to stop him retreating."

She frowned but nodded; I added. "And avoid the skillet – he'll be dead for sure if you hit him with that!" She giggled.

I turned back to the others. "He'll try to get through to the front of the house," I said, and ruthlessly overrode Hugh who wanted to ask how I knew. "Fowler, I want you just on the house side of the servants' door. Esther – " I saw Fowler blink at my use of Esther's Christian name. "Position yourself by the library doors. He won't go in but he might try to get out that way and I need to be sure he can't. Hugh, I want you opposite the drawing room door – you should be able to find somewhere to hide in the shadows of the stairs. Corelli, stand by the front door in case he tries to get out that way."

Corelli nodded. "And where will you be?"

"In the drawing room."

"Why the drawing room?" Hugh insisted. "What's so special about the drawing room!" Then he went silent. "You don't mean – Charles – he can't be! He's not from – from – "

Esther glanced round. "You mean – he does not belong here."

"I think not," I said levelly.

"I don't care who he is or where he comes from," Corelli said. "So long as we get him."

He was very quiet, had been ever since we met an hour ago at St Nicholas's Church. I knew he had not told me everything and that worried me. Clearly I would have trouble keeping him from killing the murderer; I had expected that. But there was something more.

Perhaps he was not sure of it himself – he had the air of a man trying to puzzle something through and not greatly liking the answers that suggested themselves.

I told them to get to their positions. Catherine and Esther went off upstairs, first to light candles and then to put them out again as if they were going to bed in the ordinary course of events. Tom went ostentatiously round the house showing himself at every window, checking all the locks. Fowler went briefly into the garden to piss; Hugh and Corelli walked off to the library, discussing fencing.

I pulled out a stool and sat down next to Ned in the candlelit kitchen.

"You've got to stop drinking, Ned."

"Go to the devil," he said thickly.

"You're in a fair way to finishing the work Julia started."

He showed me a sour face. "What do you mean by that?"

"Hanging Richard," I said again, brutally. "You're the danger to him now."

He laughed mirthlessly. "Perhaps I'd better hang myself then. Get myself out of his way."

"Yes, yes," I said dryly. "And you think he'll be safe on his own? How much common sense do you think he has, Ned? He was the one who told Julia, wasn't he?"

Ned stared at me then looked away, at the puddles of beer on the kitchen table.

"The Colonies – you think we'll be safer there?"

"Possibly. Or try Paris. They tend to let people get on with their own lives there, I'm told." I leant forward. "As long as you're discreet. Do you know the meaning of the word, Ned? Discreet, spelt S-A-F-E."

That sour look again. "I can spell."

"Doesn't look like it from my point of view."

"I don't speak French."

"Hugh will teach you."

"And what are we supposed to do for money?"

I hesitated, thought of the hundred guineas under my mattress and sighed. "I can lend you some."

"You'll not get it back," he said sharply.

"Surprise me. Become Monsieur Reynolds – France's greatest actor."

That brought a wry grimace. "It's been a long time since I imagined that sort of thing was possible, Charlie."

"Perhaps you'd better start thinking of it again."

Ned laughed weakly. "God, would you do all this for a fool like me?"

There was a clatter from the passageway outside; Tom came back into the kitchen, beaming with excitement. "Everything's locked except the back door, sir."

"Good. Then get to your post." I got up, leant over Ned. "Come and see me after Julia's funeral tomorrow and we'll sort out the details."

He nodded. "I keep thinking – "

"Yes?"

"That there's something I ought to be telling you." He frowned. "Something Julia said when she was telling me I had to marry her. But I didn't listen properly. I couldn't think of anything but Richard, about saving him – "

"It doesn't matter," I said. "I know who the murderer is."

He grimaced, plainly annoyed with himself. "You'd do better to kick me from here to Paris, Charlie. You'll be throwing good money away."

"That's my choice."

I thought ruefully of that hundred guineas as I left the kitchen. Esther would be furious if she knew I was giving some to Ned. And it had represented ease and a troublefree mind for at least the rest of the year. Yet perhaps I was not so distressed – it represented obligation too, and charity. Yes, perhaps that was the worst of all. Call it pride, but I wanted to meet Esther on equal terms through my own efforts.

I knew that was almost certain never to happen.

I went through the house checking that everyone was where they should be. Tom was eager for the intruder to show his face; he had even found rope with which to tie the rogue up. Esther had positioned herself in the dark library just behind the harpsichord, with one of her lethal duelling pistols close to hand.

"I was hoping to catch him alive," I said uneasily.

"No, you were not," she corrected me, coolly. "You are hoping he will go back into the world whence he came and not trouble us any more."

I could hardly see her face in the darkness – it was a pale blur – but I could smell her scent.

"I think he is from that other world, yes," I agreed. "That's why he kept trying to get in."

"He lives here in that other world?"

I nodded. "It's a shabby lodging house there. I told you that world was both like and unlike our own? Well, the key to the garden is the same in both worlds, but the house lock is different."

"I had it replaced," she said. "Last year. Tom broke the key in the lock. So when the intruder tried to break into the house, he thought he was merely trying to get back into his own lodgings?"

"Yes. That's why he kept coming back."

"Then –" She hesitated. "This is fiendishly complicated, Charles. Does that mean he does not know he is not in his own world?"

"I think that at the very least he is confused." I gestured at the pistol. "He is bewildered, uncertain and weak. You will not need that pistol."

"I do not have the least concern about the intruder," she said coolly. "It is your safety that concerns me. And that means the pistol is essential. Or may be at any rate."

"I am in no danger."

"You cannot know that," she said into the darkness. "I meant what I said, Charles, I am not prepared to live in constant fear. I do not know whether these dangers seek you out or whether you go looking for them, but I will not sit idly at home and let you deal with them alone. You must know that already."

"Esther – "

"Yes," she said. "We should talk of it later. I agree. Now is not the time. But let us be clear – the opinion of society means nothing to me. I will have my own way."

There was nothing more I could say. How could I argue against something I wanted so much, yet knew to be so foolish? But I could not agree with her. I had just come from berating Ned Reynolds for putting his lover in danger; how could I turn around and do something equally detrimental to the woman I loved?

# 39

**Shadows surround us; we are liable to be thrown into darkness at any moment. All the more reason therefore to cling to the light, to all things good and decent.**
[Letter from Lady Hubert to her eldest daughter on the death of the latter's child, September 1731]

Hugh was lingering in an ornamental alcove opposite the drawing room. A small table that held the bust of a Roman matron had originally stood in the alcove and he had moved it to one side, turning the face of the matron to the wall.

"Couldn't stand her looking at me like I'd just taken her last macaroon," he whispered. "Charles, if he gets into the house, how do we know he won't just snap his fingers and go back to his own world before any of us can get near him?"

"It's not as easy as that. Anyway, wherever he goes, I'll shadow him. I'll be no more than an arm's length away."

"So you can grab him? Damn it, Charles, you'll get drawn into this other place too!"

"I can come and go as I please," I said. Praying that it was true, and glad that he couldn't see my face in the gloom. As I said before, I am not a good liar.

Corelli, by the front door, was morose and unapproachable. "This is all my fault."

"No."

"If I had not been so stupid as to agree to Father's plottings!"

"Julia was killed by someone else," I said, not feeling up to explaining the other world to Corelli. "Her death was nothing to do with your father."

"Maybe I put the idea into his head."

"Then you can make amends by helping me catch the fellow tonight."

He said nothing. I sighed inwardly. Admirable though it was to see so much attachment to family, it was also wearisome. Corelli no doubt had many admirable qualities but cool detachment did not seem to be one of them. And was he far enough away from the drawing room? Could I get Julia's murderer back in his own world before Corelli put a shot his way. If he could deliberately miss an entire crowd, shooting one individual in near-darkness was probably child's play to him. Then I saw that he had a sword, not a pistol; I fancied he intended to toy with his victim, rather than put him out of his misery with a single shot.

I planned to wait just inside the back door, so I could follow the intruder into the house, to ensure that he did not somehow slip away from us. By the time I got to the servants' door, Fowler was leaning wearily against it, rubbing his eyes.

"Did you have trouble getting away from Heron?"

He grinned. "The opposite. Said I could have the evening off as he wanted to read Ovid. And as I was leaving – "

"Yes?"

"He said: *Give my regards to Mr Patterson and tell him not to take foolish risks.*"

"Damn it," I said, "Does the man know everything?"

"Well nigh, I reckon," Fowler said, grinning again.

I wondered if that included Fowler's *interests*.

In the kitchen, Catherine was pouring hot chocolate for herself and Ned. The window shutters did not quite meet and let in a thin line of moonlight. She nodded at the gap. "That moon's a nuisance. Will he risk coming here tonight when a casual passer by might see him clear as day?"

"I don't think he's thinking as rationally as that."

She looked sceptical.

I took up my place just outside the scullery in the kitchen

passageway. Tom hid by the door to the garden; he was to allow the intruder to pass, then lock the door and stay to guard it. He had looked mutinous at my repetition of these orders but said nothing. And there we waited while the moon drifted in and out of the gathering clouds, alternately bathing the garden in brightness, then plunging it into impenetrable darkness. The house was silent except for the chiming of the hall clock; distantly I heard it chime twelve times.

Then came the sound of the key in the door.

The fellow was ridiculously obsessive, I thought; why try the key after finding three times that it did not fit? But then I had accidentally encouraged him to try again.

Silence. Then a creak. Moonlight flooded the scullery and spilled out into the passageway, pooling on the stone flags. I stepped back quickly, afraid that the intruder would see me, retreated to the butler's pantry, standing just inside the room to try to obtain a good view of the passageway. The scullery door clicked shut; the moonlight died.

The intruder's footsteps seemed to hesitate, then came up the passageway towards me, stopping then going on. He passed – I saw a faint blur of movement in the darkness. To my horror, I heard the kitchen door creak open. Surely he must be able to see Catherine and Ned in the light shining through the ill-fitting shutters?

I heard a whisper, hardly audible, barely made it out: Julia's name whispered on an outbreath. The moonlight from the kitchen shone out faintly – I could see the intruder's figure, slight and blurred.

He moved on, through the servants' quarters, to the door that separated them from the main part of the house. Here he was again a mere blur of movement. I heard him open the door; when I followed, I could not see Fowler even though I knew he would be there. No doubt another skill he had learnt in his disreputable past. On, past the library, towards the drawing room. I had known he would go there; I should have known, or guessed, everything when the young seamstress in the other world had asked me if I knew where her father was.

An almighty crash behind me.

The shadow started, swung round. Behind me, Tom was swearing and Hugh cursing him. The table with the Roman matron on it: Tom must have disobeyed me and followed, tripped over the table Hugh had moved –

I grabbed at the shadow. He slipped free, darted for the front door. Corelli's massive shape came at him out of the darkness. I saw a glint of brightness, heard the hiss of a sword. But the intruder ducked under Corelli's arm, stumbled, headed across the hallway.

"The dining room!" Hugh cried. We all ran after him. I was cursing and yelling. "Corelli, stay by the door! Tom, back to the scullery. Now!"

Huge shadows flared as I shouldered my way into the dining room – someone behind me must have lit a branch of candles. The dancing light revealed an empty room – and a door swinging on the other side.

"Servants' stairs!" Fowler yelled. I heard his footsteps clattering back into the bowels of the house. Esther and Hugh crowded in behind me, Esther carrying a branch of candles half-lit. Corelli was staring over their shoulders in a murderous rage. "Back to the front door!" I yelled, frustrated. Was no one capable of doing what they were told! I seized Esther's arm. "Go upstairs. Make sure he can't emerge in one of the rooms up there. Maybe we'll need George after all. Tell him to keep alert. And shout your loudest if you find the intruder. You'll need help to deal with him."

She gave me a cool ironic gaze but went off into the hall, thrusting the branch of candles into Hugh's hands. I ducked into the servants' stair, tried to listen. Stairs like these climb in a narrow gap between the walls of the reception rooms. Footsteps echo in these confined spaces; servants know how to deal with this – the intruder probably wouldn't.

Hugh leant over my shoulder. We heard a clatter. "That's him!" Hugh exclaimed. "Up or down, d'you reckon?"

"Down – he'd want to get out."

We clattered down the stairs, the candles flaring wildly in the draught we created. Downstairs (in the cellars perhaps?) doors slammed, footsteps pattered. Light flickered ahead. I took the remaining steps two at a time, almost cannoning into the man at the cellar door.

Fowler. He had a candle in one hand and a pistol in the other. "He couldn't have got out this way," he said, crisply. "The doors are all locked and bolted. He's still in the house."

I swung round, pushed past Hugh. "He must have gone up after all."

"Why the devil should he do that?"

I didn't have breath to answer. I raced upwards, trying not to stumble in the uncertain light of the candles. The stair became narrower – how the devil did the servants get round the corners with scuttles of coal and all their other paraphernalia? Fowler swore as he hit his head on one low beam.

"Damn it," Hugh said, "He could have got out into any room!"

"How? He has no light, Hugh! How is he to see where the doors are?" The flaring light of our own candles barely showed the close fitting doors; no hint of light shone through from the rooms beyond. There were not even any handles – just tiny holes to curl a finger into and tug. I plunged on, gasping for breath, feeling the muscles in my legs ache. In any case, if the intruder had run into a room, then the door would still be swinging. He would hardly have the presence of mind to close it again neatly.

"How far up are we?" Hugh gasped.

Fowler, in the rear, was in a lot better shape that either of us, barely breathing heavily. "He must be heading for the roof. He's going to kill himself!"

That had all too likely a sound to it.

"Does the stair go to the roof?"

"It must do," Fowler said. "Heron's does – that way the workmen can get out on to the slates if they need to."

He was right. At the top of the stair, I came up to a blank wall, saw a thin line of brightness and grabbed at it. I caught the edge of a door; it swung open on to a roof flooded with moonlight. A wooden walkway led out across lead guttering. Behind me, Fowler blew out the candles in case the intruder decided to take a pot shot at us.

I took a deep breath and edged out. No one attacked me. I saw only slates and tall chimneys and guttering and a few straggly weeds all bathed in ghostly moonlight. A step or two further and a breathtaking view opened out before me, across the roofs of the town to the glittering gilded spires of St Nicholas's Church.

A shadow moved.

I started after him. He was over by one of the chimney stacks, ducking behind it, trying to stretch across from one walkway to another, rather than going the long way round by the parapet of the roof. But at that moment the moon slid behind a cloud and all was darkness. My foot went down into black shadow, caught the edge of the wooden walkway. My ankle turned over; I crashed down with a force that took the breath out of me.

Hugh swore – from my prone position, I saw him leap over me, dart for the place where the shadow had been. And in the next instant, the shadow emerged from between two chimney stacks –

Fowler fired. The shot whistled above my head; Hugh yelped in surprise. I saw the figure stagger. He stumbled then disappeared behind the chimney stack.

Fowler's hand closed round my arm to help me up. I was cursing inwardly. I didn't want the fellow dead! Fowler had just done what he thought best but God, the whole thing was a mess!

Hugh was edging round the chimney stacks, holding on to them by his fingertips. By the time I got there, I saw why – part of the wooden walkway had rotted through and broken away. I followed him round the stacks, with Fowler close behind me. Round the other side of the chimney, Hugh was staring blankly at the roof beyond.

There was no one there.

# 40

**One day the meaning of all these trials will be revealed to us.**
[Lady Hubert to her eldest daughter, September 1731]

"The other chimney!" I leapt for the next stretch of slates. There was no wooden walkway here and my foot came down hard on the roof. There was an ominous cracking noise, as of wooden laths breaking under the slates. I jumped for the low parapet that edged the roof, landed on a more secure section of the walkway behind it. The moon slid in and out of the clouds. Hugh was swearing, Fowler laughing.

There was no one behind the next chimney stack either, but there was a small attic window, and it was yawning wide open.

I grabbed the sill to swing myself inside and felt something warm and sticky under my fingers. "He's bleeding," I said to Fowler. "You hit him all right."

"I never miss," he said in a matter of fact way. "Except that once, with Heron."

Hugh climbed through the window behind me, blocking the moonlight briefly. The room was unlit and unoccupied, a lumber room, neatly piled with boxes and trunks. A path led to the open door. We piled out into a maze of tiny rooms. The servants' quarters.

Fowler pulled a stump of candle out of a pocket, struck tinder and lit it. His past might be questionable but he was plainly a good man to have beside you in a fight; he seemed prepared for everything. He lit a second stub from the first and handed it to me.

"Check all the doors," I told him. "If you find him, don't put yourself at risk but shepherd him towards the ground floor."

He nodded, went off to the first door. Hugh and I went down the bare wooden steps to the storey below, shielding the candle flame against draughts. I was wondering where George's spirit was; he should have warned us when the intruder reached the roof. Thank God I had not relied on him.

On the banister towards the bottom, I felt the hot stickiness again. "He's down here all right."

A figure loomed out of the darkness, the metal of a pistol glinted. The candlelight showed me Esther. Her pale hair had fallen about her shoulders; she was a little out of breath. "Did you find him?"

I stared down at her. "He came this way. Didn't you see him?"

She shook her head. "I've just got here. I came through the servants' passageways."

"The main stair," I cried. "He must have gone down the main stair!"

We plunged through the darkened rooms. These were not the fine rooms of the lower storeys, but they were neat and pleasant nevertheless, with comfortable chairs and beds, and clean curtains shining bright in the moonlight. The sort of rooms the governess gets in the more considerate families, or the room the companion lives in.

Brightness blossomed as the moon came out again and shone in through an elegant floor-length window on a half-landing of the main stairs. I went headlong down, jumping two or three steps at a time. Below I heard raised voices. Was that George? Yes, an excitable boyish treble calling enthusiastically. A shriek. Corelli shouted. Running footsteps. A banging of doors. By the time we got to the hallway, Corelli was nowhere to be seen but there was uproar at the back of the house. I threw myself at the servants' door.

Beyond was chaos. Tom was sprawled against a wall, dazed

and bleeding. Catherine was shouting from the scullery – I heard Ned's sharper tones. George was some way off, shouting: "Here! Here!" Where the devil was Corelli?

"Hugh," I said, struggling for breath. "Stand by the drawing room door. If he tries to get in there, stop him. Esther – the library door." I didn't wait to see if they obeyed me; I ran on.

A shot. Catherine cried out in alarm. Someone hurtled out of the kitchen and crashed into me. Ned Reynolds. "Butler's pantry!" he yelled and ran on. I followed him into the cellars, into the chill and dank corners of the house. George was still shouting. In heaven's name, could he not say something useful – like – we're in the scullery! Ahead, I thought I saw a shadow twist and turn.

We stumbled to a halt. Cellars stretched on either side of us; dusty wine racks to one side, a few barrels of beer, one or two broken pieces of pottery, dented saucepans. Shelves of jams and preserves.

Ned was heaving for breath. "Damn, damn! He must know the house well to get away so easily!"

"He should do," I said, cursing myself for not having thought of it before. "He lives here."

Ned stared at me in astonishment. "One of the servants? I thought there was only one male serv – "

I was already running back towards the scullery.

At the back door, Catherine was standing with a heavy skillet menacingly raised. She pointed urgently towards the front of the house. I ran on, hearing her call after me. "He was bleeding! His arm!"

Ned was close behind me again. "I thought my shot missed him."

"Fowler got him when we were on the roof."

We headed back to the main part of the house. Corelli was just inside the servants' door. "He tried to get out the front again – I stopped him and he ran back."

"Go back to the door," I said urgently.

He hesitated but went, passing Fowler who had just come to the bottom of the main stair. "Where the devil can he have gone?"

I was looking about. Something was wrong. Something was not as it should be. I heard the murmur of voices in the hallway – Corelli's voice and Hugh's. I crunched through the fragments of the Roman matron who lay shattered in pieces on the floor, and came to an abrupt halt.

The library door was up ahead. Closed and silent.

Where was Esther? Surely she must have come down the stairs when she heard all the shouting...

I pushed gently at the library door. It swung open almost soundlessly. The room was unlit but then the erratic moonlight slid into the long room and showed me two vague figures, across the far side of the room by the bookshelves and the angular shape of the ladder that gave access to the higher shelves. The light gleamed on Esther's face and on her hands clutching at the arm of the man behind her. And on the knife held at her throat.

Hugh appeared behind me, with one of Fowler's candle stubs. The figures were too far away to be illuminated by the candlelight. I gestured to him to stay back and advanced slowly into the room, hands held out in front of me to show I had no weapon. The face of the man holding Esther was shadowed, half obscured by her; he was slight and not particularly tall. My attention was on the man's hand and the knife – a kitchen knife by the looks of it – that lay across Esther's throat, but even in my preoccupation I noticed the edge of slight amusement that curved Esther's lips. What the devil was there to be amused at? She was as bad as Heron.

I was careful to pitch my voice low and reassuring. "There's no need to hurt anyone – "

Esther moved faster than I could see. Seizing the moment

when her assailant was slightly distracted, she heaved on the arm she clutched, tugged, shifted her weight. The next moment, her assailant was falling and the knife was hitting the ground with a clatter. He yelled.

No mistaking that voice.

Matthew Proctor.

# 41

**Nothing can prepare us for such events;
all we can do is go blindly on.**
[Lady Hubert to her daughter, October 1731]

He scrambled to his feet – Esther grabbed at him but missed. At the last moment she put out a foot to try and catch his ankle; he stumbled but ran on. Heading for the drawing room door.

I went after him. As I passed, I dipped to catch up the knife but misjudged the distance in the erratic candlelight and only managed to kick it further away. I left it. With Esther and Hugh close behind me, I plunged after Proctor.

As I ran through the door into the drawing room, the smell of mildew and decay almost overwhelmed me. I gagged. Hugh swore; Esther drew in a sharp breath.

Proctor fell over; a clatter of small things tumbled to the floor. Then Hugh's candle cast its dim light. I made out a curtain with the shape of a couch behind it, a large table with bread covered by a cloth. And Proctor stumbling to his feet again in a tangle of threads and needles and ribbons.

We had stepped through to the other world.

Proctor was heading for the further door, the one out into the hallway, and in this world it was not guarded by Corelli. I yelled to Hugh to cut Proctor off; he pushed the candle stub into Esther's hand but tripped over the tumbled work table, managed to right himself. He and Proctor arrived at the door at almost the same time; Hugh flung his weight against it and it slammed shut.

Silence. The shutters were closed and only a thin band of bright light shone underneath. I glanced around, relieved to see that the girl – Proctor's daughter, Flora – was not here. Esther, by the door to the library, was composedly holding the candle stub and looking round with wary interest.

And in the middle of the room stood Proctor, breathing heavily, blood darkening his left sleeve and oozing down over his fingers. He looked about him with little darting glances, at Hugh, at me, at Esther, backed away towards the window. I held up my hands to try and calm him.

"Proctor," I said, as soothingly as I could. "We must talk."

He was watching me with febrile energy, as if he thought me about to pounce on him.

"Where the devil are we?" Hugh demanded.

"In that other world. We've stepped through."

"In my house," Esther said with a trace of exasperation. She tilted the stub of candle, poured wax on the table edge and stuck the candle to the wood. Hugh sighed and said heavily, "For heaven's sake, will someone explain all this?"

"You trapped me," Proctor said accusingly. Blood dripped from his fingers on to the bare floor. "You told me to come back and try again so you could trap me!"

"Actually, I didn't," I said. "I meant something else entirely. I only realised how you might take it when I knew you had attacked Julia."

"*He* did it?" Hugh said amazed. "Proctor? Damn it, Charles, I've known the fellow for years. He even hates killing wasps – all God's creatures and all that!"

"The Matthew Proctor you know is in Carlisle," I said. "This is a different person altogether."

Proctor had taken hold of the back of the one rickety chair in the room – I was half afraid he might decide to pick it up and try to throw it at us. "I didn't kill Julia," he said fiercely.

I shook my head. "You told me yourself that you'd been watching the house," I said. "You were there almost the whole time, every night."

"To keep her safe!"

I sighed; I had hoped that, once cornered, he would simply admit his guilt.

"On the night of Julia's death," I said, "you had an argument with Mazzanti at about nine o'clock. He came home drunk and shouted at you. You told me yourself that he sent you packing then. Mrs Baker told me the same story. But several other people also saw you outside the house – at *midnight* – at about the time Julia was waiting for her lover."

"They were wrong!" he said wildly.

"No," I said. "At nine o'clock you did indeed leave the street but once Mazzanti was in the house you went back to resume your vigil. And you saw Julia come out of the house and hang about as if waiting for someone. She didn't see you because you hid – there were other people in the street you didn't want to see you. Three drunks for instance. And Mazzanti himself was peering out of the window. Then you saw Julia walking off."

Proctor gripped the chair as if it was the only thing holding him up. "She was running away. Eloping with some fortune hunter! After everything she had said to me!"

I thought of the Julia I had met in this world, the Julia dressed in a mature woman's finery, who had been waiting in the kitchen with two glasses of wine for a man who never returned. The Julia who had asked me anxiously if I knew where Proctor was.

"She wasn't your Julia, Proctor," I said gently. "This was a different woman."

I took a deep breath. How in heaven's name was I to explain to him what had happened? How could I tell him that he had accidentally stepped from his own world into another that bore a resemblance that was in many respects so close that a distraught man might not notice it? How could I explain that he had fastened his attentions on a girl who was not the woman who was already his lover?

"Have you never wondered," I said, "why your key no longer fits the door of the house?"

"Damn landlord," he said with uncharacteristic spite. "Changes the locks all the time. Then we have to pay for new keys."

I glanced at Esther and Hugh; they were standing silently, almost as unnerved as Proctor. I tried again.

"What about your daughter? Flora? She should have been sitting here at home doing her fine needlework to supplement your income, shouldn't she? When your key didn't fit, did it not surprise you that she didn't come to let you in?"

He looked about him helplessly. The girl's workbox lay overturned on the floor, spilling out pins and threads and scissors. He darted a look at Hugh keeping watch near the door, then at Esther. She was looking at the window with an air of puzzlement. I couldn't see what was perplexing her.

"Proctor." I started again. If a roundabout way would not work, then I must try directness. "You have, by chance, stepped through to another world – "

He began to laugh, almost hysterically; I could not blame him. I persisted. "You saw and heard the spirits there, Proctor." I remembered how they had frightened him so much. "Spirits do not exist in this world, do they? But they have surrounded you this last week."

He stopped laughing, gasped for breath. "Demons! Legions of demons rising from the very stones!"

"It's no good," Esther said. "He cannot believe."

Proctor was not seeing any of us. "She was so beautiful," he whispered. "And she turned away from me. I pleaded with her not to be unfaithful but she wouldn't listen. It was the demons. They spoke to her and she laughed."

I thought of the spirit on the house next to Mrs Baker's. The spirit who liked a good-looking woman, who had been unable to resist a little flirtation with Julia.

I said softly: "You were lovers?"

"We were going to marry," he said. Hugh snorted in derision and I signalled furiously to him to keep quiet. "We talked about how we could afford it. She was going to save all she could from the money she got for playing Lucy in London. She was going to sell her jewels and her lace – "

"What were you going to contribute?" Esther said tartly. The candle stub began to splutter and die.

"We were going to travel the country – I would teach the congregations their psalms, she would teach the ladies the latest songs from the London operas."

Oddly, I could imagine the Julia in this world actually making such an impractical idealistic plan work, although I wondered what would have happened to the daughter, Flora, in this idyll.

"But she tried to pretend she didn't know me!" He battered at the back of the chair with his fist. "When I tried to embrace her, she pushed me away, said she'd call for help! She said she didn't know me!" He almost shook the chair in his fury. "And then she walked away from me. I told her she had to go home." He turned his face pleadingly towards me. "It wasn't safe! But she said she had to find him. *Him*! That weedy fellow. Just because he was a gentleman. She was going to his house, she said."

Julia had been going to knock on Ord's own door! Had she been as desperate as that?

"This was outside her lodgings?" I asked. "Did her parents not hear you argue?"

He stared at me, apparently disorientated. "No – it was a street or two away."

"Which street?"

The only sound in the room was the sparking of the dying candle and our own breathing.

He swallowed hard. "I could not let her go, I could not!"

"You caught up with her. You took hold of her."

"I thought – " He hesitated. "I thought a kiss would bring her to her senses."

"But it did not," Esther said, dryly.

"I didn't mean to hurt her!" he insisted. "I thought I could make her remember how we loved each other. But she kept trying to push me away, kept hitting me."

"She struggled and fell," I said.

"She hit her head," Proctor said, "on a stone at the base of a wall. She was dazed. I thought I could comfort her."

"Yes, yes," Hugh said derisively. "I've heard it called that before. You raped her."

Proctor was weeping, great silent tears rolling down his cheeks. He wiped his eyes and left a smear of blood across his nose. "She said she didn't know me!" He looked at me pleadingly. "I didn't know what to do. I ran away. Then I thought I should go back. And then – " A great convulsion of tears overtook him; Hugh muttered contemptuously, Esther shifted impatiently. "I didn't know what to do!" Proctor insisted. "And then – I found her dead. And – and – God help me, all I could think of was that she couldn't now tell anyone what I had done." He gave us all desperate glances. "I was scared!"

"You took one of her ribbons," I said.

"To remember her by." He added listlessly, "I lost it."

"You raped her and then you killed her," Esther said with contempt. "And then you ran away. You left her body in the street for anyone to find and take advantage of."

"No, no," he protested. "I didn't – You don't understand."

"And it wasn't even the right woman," Esther said.

"Julia," he whispered.

"Not your Julia." Esther strode across the room and lifted the heavy bar securing the shutters. It dropped with a heavy clatter. She pulled one side of the shutters open.

We were drenched in sunlight. That line of light below the

shutters had not been moonlight but the full sun of midday. The sunshine flooded into the room, setting dust motes dancing. As I squinted against the dazzling brightness, I saw the dim shapes of carriages in the street outside, the blurs of people passing the window. Then my eyes adjusted and I turned to look at Proctor. He was staring out into the daylight.

"Midnight?" Esther said mockingly. "In our world, yes. Here it is full day. Now do you realise we are telling you the truth? You were not in your own world. It was not your Julia you killed."

Proctor stared out into the street. We heard the clatter of horses' hooves, the call of a carter, the barking of dogs.

"She was not betraying you," Esther said. "She genuinely did not know you. You killed an innocent stranger."

"No, no," he protested.

There was a noise at the door. The door opened inwardly, bumping into Hugh. He shifted aside, startled, started to raise his pistol. I called out to stop him.

It was Julia Mazzanti, the still-living woman. She stood in the doorway with the gossamer-thin shawl over her lace-bedecked dress, fake jewellery sparkling at her ears and around her neck. Yellow embroidered ribbons hung through her hair.

Hugh was staring in blank amazement; Esther, by the window still, was startled into immobility. I thought that Julia Mazzanti saw none of us. She was staring at Proctor with a face alive with joy.

"Matthew!"

Proctor shrieked. He started away from Julia who stared at him in astonishment, backed away round the chair, half-lifted it as if in defence.

"Matthew?" Julia said bewildered. "You're hurt!" She reached for him then seemed to see me for the first time. "Mr Patterson? What's happening?"

She took one step towards me. It was enough to clear Proctor's way. He threw down the chair, cannoned into Esther, sending her stumbling aside, darted for the door.

I knew I was too far away but I tried to catch him anyway. I pushed unceremoniously past Julia, vaulted the fallen chair and ran for the hallway. The door to the street was open to the warm autumn sunlight and the rattling carriages. Proctor was just disappearing through it.

I almost caught him. My fingers snagged on his coat tails as he dashed out into the street in panic. Someone shouted a warning, a dog set up a furious yapping. A woman screamed. Then horses were rearing and Proctor was under the wheels of a brewer's wagon.

## 42

**Somehow, true satisfaction always seems to elude us.**
[*Instructions to a Son newly come of Age*, Revd. Peter Morgan
(London: published for the Author, 1691)]

I knelt and reached under the wheels to touch Proctor. One glance was enough to tell me he was dead; his neck was twisted, his eyes wide open and blank.

The carter was murmuring soothing noises to his nervous horses; a woman, clearly a farmer's wife, said comfortably, "It was his own fault. He ran out as if all the demons in hell were after him."

"They were," I said.

I turned to look back at the house. On the doorstep, Julia Mazzanti was standing dry-eyed and rigid. Esther murmured something in her ear; Julia shook her head. I went back to them.

"I thought everything was going to be all right," Julia said. "I thought I'd found happiness after all that had happened to me. A husband and a child. After everything so dreadful and sordid, I thought there was one man in the world who believed in God and in love."

I searched for words that might comfort her but she turned her head and looked on me with contempt. "Are you not going to ask me what I mean, Mr Patterson? Or are you going to change the subject or keep silent too?" She smiled mirthlessly. "Like my mother."

And then to my fury we were crashing back into darkness. The daylight winked out, the chattering crowd was silenced, the dog's barking cut off. A great chill overtook us, and left me shivering and trembling and cursing and railing against the perversity of whatever force it was – fate, or God, or chance – that controlled the links between the two worlds. I found I had shut my eyes; when I opened them again, I was standing in the drawing room of Esther's house, with candles flickering in the doorway and Corelli shouting.

I knew I would not see Julia Mazzanti again.

I got my breath back, felt warmth seeping back into my bones. Flickering candlelight showed me Hugh sprawled on the floor, tangled in a chair; I looked round for Esther and found her by the library door, staring blindly into space.

The door to the hall burst open; Corelli rushed in, flourishing his sword. "What happened?" he demanded. "Where the hell is he? Devil take it, he didn't get away? He didn't go out the front door. He must still be in the house!"

Fowler came up behind him. "He didn't go through the servant's door to the back of the house."

"How about the library windows?" I said brightly. "They overlook the gardens. If he could get out there, he would have been able to get out into the street."

Corelli plunged through into the library. Fowler gave me a hard look but followed the Italian; like master, like servant, I thought – more perceptive than I would have liked. But then Heron could never stand fools about him.

Esther pushed past me, hurriedly unlatched the drawing-room window shutter and dragged the window up an inch. Corelli and Fowler in the library were making enough noise to awaken the dead; Catherine's voice came through from the kitchen. Esther pulled the window up a little further and called out. "This way! He must have got out here!"

Corelli came back, cursing and swearing. He took one look at the window and dashed for the front door. Fowler and Ned went after him; Ned was grinning with all his old recklessness.

Catherine hovered in the library door. "Tom's gone out to check the garden. Shall I call him back?"

"No," I said. "Tell him to check everything."

She went off to do my bidding. Hugh and Esther exchanged glances. The noise and heat of excitement died away; I could hear Corelli and Ned shouting out in the square, waking half the neighbours no doubt. I sensed that while half an hour or so had passed for us in the other world, for Corelli and the others no time at all had passed; they had seen us go into the drawing room and followed us there at once. That discrepancy in time seemed to work both ways.

"Proctor," Hugh said. "Who'd have thought it?"

"You could say that he murdered her for love," Esther said.

Hugh snorted. "He conducts a secret affair with her, gets her with child, then kills her when she won't talk to him. Funny kind of love."

Esther flushed. "You are harsh, Mr Demsey."

"I'm right," he retorted.

"But Julia was not unfaithful," she pointed out. "It was a tragic error that Proctor could not have known he was making. He did not know he had slipped through to another world and that the woman he saw was not his lover."

"But if he'd never started the affair in the first place," Hugh said ruthlessly, "the confusion would never have arisen. That's what comes of doing things in an underhand way."

I let them talk. I had not wanted to leave Julia Mazzanti so suddenly. How mysterious the whole affair must seem to her; she was owed an explanation for her lover's strange brief disappearance and for the panic in which he had run from her. All her life she would agonise over that mystery. But perhaps I had never any choice in the matter once Proctor was dead; perhaps the reason for my stepping through at this time was concluded. The worlds had moved away from each other and would not touch again until another crisis.

And there was a taste of bitterness in my mouth. I had speculated that I had been transported to that other world in order to save Julia Mazzanti from the fate that had overtaken her counterpart in my own world. But I had not. I had not saved her life – I had destroyed it.

# 43

**In the midst of life...**

I woke with a start as sun touched my eyes. I was hot and uncomfortable. Blankets were rumpled around me. I struggled to sit up, nearly fell out of the armchair, clutched at the arms.

I was in Esther's tidy estate room, my feet up on a footstool almost under the table Esther used as a desk, the chair back up against the shelves. A dish of cold chocolate stood on the table at my elbow. I stared with bleary eyes at the massive tomes of accounts, at the boxes of legal documents – titles to estates here and there, maps of farmland, correspondence with agents –

Groggily, I stretched, rubbed at my eyes, extricated myself from the chair and the blankets. I felt sticky and grubby, as if I needed a good wash. My chin prickled with stubble.

With difficulty, I pieced together the events of the previous evening: Proctor's panicked flight, his death, Julia Mazzanti's bitter grief. The makeshift story we had invented to fool Corelli and the others. Esther's quietness and Hugh's loud scorn. That was what unnerved me most. They had both been shaken by their experiences in the other world – that was natural enough – but I sensed something more, in Hugh particularly. As if his faith in the solidity of the world had been overset; he kept putting out a hand to touch things – chairs, walls, windows – as if to make sure they were real.

The door opened. Esther came in bearing a tray which held two dishes of chocolate and a plate of bread and cheese. She was in deshabille again, wearing an elaborate beribboned, belaced robe over her nightgown. Her hair was loose about her shoulders.

Through the open door, I heard the hall clock chiming.

Ten o'clock. I started up. "I must go!"

Esther set the tray down on the table. "We must talk, Charles." She interrupted as I started to speak. "Don't give me any more of your ifs and buts – "

"It's Julia Mazzanti's funeral today," I said. "It's at eleven and I am playing the organ."

She sighed, said nothing for a moment. "Very well," she said at last. "We will talk tonight instead."

She paused a moment. I was searching for something to say. The memory of those hundred guineas nagged at me.

Esther regarded me for a long moment, then handed me a dish of chocolate with the utmost composure. "I wish you would understand, Charles," she said, "that the choice is not merely yours."

By the time I had got home, washed and put on my best clothes, I was late and had to go to the church unshaven. Fortunately, all the music I needed for the funeral service was already locked in the cupboard beside the organ, but it would be a close-run thing whether I got to the church before the mourners.

I had hardly got to Pilgrim Street before I came up with the funeral procession; I heard it before I saw it. A trumpet blared through the hot narrow streets and drums thudded hollowly, setting loose shutters rattling. Mazzanti must have enlisted the help of some regiment from Tynemouth.

I caught up with the tail end of the affair where the sightseers strolled along with the children and the beggars – funerals were good times to earn a little money; there were always plenty of people willing to give tangible thanks it was not them in the coffin. The front of the procession was somewhere ahead; I cut through an alley or two and spied the corpse in a carriage laden with flowers. The horses were weighed down with plumes. And dear God, he had hired a couple of choristers and two singing men from Durham Cathedral to sing some anthem in Italian, some Romish music, I guessed. I stood listening for a moment with great pleasure to a boy with the voice of an angel. Now, if Julia Mazzanti could have sung like that!

Behind the coffin and the choristers came the chief mourners. John Mazzanti was impressive in a very new black coat, pressing a black silk handkerchief to his eyes and occasionally letting out a sob, horribly embarrassing Mr Jenison and the other directors of the concerts who had turned out to lend their support. No doubt Mrs Jenison and the ladies were having an equally difficult time coping with the abandoned grief of Signora Mazzanti. They say of course that foreigners are more demonstrative than the English, but nevertheless there was something that seemed staged about the whole affair. The Mazzantis were weeping for the loss of their own future rather than the loss of a daughter.

Mrs Baker materialised beside me, watching in amused contempt. "All the gentlemen of the concerts are here, I see," she said, admiring the solemn posse immediately behind the carriage. About tenth in line was Philip Ord, pale and respectful; he saw me, looked arrogantly away. None of the theatre company were there, I noted. "They haven't found her spirit then?"

"Not that I've heard," I agreed. "I'm told Bedwalters has had men out, scouring the streets."

"It happens," Mrs Baker said. "Sometimes they just don't want to talk."

Sometimes, I've even heard it suggested, a spirit never disembodies at all. I've never known that happen myself – perhaps it's just a tale.

"I knew a fellow once," Mrs Baker said. "When I was a girl, oh, nine years old. A vagabond who killed another in a drunken stupor. He thought he'd hide the deed by carrying the body off somewhere else."

On the principle of course that the spirit remains in the place of death; move the body and the law may never discover the spirit, and thus never know what has happened. That was what the murderer had done with Julia's body, of course, in moving it to Amen Corner. I had an uneasy picture of Proctor staggering along under Julia Mazzanti's weight; she had been a slim thing but he was not particularly large himself.

"What happened?" I asked, half-distracted.

"Silly fool never made sure his victim was dead. Came round and started shouting for vengeance – right outside our front door!"

I laughed dutifully. Proctor must have managed it somehow because that was what had happened.

Mrs Baker nodded at the singers. "I'd have thought Mr Proctor would be there – he was so gone on the child."

"He had an engagement in Carlisle," I said hurriedly.

It was time I went off to the church; I turned away just as the singers started on another ornate anthem. Then I heard my name called and turned to see Ned Reynolds hurrying up behind me.

"I'm glad to see you," he said breathlessly. "I've remembered!"

"Remembered what?" I asked blankly.

"What I had meant to tell you. Remember, I told you last night? Something Julia said puzzled me – I thought it might be of use to you in solving this puzzle."

I opened my mouth to tell him it was too late, that the matter was settled. Then I thought better of it. As far as Ned was concerned, Julia's murderer and Esther's intruder was still at large.

"Go on."

"It was that time Julia made it clear she knew about Richard and me," Ned said. He glanced round but the crowd were all intent on the funeral procession; nevertheless he drew me aside, and looked round closely for spirits who might overhear us. "The time she said I had to marry her. We were in the theatre – in a back corner where no one could hear. She'd just put her deal to me and I didn't know what to say or do. And as I was staring about, I saw Mazzanti come in from the timber yard. I was hoping he'd see us and come across to separate us. To rescue me." His mouth twisted unpleasantly. "I told you, Charlie, I've always been one to hope trouble will go away if you ignore it."

What did that remind me of? I wanted to stop him, to grasp at that fleeting memory, but he went on. "But he didn't see us. He spotted Proctor, the psalm teacher. The poor fellow was doing nothing much, just hanging around in hope of a word with Julia, but Mazzanti went across to him straightaway and began to berate him."

The memory would not return. "What did he say?"

"Don't have the least idea – they were too far away. But that's not what I wanted to tell you." He shifted to allow a gaggle of excited children to rush past. "Julia saw me looking and turned to see what was interesting me so much. She said –" He frowned, obviously trying to remember the exact words. "*Look at them both. Two bullocks fighting over the same heifer.*"

I stared at him. A host of disparate facts suddenly flooded in on me. Corelli's mother – a young servant girl; Ciara Mazzanti's aging, plump helplessness. Her dependence on her husband to manage her career and their joint reliance on Julia's income. Proctor's repeated protestations that he had not killed Julia. Someone else who like Ned dealt with troubles by pretending they did not exist. Julia's desperation to find a husband; Ord's sarcastic comments about her lover – *Married, I suppose*. And the living Julia's last comment. *Are you going to keep silent too? Like my mother.*

Her mother. Dear God.

## 44

**Marriage, my dear, is only a means to an end.
It is our way to comfort and to security and, if we let it,
it can be our way to happiness and even joy too.**
[Lady Hubert to her eldest daughter on her wedding day,
12 October 1730]

St Nicholas's church clock was striking two in the morning as I came up to the door of Mrs Baker's lodging house. The lanterns in the street had almost all burnt out and the full moon was drifting in and out of gathering clouds. The night was as hot and stifling as ever.

I didn't think it mattered that Julia Mazzanti's spirit had not been found. I knew what she would say. She would tell us that she had met with Proctor in the street, that he had been mad, he had claimed to be already her lover and had then attempted to assault her. She had fallen as she struggled and hit her head on the cobbles. She had been dazed, perhaps even unconscious, so she had known nothing more. Everything would point to Proctor as a killer. And given that the innocent Proctor of this world would sooner or later return to the town, it was just as well Julia could not accuse him.

Everything seemed plain. Julia's killer had been tragically confused and deluded; we had caught him and he had died. Yet one thing could not be denied. Proctor had said he had not killed Julia. He had admitted to raping her and to running off scared, leaving her unconscious. Then, he said, his conscience had prompted him to go back and he had done so. And he had found her dead. That was what he had said: *I found her dead.*

Proctor had not killed Julia. Someone else had come along

and taken advantage of Julia's unconscious state to strangle her. But I didn't think for one moment that the murderer had been an opportunist thief or a casual passer by. Like Heron, I don't believe in coincidence. I believe in a wily man keeping an eye open for an opportunity to solve a problem that is beginning to threaten all too urgently.

The knocker on Mrs Baker's door was still shrouded in crepe; I lifted my hand to knock then changed my mind. The last thing I wanted was to raise the whole household. Let Mrs Baker sleep on. The spirit of the maid was reclusive and would not leave the attics. Good – I had business I didn't want interrupted. With one last glance back at the corner of the street where Hugh and Esther lingered, I peered in at the drawing room window. The shutters had been drawn and barred but there was enough space where they met to allow a thin gleam of candlelight to shine out. Mazzanti must still be up. I tapped on the glass.

It took four attempts to rouse him. At the last attempt, one of the shutters folded back and I saw his face, grotesque in the candlelight. He looked haggard, which was hardly surprising in a man who had lost a daughter and his only source of income in one fell swoop. He was not wearing his wig and the grey stubble on his head shadowed all the bumps and hollows of his skull.

I gestured towards the front door. He mouthed obscenities and waved to me to go away. I mimed banging on the front door. He swore again, hesitated, then dragged himself towards the door of the room. He was far more drunk than Ned Reynolds had ever been.

After what seemed an age, I heard the bolts being drawn on the front door. He turned the key with such a clatter that I thought Mrs Baker would come down anyway. She did not – perhaps she was used to Mazzanti's clatterings during the night. The door was dragged open and I confronted him face to face; he was hollow-cheeked, red-eyed and slack-mouthed.

He stank of brandy.

He dragged himself back towards the drawing room, leaving me to shut the door; when I went into the room after him, he was pouring himself another brandy. The stench in the room almost made me gag.

"Despise me, eh, Patterson?" he said. He turned and pointed a wavering finger at me. "Yes, I know you do. I've always known it. That's why I set that constable after you."

"A little contempt hardly seems sufficient motive to do something that might send a man to the gallows."

He laughed raucously. Yes, very drunk. "It's because I'm Italian, isn't it?" he said loudly. The drunk always misjudge how loudly they are speaking. "You English always despise foreigners."

"You're as English as I am," I said. "And accusing an innocent man – however much you may dislike him – seems rather odd under the circumstances. It might have got the real murderer off scot-free."

He said nothing, tried to find his mouth with the brandy glass.

"Don't you want to find who killed your daughter?" I asked.

He sneered.

"Or even," I added, "who has taken away your sole source of income and left you and your wife paupers?"

"We'll manage."

I shook my head. "Your wife has a year or two left. There are still some genuine music-lovers who know how good she is. But even that won't last long." I perched myself on the arm of a chair. "I know who Julia's murderer is," I said softly.

He turned, his gaze uncertain, meeting mine, then flickering away into some corner. "Long gone," he mumbled into his brandy. "Left the town days ago. Some Italian fellow, Bedwalters says."

"Corelli? No, he's innocent of everything except family feeling."

He did not seem to understand me; I pressed: "I refer of course to your son, Domenico."

He snorted in derision.

"All he wanted," I said, "was a little acknowledgement."

"He wanted money," Mazzanti said loudly.

"How much did you pay him for pretending to shoot at you?"

He said nothing; I suspected no money had passed at all. I let a few moments pass but either Mazzanti had nothing to say or he was incapable of saying anything. I wondered if I was going to get any sense out of him at all. He was a man who would be drunk, or on the verge of it, the rest of his life.

Outside, in the street, I heard a faint noise like footsteps. Damn Hugh and Esther. Could they not keep quiet?

"The real murderer is still in the town," I said, breaking the silence.

"Devil he is," he mumbled.

"Do you not want to know what happened?"

A long silence. He drank like a man who has a bottle or six to get through and must do so, as a duty.

"Well?" he said at last.

"Julia was pregnant."

He said nothing. In the silence I thought I heard a noise upstairs; perhaps we had disturbed Mrs Baker after all. I prayed silently that she did not come down.

"She was desperate for a husband," I pursued. "Desperate enough to keep at least two men in view. One was Ord."

Mazzanti snorted in derision. "That fool."

"Yes, he is, isn't he?" I agreed. "He was in love with her, but I don't know how she could imagine that would have lasted when she gave birth to a child that plainly could not be his. Then there was Ned, but he was a last resort – Julia had become used to a comfortable existence and Ned would never have the money to support her as she would like. The strange thing is that she never looked twice at the one man who would have married her as soon as he could get a licence. Matthew Proctor."

Mazzanti laughed scornfully. "The psalm teacher! Devil take it, the man's a weakling."

"He was genuinely in love with her – that's why he was so insistent in keeping watch over her. Too insistent. The night she died he tried to force his attentions on her, she resisted and he lost all control. He was the one who raped her!"

Mazzanti was slow to react but he lifted his head, turned on his heel and gave me the most astonishing look I had ever seen. It was a look of hope.

That look floored me. Abruptly I saw what he had been drinking away: despair. Not anxiety about the future, certainly not grief at the loss of a daughter, not even bitterness at a life gone hopelessly out of control. Despair. The absence of even the slightest spark of life. Until now. I had given him hope.

But how?

I felt I was walking through a fog. I was almost at my destination but not quite, yet I didn't know which way to turn. One step might take me further away, not nearer. I went on more cautiously.

"There was a struggle. Julia was knocked unconscious. The one mercy in this whole business is that in all probability she was not aware of the attack that killed her."

He ran his hand across his face. "Thank God," he said. "Thank God." He sounded as if he meant it.

I started to speak again then heard the faintest of creaks. I had left the front door slightly ajar so that Hugh and Esther could get in if necessary. This sound was closer however; I looked to the door of the room – it was open a crack. Through the gap I saw a pale blur, a gleam of gold. I called out: "Would you care to come in?"

Ciara Mazzanti was wrapped in a gauzy nightgown with a lace overwrap and a shawl of figured silk. Her golden hair was haloed around her head; the long plait in which she plainly dressed it for bed, hung over her shoulder almost to her waist. She was, even for her age and weight, a magnificent figure.

The ever-present handkerchief was clutched in her hand. "It's his fault," she said, convulsively. "If he had been a better father, none of this would ever have happened!"

"Yes, yes," I said. "Very dramatic, Signora. If you wish to talk, pray sit down. I'm tired, very tired, and I don't wish to watch one of Mr Handel's operas at this time."

She turned on me a look of pure hatred. I applauded. "You hated her, didn't you," I said. "Both of you?"

They said nothing. Mazzanti smiled into his brandy, his wife looked down at her hands and played with the fringe of her shawl. "To you, Signora," I said, "she represented youth and beauty, and the success that was rapidly slipping through your fingers. And you, Signor, hated being reminded that you had never had any talent. You both hated being dependent on her. And there was no security in it – if she married or was courted by an admirer, you would lose your only source of income."

"It is time," Ciara Mazzanti announced, "to concentrate on my career."

Mazzanti and I both looked at her. He was gripping his brandy and swaying slightly. The brandy gleamed in the candlelight and cast bright glints on the hand that held the glass. "You?" he said. "What good are you? Who wants a fat old woman?"

"Not you," she retorted. "You were after fresher bait."

"Damn you, woman!" he shouted. "If you'd been half the woman you should have been, none of this would ever have happened!"

"That's enough," I said sharply. "You took out your hatred on Julia in a way no father ever should."

"Ask him how old she was!" Ciara Mazzanti said stridently. "Ask him!"

"But she was very like you, wasn't she?" I said, trying to fix Mazzanti's wavering gaze. "Devious, sly and manipulative. She hated what you did to her, but she enjoyed the power it gave her over you and made sure you knew it. And then she found out she was with child."

"My poor lamb," Ciara Mazzanti said, stifling a sob with her handkerchief.

I lost my temper. "Don't give me that hypocrisy! You knew exactly what was going on! And you decided to say nothing. Best to keep quiet, isn't it? It might go away. And of course it gave you power too, didn't it? It meant your husband had to keep negotiating deals like the one you have with the concerts here to make sure that you kept quiet."

She put up a hand as if to brush my words away. Her hand went to her mouth to cover it. After a moment, she started to sob.

"Be quiet!" I said, furiously. "Playing the fond mother now won't help!"

She sobbed noisily.

"You're not a fool," I said. "You knew she was pregnant."

Mazzanti put down his brandy very carefully. "I see how it was." He was pronouncing his words very precisely. "Ciara killed Julia."

Ciara Mazzanti stopped crying, snatched her handkerchief from her mouth, snarled at him. "You wretch! First you humiliate me by bedding every actress in London – and the younger the better! Then you bed your own daughter, then you accuse me – me! – of killing her. Wretch, wretch, wretch!"

For one brief moment, I felt sorry for Mazzanti. Fury twisted Ciara Mazzanti's face into the mask of a vicious, embittered woman. I tried to intervene but Mazzanti was laughing hysterically, wagging his finger at his wife. "Take her away!

"Be quiet!" I snapped. There was an unpleasant taste in my mouth. These people had been embittered by long years of uncertainty, by the condescending patronage of people like Jenison, and their state might, who knows, might in future years be mine too.

"Oh really," I said, in disgust. "Think, man! Does your wife have the strength to strangle a young healthy girl? She wanted Julia to be married! Or at the very least to run off with someone. I'd wager she was relying on Philip Ord. He had surprisingly easy access to Julia in London – that must have been her doing."

Ciara Mazzanti reddened.

Mazzanti stared at me, then started to laugh again, throwing back his head. He turned back to the brandy bottle. It was empty – he picked it up, looked at it, tossed it away. It hit the fire grate and shattered, showering the hem of Ciara Mazzanti's night gown with tiny shards of glass.

In the silence that followed, the door shifted open a little further and I saw Esther, sedate and respectable in a dark gown and mantle, on the threshold. She raised her eyebrows at me in query. I nodded. I had asked her to leave her intervention as late as possible but I didn't think there was any point in having Ciara Mazzanti here any longer. We could deal with her later.

Esther touched Ciara's arm. "Let's go," she said with the firmness of a schoolmistress. "We'll go to my house. You can be comfortable there."

Ciara leant gratefully on her, murmuring something in broken terms. She started to turn away then swung back, her gaze darting from me to her husband. She pulled away from Esther, came across to me, putting a plump hand on my sleeve. "Mr Patterson." She had to look up at me for she was not particularly tall. "Mr Patterson, thank you."

"For what?" I said startled.

"For rescuing me. Alas – " She seemed to consider dabbing her eyes with her handkerchief then thought better of it. "Alas, it is too late for my daughter."

"Much too late," I said brutally. "You could have rescued her years ago if you'd had a mind to."

She continued to look up at me with mute appeal. Then something slipped in her face. "You don't know what it's like," she said pleadingly. "I didn't like what he was doing, but I had no other choice but to accept it. How could I survive without him?" She turned to Esther. "You know, don't you? We women all know what it's like to be dependent on a man."

"Better to live without money than without conscience," Esther said, with all the no-nonsense of a woman who has never had to worry about such sordid things.

Signora Mazzanti gave her a mocking smile. And went off with her, as docile as a doll.

The room was silent after the two women had gone. Mazzanti ground shattered glass underfoot and cast me a sidelong glance. "No point in my trying to put you off any more, is there, Patterson?"

"No," I said. "You killed Julia."

He shrugged. "If Ciara had been a different woman, none of this would have happened."

His indifference infuriated me. I said, as coolly as I could, "Julia was pregnant and desperately looking for a husband, and she wasn't above using blackmail to find one. She couldn't marry the father of her child, of course, because that was you."

He pretended to yawn. "I doubt we can be certain of that. My dear Patterson, do you honestly think she gave me no encouragement?"

I balled my fist, digging my nails into my flesh to prevent myself shouting. "But you knew that marriage wouldn't necessarily be the end of the matter. Once Julia was out of your hands, she might say anything to anyone. Suppose she married Ord, for instance, and he realised the child was not his – might she not try and fend off his anger by confessing to him what had really happened? She might even – shall we say, overdramatise – in an attempt to deflect his anger. No, sir, you knew that you could not relinquish her to any other man."

He contemplated the wall.

"You heard her leave the house," I said. "You looked out of the window and saw her. You saw her walk off, and Proctor walk after her. So you followed." I bit back revulsion. "Did you watch Proctor raping her?"

"I lost them," he said grandiloquently. "Such a rabbit warren of streets in this town." He looked only mildly interested. "She was dead when I found her."

"No," I said. "Proctor raped her, but he didn't kill her. *You* did that. You must have been desperate if you were willing to destroy your sole source of income."

He betrayed his first sign of unease, running his tongue across dry lips. "Desperate," he said. "Yes, mad with despair. It was an accident. She died when she hit her head against the wall."

"She was strangled," I said, uncompromisingly. "And if you are trying to convince me that you killed her in an excess of emotion, on the spur of the moment, you may as well desist now. This was a planned murder – you decided on it the moment you knew she was pregnant."

I saw his fists clench. The candlelight shone on a ring on his little finger.

"You hatched a plot," I said. "You hired your son to shoot at you. You told him it was for the sake of publicity, to bring you to the attention of sensation-loving audiences – but that was not your chief motive, was it?"

He said nothing.

"You wanted to create the impression that your life was in

danger. You suggested that it was some aristocrat you had offended by being over-familiar – though innocently so, of course – with his mistress. Julia's death might then be construed as part of a campaign against you. That's what you claimed was happening, wasn't it? Of course, your son might give you the lie but he is hardly a credible witness in view of his political activities."

The silence this time was very long indeed. The old house creaked a little, and outside the owl hooted again. I could hear my own breathing. I waited. Mazzanti had his back to me. I rested my hand on my coat pocket, feeling the hard edge of the heavy pistol. I had not discounted the possibility that Mazzanti would try to get away by violence and I was prepared to shoot if he attacked me, though given my incompetence with pistols, I hoped he would not.

He turned to me at last. "So," he said, "you are going to tell the constable I killed my daughter." He sneered at my silence. "No, of course not. You cannot prove your allegations. And if you could – " He swaggered a step or two towards me. "I know all about the lady, sir." He nodded at the door, as if Esther still stood there. "I have been asking some questions of my own, sir. You give the lady a music lesson every day." He smiled maliciously. "That was my own name for it, sir. *I am giving my daughter a music lesson – pray do not disturb us on any count.*"

I said nothing.

"I will tell all I know," he said. "You dare not give me away!"

I walked to the door. "Are you certain, sir?"

In the hallway, I heard him call after me but I did not go back. He was right – I would not risk Esther's reputation and he knew it. All I could do was leave him in fear, the sort of fear his daughter must have lived in. He called once more but I was already in the street.

Esther's carriage had already gone, taking Esther and Ciara

Mazzanti to the house in Caroline Square. But Hugh was still waiting for me, standing in the shadow of the doorway, pistol in his hand, glancing about for any danger.

"Have you left him?"

"What else can I do?"

"You can't let him get away with it! He killed his own daughter."

I rubbed my eyes wearily. "What do you suggest I do then?"

"Tell Bedwalters."

"We've no evidence."

"Then – " Hugh gestured with the pistol.

"Then we'd be the ones strung up. And for filth like Mazzanti? I think not."

I started walking down the street, knowing that Hugh would follow me. After a moment's hesitation, he did so.

"What if he slips off to this other world?"

"There's no evidence he can do that." I glanced at him. In the moonlit darkness, his face was shadowed and unhappy. I stopped and turned to face him. "Hugh, about that other world… "

"I don't want to talk about it," he said sharply, putting out a hand to touch the nearest wall. He added, "You haven't told anyone else about it? It's just Mrs Jerdoun and I who know?"

"And Heron," I reminded him.

"You mustn't tell anyone else," he said insistently. "Devil take it, Charles, what in heaven's name do you think other people would make of it – the ruffians who've been after you, for instance – what would they make of it?"

I kept silence. Ruffians like that are no more and no less superstitious than the rest of mankind; they are merely more open about it. They'd say it was a manifestation of evil and I was in league with the devil. And sooner or later, someone would decide to take action on the matter.

We turned up the street.

"His wife will talk," Hugh said, as if struck by a new hope.

"She'll give him away."

I thought not. Ciara Mazzanti was after vengeance and her own safety today but tomorrow she would be comfortable again and basking in the sympathetic attentions of Mrs Jenison and the other ladies. And she would decide there was no point in dwelling on unpleasantness.

I glanced back. The moonlight was shining down the length of the street, catching on something bulky, striking small metallic glints. A shadow moved in a doorway. Then the moon slid behind the clouds and when it rode out again a moment or two later and I looked again, the shadow was gone.

# 45

**All will be clear one day.**
[Lady Hubert to her eldest daughter, September 1733]

Claudius Heron pulled out the chair opposite mine and signalled to the serving girl to bring him coffee. Nellie's coffee-house was crowded and abuzz with the latest political gossip; no one paid any attention to me as I sat and wrestled with scribbled sums to see how much I could afford to give Ned and Richard, without leaving myself short of money before my next bills were due to be paid. I had been in possession of what was for me wealth for precisely one month and a half.

Heron waited until the girl had brought his coffee. Then he said bluntly: "Mazzanti's dead."

It was extraordinarily difficult to know how I should react to this news. "Oh?"

"Stabbed. In his own house, in the early hours of this morning. One thrust of a sword, straight through the heart."

Heron waited; I said: "I always thought he was born to be murdered."

He leant back in his chair. "Rather odd, do you not think?"

"How?"

"Three previous attempts had been made on his life, all attempted shootings. Yet now he falls victim to a mysterious swordsman."

"Perhaps his attacker decided a pistol was not very effective."

"He was remarkably effective at missing, certainly," Heron said.

Damn the man's perspicacity. "I was very grateful for that myself," I said lightly.

Heron lounged at his ease. He was in one of his light-coloured coats and looked rather cooler than he had recently. A trifle relieved too, as if a weight had been taken off his mind. "You do not ask after his wife."

"Do you think she stabbed him?"

"Hardly," he said dryly. "Where would the Signora have found a sword? In the theatre costume box?"

"They're all wooden," I said absently.

"Though she does say that there is more than one wronged husband who would have been glad to see him in his grave. Personally, I find that a rather unconvincingly melodramatic response – after all, the divorce court does exist."

Someone close by raised his voice to say that Walpole was the greatest fool living; half a dozen others shouted him down.

"Come, come, Patterson," Heron said. "You will not convince me that Mazzanti's relationship with his daughter was a good one. It is merely a question of how bad it was."

I met his gaze. "As bad as it could be."

He nodded. "Then he is better dead." He was silent for a moment, toying with his dish of coffee. "You will not be pleased that I ask, I know, but it is best to know what one faces. You did not – "

"No, I did not," I said, forcibly.

He was not perturbed by my annoyance. He said, "Then Mazzanti's killer has escaped. It is regrettable, but not necessarily a bad thing."

"No," I said shortly. Particularly as I was certain it meant there was one less spy in England.

He said nothing for a moment, nodded acknowledgement to an acquaintance who passed. "Did Fowler tell you how we met in London?"

"No."

He half-smiled. "He was in despair, I think, and reckless who knew or saw what. I persuaded him that that was a foolish point of view. I persuaded him that what you do in private has no meaning or significance – unless it is known."

I stared at him. It was hardly a Christian viewpoint; the Bible says clearly otherwise. It says moreover that God knows all the secrets of our hearts, that ultimately nothing can be a secret from Him. "That is a very bleak philosophy," I said.

He nodded. "But a very practical one. The Mazzantis lived by it very successfully for some time. Not happily, I grant you, and not morally, but nonetheless they survived in a harsh world. It was only when matters threatened to become public, when the girl became pregnant, that their affairs started to unravel. If they could have found a husband for the girl, perhaps they would all survive still."

"And what about the matter of conscience?" I demanded.

"Mazzanti does not seem to have had one."

"He committed a crime against his daughter," I said shortly. "That's the kind of secret that should never be allowed."

Heron turned his cool gaze on me. "Secrets are much maligned, Patterson. It is only by keeping secrets that society holds together. Do you understand me?"

I wasn't sure I did.

He drank his coffee and took his leave, pausing on his way out to exchange a word or two with another gentleman. Was Heron referring to Mazzanti's death, or to the matter of the other world? Well, he need have no fear on either account, for I had no intention of speaking out on either matter.

But there was one thing left. I reached into my pocket and took out the note that I had found pushed under my door this morning. It was the politest of notes.

*Mrs Jerdoun expects the honour of Mr Patterson's company at dinner…*

That was almost all it said. There was a date, a time for dinner, a conventional sentiment or two. And the added note: *We will be alone.*

Like Ord, but with more calculation, Esther had put her feelings in writing.

*What is done in private has no meaning or significance – unless it is known.* Was I to live by Heron's bleak philosophy? With Ciara Mazzanti's dreadful example before me? This was not the same situation surely? Who could be hurt by this besides ourselves?

No doubt Ciara Mazzanti had said much the same.

I folded the note, put it in my pocket and went out into the street where the sun blazed hot as ever.

# THE PREVIOUS ADVENTURES OF CHARLES PATTERSON, HARPSICHORDIST, CONCERT ARRANGER AND ACCIDENTAL INVESTIGATOR
## by
## ROZ SOUTHEY
### are available from a bookshop near you

### BROKEN HARMONY
Patterson is accused of stealing a valuable book and a cherished violin. Then the apprentice he inherited from his flamboyant professional rival is found gruesomely murdered. As the death toll mounts Patterson starts to fear for his health and sanity – and it becomes clear to characters and readers alike that things are not quite as they seem...

**Published by Crème de la Crime**
**ISBN: 978-0-9551589-3-3** £7.99

### CHORDS AND DISCORDS
Winter is a bad time for jobbing musicians. The town has emptied, and Charles Patterson is down to his last few shillings.

When an unpopular organ builder thinks his life is in danger and a shop-boy dies in dubious circumstances, a substantial fee persuades him to seek answers to difficult questions.

Like, who stole the dancing-master's clothes? Why is a valuable organ up for raffle? And will Patterson escape whoever is trying to kill him?

**Published by Crème de la Crime**
**ISBN: 978-0-9557078-2-7** £7.99

**You can also meet Charles Patterson again in**

## CRIMINAL TENDENCIES

**a diverse and wholly engrossing collection of short stories from some of the best of the UK's crime writers.**

**£1 from every copy sold of this first-rate collection will go to support the NATIONAL HEREDITARY BREAST CANCER HELPLINE**

She lay on her face, as if asleep. I turned her over and saw the deep wound on her brow…
- Reginald Hill, *John Brown's Body*

Her mouth was dry and she was shaking badly. Terror was gripping her; the same terror she previously experienced only in her dreams…
- Peter James, *12 Bolinbroke Avenue*

His lips were thin and pale. "She must be following us. She's some sort of stalker."
- Sophie Hannah, *The Octopus Nest*

When he thought he was alone, he squatted down and opened the briefcase. I was interested to see that it contained an automatic pistol and piles and piles of banknotes.

- Andrew Taylor, *Waiting for Mr Right*

**Published by Crème de la Crime**
**ISBN: 978-09557078-5-8** £7.99

# MORE GRIPPING TITLES FROM CRÈME DE LA CRIME

### DEAD LIKE HER — Linda Regan

It seems like a straightforward case for newly promoted DCI Paul Banham and DI Alison Grainger: the victims all bore an uncanny resemblance to Marilyn Monroe. But they soon unearth connections with drug-running and people-trafficking.

**ISBN: 978-09557078-8-9** £7.99

### BLOOD MONEY — Maureen Carter

Personal tragedy has pushed Detective Sergeant Bev Morriss into a dark place. But there are bad guys to battle as well as demons – like the Sandman, a vicious serial burglar who wears a clown mask and plays mind-games with his victims.

And Bev is in no mood to play...

**ISBN: 978-095570878-7-2** £7.99

### THE FALL GIRL — Kaye C Hill

Accidental P I Lexy Lomax is investigating a suspicious death in a decidedly spooky cottage. Kinky, her truculent chihuahua, hates the place, but he seems to be in a minority.

She's hindered by her obnoxious ex, and a mysterious beast dogs her footsteps. And dark forces are running amok...

**ISBN: 978-095570878-9-6** £7.99

### LOVE NOT POISON — Mary Andrea Clarke

The death of ill-natured Lord Wickerston in a fire leads Georgiana Grey to ask questions.

Who would want Lord Wickerston dead? Does her brother Edward know more than he is willing to say? And how is the notorious highwayman known as the Crimson Cavalier involved?

**ISBN: 978-0-9560566-0-3** £7.99